I0583227

Earl Stanhope

Life of the Right Honourable William Pitt

Vol. II

Earl Stanhope

Life of the Right Honourable William Pitt
Vol. II

ISBN/EAN: 9783337189921

Printed in Europe, USA, Canada, Australia, Japan

Cover: Foto ©Raphael Reischuk / pixelio.de

More available books at **www.hansebooks.com**

LIFE

OF

THE RIGHT HONOURABLE

WILLIAM PITT

WITH EXTRACTS FROM HIS MS. PAPERS

By EARL STANHOPE

NEW EDITION

IN THREE VOLUMES—VOL. II.

With Portraits

LONDON

JOHN MURRAY, ALBEMARLE STREET

1879

CONTENTS

OF

THE SECOND VOLUME.

CHAPTER XX.

1795.

CHAPTER XXI.

1795.

CHAPTER XXII.

1796.

CHAPTER XXIII.

1796–1797.

CHAPTER XXIV.

1797.

CHAPTER XXV.

1798.

LIFE

OF

THE RIGHT HONOURABLE

WILLIAM PITT.

CHAPTER XVII.

1793.

Retrospect of the first part of Pitt's Administration—Controversies on the second part—Pitt's Speech on the Address—His French policy supported by Parliament—Commencement of campaign—Defeat and defection of Dumouriez—Robespierre—Reign of Terror—Rising in La Vendée—Surrender of Condé, Valenciennes, and Mayence—Siege of Toulon—Dispersion and slaughter of the Vendéan army—Conquests out of Europe—Political Trials.

WITH the Declarations of War by France in February, 1793, or with the preparations for that war a few weeks before, the first and the peaceful part of Pitt's administration ends. It was a period of nine years—the most prosperous and happy, perhaps, that England ever yet had known. I have related how the consummate financial skill of the young Prime Minister converted deficiency to surplus, and augmented the revenue while lessening the taxes. I have related how a firm and most resolute tone to foreign powers—as to France in the case of Holland, and to Russia in the case of Ockzakow—was found not inconsistent with the rapid expansion of commerce and the almost unexampled growth of credit at home. And let me add, that the benefit of these measures was by no means limited to the period thus described, since it was mainly the sap and strength imparted by them which enabled the nation to sustain and finally triumph over the perils of the conflict that ensued.

The second part of Pitt's administration, commencing in 1793, was of nearly the same length as the former. 'From this time,' says Bishop Tomline, 'to the end of his life, we shall have to follow him in the wise and vigorous conduct of a war attended with circumstances and difficulties unexampled in the history of the world.' Bishop Tomline did not live to fulfil his design, and the sentence from which I have quoted is the last that he ever published. But, as I conceive, he has rightly described the nature of the task before him.

At the time the first part of Pitt's administration was, as I have shown, inveighed against by Fox and Fox's friends on many grounds of censure and with the utmost force of invective. At present, on the contrary, Fox's followers in politics seem rather inclined to represent it as free from blame—nay, even as entitled to praise. They reserve their fire to assail the position of Bishop Tomline as to the 'wise and vigorous conduct of the war.' Thus it is almost exclusively the second part of Pitt's administration on which the more recent controversies turn. Two accusations of especial weight have been brought against it by Lord Macaulay. His short biography of Pitt, to which I have already more than once referred, seems to me, when taken as a whole, distinguished by candour and judgment as much as by eloquence and genius. But even from such a quarter grave imputations are not to be implicitly received. In the task which I have undertaken they ought to be frankly discussed. Therefore, though with all due deference, with all the respect that I owe to the memory both of a great historian and of a departed friend, I shall here insert some observations written in his life-time, and designed to meet his own eye, in reference to both his heads of charge.

In the first place, then, Pitt is accused of showing an undue severity. He is charged (let me give the very words) 'with harsh laws harshly executed, with Alien Bills and Gagging Bills, with cruel punishments inflicted on some political agitators, with unjustifiable prosecutions instituted against others.' These acts of the Legislative or of the Executive Powers may perhaps require to be separately judged. They will be seen and they may be estimated one by one in my subsequent pages. I by no means stand up for them all as carried into practical effect throughout the country. I do not conceive the fame of Mr. Pitt involved in every act of every Magistrate or every Judge. I do not even think it bound up with all the judicial decisions of Lord Chancellor Loughborough. In several cases, then, which the adversaries of this Government have held forth and selected out of many, I do not deny, and on the contrary intend to show, that the zeal of some men and the fears of others transported them beyond the bounds of right. But that is not the point which Lord Macaulay puts. He passes sentence on them together and as a whole. Taken together, then, it may be asked—when, even at the outset of the struggle, such scenes occurred as I have commemorated, for example at Dundee—a tree of Liberty planted and a cry of 'No King!' raised—when the frenzy of the Jacobins, like some foul infection, spread from shore to shore—when thousands upon thousands of well-meaning and till then sober-minded men were unhappily misled and caught the fever of the times— when French gold was as lavishly employed to corrupt as were French doctrines to inflame—whether the same mild and gentle measures would still suffice as in mild and gentle times? It is the well-known saying of a Frenchman at that period active on the side of the new system, and zealous to excuse its excesses, that Revolutions are not to be made with Rose-water. This plea will not hold good for deeds of massacre and robbery, but in a more limited and lawful sense it must be acknowledged to have truth on its side. But if this be truth, surely it is full as true that Revolutions are not to be put down with Rose-water. There are times when new and unparalleled dangers are only to be met by rigorous and extraordinary stretches of power. There are times when the State could be saved by no other means.

I may add that the view of the subject which I have just expressed was in thorough accordance with the temper of the times. This, I think, can scarcely in any quarter be denied. The great majority of the people of England in 1793 and 1794 felt everything that they most prized imperilled by the French Revolutionary school, and far from deprecating, they demanded a course of most rigorous repression.

But there is another charge no less heavy which the same critic, speaking of the same period, alleges. Pitt is accused of showing too little vigour. It is said that, ' since he did not choose to oppose himself side by side with Fox to the public feeling, he should have taken the advice of Burke and should have availed himself of that feeling to the full extent. He should have proclaimed a Holy War for religion, morality, property, order, public law, and should have thus opposed to the Jacobins an energy equal to their own.' Let it, however, be remembered to what the policy of Burke in its full extent would lead. Look to his ' Thoughts on a Regicide Peace.' See how we might deduce from them the duty of making no terms with France unless the Bourbons were restored—of shunning as a pestilence such a pacification as we attempted at Lille and actually achieved at Amiens. Surely that is not the course which a philosophic historian of the nineteenth century, writing with a clear view of the succeeding events, is prepared to recommend.

Nor should it be forgotten that he who preaches a crusade stirs up not only the good but also the evil passions of a people. Had Pitt chosen to exchange the part of statesman for that of Peter the Hermit, he might no doubt have aroused in England a frenzy against the Jacobins almost equal to theirs against priests and Kings. But could this object have been effected without numerous outbreaks of that new frenzy —without such conflagrations of chapels and dwelling-houses as the political dissenters had already sustained at Birmingham? Would not, in such a case, the memory of Pitt be deeply tarnished with blood—blood, not shed in foreign warfare, but in strife and seditions at home?

There are still some further questions to be urged. Are the first and the second of these charges in truth quite consistent with each other? Would it have been possible to 'proclaim a Holy War,' which Pitt is arraigned for not proclaiming, and at the same time to avoid 'the Alien Bills and Gagging Bills' which Pitt is arraigned for having passed?

But there is yet another branch of this second charge. We are told that 'the English army under Pitt was the laughing-stock of Europe.' We are told that, 'great as Pitt's abilities were, his military administration was that of a driveller.' We are required to believe that a statesman acknowledged as pre-eminently great in peace, became at once ridiculously little in war. Yet, in truth, History bears no Magician's wand, and displays scarce any of such sudden and surprising changes. No doubt that during Pitt's administration there were many miscarriages by land to set against our victories at sea. The same fate attended all the armies which at that period were arrayed against France. It was no easy matter to prevail over a nation at all times most brave and warlike, and then inflamed to a preternatural strength by its revolutionary ardour. When, therefore, the English army is declared to have been at that period the laughing-stock of Europe, it may be asked what other European army had permanently enjoyed better fortune or was justly entitled to smile at ours?

It is also to be borne in mind that the military failures here laid solely to the charge of Pitt, continued long after Pitt had ceased to be. With the greatest of all, the expedition to Walcheren, he was not at all, except in kindred, connected. The truth is that our Generals at that period were for the most part anything but men of genius. Lord Grenville, writing to his brother in strict confidence on the 28th of January, 1799, asks: 'What officer have we to oppose to our domestic and external enemies? . . . Some old woman in a red riband.' The truth is then that these miscarriages in our military enterprises, far from being confined, as Lord Macaulay's statement would imply, to Pitt's administration, went on with few exceptions in regular and mortifying series, till happily for us and for Europe there arose a man as great in the field as was Pitt in the Council—till the valour which had never failed our troops, even in their worst reverses, was led to victory by the surpassing genius of Wellington. If then it can be shown that Pitt as Prime Minister strove with unremitting toil by day and night for the success of that war in which he had reluctantly, but on a high sense of duty, engaged—if in his plans he consulted the most skilful officers in his power—if in his diplomacy he laboured to build up new coalitions when the first had crumbled away—if for that object he poured forth subsidies with a liberal, nay, as his enemies alleged, a lavish hand—if he sought to strike the enemy whenever or wherever any vulnerable point lay bare, on the northern frontier when in concert with the Austrian armies, on the southern coast when Toulon had risen, on the western coast when a civil war broke out in La Vendée—it seems hard that, having striven so far as a civilian could strive for the success of our arms both by land and sea, the reverses on the former should be cast upon his memory, whilst at the same time he is allowed no merit for our triumphs on the latter. That merit is declared by the same critic to belong to 'one of those chiefs of the Whig party, who, in the great schism caused by the French Revolution, had followed Burke.' This was Earl Spencer, as First Lord of the Admiralty since the close of 1794. 'To him,' continues Lord Macaulay, 'it was owing that twice in the short space of eleven months we had days of thanksgiving for great victories.' There is no doubt that Lord Spencer at the Admiralty was an excellent administrator. There is no doubt that Lord Chatham was far from a good one. Still, however, Lord Macaulay's statement, as I have cited it, does not seem to recognise the fact that the greatest of our naval victories at that period—the battle of the First of June—was fought not with Lord Spencer but with Lord Chatham at the head of the Admiralty Board. But, waiving that point, is this the one weight and one measure? When our armies retreat, the Prime Minister is solely to be blamed! When our fleets prevail, the Prime Minister is to have no share in the praise!

These few remarks, which I make unwillingly, may, however, tend to show that Mr. Pitt in his conduct of the war against Revolutionary France was as far removed from the 'driveller' that Lord Macaulay calls him, as from the 'demon' whom some French writers have portrayed. But from this more general survey I now resume the progress of my narrative.

On the dismission of M. de Chauvelin, papers were presented to both Houses in the name of the King, showing the great probability of an impending rupture with France. Addresses in reply to assure His Majesty of their cordial assistance were moved in the Commons by the Prime Minister, and in the Lords by the Foreign Secretary. It was the 1st of February—the same day as it chanced on which at Paris war was actually

declared. Mr. Pitt began his speech by an eloquent
denunciation of the calamitous event of the 21st, 'the
foulest and most atrocious deed,' he said, 'which the
history of the world has yet had occasion to attest.'
And he recited against it some lines of Statius, which
the great historian De Thou had formerly applied to
another dark scene in his country's annals, the Massacre
of St. Bartholomew :—

> Excidat illa dies ævo, nec postera credant
> Secula ; nos certè taceamus et obruta multâ
> Nocte tegi nostræ patiamur crimina gentis.[1]

With no less eloquence he went on to contrast the
ruinous anarchy of France with our own prosperity and
freedom. He compared the situation of England—a
comparison which since his time has been frequently
repeated—to the situation of the temperate zone on the
surface of the globe, ' formed by the bounty of Providence for habitation and enjoyment, being equally removed from the Polar frosts on the one hand and the
scorching heats of the torrid region on the other. In
this country,' he added with just pride, ' no man in consequence of his riches or rank is so high as to be above
the reach of the laws, and no man is so poor or inconsiderable as not to be within their protection.'

The course of Mr. Pitt towards Revolutionary France
received the cordial support of by far the greater part
of the Opposition in both Houses. In the Lords scarcely
more than four Peers voted or signed protests against it
—the Earls of Lauderdale, Derby, and Stanhope, and the
Marquis of Lansdowne. In the Commons, before this
Session closed, Mr. Fox brought forward two motions for
peace, and on neither occasion could he muster so many
as fifty votes.

Thus also a Bill, which Fox with great warmth
denounced, providing new restrictions and penalties on
any traitorous correspondence with the enemy, was

---

[1] These lines are from the *Sylvarum* of Statius, lib. v. div. 2,
verse 88.

nevertheless carried through Parliament with a high hand. It was introduced on the part of the Government by the Attorney-General. Since the beginning of the year that office was no longer held by Sir Archibald Macdonald. He had been promoted to the Bench and been succeeded by Sir John Scott, while the new Solicitor-General was Sir John Mitford, afterwards Lord Redesdale.

The campaign commenced early on the side of Flanders. Scarce a fortnight from the Declarations of War, Dumouriez crossed the frontier and invaded Holland, but he was soon recalled to the Meuse by the advance of the Prince of Saxe-Coburg at the head of some Austrian forces. On the 18th of March the two armies engaged at Neerwinden, when, in spite of great exertions, Dumouriez found himself defeated. The result of the battle was that the Austrians recovered the whole of Belgium almost as rapidly as they had lost it. From the Lower Rhine also the French were driven back to Alsace. The city of Mayence, in which they left a considerable garrison, was besieged, and after an obstinate resistance taken by the Prussians.

The mind of Dumouriez was filled with chagrin at his reverse of fortune, which he ascribed wholly to the ruling Jacobins. 'See,' he cried to all comers, 'how these foolish men neglected my requisitions and controlled my plans!' He determined to make a stand against their authority, and to restore the Constitution of 1791 with a Prince of the House of Orleans at its head. His first step was to enter into secret communications with the chiefs of the Austrian army—the Prince of Saxe-Coburg and General Mack. His next was to seize and send over to his new friends as captives Beurnonville, the Minister of War, with four deputies of the Convention who had come to his camp and who summoned him to Paris. But the French troops were now far better inclined to their own Government than they had been some months before. Dumouriez found it impossible to draw the great mass along with him, and thus, with abilities so far superior to La Fayette's, he was reduced to the same poor part that La Fayette had played. On the 5th of April he rode away into the enemy's country attended only by a single regiment and by a few personal friends, among whom was the young Duke de Chartres, in after years King Louis Philippe. Dumouriez was received with great respect by the Austrian chiefs, but refused to take any further part with them, or to serve anywhere unless at the head of a French army.

During the greater part of his remaining life, which extended to 1823, the victor of Jemmapes fixed his residence in England, and received a yearly pension of 1200*l.* from the English Government. Some writers in France, rather than allow any merit to the Duke of Wellington, have been inclined to give Dumouriez the honour of conducting from his English country-house our chief Peninsular battles, as some learned counsel sitting in his London chambers might direct a trial at Exeter or Carlisle. So that when viewed through these Parisian glasses, our great victories in truth were not won by an English, but by a French commander![1]

The defection of Dumouriez led to the downfall of the less extreme party at Paris, which was known by the name of the Gironde. Every man who desired to stop short of the most furious excesses was hooted at as a friend of the fugitive General, as an adherent of 'Pitt and Coburg,' for by that strange amalgam was the foreign Coalition expressed. The Jacobins succeeded in vesting all the powers of the State in a small Committee of the Convention called the 'Committee of Public Safety,' and in that Committee Robespierre had the main ascendant. Robespierre was now in truth the master of France, and his ferocious reign is well described in the

[1] 'On lui attribue la meilleure partie des succès de Vittoria,' &c. See in the *Nouvelle Biographie Générale* of Didot the article 'Dumouriez' by M. Paul de Chamrobert.

expressive phrase which his countrymen have ever since applied to it—the Reign of Terror. His system of government as against his enemies was clear and simple, and invariably the same—the Guillotine. No rank, no age, no sex was spared. In October were sent to the scaffold the young and eloquent chiefs of the Gironde, in the same month Marie Antoinette, once Queen of France, in November Philippe Egalité, once Duke of Orleans, who met his doom in utter silence:[1] in November also Madame Roland, who in passing by bowed her head before the statue of Liberty, and spoke these memorable words : ' Oh Liberty, how many crimes are committed in thy name !'

The Guillotine was by no means the only expedient for clearing the prisons in France. Not, of course, that there was any release or mercy to the prisoners. But in the provinces the executions were marked by agreeable varieties denoting a playful wit. Thus at Nantes, for example, the political prisoners, male and female, being drawn from their cells and pinioned, two and two together, were cast into the river, these executions being known by a jocular byword as the ' Marriages of the Loire.' By confiscations and heavy fines upon the rich, as well as by large issues of depreciated Assignats, it was sought to supply the failure of regular taxes and the ruin of public credit. The Christian Religion was declared to be abolished with all its rites and ceremonies, and in their place was substituted the worship of the Goddess Reason. To personify this Goddess a courtesan not too much encumbered with attire was conducted in solemn state to the high altar of Notre Dame, there to receive the homage of the crowd. The bust of Marat, one of the vilest of the mob-pamphleteers, who had been stabbed in his bath by Charlotte Corday, an enthusiast on the opposite side, was carried round as another fitting object of devotion. And this among the countrymen of Pascal and Fénelon !

[1] See the *Journal of Mrs. Dalrymple Elliott*, p. 181, ed. 1859.

Yet in many places of France and by many persons this abominable Reign of Terror was most bravely opposed. The great commercial cities of Lyons and Marseilles, the important maritime fortress of Toulon, cast off the yoke of the Jacobins, though without proclaiming Royalty, and sooner than submit prepared to stand a siege. Still more important was the rising in La Vendée. There some forty thousand of the peasantry gathered in arms for the defence of their Church and King, and they gained some brilliant successes in their first conflicts with the Republican troops. Their leaders were in part of their own rank, like Stofflet, who had borne a gun as gamekeeper, and Cathelineau, who had driven a team of horses; and in part of nobles from the neighbouring *châteaux*, as Messieurs d'Elbée, de Lescure, and above all Henri de la Roche Jaquelein. But all of whatever rank displayed the most ardent and devoted courage. Once as La Roche Jaquelein led on some of his new levies, equipped with little beyond scythes and staves, he pointed to an advancing regiment of 'the Blues,' for so they always called the regular troops. 'I promised you,' he cried, 'arms, ammunition, and artillery. Yonder they are—let us rush forward and take them!' And take them they did.

Such was the young hero, let me say in passing, who when struck dead by a musket-ball before he had attained the age of twenty-two, left behind him, even at that early age, a dear and imperishable memory among his countrymen of La Vendée. 'Even now,' so wrote in 1816 one of the partakers of his perils, 'there is not a peasant whose eye does not light up when he relates how he served under *Monsieur Henri*.'[1]

Still, however, in many parts of France, and especially in Paris, which was permitted to guide them all, the frenzy of the multitude kept pace with the frenzy of their rulers. As the deadly axe fell from day to day on hundreds after hundreds of innocent victims, there was

---

[1] *Mémoires de Madame de la Roche Jaquelein*, p. 465.

no softening of compassion towards them, but only the louder cries against 'Pitt and Coburg'—against the tyranny of Kings—the insolence of the Nobles—and the juggler's play of the Priesthood! Against the English Minister especially the violence of popular declamation knew no bounds. Even among the more moderate Girondins we find him designated as 'that monster Pitt.' But although the democratic rage against him continued in full force during the next few years, it is remarkable that the grounds of accusation were from time to time completely changed. During the Reign of Terror it was said that he had in his pay all the chief Royalists of France, exciting them not only to open resistance as at Lyons and Toulon, but also to such evil deeds as the assassination of Marat. After the Reign of Terror it was said that he had in his pay all the chief Jacobins of France, urging them forward by dint of English guineas, and trusting by their excesses to cast more and more disgrace on the Revolutionary cause. And so far as we now can gather, these opposite charges were received by the same public with an equal credulity.

It may be asked how with France thus distracted and divided the Coalition against her could fail of rapid and complete success? But the Coalition was by no means so large or so formidable as at first sight it seemed. Russia and Sweden stood aloof in an ambiguous state between peace and war. Spain and Sardinia did no more than nibble at the southern frontiers. Prussia appeared to be fully satisfied with the siege of Mayence, and resolutely bent against any new aggressive operations. The Dutch looked only to the protection of their own territories. And thus the brunt of the war fell mainly on the Austrians and the English.

As regards the latter there were about ten thousand troops ready for the defence of Holland when invaded by Dumouriez. Being now free of that duty, they were designed to take part in the campaign of Flanders, and accordingly they were landed at Ostend. Their commander was Frederick Duke of York, who from early youth had applied himself with zeal to the military service. It was hoped that his position as one of the King's sons would cheer and please the troops, while his want of experience might be supplied by older officers at his side.

The Duke of York having joined the Prince of Coburg, the two commanders found themselves opposed to General Dampierre as successor of Dumouriez. He had taken post at the camp of Famars in front of Valenciennes, and desired to remain on the defensive till reinforcements should arrive; but being urged forward by deputies from the Convention, he attacked the Allies on the 1st, and again on the 8th of May. On both occasions his troops were repulsed : on the last he was mortally wounded.

The French army, much weakened, retired shortly afterwards to another position in front of Bouchain, called from some old intrenchments the Camp of Cæsar; and the Allied Chiefs held a Council of War. There General Clerfait and the Duke of York strongly pressed an immediate advance into the heart of France. On the other hand it was contended by the Prince of Coburg and General Mack that the safer and surer plan, and such as was prescribed by ' the best writers,' would be in the first place to reduce the border fortresses. These counsels of dry routine prevailed. With one body the Prince of Coburg undertook to observe the French in Cæsar's Camp, while another division was to blockade Condé, and another to besiege Valenciennes. The latter and most important operation was entrusted to the personal command of the Duke of York. But Valenciennes, though most warmly attacked, was with equal ardour defended. The French Commander, General Ferrand, sustained forty-one days of bombardment, until the greater part of the town was laid in ashes and nearly half his garrison had perished. He did not surrender until towards the close of July, when his remaining troops were allowed to march out with all the honours of war. Shortly before, the small town of Condé, closely blockaded, had been compelled to yield to famine.

Even after the successful termination of these sieges the Allied Chiefs could not decide on any movement in advance. They did, indeed, by a joint operation drive the French from the Camp of Cæsar, as they had already from the Camp of Famars. But then they once more divided. With the English, the Hanoverians, and some regiments of Austrians, the Duke of York undertook the siege of Dunkirk, while General Clerfait led another body to the siege of Le Quesnoy.

But besides the hesitation of the Allies upon the frontier, there were other points in their conduct most unfavourable to their cause. The city of Mayence had surrendered on nearly the same day as the town of Valenciennes. From Mayence there marched out a garrison of twenty thousand excellent troops; from Valenciennes a garrison of eight thousand. On both the same terms had been imposed—freedom to go home, with an engagement not to serve against the Emperor or his allies for the period of one year. But no thought was taken, no condition made in behalf of those brave men who in La Vendée or along the Rhone had risen against the tyranny of the Convention. Against them, as though unworthy the care of the Allies, the two garrisons were left at full liberty to turn their arms. Barère, as the mouth-piece of the ruling Jacobins, hastened to point out and to gloat over this omission. The garrison of Mayence was despatched by forced marches to La Vendée, and the garrison of Valenciennes to the Rhone—with what fatal effect will presently be shown.

Still worse in its moral influence, if worse be possible, was another act of the Austrian chiefs. On the surrender of Condé and of Valenciennes they had taken possession of both towns in solemn, nay, ostentatious form, not as places to be held during the war—not in the name of the captive King Louis the Seventeenth, but as conquests of their own, as permanent additions to the Austrian Netherlands. In vain did Monsieur in the name of the French Princes protest against this act; in vain did Dumouriez, then at Brussels, arouse the indignation of the later exiles. It was plain that the early views of moderation had been laid aside by the Austrian Cabinet; that the counsels of Pitt had not prevailed; that the curtailment of the French territory at least, if not the partition of France, was now in view.

Supposing for a moment that the Allies had pursued no such suicidal course—that the spirit of greedy self-interest had been withheld—that the system of old routine in the frontier sieges had been cast aside—what result, it may be asked, would have attended a forward movement to the capital? In all probability it would have been crowned with complete success. With English, Dutch, and Hanoverians, in addition to the Imperial troops, the Prince of Coburg could have mustered full eighty thousand men. The French in the Camp of Cæsar had scarcely more than half as many. First, then, defeating the French army, or leaving behind a large division to keep it in check, the remaining forces might have boldly advanced, and would have found no obstacle of any kind on their road to Paris. Paris itself at their approach would have probably risen, in part at least, against its tyrants. At all events, it had then no fortified works and no regular troops to defend it. And for the Allies to enter Paris would be to end the Revolution. To put down the bawlers of the Jacobin Club and the pikemen of the Faubourg St Antoine would be to put down at that time the acknowledged rulers of France.

It must be owned, however, that the project of a rapid advance into the heart of France as urged in

1793 seemed wild and rash, and in fact did startle the common run of politicians as well as the common run of Generals. When in April, 1794, Mr. Jenkinson ventured in the House of Commons to declare his approval of it, the idea was received with derision. Long afterwards, and since by the promotion of his father to an Earldom in 1796 he had become Lord Hawkesbury, the words ' Lord Hawkesbury's march to Paris ' were the burthen of many a jest or satirical song against him.

It must likewise be owned that the most favourable opportunity to strike this blow, like all favourable opportunities, quickly passed away. The indignation aroused by the conduct of the Allies on the surrender of Mayence and Valenciennes lost them the prospect of French adhesions, and tended in no small degree to recruit the opposite ranks. Moreover, as regards the last point we must bear in mind that the effects of the French Revolution had been in part for good. The abolition of grinding taxes like the *Gabelle*, and of arbitrary arrests as by the *Lettres de Cachet*, and the substitution of equality before the law in the place of seignorial privileges and immunities, had stirred up in many places a powerful enthusiasm, above all with the young and the bold. Under all these circumstances new levies in great numbers flocked to the Tricolor standard, and filled the ranks of the Revolutionary armies. Fired with no common ardour, and never for a moment belying the martial spirit of their race, they seemed careless alike of danger, privation, and fatigue.

The fruits of this new spirit soon appeared. When the Duke of York proceeded with the siege of Dunkirk, he found two brave Generals against him—Hoche within and Houchard without the walls; and he was assailed both by sallies from the garrison and by attacks from the large relieving force. His own army was divided into two corps: the one of observation under the Hanoverian Marshal Freytag and the Hereditary Prince of Orange ; the other of siege, which was commanded by himself. But with the latter he could make no real progress for the want of a battering train which he impatiently expected from England. On the 18th of August the Prince of Orange gained an advantage over the French at the village of Lincelles, but on the 8th of September was worsted at the village of Hondschoote. This action and the continued want of heavy cannon compelled the Duke of York to raise the siege.

Nor had the Prince of Coburg any better success. The small place of Le Quesnoy did indeed surrender to General Clerfait, but immediately afterwards the French, having received large accessions of new levies, compelled both Clerfait and Coburg to raise the siege of Maubeuge and to fall back behind the Sambre. Some smaller operations followed with but slight result. And thus indecisively ended this campaign.

Meanwhile the chiefs of the Convention displayed a terrible energy against the insurgents within the limits of France. Lyons was retaken and laid waste with fire and sword. Its buildings were ordered to be razed to the ground ; its very name was declared to be obliterated, and changed to *Commune Affranchie*. Marseilles in like manner was compelled to yield to the Revolutionary troops ; and Toulon only for a time escaped the same fate by proclaiming Louis the Seventeenth, and calling in the aid of an English squadron under Admiral Lord Hood.

Lord Hood could land no more than fifteen hundred men as available for the defence of the town. But, besides some small succours from the Sardinian and Neapolitan armies, the Spanish Admiral Langara brought three thousand men from the coast of Catalonia, and General O'Hara two foot regiments from the garrison of Gibraltar. Sir Gilbert Elliot also arrived from England for the civil direction of affairs, being associated in that object with O'Hara and Hood. The

three Commissioners lost no time in issuing a joint
Declaration containing a solemn promise in His Majesty's name, that on the restoration of monarchy in
France, and the conclusion of a treaty of peace, the
fortress of Toulon, with all the ships and supplies,
should be faithfully restored.

But however inspiriting might be this promise to
the Royalists of Toulon, they found themselves by no
means able to maintain their ground. Their ill-assorted
allies—English, Sardinians, Neapolitans, and Spaniards
—even when added to themselves, were far outnumbered by their Republican besiegers. And although
the great importance of assisting them was both felt
and acted on by the English Government, their fate
came to a decision before fresh succour could arrive.
The attacks made upon their posts were frequent and
formidable; and the artillery against them was under
the direction of a young Corsican officer, whose name,
then first rising to distinction, was ere long to resound
with surpassing fame throughout the world. This was
Napoleon Bonaparte.

General O'Hara, being closely pressed, tried a sudden
and vigorous sally, but he was wounded and taken
prisoner, while his troops were repulsed. On the 18th
of December the besiegers obtained possession of the
fort which commanded the inner harbour, and the Allied
troops found themselves compelled without delay to
relinquish the town and re-embark. By great exertions
on the part of the Spanish and English Admirals, several
thousands of the Royalists—and the Royalists had
flocked to Toulon from all parts of Provence—were put
on board, and secured from the vengeance of their countrymen. Some French ships ready for sea sailed forth
under Admiral Trogoff, one of their own chiefs; the
remainder, with the arsenal and stores, were committed
to the flames. It was a night of terrible havoc and
affright, and of slaughter also when the infuriated Republicans marched in.

Not less afflicting were the scenes in La Vendée. The ferocious troops from Mayence had been let loose upon the open country, and had treated it much as a tribe of Mohawks might have done. At Chollet they had given battle to the insurgent army, when the latter had been worsted. D'Elbée, Bonchamp, Lescure, nearly all the insurgent chiefs, were mortally wounded. The remainder, drawing along with them a confused multitude of women and children, who would have been slaughtered had they stayed, crossed the Loire and marched, half fugitives and half invaders, through Anjou. There might be eighty thousand in all. Their object was to reach some point upon the northern coast, where they might receive the expected succours from England. Accordingly they repulsed their pursuers at Laval, and pushed onward to the fortified sea-port of Granville, which they attempted to reduce by a *coup de main* on the 14th of November.

In England their interests were not forgotten, as they had been at Mayence and Valenciennes. An expedition for their aid was fitted out under Lord Moira's command. But whether from any delays that might have been avoided, or from the inherent difficulties of the service, that expedition came too late. When Lord Moira at last appeared off the coast of Normandy, he found that the Vendéans had left it ten days before.

Failing in their attempt upon Granville, and suspecting their chiefs of a design to escape by sea, these armed peasants, never at any time very amenable to discipline, insisted with loud cries on marching back to the Loire. Henri de la Roche Jaquelein strove against them in vain. He boldly marched forward and took the town of Villedieu, but he found no more than a thousand men beside him, and was compelled to rejoin the main body in retreat. Famished and footsore they were overtaken at Le Mans by the main Republican army, including a division from Mayence. An action ensued; the Vendéans were utterly routed, and great numbers of them put to the sword. The remainder continued their dismal flight beyond Nantes to Savenay. There, in a second action, the rout was renewed and the work of slaughter completed. Little mercy was shown even to the women and children, and of the vast multitude which had crossed the Loire a few weeks since, only a few scattered fugitives ever again set foot upon the southern shore.

By sea there was not in the course of this year any general action, but many a single ship of the French Republic after a gallant fight struck its flag to ours. And out of Europe we made several conquests. In India we took Chandernagore and Pondicherry, in North America St. Pierre and Miquelon, and in the West Indies Tobago, while St. Domingo and Martinico were attempted in vain. But these conquests, though important, were easy, and did not suffice to counterbalance the ill-impression which had been produced by the indecisive European campaign.

At home, and as regards the members of the secret societies and their abettors, the years 1793 and 1794 were marked by a vigorous, nay severe exertion of the law. So rife and unrestrained had become the projects of treason, that the strongest measures of repression seemed to be required by the public safety, as most certainly they were called for by the public voice. The licence of the press, above all, had far outrun all customary bounds. Hence in every part of the island there ensued frequent prosecutions for political offences. Hence throughout the country many persons concerned in the book or newspaper trades were brought to trial, and convicted for either reprinting or selling Thomas Paine's 'Rights of Man,' and his 'Address to the Addressers.' Amongst them were Mr. James Ridgway of London, Mr. Daniel Holt of Newark, and Mr. Richard Phillips of Leicester. A Dissenting Minister of Plymouth, Mr. William Winterbotham, was found guilty of some seditious expressions in two sermons which he had preached. Another prosecution was directed against Messrs. Lambert, Perry, and Gray, as printers and proprietors of the *Morning Chronicle*. The charge against them was for inserting the Address of a political society at Derby, which heaped opprobrious terms on all the institutions of the country. Sir John Scott, the Attorney-General, exerted himself on the one side, as did Mr. Erskine on the other, and finally, after long deliberation and many doubts on the part of the jurymen, a verdict of Not Guilty was returned.

In some of these transactions it is hard entirely to vindicate the conduct, or at least the language, of Lord Chancellor Loughborough. He had alleged his horror of the French Revolutionary principles as his only reason for joining the Government in advance of his party friends. To justify his politics he a little strained his law. He rather inclined to fall in, at least as to minor cases, with any severity to which that horror in the minds of others might give rise. The strongest of all such cases perhaps is one which occurred in Kent. An honest yeoman, most certainly drunk, was pushed aside by a constable as drunk as himself, and ordered to keep the peace in the King's name. The answer was in these words: 'D—— you and the King too!' For this foolish expression the Quarter Sessions condemned the poor man to twelve months' imprisonment, and the Chancellor on being appealed to refused to interfere. 'To save the country from Revolution'—thus spoke his Lordship—'the authority of all tribunals high and low must be upheld.'[1]

But it was in Scotland that we find the most of violence, both in the Revolutionary spirit and in the measures against it; and all the other trials of 1793 are cast into the shade by the superior interest of the cases of Muir and Palmer.

Thomas Muir was a Scottish Advocate, the son of

[1] See Lord Campbell's *Lives of the Chancellors*, vol. vi. p. 265.

a bookseller at Glasgow. He had taken an active part in politics as a speaker at public meetings, and as a member of the society called 'the Friends of the People.' Finding a charge of sedition brought against him, he had retired to France and undergone a sentence of outlawry. But in the course of this summer, coming back by the way of Ireland to his native country, he was discovered and arrested at Port Patrick. Next, he was indicted for having published by distributing several seditious works, particularly those of Thomas Paine, and also for seditious words and speeches. In the trial which ensued at Edinburgh he conducted his own defence. Overlooking, since he could not vindicate, some language of a seditious tendency which was certainly brought home to him, he declared that his object had only been to effect a reform of the House of Commons, and he quoted—as was the usual course of the defendants for sedition at this period—the early speeches of Mr. Pitt and the Duke of Richmond in support of the same cause. On the whole he defended himself with eloquence, skill, and courage, and when he sat down the sympathy of the audience was shown by repeated bursts of cheers.

On the other hand, the Lord Justice Clerk—and here not merely the office which he sullied, but also his name and title should be recorded; it was Robert MacQueen of Braxfield—in summing up the evidence with a strong bias against the prisoner, used some most unjustifiable expressions. He said that the Government of the country was made up of the landed interest, 'which alone had a right to be represented. As for the rabble,' he continued, 'who have nothing but personal property, what hold has the nation of them?' Some months later, Mr. Fox, with his usual force, denounced in the House of Commons this most discreditable Charge.[1]

At Edinburgh, however, the jury returned a verdict

[1] Howell's *State Trials*, vol. xxiii. p. 231, and Debate on Mr. Adam's motion, March 10, 1794.

of Guilty, and the Judges concurred in a sentence that Thomas Muir should be transported beyond seas for the term of fourteen years. And here another grave charge arises against Lord Braxfield. It appears from his speech that the cheers at the close of the prisoner's address were admitted, most unjustifiably, as an argument against the prisoner himself. 'I must observe'—thus spoke Lord Braxfield—'that the indecent applause which was given Mr. Muir last night convinces me that a spirit of discontent still lurks in the minds of the people, and that it would be dangerous to allow him to remain in this country. This circumstance, I must say, has no little weight with me when considering of the punishment which Mr. Muir deserves.'

In fulfilment of this sentence, Mr. Muir, after being confined for some months in the Tolbooth at Edinburgh, was transported to Botany Bay. There he had fresh opportunity to show his courage and skill. It was a matter of extreme difficulty to escape from that settlement, visited at that time by scarce any besides convict and strictly-guarded ships. Mr. Muir, however, found means to embark undiscovered for Nootka Sound, thence travelling along the coast of Panama, and across the Isthmus of Darien, and after a short detention in the island of Cuba, finding in a Spanish frigate a safe conveyance to Europe. But during this last passage he received a wound that was never perfectly cured, and to which was ascribed his death at Paris in the year 1799.[1] Wolfe Tone, who saw him there in the preceding years, describes him in far from favourable terms: 'Of all the vain, obstinate blockheads that ever I met, I never saw his equal.'[2] Since his death, on the contrary, some of his own countrymen in Scotland have been disposed to look on him with great veneration, as 'one of the Martyrs.'

[1] *Ann. Registers*, 1797, p. 14; and 1799, p. 9.
[2] *Diary*, Feb. 1, 1798.

A much shorter statement will suffice for the case of the Rev. Thomas Fyshe Palmer. He was of an old gentleman's family in Berkshire, but having renounced the tenets of the Church of England, he became a writer and preacher of the Unitarian party, and a resident of Dundee. Having distributed some papers of a seditious character, he was brought to trial in September before the Circuit Court of Justiciary at Perth. His Counsel greatly relied on the objection, that on the record his name was spelt Fische instead of Fyshe, and to an English lawyer of that period the objection would have seemed insuperable. But in Scotland it was with better reason overruled. The main defence of Mr. Palmer was made up of the usual topics—assertions that his objects were limited to Parliamentary Reform, and extracts from the early speeches of Mr. Pitt and the Duke of Richmond. The verdict was 'Guilty,' and the sentence, as in Mr. Muir's case, was of transportation, but for a lesser period, namely, seven years. It is alleged that in this case as in Muir's, there had been stretches of the law on other points besides the sentence—jurymen admitted in spite of just grounds of challenge—witnesses unduly heard for the prosecution, or unduly shut out from the defence.

In the same part of the country, and before the close of the same year, there was a further aggravation of the popular violence. Delegates from various parts of Scotland assembled at Edinburgh at the call of the 'Friends of the People,' and in concert with the London Corresponding Society. At their first meeting one hundred and fifty-three duly qualified members appeared. Subsequently there came to be added a few more. Among them were Maurice Margarot and Joseph Gerrald, who were the Agents of the London Association, and who quickly took the lead in the proceedings of this new body. Among them there was also one person of rank and fortune, Lord Daer, eldest son of the Earl of Selkirk, a young man of ardent temper and extreme opinions. Condorcet, in his Will, dated March, 1794, mentions Lord Daer as one of the two persons in Great Britain on whom his infant daughter might, he thought, rely.[1] Several of his contemporaries speak of his abilities in very high terms, and he might, not improbably, have played a considerable part in the politics of this period had he not fallen a victim to a lingering illness, when on his voyage to Madeira in the course of the ensuing year. The Delegates at Edinburgh assumed the name of Convention, and sought in nearly all respects to ape the Convention at Paris. Thus because the French had proscribed all titles, even that of Monsieur, they gave to every Member's name the prefix of 'Citizen.' Thus again, because the French had established a new Republican Era, they dated their own reports in the same style, 'First Year of the British Convention, One and Indivisible.' But there was one difference strongly characteristic of the countrymen of Knox. While the Republicans of Paris in their new Calendar had abolished the observance of Sunday, and instituted in its place a tenth day of rest, the Republicans at Edinburgh adhered to their ancient forms of worship. They would transact no business on 'the Sabbath.' They began and ended every meeting with prayer. And when a clergyman joined them, and sent in a present of books, they blended his old title with his new one, and returned thanks to him as 'the Rev. Citizen Douglas of Dundee.'

The Minutes of the Edinburgh Convention have been published, and display a curious mixture of simplicity and shrewdness.[2] Considerable jealousy appears

[1] 'En cas de nécessité elle trouverait de l'appui en Angleterre chez Mylord Stanhope ou Mylord Daer, et en Amérique chez Bache, petit-fils de Franklin, ou chez Jefferson.' (*Œuvres de Condorcet*, vol. i. p. 624. ed. 1849.)

[2] These Minutes were produced as evidence on the trial of William Skirving. See Howell's *State Trials*, vol. xxiii. p. 391–471.

to have been felt by the delegates at any delegation from themselves. ' It will be proper,' said Lord Daer, ' to avoid an aristocratical dependence on Committees.' On the other hand, Citizen Gerrald, not perhaps without a side-blow at Lord Daer, warned the Convention against ' the choice of any other than known and plain men like ourselves; men uncontaminated by the pestilential air of Courts.' It had been proposed to hold the next Convention at York, as a central point which might combine delegates from Scotland with delegates from every part of England. But here an important objection was started by Citizen Gerrald :—' I can assure you,' he said, ' that the city of York is the seat of a proud aristocracy—the seat of an Archbishop!' However, on reflection, Citizen Gerrald thought that this difficulty might be waived. He might perhaps be prevailed on to meet even the Archbishop himself. ' I would not object,' he added, ' to go there, because the Saviour of the world was often found in the company of sinners. . . . Let us then, fellow-citizens, unite heart and hand to bury the hatchet of natural antipathy, which the wicked policy of Courts once instigated us to wield.'

Another favourite topic in this Convention was the alleged tyranny of the chiefs in the Highlands. ' Let me give an instance,' said Citizen Wright. ' A Highland gentleman had an avenue about a mile long, into which none of his tenants dared to enter without taking off his bonnet; and if they had occasion to go to the house, though in the midst of a hurricane, they were obliged to walk all the way bare-headed!' Such were the Mother Goose tales that found credit with these foolish men.

The Convention continued its debates for upwards of a month. But early in December these were cut short by the magistrates. The Lord Provost entered the room with a sufficient force, bid the ' Citizen President ' leave the Chair, and dissolved the meeting. Skirving, who had acted as Secretary, with Margarot and Gerrald, the delegates from London, were brought to trial. All three were found Guilty, and sentenced to be transported for fourteen years.

CHAPTER XVIII.

1793-1794.

Retirement of Mr. Eliot—Trial of Hamilton Rowan—Public approval of the State Trials and the prosecution of the war—Schemes against the Government—Suspension of the Habeas Corpus Act —Energy of the French Republicans—Operations of the Allies— Sanguinary Decree of the Convention regarding prisoners of war —Duke of York's General Order—Corsican revolt—Heroism of Hood and Nelson—Victory of the First of June—Accession to office of the Duke of Portland and his friends—Provision for Mr. Burke—Death of his son—Mr. Windham—Misunderstanding with the Duke of Portland—Close of the Reign of Terror in France—Execution of Robespierre—Recall of the Duke of York.

In June of this year Mr. Pitt was grieved at the retirement of a dear friend and kinsman. A seat at the Board of Treasury was given up by Mr. Eliot. Delicate health, and a more serious temper resulting from his family bereavement, led him to this step. Yet he did not altogether withdraw himself from public life, since he continued in the House of Commons.

So full of anxieties was the whole of this year that Mr. Pitt could not venture to leave London for any long time. Sometimes he had a day, sometimes only a few hours, at Holwood. Thus writes Wilberforce: ' June 22. To Holwood with Pitt in his phaeton—early dinner, and back to town.' We can imagine the Minister most frequently in Downing Street, as another entry of the same journal describes him, ' To town, 14th of September, to see Pitt—a great map spread out before him.'

In August, however, Pitt was able to go for a few days to Burton Pynsent, and in September to his new possession as Lord Warden of the Cinque Ports, Walmer Castle. The King had some fears for his Minister thus in the very sight of the French coast. Without Mr. Pitt's knowledge he sent orders to Lord Amherst to stockade the ditch of the castle, and station in it a picket of soldiers.[1]

At that busy period the private letters of Pitt are but brief and few. Here are some to his mother, either in extract or entire :—

Holwood, June 7, 1793.

I have just received your letter, and must disobey the kind injunction it contains by writing a single line to thank you for it, and to tell you that the gout, after having made a visit in due form, and stayed a reasonable time, is now taking its leave. I was able without any inconvenience to come here yesterday evening, and your letter found me enjoying a fine day from my window, so much as almost to be glad of my present excuse for being out of London. If I was to ascribe entirely to the same circumstance the delay of my visit to Burton, I should think of it very differently. I believe, however, that in fact if I had not been a prisoner to gout, the state of things in Flanders would hardly have left me at liberty at the time I first intended; as we are flattering ourselves that a few days may possibly bring us very favourable news from Valenciennes; and I should hardly be able to absent myself till the consequences are more ascertained.

Holwood, July 2, 1793.

I am still kept from week to week in the expectation of some melancholy event either on sea or land, of which I should not like to be out of the way of receiving the earliest news. The surrender of Valenciennes and Lord Howe's sailing, both of which will probably happen very soon, may set me more at liberty.

In the meantime I have holidays enough for a good deal of country air, and have the advantage of having parted with my gouty shoe, and found the full use of my legs.

[1] The King to Mr. Pitt, July 13, 1793.

Holwood, July 15, 1793.

My dear Mother,—I am very sorry that I have had an application some time since about Lampeter, which will perhaps not itself be successful, but being from one of my constituents, would make it impossible for me to intercede in favour of Mrs. Lewis's request.   Lord Stanhope's notification of his visit[1] certainly comes at a singular time, but so many miles from the House of Lords, he will be very harmless and well-behaved, and I cannot help rejoicing on account of the companions of his journey.   Besides answering these two points, I have another reason for making use of the leisure of Holwood to write to you.   A vacancy has just happened in the office of housekeeper to the Excise, which is executed by deputy, and worth above 100*l.*, I believe 150*l.* per annum. This is so much better than that which is now held by poor Mrs. Sparry, that I think the offer of an exchange would probably be very agreeable to her, as a mark of attention and remembrance, though in any other view I am afraid the prospect of her enjoying it cannot make it much an object. I have, therefore, in my own mind destined it for her, and I conclude you would wish Mrs. Arden, whom you mentioned some time ago, to succeed to Mrs. Sparry's office at the Treasury.   I should add that the last housekeeper of the Excise was a widow of one of the Commissioners, and her predecessor an old Mrs. Cavendish, who was, I believe, a distant connection of the Devonshires.   This gives a sort of credit to the office which may make it the more welcome ; at the same time it does not make the way of disposing of it at all improper.

The fall of Condé will, I hope, soon be followed by Valenciennes, but the prospect is not yet certain enough to let me fix my plans positively.   I think I may be at liberty in about a fortnight, but I should wish to regulate my motions a little by Eliot's and Lord Stanhope's, though not exactly in the same way by each of them.   I have written to Eliot, and take the chance of my letter finding him in Cornwall, to tell him that it is of no consequence whether he comes to town a little sooner or later.

Your dutiful and affectionate son,   W. Pitt.

I have been enjoying a great deal of this unusual sum-

---

[1] To Burton Pynsent, on returning with his daughters from a visit to his estate in Devonshire.

mer, and should like it still better if it had not burnt all my grass, and parched a good many young trees.

Downing Street, Aug. 31, 1793.

After the interval of a week's holidays, and preparing for another, I have not till now found time for writing, though I have intended it every day. It would now be rather late to tell you that I performed my journey and arrived as I intended; for probably the newspapers will have told that for me already.

Downing Street, Nov. 11, 1793.

My dear Mother,—I trust I need not say that my first wish must always be to contribute to your ease and convenience, and I am only sorry you should have given yourself so much trouble, where a single word to convey your wish would have been sufficient. I can furnish without difficulty three hundred pounds, and will immediately desire Mr. Coutts to place that sum to your account. Indeed, I should not feel satisfied with myself in not naming at once a larger sum, if it were not that my accession of income has hitherto found so much employment in the discharge of former arrears as to leave no very large fund which I can with propriety dispose of. This, however, will mend every day; and at all events I trust you will never scruple to tell me when you have the slightest occasion for any aid I can supply.

. . . .

Ever, my dear Mother, &c.,   W. Pitt.

To the State trials during 1793 as told in my last chapter may be added another at the beginning of 1794 —that of Hamilton Rowan. It was brought before the Court of King's Bench at Dublin by Arthur Wolfe, the Irish Attorney-General. Mr. Rowan had acted as secretary of the new political combination first formed in 1791 under the influence of French examples, and calling itself 'The Society of United Irishmen.' As secretary Mr. Rowan had signed and issued an address of seditious character to the Volunteers of Dublin, and of this act he now stood accused. His Counsel, John Philpot Curran, conducted his defence with great eloquence and undaunted spirit, thus laying the foundations of his own subsequent renown ; but Hamilton Rowan was found Guilty. The sentence passed upon him was, to be imprisoned for the term of two years. Within four months, however, he found means to escape from Newgate Gaol in Dublin, and made his way to France.

Although in a few of these cases an eloquent address, as of Muir or Curran, on the defendant's side, might stir the audience to applause, and although undoubtedly some Judges, the Chancellor included, did sometimes degenerate to partisans, it does not appear that the main course of these prosecutions in any degree outran the general temper and opinion of these times. Among the middle and upper classes more especially, as also in the entire rank of yeomen, there was a detestation of the French excesses ; and dread might well be felt when they saw such excesses held up for examples. Among those who in England or in Scotland still for safety called themselves Reformers, their open violence was plain to view and their secret conspiracy was feared ; and the public voice was loud in calling for activity and firmness, nay, even for rigour, against them. In such extraordinary circumstances can we, it was asked, expect that mere ordinary measures would suffice?

This temper of the public in regard to the State Trials was further manifested in the deliberations of the Legislature. Parliament met on the 21st of January, and within ten days Lord Stanhope appealed to the Upper House upon the case of Muir. A few weeks later Lord Lauderdale brought forward the cases of Muir and Palmer conjointly, and in the Commons there were no less than three motions on the same subject from Mr. Adam. But they met with no success. In the motion of Lord Stanhope, which was irregular in point of form, the mover stood alone, and Lord Lauderdale did not venture to call for a division. Mr. Adam, though warmly supported by Fox and Sheridan, was as warmly withstood by other members of the old Whig party; and the highest number of votes that he could muster was thirty-two.

Nor had the same politicians any better success in their endeavours to put an end to the war with France. Lord Stanhope brought forward two motions with that view, couched in speeches so extreme as in a great measure to defeat themselves. The same object was zealously pressed by Lord Lansdowne and the Duke of Bedford among the Peers; in the Commons by Fox, Sheridan, and Grey. But they had left to them only a handful of adherents. The minority on Fox's motion was no more than fifty-five.

On the other hand, there was a cheerful acquiescence in all the measures proposed by the Prime Minister for the vigorous prosecution of the war. When he laid upon the Table subsidiary Treaties with several Foreign Powers, they were approved. When he asked a loan of eleven millions, it was voted. When he asked for some additional duties on various articles, as rum and spirits, bricks and tiles, plate-glass and attorneys, not even the attorneys complained. When, a King's Message being first presented, he called for an augmentation of the land-forces, that augmentation was agreed to.

On all these questions Mr. Pitt could rely on the Duke of Portland's friends as much as on his own. Still, however, the chiefs of the remaining Opposition struck at him boldly whenever they saw, or fancied that they saw, any vulnerable point. Thus Mr. Dundas, as Secretary of State, had sent round in circulars a plan ' to provide more completely for the security of the country.' He recommended that bodies of volunteers, both infantry and cavalry, should be formed, and that for these objects a public subscription might be raised. Hereupon Mr. Sheridan in the one House, and Lord Lauderdale in the other, brought forward motions declaring that it was a dangerous and unconstitutional measure for the Executive Government to solicit money

for public purposes without the consent of Parliament.
But with every exertion Mr. Sheridan could muster no
more than thirty-four votes, and Lord Lauderdale no
more than seven. As zealously, but with equal ill
success, was the progress of the Volunteer Corps Bill
resisted.

In like manner, when some Hessian troops in British
pay were landed in the Isle of Wight, or when a Bill
was brought in enabling the Government to enlist some
of the French Royalists in the British army, the Opposition raised a loud cry of Constitutional alarm. ' I
firmly believe,' said Colonel Tarleton —this eager politician afterwards became Sir Banastre and a General
Officer—' that the passing this Bill will destroy the privileges of Magna Charta, undermine the Bill of Rights,
and finally annihilate the British Constitution!'[1]

An argument of real weight against the Bill was,
however, supplied by Mr. Sheridan. 'Suppose,' he
said, ' any of the French emigrants in our service are
taken prisoners and are put to death. What then?
Are we to avenge their fate by retaliation?'— Here
across the House Mr. Burke exclaimed ' Yes.'—' Good
Heavens!' cried Mr. Sheridan, ' consider that the lives
of millions may depend upon that single word!'

On a subsequent day the same argument was farther
pressed by Mr. Fox. ' If,' he said, ' the French were
to land in this kingdom, and there chanced to be any
body of the people so lost to all sense of duty as to join
them, should we pardon those who produced Commissions from the Convention? We should not. Nor
would the French in the like case respect Commissions
granted by our King. Then, if we determined not to
retaliate, in what a calamitous situation did we place
those whom we employed! And if we did retaliate,
good God! in what horrors would Europe be involved!'

Mr. Burke in reply—and this speech deserves the

----

[1] *Parl. Hist.* vol. xxxi. p. 387.

more attention as the last of Burke's great efforts in the House of Commons—defended his former cry of 'Yes,' and boldly avowed that in the case supposed his voice would be for retaliation. 'God forbid,' he said, 'that the authors of murder should not find it recoil on their own heads. But fears are expressed that we may inflame the Jacobins by severity. Inflame a Jacobin! You may as well talk of setting fire to Hell! Impossible!'

It is not easy to see how any Government could have displayed greater energy in all its Parliamentary measures for the effectual prosecution of the war. Nor was there less of vigour for the repression of treasonable practices at home. Early in April Thomas Walker, a merchant of note at Manchester, with six other persons of inferior rank, were brought to trial for conspiracy, at the Lancaster Assizes. But this prosecution most signally failed. The principal witness was Thomas Dunn, a weaver, who was shown to have forsworn himself on several points, and to be wholly undeserving of credit. Mr. Law, as Counsel for the Crown, threw up the case, and the Jury returned an immediate verdict of Not Guilty, while Dunn, being detained and indicted for perjury, was soon afterwards convicted. The sentence passed upon him was, to stand once in the pillory, and be imprisoned for two years in Lancaster Castle.

It is worthy of note that among the records of the first of these Lancashire trials will be found, dated 1793, a letter of reproof and admonition from Mr. William Cartwright of Shrewsbury, 'who,' it is added, 'is a surgeon and apothecary, and a non-juring Bishop.' Here, according to Mr. Hallam, is the latest trace in our history of these successors to Sancroft and Lloyd.[1]

But this last of the non-jurors had now become a most loyal subject to King George. In his letter he says : 'The one family being as good as entirely extinct,

---

[1] *State Trials*, vol. xxiii. p. 1073; *Constitutional History*, vol. iii. p. 341.

and the other having been so long in uninterrupted possession, surely we need not now hesitate which of these God has chosen to reign over us.'—Then why not conform ?

Of all the schemes against the Government, however, London was the main and directing point. There the two Societies—the 'Corresponding,' and the Society 'for Constitutional Information '—had lately combined their efforts and extended their designs. It was desired to call a Convention of the people, to sit in London, and to supersede as far as possible the authority of Parliament. With this view, not merely were the workmen instigated to hold meetings at the chief manufacturing towns, and delegates sent down to attend them—not merely were the most inflammatory topics and the most malignant misrepresentations urged in their harangues—but songs were put in circulation designed for popular impression, and breathing the very spirit of the Regicides.[1] Take, for instance, the song which had for chorus—

> Plant, plant the tree, fair Freedom's tree,
> Midst dangers, wounds, and slaughter :
> Each patriot's breast its soil shall be,
> And tyrants' blood its water.

Such mere moral weapons were not alone relied on. Arms—as muskets and pikes—were also, it appears, in some places collected and kept ready ; and a seizure of such was made at this time by the Government at Edinburgh.

But this did not suffice. It was not enough that the leaders in such projects should be stopped short in their course. The Government deemed it further indispensable, as a warning to others, that they should be brought to trial for High Treason. Early in May, therefore, eight members of the two Societies were apprehended and, after an examination before the Privy

[1] See the evidence adduced on the trial of Thomas Hardy. (*State Trials*, vol. xxiv. p. 977.)

Council, sent to the Tower. At the same time the books and papers of the two Societies were secured.

The eight persons thus committed for trial were as follow :—Thomas Hardy, secretary to the Corresponding Society, and a shoemaker by trade ; Daniel Adams, secretary to the Constitutional Society, and lately a clerk in the Auditor's Office ; John Horne Tooke, so well known from his former controversies in the days of Junius and during the American war ; the Rev. Jeremiah Joyce, private secretary to Lord Stanhope and tutor to his sons. Mr. Joyce is still remembered as the author of the 'Scientific Dialogues,' in four volumes, which appeared between 1800 and 1802, and which convey a great amount of knowledge in a very agreeable form. There was also John Thelwall, of some note as a political lecturer. The others were John Augustus Bonney, John Richter, and John Lovett.

The books and papers thus seized were announced in a Message from the King to the House of Commons, and referred by Mr. Pitt to a Committee of Secrecy. That Committee, to consist of twenty-one members, was selected by ballot. Within four-and-twenty hours they presented their first Report, declaring themselves convinced that the papers before them afforded ample proofs of a traitorous conspiracy. 'However,' they added, 'at different periods the term of Parliamentary Reform may have been employed, it is obvious that the present view of these Societies is not intended to be prosecuted by any application to Parliament, but, on the contrary, by an open attempt to supersede the House of Commons.'

Fortified by this Report, and, it may be added, by the public feeling out of doors, Mr. Pitt deemed it his imperative duty to bring in, without a moment's delay, a Bill for the suspension of the Habeas Corpus Act. That Bill received the ready and rapid concurrence of the House of Commons, though resisted with

the utmost energy by Fox and Sheridan. On the day
when it was pressed forward through its various stages
they tried no less than eleven divisions against it,
though their highest numbers in any of these were but
thirty-nine. In the other House the Bill was opposed
only by Lords Stanhope, Lauderdale, and Lansdowne,
and six Peers present besides.

Shortly afterwards the Committee of Secrecy presented a second Report, comprising copies of many of
the original papers seized. The letters from various
parts of the country, as here produced, are a strange
amalgam of treasonable schemes with silly gossip. Thus,
on the one hand, from Sheffield :—' Fellow citizens, the
barefaced aristocracy of the present administration has
made it necessary that we should be prepared to act on
the defensive. A plan has been hit upon, and, if encouraged sufficiently, will, no doubt, have the effect
of furnishing a quantity of pikes to the patriots. The
blades are made of steel, tempered and polished after
an approved form, and each, with the hoop, will be
charged one shilling.' And thus, on the other hand,
from Tewkesbury :—' The burning of Thomas Paine's
effigy, together with the blessed effects of the present
war, has done more good to the cause than the most
substantial arguments. 'Tis amazing the increase of
friends to Liberty and the spirit of inquiry that is
gone abroad. Scarcely an old woman but is talking
politics.'[1]

Throughout this winter the most strenuous exertions had been made in France for the prosecution of
the war. The Committee of Public Safety, with Robespierre for its leader, seemed to imprint its savage
energy on everything around it. Above a million of
Frenchmen—so, at least, was computed or guessed at
—took up arms. Thus every frontier of the new Republic was lined with numerous and ardent levies. The
Army of the North, as it was termed, that is, in front

---

[1] See the *Parliamentary History*, vol. xxxi. pp. 689 and 822.

of Flanders, was, including the garrisons, of two hundred and fifty thousand men. Its command had been entrusted to General Pichegru, while General Jourdan was at the head of the Army of the Moselle.

On the side of the Allies the Duke of York had, in the month of January, returned to London for fresh instructions, accompanied by General Mack, an excellent officer on paper. By Mack there was formed a plan, most ingenious and most impracticable, for the next campaign. The siege of Landrecies was first to be undertaken, and then a combined march to Paris was to be made. Great hopes were, moreover, founded on the arrival of the Emperor at Brussels. It was thought that his presence might serve to restore the loyalty of his ill-affected subjects, and to compose the dissensions of his jarring Generals. But neither of these aims was effectually attained.

In the middle of April the young Emperor reviewed his army in the plains of Cateau, where it is said that no less than one hundred and forty thousand men were mustered before him. But immediately afterwards these troops were parted for active operations. The Prince of Saxe Coburg, as Commander-in-Chief, led the main body to the siege of Landrecies; the Duke of York with one division covered his right flank in the direction of Cambray; while General Clerfait, to protect the frontier, took post on the side of Lille.

While Landrecies was thus invested the Republicans were not at rest. They made several attempts to raise the siege. With great spirit they assailed the lines of the Prince of Coburg, but altogether failed in piercing them. Still more unsuccessful was their onset on the position of the Duke of York at Troisville, when they lost thirty-five pieces of cannon and at least three thousand men, their chief, Chappuis, being himself among the prisoners. On the other hand, General Clerfait, being attacked by Souham and Moreau, was defeated and driven back with loss to Tournay. Still, however, Landrecies, not being relieved, was compelled to surrender, with its garrison of four thousand men, after ten days of open trenches.

The French were far from dispirited. Confident in their superior generalship and growing numbers, they resumed the offensive and crossed the Sambre. They gained an advantage at Turcoing on the 18th of May, and another on the 22nd at Pont-à-chin. In the former engagement the Duke of York was nearly surrounded, and owed his safety to the fleetness of his horse, a fact which, with a frankness well becoming a brave soldier, was acknowledged by the Duke himself in his despatch.

It was at this period that the French Convention by the instigation of Barère passed a Decree well worthy the Mohawk Indians, from whom indeed the first idea of it may have been derived. It was argued that 'the slaves of York and George' ought not if taken in battle to escape with life. It was commanded that henceforth no quarter should be given to any English or Hanoverian soldier. No sooner had this sanguinary Decree reached the English camp than some excellent General Orders upon it were issued by the Duke of York. 'His Royal Highness anticipates the indignation and horror which have naturally arisen in the minds of the brave troops whom he addresses. He desires, however, to remind them that mercy to the vanquished is the brightest gem in a soldier's character, and exhorts them not to suffer their resentment to lead them to any precipitate act of cruelty. . . . The British and Hanoverian armies will not believe that the French nation, even under their present infatuation, can so far forget their character as soldiers as to pay any attention to a Decree as injurious to themselves as it is disgraceful to the persons who passed it.'[1]

[1] These General Orders, which bear date June 7, 1794, are printed at full length in the *Annual Register* for that year, part ii. p. 168.

The generous confidence expressed in this last sentence was most justly founded. It is gratifying to learn that this inhuman Decree caused nearly as much disgust in the French as in the English camp. 'Kill our prisoners!' said an honest serjeant to his officer, 'no, we will never do that. Send any prisoner we make to the Convention, and let the Deputies shoot him if they will, ay and eat him too, savages as they are.'[1] Thus, to the honour of the Republican army, this order was never executed, and on the fall of Robespierre it was one of the first to be rescinded. The whole transaction may serve to show how much thirst of blood there may often be in a civilian's breast, and how much gentleness in a soldier's.

In the middle of June the Emperor set out on his return to Vienna with slight hopes of retaining the dominion of the Netherlands, and leaving his troops outnumbered and disheartened. General Clerfait and the Duke of York were in West Flanders, where they could not prevent Pichegru from reducing Ypres, and the Prince of Coburg was recalled to the Sambre by the advance of Jourdan from the Meuse. Finding the French army invest Charleroi before him, Coburg determined to fight for its relief, but the battle which he gave upon the plains of Fleurus on the 26th of June proved adverse to him and decided the campaign. Pichegru and Jourdan advancing in concert entered Brussels, and the recent conquests of the Allies, Landrecies, Condé, Valenciennes, and Le Quesnoy, were rapidly recovered by the French.

In the Mediterranean and in the Channel we had more success. The Corsicans had risen in revolt against the French Republic. They had once more at their head the veteran patriot General Paoli, returned from his exile in London, where during twenty years he had enjoyed the intimate friendship of such men as Johnson, Reynolds, and Burke. On his journey homewards, at the

---

[1] Thiers, *Hist. Révol.* vol. iv. p. 68.

commencement of the French Revolution, he had passed through Paris and been presented by La Fayette to the Constituant Assembly. Both there and in Corsica, averse as he was to civil war, he had shown an honourable willingness to accept the dominion which he found established. But the atrocities of the Reign of Terror stirred up his countrymen and himself to arms. A meeting of deputies under the name of a Consulta was held at Corte, where Paoli was proclaimed General in chief and a military force was provided. Of the principal men in the island, some, like Pozzo di Borgo, took the part of Paoli, while others, like the Bonapartes, adhered to France.

In the first instance the success of the insurgents was complete. They drove the few French troops from all the open country, and confined them to the three maritime posts of San Fiorenzo, Bastia, and Calvi. And to complete their conquest they solicited aid from England. Accordingly after our evacuation of Toulon, it was to this quarter that the next effort of our forces was directed. Lord Hood with his fleet appeared off the northern coast. Sir Gilbert Elliot, as the King's Commissioner for the Mediterranean, went on shore and held a satisfactory conference with General Paoli. In the result the English ships co-operating with the Corsican levies reduced first San Fiorenzo; next, in May, 1794, the important town of Bastia, the capital of the island; and lastly, after a long resistance, Calvi.

It should not be omitted that in these three sieges much prowess was shown and much distinction acquired by an officer destined to become the greatest of our naval heroes, but as yet plain Captain Nelson of the Agamemnon. His zeal and energy—as also the veteran Lord Hood's—stand forth in striking contrast to the indecision and slackness which at this period had beset too many chiefs of our land service. Thus before the walls of Bastia General Sir David Dundas, who commanded the troops, appeared upon the heights, but, satisfied with having reconnoitred the place, returned to San Fiorenzo. 'What the General,' said Nelson, 'could have seen to make a retreat necessary I cannot conceive. A thousand men would certainly take Bastia; with five hundred and Agamemnon I would attempt it. My seamen,' he adds, 'are really now what British seamen ought to be— almost invincible. They really mind shot no more than peas.' General Dundas was far from having the same confidence. 'After mature consideration,' thus he wrote at this time to Lord Hood, 'and a personal inspection for several days of all circumstances, local as well as others, I consider the siege of Bastia, with our present means and force, to be a most visionary and rash attempt, such as no officer would be justified in undertaking.' Lord Hood replied that he was ready and willing to undertake it at his own risk. He did undertake it accordingly, but neither from Dundas nor from another officer who at this time succeeded to the chief command could he obtain any aid except only some artillerymen. 'We are but few,' said Nelson, 'but of the right sort: our General at San Fiorenzo not giving us one of the five regiments he has there lying idle.'

Yet even unassisted see what Hood and Nelson could achieve. 'On the 24th of May, at daylight,' thus again writes Nelson, 'there was exhibited the most glorious sight that an Englishman could experience, and that I believe none but an Englishman could bring about—four thousand five hundred men (the garrison of Bastia) laying down their arms to less than one thousand British soldiers, who were serving as marines!' All this while General Dundas might be no doubt composing a most able despatch to the Secretary of State proving, by irresistible arguments, and on a full review 'of all circumstances, local as well as others,' such an exploit to be beyond all bounds of possibility.[1]

---

[1] See the *Life of Nelson*, by Southey, p. 71, ed. 1857; and by Pettigrew, vol. i. pp. 50–54.

On the fall of Bastia expression was forthwith given to the common, nay, almost unanimous wish of the insurgents. They desired that the island should henceforth be annexed to the Throne of England, but as another kingdom, and with a free constitution of its own. A Council was employed in framing the articles of that Constitution with ample powers to a representative assembly, and the sovereignty thus tendered with the title of King was accepted in His Majesty's name by Sir Gilbert Elliot. In his despatch on this occasion Sir Gilbert thus sums up the affair, or rather his own hopes of it : 'His Majesty has acquired a Crown—those who bestow it have acquired liberty.'[1]

In the British Channel a formidable French armament was cruising. It had left the harbour of Brest in pursuance of orders from Paris, and for the purpose of protecting a large convoy laden chiefly with flour which was expected from America. The armament consisted of twenty-six sail of the line, equipped with great care, and having for its chief Admiral Villaret Joyeuse. But his authority was often overruled by a Commissioner from the terrible Convention—Jean Bon St. André, who, though wholly ignorant of seamanship, and indeed at one time a Calvinist Divine, had come on board and assumed the tone of a great commander. Nor was the Admiral adequately supported by all the captains and crews. The French Revolution had been the means of driving the best sea-officers from the service; for under the influence of the new ideas every attempt at maintaining discipline in a ship of war was denounced by Jacobins at the seaports as savouring of aristocracy —as an inroad on the rights of the people. It has been calculated that even before the close of 1791 three-fourths of the officers of the Royal Marine had either retired or been dismissed. Their place was supplied from the merchant service, with a very searching

[1] See this despatch, with some other papers on the same subject, in the *Ann. Reg.* 1794, pp. 95–111.

test as to politics, with a very slight test as to science
and skill.[1]

The commander of our Channel Fleet was at this
time Earl Howe. Like Lord Hood, that veteran chief
had now reached the verge of threescore years and ten;
but it might be said of him as Nelson at the same period
does say of Lord Hood, that, ' upwards of seventy, he
possesses the mind of forty years of age, and he has
not a thought separated from honour and glory.' Lord
Howe had also under him several gallant admirals, as
another Hood, Sir Alexander, afterwards Lord Bridport,
and Graves and Gardner, both subsequently raised to
the peerage. In the action which ensued the French
were superior to the English by one line-of-battle ship
and considerable weight of metal. That action, unlike
most others at sea, does not derive its name either from
the chiefs in command or from the coast in sight, but
is known in history as the battle of the First of June.

Soon after daybreak the English ships bore down
together for close action, and the onset was begun by
the English Admiral. His object was to repeat the
manœuvre of Rodney in 1782, and break the enemy's
line. On the French side a heavy fire was opened
against the English as soon as they came within range.
But Howe in his own ship, the Queen Charlotte, of 100
guns, forbade his men from returning any of the volleys
poured upon them until his pilot could place him alongside of the French Admiral's ship, the Montagne, of
120 guns, the largest vessel at that time in the whole
French navy. Thus piercing through the French line
of battle, and closely followed by five ships of his own
fleet, he drew nigh to the Montagne. So terrific was
the sight and sound on board the enemy's flag-ship that
Jean Bon St. André, who was wholly wanting in the
high spirit of his countrymen, ran down for safety to

[1] See on these points the " Souvenirs d'un Marin, par l'Amiral de
La Gravière," part ii., in the *Revue des Deux Mondes*, Sept. 15, 1858,
p. 213.

the hold. It is to this that Mr. Canning alludes in his well-known song upon St. André :—

> Poor John was a gallant captain,
> In battles much delighting :
>   He fled full soon
>   On the first of June,
> But he bade the rest keep fighting ![1]

The battle now raged furiously, both parties striving with their customary ardour. But after an hour's conflict the French Admiral gave way, and, followed by all his ships still in sufficient order, made sail. One of his seventy-fours, Le Vengeur, went down during the action with many hundred men on board, as also some other nearly disabled ships that might perhaps have been secured; but still five were left as prizes, and brought home in triumph by Howe.

This victory was most seasonable in its influence on England. It proved our continued ascendency on our own element, as we love to call it, the sea; and it revived the spirits that were drooping from the adverse or indecisive results of the last Continental campaigns. The joy in London and in some other cities was manifested by a general illumination for three successive nights. The joy at Court was manifested by a visit which the King, the Queen, and some of the Princesses paid to Lord Howe and the fleet at Spithead, when His Majesty presented to each Admiral and Captain a medal struck in commemoration of the day. Lord Howe himself received on that occasion the further gift of a sword richly set in diamonds. Parliament was still sitting when there came the news of this success, and of that at Bastia. Votes of thanks were most cheerfully passed, and there was a vote also for a monument in Westminster Abbey to Captain Montagu, the only one of Howe's Captains who had fallen.

On the 11th of July the Session closed, and on the same day another event of importance was announced

[1] *Poetry of the Anti-Jacobin*, p. 146, ed. 1813.

—the long expected accession to office of the Duke of
Portland and his friends. This was another token of the
general desire for an united and vigorous prosecution of
the war. This was another token of the general disapprobation of the doctrines which Mr. Fox had recently
professed. The third Secretaryship of State, suppressed
at the Peace of 1782, was on this occasion restored.
Thus while Lord Grenville continued to be charged
with Foreign Affairs, and Mr. Dundas with War and
Colonies, the Duke of Portland received the Seals for the
Home Department. Earl Fitzwilliam became Lord
President, and Earl Spencer Lord Privy Seal; these
vacancies being caused by the death of Earl Camden,
and the retirement of the Marquis of Stafford. Mr.
Windham became Secretary at War with a seat in the
Cabinet. In the first instance he had been designed
for Secretary of State, and the negotiations had for a
long time continued on that footing. But at the very
last the friends of the Duke of Portland grew anxious
to give greater prominence to their former Premier;
Mr. Pitt acquiesced; and His Grace was prevailed upon
to accept the arduous post.

Besides these appointments, two or three peerages,
and two or three places of less amount, gratified some
less leading members of the same connection. Thus
Welbore Ellis became Lord Mendip, and Lord Por-
chester Earl of Carnarvon. Among those who now
became supporters of the Ministry without accepting
any promotion for themselves, was a gentleman of
most accomplished mind and most amiable manners,
Mr. Thomas Grenville, brother of Lord Buckingham
and Lord Grenville, who up to this time had detached
himself from the politics of his family, and been numbered among the adherents of Mr. Fox. As further
and outward tokens to the public of the new alliance,
the Duke of Portland was invested with the Garter,
and his eldest son, Lord Titchfield, received the Lord
Lieutenancy of Middlesex.

It was moreover intended, and with no more than strict justice, to make a suitable provision both in rank and in fortune for Mr. Burke. Some time since he had announced his approaching retirement from the House of Commons. He had declared that he only lingered to see concluded the greatest object of his public life—the prosecution of Warren Hastings. Accordingly, his last appearance in the House was on the 20th of June, when, after a long debate and two divisions, thanks were returned from the Chair to the Managers of the Impeachment (they standing up severally in their places) for their faithful discharge of the trust reposed in them. Immediately afterwards Burke took the Chiltern Hundreds. Then the Writ for Malton was moved, and in that representation, through the continued friendship of Lord Fitzwilliam, his son was chosen to succeed him.

It was now desired—I cannot say with truth to honour Mr. Burke, but rather to honour the peerage by his accession to its ranks. There was also, as I have heard, the design, as in other cases of rare merit, to annex by an Act of Parliament a yearly income to the title during two or three lives. Already was the title chosen as Lord Beaconsfield. Already was the patent preparing. Just then it pleased Almighty God to strike the old man to the very earth by the untimely death of his beloved son, his only child. Richard Burke expired on the 2nd of August, 1794. There ended Burke's whole share of earthly happiness. There ended all his dreams of earthly grandeur. Thenceforth a Coronet was to him a worthless bauble which he must decline to wear. But of the Ministers he speaks as follows, in one of the last and greatest of his works: 'They have administered to me the only consolation I am capable of receiving; which is to know that no individual will suffer by my thirty years' service to the public.'[1] In that long term he had contracted

---

[1] First Letter on a Regicide Peace, 1796. (*Works*, vol. viii. p. 206, ed. 1815.)

divers debts and obligations which his own scanty
means could not discharge. And moreover, how doubly
hard under the pressure of sorrow to have to cut down
expenses and retrench from personal ease! He therefore gratefully took what was freely and honourably
tendered—a signal and suitable token of the Royal
bounty. But the course that was designed will best
appear from the correspondence that ensued. Here is
Pitt's first letter to Burke:—

Downing Street, August 30, 1794.

Dear Sir,—I have received the King's permission to acquaint you that it is His Majesty's intention to propose to
Parliament in the next Session to confer on you an Annuity
more proportioned to His Majesty's sense of your public
merit than any which His Majesty can at present grant.
But being desirous in the interval not to leave you without
some, though an inadequate, mark of the sentiments and disposition which His Majesty entertains towards you, he has
further directed me to propose an immediate grant out of
the Civil List of 1,200*l.* a-year (being the largest sum which
His Majesty is enabled to fix), either in your own name or
that of Mrs. Burke, as may be most agreeable to you. I
shall be happy to learn your decision on this subject, that I
may have the satisfaction of taking the necessary steps for
carrying His Majesty's instructions into immediate execution. I have the honour, &c., W. PITT.

Mr. Burke replied in two letters—the first ostensible
and intended to be laid before the King, while the
second expressed his personal thanks to Mr. Pitt.

Beaconsfield, August 31, 1794.

Dear Sir,—This morning I received your very obliging
letter of the 30th of this month, acquainting me with His
Majesty's most gracious dispositions towards the remains of
this afflicted family.

You will be so kind as to lay me, with all possible humi-
lity, duty, and gratitude, at His Majesty's feet, and to express
my deep and heartfelt sense of His Majesty's bounty and
beneficence, and the gracious condescension with which His
Majesty has been pleased to distinguish me; at a time too

when neither I, nor any person to represent me, can aspire to the honour and happiness of rendering him any service whatsoever.

I have never presumed to apply for anything. I never could so far flatter myself as to think that anything done by me, in or out of Parliament, could attract the Royal observation. In some instances of my public conduct I might have erred. Few have been so long (and in times and matters so arduous and critical) engaged in affairs, who can be certain that they have never made a mistake. But I am certain that my intentions have been always pure with regard to the Crown and to the country. It is upon these intentions that His Majesty has been pleased to judge of my conduct, and to reward them with his Royal acceptance and Royal munificence. I could wish for ability to demonstrate the sincerity of my humble gratitude by future active service. But I am denied this satisfaction. My time of life, my bodily infirmity, and my broken state of mind, leave me no other capacity than that of praying, which I do most fervently, for the prosperity and glory of His Majesty's reign, and that he may be made the grand instrument in the hand of Providence for delivering the world from the grand evil of our time, the greatest with which the race of man was ever menaced.

I have the honour to be, &c., EDM. BURKE.

P.S. For obvious reasons, if it is indifferent to His Majesty's service, I should wish the pension on the Civil List to be made for Mrs. Burke's life.

Beaconsfield, August 31, 1794.

Dear Sir,—I do not know whether in propriety I could make my personal acknowledgments to a subject in a letter in which I was to return my thanks to the King for a favour derived from the Crown. But it would be full as contrary to propriety, and more contrary still to the dictates of my heart, if I were to omit my thanks to you very particularly for the kindness, the generosity, the delicacy with which you have conducted the whole of this business. I am obliged to such an architect as you are for undertaking, not the reparation (that is impossible), but the conservation of a ruin.

I cannot dissemble that what you have done is not only convenient but necessary to me. Nothing short of what I hear it is your plan to execute can give me such quiet as I am capable of enjoying during the few melancholy years, months, or perhaps weeks that I may have to linger here. I should be sorry to leave just creditors unsatisfied, and just obligations wholly unreturned. I should be more miserable still than I am if I were obliged to mix very unsuitable solicitudes and very mortifying occupations in my struggle with other less degrading but much sorer griefs. But you have done everything for me which can be done by any human hands. From these additional vexations (which had already begun to beset me) the present plan - that is, the gracious message proposed to Parliament and what the King is by law enabled to grant—will afford me what will be deemed a security for the advance of some of the money which will be necessary for my present repose, as the rest will suffice for my comfortable retreat after the meeting of Parliament shall have enabled you to propose the larger plan for my liberation. If I were to presume to suggest anything, it would be the antedating the grant of the pension on the Civil List, for otherwise the state of the payments there will hardly make the relief so immediate as I am sure you wish it. My mind is much troubled, so that I do not know whether I express myself with any tolerable clearness. But be assured that, express myself how I will, I feel just as I ought to do for your very noble proceeding on this occasion, and that it is impossible for any one to wish more sincerely honour and success to your administration, and everything which can be satisfactory to you as a man or as a statesman.

I have the honour to be, with sentiments of the most perfect gratitude and regard, &c., EDM. BURKE.

Some further explanations passed on the details of the intended arrangement, the channel of communication being the Rev. Walker King, a personal friend of Burke. In consequence Pitt addressed to Burke a second letter in the following terms :—

Downing Street, September 18, 1794.

My dear Sir,—It was not till yesterday that Mr. King had an opportunity of showing me your letter to him of the 14th. I flatter myself I shall have best met your wishes with respect to the present grant out of the Civil List by directing it to be made out to yourself, for your life and that of Mrs. Burke, to commence from the 5th of January, 1793. With respect to the remaining part of the arrangement, which requires the assistance of Parliament, my idea of it has been exactly what you understood, and it will be a very honourable and gratifying part of my duty to take the first opportunity of conveying the King's recommendation for carrying it into effect.—Believe me, dear Sir, with great regard and esteem, &c.,   W. Pitt.

Burke replied as follows:—

Beaconsfield, September 19, 1794.

Dear Sir,—The unfortunate inhabitants of this house are much obliged to you for the very kind and consolatory letter which I received from you this morning. You have conceived everything in a very kind and liberal manner, with regard to the lives, to the date given to the pension on the Civil List, and to your resolution to bring the message from His Majesty early in the Session.

As for us, though we can feel neither this nor anything else with real pleasure, we feel it with very sincere gratitude. If I were to consider myself only, whatever was the most obscure and the least ostentatious would be most suitable to the present temper of my mind, and what must continue the same to the end of my short existence. Whilst my dear son lived, there were certainly objects which I had at heart, the smallest desire of which, in my present forlorn state, would only argue the most contemptible vanity. As to other things I cannot be equally indifferent, nor indeed ought I.

My first object is the payment of my debts, that I may stand as clear with individuals as I trust I do with the public. I know this object enters into your plan. I am to say that these debts were stated by my son below their real amount. When I came to examine them with accuracy I found it so. He too was sensible of this. But he was delicate with regard to you and the public; and having a resolute and sanguine mind, he was willing to take his succession a little encumbered, and to trust to good management and good fortune to support those debts, or to clear them off. I hope, however, this affair has not been so much below the mark as to make any serious difficulty in your arrangements.

As to the provision to be made by Parliament, I wish for no augmentation in this respect. If the whole pension be

made up to twenty-five hundred clear, to our personal case
it is sufficient, without obliging us late in life to change its
whole scheme, which, whether wise or justifiable or not, is
now habitual to us; and, in truth, we are little in a condition to make any new arrangement. Without therefore
troubling you further, we leave the whole matter entirely to
your generosity, and your liberal sentiments. I am heartily
sorry to be thus troublesome.

I have the honour to be, with the most sincere respect
and gratitude, &c.,   EDM. BURKE.

To Mr. Pitt these new allies were of high importance.
They rallied for a time around his standard one, and
that the larger, share of the Whig party. They gave
him fresh strength in the country to resist the advance
of the Republican arms abroad, and of the Republican
doctrines at home. They gave him also in some cases
the accession of considerable talents. The Duke of
Portland, indeed, viewed either as a statesman or an
orator, was certainly not in the first class. But he was
justly respected as a man of probity and honour, and he
had considerable weight as once the chosen Minister of
the united Whigs. Therefore though the King, referring
to the Garter, might at that time write, ' I cannot see
why on the Duke of Portland's head favours are to be
heaped without measure,'[1] yet certainly it was of high
importance to connect His Grace with the Government.
Lord Spencer was not conspicuous in debate, but, as I
have already stated, he had very great ability in administration; and Mr. Windham had already attained a
foremost rank in the House of Commons. Born in
1750, of an old family in Norfolk, and Member for Nor-
wich since 1784, he had also filled the office of Secretary for Ireland in the Coalition Government. In
his character Windham has been described, and with
truth, as the model of a true English gentleman. Fond
of field-sports and of all manly exercises, he applied himself with zeal at his seat of Felbrigg to the county busi-

[1] To Mr. Pitt, Windsor, July 13, 1794.

ness. But in town he showed other tastes and talents not always combined with these. He delighted in scholar-like studies and in literary friendships, and attached himself in an especial manner first to Johnson and then to Burke. To all affairs, whether of public or private life, he brought a high, nay chivalrous sense of honour. His oratory was distinguished not only by graces of manner, set off by his fine person and beaming countenance, but by ingenuity in his arguments and fearlessness in his opinions. Sometimes he might be accused of affecting singularity, but never of courting power.

This alliance of statesmen, formed with considerable difficulty, was in peril of disruption almost as soon as it was formed. There was a misunderstanding on the part of the Duke of Portland. When the third Secretaryship of State was renewed, Pitt had resolved to divide as follows the duties and the patronage of late combined :—Dundas was to have the Colonies and the East India Department, with the conduct of the war. The Duke of Portland was to have Great Britain and Ireland, that is above all the care of the internal peace and police of the country. But either Mr. Pitt did not clearly explain this matter to the Duke, or the Duke did not clearly understand his explanation. It appeared at the last moment that His Grace expected to have the whole power and patronage which Dundas had lately possessed. Under these circumstances Dundas, in a generous spirit, desired to give way. But he declared that he should resign the Seals, and relinquish the conduct of the war. Pitt, in great anxiety and distress, wrote to Dundas as follows. The original is now preserved, not at Melville Castle, but at Arniston :—

Downing Street, Wednesday,
July 9 (1794), ¾ past 11.

Dear Dundas, - The Chancellor has sent me the letter which he had received from you, and I really cannot express to you the uneasiness it has given me. I shall give up all hope of carrying on the business with comfort, and be really completely heart-broken, if you adhere to your resolution. Had I had the smallest idea that it would be the consequence, no consideration would have tempted me to agree to the measure which has led to it; and yet, after all that has now passed, it seems impossible for me to recede. Under these circumstances you must allow me to make it a personal request in the strongest manner I can, that you will consent to continue Secretary of State in the way proposed. On public grounds, and for your own credit, I feel most sincerely convinced that you ought to do so; but I wish to ask it of you as the strongest proof you can give of friendship to myself; and of that you have given me so many proofs already that I do flatter myself you cannot refuse this, when you know how anxiously I have it at heart. At all events, let me beg of you to give me an opportunity of talking it over with you. I dine at the Chancellor's. Possibly you can contrive to come to town to dinner, and return in the evening. If you do, be so good as to call here, and we may go to Bedford Square [1] together.

Ever yours,   W. PITT.

I hope, if possible, to get your answer before I go to St. James's, and to be relieved by it from the anxiety I shall be under in the interval.

Here is Dundas's reply :—

Wimbledon, July 9, 1794.

My dear Sir,—The letter I have just received from you has given me the most poignant concern. My only consolation is, that upon the perusal of the letter I wrote to you this morning, you must be satisfied that neither the public service nor your own comfort are at all concerned in the matter, whereas my feelings and public estimation would be deeply wounded by the line of conduct you suggest. As for your receding, it is quite out of the question. Indeed, the moment I heard the probability of a misunderstanding, which I first did from Nepean, he can inform you that my resolution was taken to render it impossible that there should be any question about my situation.

Yours ever,   HENRY DUNDAS.

---

[1] The Chancellor's house, 15 Bedford Square.

Mr. Pitt, however, did not yield the point. Going to St. James's, he induced the King himself to address Mr. Dundas.

The King to Mr. Dundas.

St. James's, July 9, 1794.

Mr. Pitt has just informed me of Mr. Secretary Dundas's most handsome conduct on the want of the Duke of Portland's clearly understanding the foot on which he is to hold the Seals of the Home Department. Though I do not quite approve of the West Indies being added to the Home Department, I will reluctantly acquiesce in the arrangement; but I at the same time, in the strongest manner, call on Mr. Secretary Dundas to continue Secretary of State for the War, namely, to keep up the correspondence wherever the war is carried on. I have desired Mr. Pitt, who will further speak on the subject, to deliver this to Mr. Secretary Dundas.

GEORGE R.

Going himself with this letter to Dundas, whom he found at dinner with his family, Pitt again most earnestly appealed to his friend, and he prevailed. 'Here, then, I am still,'—so writes Dundas to his kinsman, Robert Dundas, Lord Advocate,—'I must remain a very responsible Minister with a great deal of trouble, and without power or patronage, all of which I have resigned into the hands of the Duke of Portland.'

There were also other friends of Pitt to whom his new alliance gave some concern. 'Have you no fears upon the subject?' said the Speaker to him. 'Are you not afraid that you might be outvoted in your own Cabinet?' The reply of Mr. Pitt, as long afterwards recorded by Lord Sidmouth, was as follows: 'I am under no anxiety on that account. I place much dependence on my new colleagues; and I place still more dependence on myself.'[1]

The month of July, 1794, in which the English Government was strengthened, beheld the French subverted. For some time past the authority of Robes-

[1] *Life of Lord Sidmouth*, by Dean Pellew, vol. i. p. 121.

pierre had been in fact supreme. But several of his own colleagues in the Committee of Public Safety had become his secret enemies. Collot, Billaud Varennes, and Barère were jealous of his power. Many others, both in the Convention and outside it, were weary of his cruelties. At last the day of deliverance came. It was long remembered in France as the 'Ninth of Thermidor' according to the new Republican calendar, or according to ours the 27th of July. Tallien led the attack on the tyrant. Even the recent abettors of his crimes slunk one by one from his side. With Couthon and St. Just, the two colleagues of the Committee who still adhered to him, Robespierre was outvoted in the hall of the Assembly, and overpowered at the Hôtel de Ville. A pistol which he discharged at his own head failed of its fatal effects. Next day, still half alive, his broken jaw tied up in a crimsoned handkerchief, he was drawn amidst the roar of liberated thousands to the avenging Guillotine.

With this Man of Blood the Reign of Terror fell. The Government which succeeded might not indeed deserve in other countries or at other times to be called either merciful or wise, but it was both in a high degree when compared to the rule of Robespierre. The prison doors were opened. The Guillotine ceased its daily work. The worst of the recent Decrees were annulled. The Jacobins, who more than once rose in arms and fought in the streets of Paris to recover their lost sway, were put down with a strong hand. And thus in some measure, though slowly, the public confidence returned.

But whatever might be the Government of the Republic, there was no change in the martial and enthusiastic spirit of its armies. Towards the Pyrenees one body of French troops invaded Catalonia and another Biscay, putting the Spanish forces to the rout, and pushing forward, the one to Figueras and the other to Tolosa. Thus ere long the Court of Madrid, completely humbled, was reduced to sue for peace. Towards Italy the Sardinians were driven from the passes of the Alps. In Belgium, Generals Jourdan and Pichegru, already possessed of Brussels and of Ghent, paused only while the strongholds in their rear, as Landrecies and Condé, were besieged and taken. In the beginning of September they again pushed forward, compelling the Duke of York to retire beyond the Meuse, and General Clerfait beyond the Roer.

At this period General Clerfait was in full command of the Austrian army, having replaced the Prince of Coburg, who was held responsible for the failure of the previous spring. But the evils of divided and not very effective leadership were only too apparent. They were strongly felt by Mr. Windham, who had gone to visit the English head-quarters, and by Lord Cornwallis, who had recently returned from India, and who had been requested by Mr. Pitt to confer with the Imperial Ministers at Brussels. From neither were the reports in any degree re-assuring.

Under these unwelcome circumstances a scheme was framed by the English Cabinet that Lord Cornwallis, as enjoying, and justly, a considerable reputation, might be named Commander-in-Chief of all the forces that lately occupied Flanders. The new Lord Privy Seal, who had been sent on a special embassy to Vienna, was instructed to make this proposal to the Austrian Prime Minister. This was no longer Kaunitz, but Thugut. He was born in 1739; the son of a shipper at Linz. The real name was Thu nig-gut (Do no good), but this, as of ill omen, had been changed by Maria Theresa to Thu-gut (Do good).[1]

To this scheme, however, two obstacles arose. In the first place, the Duke of York declared that in such a case he must quit his post and return to England, and the King warmly approved the determination of his favourite son.[2] Next, the Court of Vienna showed

<hr>

[1] See the *Oesterreich* of Dr. E. Vehse, vol. ix. p. 78.

[2] The Duke of York to the King, Sept. 4, and the King to Mr.

a strong though not perhaps invincible repugnance to place a foreigner at the head of its armies. But perhaps the best summary of the state of affairs at that juncture is comprised in the two following letters from Mr. Pitt ; the earliest in date, with only one exception, that I have found among his papers as addressed by him to Lord Chatham :—

Downing Street, Monday, Sept. 22, 1794.

My dear Brother,—I enclose you a letter which was left with me this morning by Prigent, who is just come through Jersey from the army of the Chouans. The letter, I understand, is from Captain D'Auvergne. Prigent has brought with him the Count de Puisy,[1] one of the Royalist Generals, whose arrival is of course to be kept if possible an entire secret. As the Count de Puisy is unwell, I have not yet seen him ; but Lord Balcarres' letters speak of him in high terms. If he is to be depended upon, his information will be very valuable.

Prigent's general accounts are that the Royalists are in great force, and the Republicans in very little. He is to put the particulars in writing. In the meantime I rather suspect exaggeration in his account, which was clearly the case in that which we had just received when I last wrote. Indeed the bearer of that intelligence turned out to be a person on whom there could be no reliance. When I know the result of the present intelligence more precisely, I will send it you. In the meantime I am not sure whether I am to understand from your answer to my former letter that the throwing in supplies would probably be executed by some of the cruising squadrons without Admiral Vandeput being employed in that service, or whether you meant that a part of any of those squadrons might be put under his direction for that purpose. Possibly the circumstances we may now learn may be material in deciding on that point as well as every other part of the subject.

Yours affectionately,   W. Pitt.

The accounts from Flanders continue, as you see, very unfavourable ; and though the Duke of York's retreat was,

Pitt, Sept. 9, 1794, both in the Pitt MSS., and the last in my Appendix.

[1] This should be Puisaye.

I believe, perfectly necessary, there is more and more reason
to fear that his general management is what the army has
no confidence in, and while that is the case there is little
chance of setting things right.

Downing Street, Sept. 24, 1794.

My dear Brother,—The Count de P.'s information, the
detail of which he has promised to give me in writing, seems
likely to be very material; but it will relate only to Brittany, and not to Poitou. Supplies for the latter will still, I
conceive, require a separate expedition. With respect to
Brittany, he says he can point out practicable places of landing either for troops or stores, both in the neighbourhood of
St. Cast and St. Brieux, and will undertake that the Royalists shall bring a considerable force near the coast to receive
them. He gives very strong reasons for attempting to land
some force, even a few thousand men, before the winter, and
with that aid has no doubt of the Royalists maintaining themselves till spring, when we may act on a larger scale. Considerable facility will certainly arise from these operations
being so near home, and I think the prospect seems at first
view a tempting one, if we can find the force, which, though
difficult, is, I trust, not impossible. Windham will probably
be back in a few days. It seems clear that if Lord Cornwallis has the chief command, the Duke of York will come
away entirely. All the accounts, however, which we have
received of the Austrian Cabinet and army since we formed
the idea of sending Lord Cornwallis have made us doubt
whether, even if we purchase their acquiescence in that arrangement, we shall be sure of any active exertions. Lord
Spencer has therefore been instructed, if the Court of Vienna
had not accepted the proposal, not to press it further; and
in that case we think we must look to more limited exertions on the side of Flanders, and turn our principal efforts
to the French coast.   Yours affectionately,   W. Pitt.

As regarded the accounts from the Continent,
nothing, indeed, could be more unpromising than the
prospects of this uncoalescing Coalition. Prussia openly
withdrew from any active share in the war, and sought
to open negotiations for a separate peace. Austria,
despairing of the retention of Flanders, required as it
were to be bribed to her own defence. It was only by

means of enormous and repeated subsidies from England
—one about this time of no less than 6,000,000*l.*—
that any Austrian army after the first campaign was
sent into the field.

Meantime the French, in two main divisions, were
pursuing their successes. On the 2nd of October
General Jourdan, giving battle to Clerfait at Rure-
monde, obtained a complete victory. The Austrians
were driven in disarray across the Rhine, while the
French in triumph took possession of Cologne and
Bonn. To the left, General Pichegru, passing the
frontier of Holland, besieged and reduced the important
fortress of Bois le Duc; and the Duke of York, after
several checks, found it necessary to fall back behind
the Waal. Holland was now in imminent peril. The
best chance of saving it was, as Mr. Pitt conceived, to
place the military operations under one general direction. With the King's sanction he proposed to the
Dutch Government, early in October, to offer to the
Duke of Brunswick the joint command both of the
King's troops and of theirs. Under him it was understood that the Duke of York was still willing to serve.
The Dutch acquiesced, and the offer was made accordingly, but the Duke of Brunswick declined.

Six more weeks passed in Holland—six weeks marked
by increasing difficulties from the rank and pretensions
of the Duke of York, combined with his youth and
inexperience. At this most critical juncture Mr. Pitt
determined to risk the displeasure rather than neglect
the service of his Master. He addressed a letter to the
King, no copy of which is preserved among his papers,
but the drift of which may be discovered from the
King's reply.[1] The object was to urge upon His
Majesty the recall of his son from the command. The
King received this communication with pain, nay even
anguish of mind, but did not oppose it. Early in
December accordingly His Royal Highness came back

---

[1] See at the close of this volume the King's letter, bearing date
Nov. 24, 1794.

to England, leaving the English and Hanoverian troops under the command of the Hanoverian General Walmoden.

In the West Indies the war continued to be waged. An English armament had been sent to this quarter, the ships under Admiral Sir John Jervis, and the troops under General Sir Charles Grey. By their joint exertions Martinico, St. Lucia, and Guadeloupe were successively reduced. But some regiments being then detached for a descent upon St. Domingo, an opening was left to a squadron which had been despatched from France with about fifteen hundred soldiers on board. These were under the direction of Victor Hugues, a delegate of the Convention. On the other hand, the British troops in Guadeloupe were thinned, not merely by the detachment from them, but by the dire effects of the yellow fever. Under such circumstances Victor Hugues succeeded in recovering that island, inflicting dreadful severities on the members of the Royalist party who fell into his hands, or, whenever he failed to seize them, burning and laying waste their estates.

CHAPTER XIX.

1794.

Riots in London—Crimps and Recruits—Prosecutions for High Treason—Trials of Hardy, Horne Tooke, and Thelwall—Discomfiture of the Government—Mr. Pitt's efforts to strengthen his administration—Retrospect of Irish affairs—Interview between Pitt and Grattan—Correspondence of Pitt and Windham—Pitt's 'Memorandum'—Retirement of Lord Westmorland and appointment of Lord Fitzwilliam as Lord Lieutenant of Ireland—Meeting of Parliament—King's Speech—Wilberforce's Amendment—Subjugation of Holland by the French—Lord Cornwallis added to the Cabinet.

In London the summer was marked by several riots, caused, if not by the reality, at least by the rumour, of

'crimping houses.' Dens of this kind, in which men
were caught and forcibly enlisted as soldiers, had existed
in England since the commencement of the war; as
in Holland they existed even in time of peace for the
service of the colonies. There the crimps were known
by the expressive name of *Seelen-Verkäufer*, the
'sellers of souls.' There the horrors of the system have
been described with terrible force in a well-known work
of Nicolai.[1]

In London, as it chanced, a young man named
George Howe threw himself from an upper window in
a court near Charing Cross and was killed on the spot.
It was alleged that this was no other than a crimping
house, and the report was implicitly believed. At the
Coroner's Inquest it appeared that this was a house
of ill-fame, and had no connection of any kind with the
recruiting service. But meanwhile the mob had taken
the law into their own hands. They demolished the
inside of this house and damaged several others, and
were proceeding to other acts of violence, when they
were, happily without bloodshed, dispersed by a party
of soldiers.

These riots were renewed by another incident of a
similar kind. At Banbury one Edward Barrett was
brought up as a duly enlisted recruit. But on being
presented he declared that he had been made drunk by
two recruiting officers in London, inveigled into a public-
house called the White Horse, in Whitcomb Street,
compelled to sign an attestation, and robbed of his silver
watch and silver shoe-buckles. This complaint being
made in due form, the two recruiting serjeants whom it
involved were sent in custody to London. There was
first an examination in Bow Street, and subsequently a
trial at the Old Bailey. Upon the first tidings, however, of this case the mob rose again. They wreaked
their vengeance not only on the White Horse in Whitcomb Street, but on other houses kept for the recruiting

<hr>

[1] *Sebaldus Nothanker*, vol. iii. p. 12, &c., ed. 1799.

service in Holborn, Barbican, and Clerkenwell. These disturbances, though stopping short of bloodshed, continued during several days, and had they not been met with firmness, might have led to the same results as in 1780. But on this occasion the great city was effectually protected not merely by regular troops, but by the newly-associated volunteers—'those Aristocrats,' as the Revolutionary party termed them. For at this period, in England as in France, 'Aristocrat' was the nickname they commonly gave not only to any men of rank and fortune, but also to any friends of law and order. These on their part retorted with the nickname of 'Jacobin.'

The reader will not fail to have observed that in Barrett's case, as in Howe's, there was, as exerted by the multitude, true 'Jedburgh Justice,' as it used to be called upon the Borders. First comes the execution—then the charge accurately stated—and then, at last, the evidence! When in due course the case of Barrett was brought on for trial, it then plainly appeared how much the anger of the multitude had been misdirected. It was shown, for example, that at the time when Barrett declared himself to have been robbed of his watch and buckles, he had neither watch nor buckles upon him. At last the Jury, declaring themselves quite satisfied, requested the Judge to spare himself the trouble of summing up the evidence, and returned a verdict of Not Guilty, Barrett being then in his turn sent to prison to be tried for perjury.

The Revolutionary ferment in this country, as too plainly derived from France, was by no means most dangerous when it broke forth in riots and tumults; it was far more to be dreaded when lurking in plots and conspiracies. Against the leaders of these, so far as they could be detected or convicted, the Government had determined to proceed with the utmost rigour by bringing them to trial for High Treason. Two cases of this kind—those of James Watt and David Downie—came before the High Court at Edinburgh in August

and September. Both prisoners belonged to the Society
of the Friends of the People, acting in secret concert
with the Corresponding and Constitutional Societies in
London. Both prisoners, as was shown, had been active
in the preparation of pikes and other measures for a
combined popular rising. Both were found guilty, but
Downie was recommended to mercy, a recommendation
which was of course complied with. Watt, on the contrary, was hanged in front of the Tolbooth.

In England the prosecutions for High Treason had
begun much earlier, but were clogged by greater delays.
Besides the eight persons sent to prison on this charge in
May, there were in September five more included in the
same indictment. Among them was Thomas Holcroft,
who had been a member of the 'Constitutional Society,'
and who, as a dramatic writer, is still remembered.[1]

While the trials were thus delayed, the party in
Opposition did its utmost to decry them. All these
plots, it was said, were but imaginary—the mere offspring of popular credulity and Ministerial malice.
And, as it chanced, there was just before the trial an
incident which seemed not unfavourable to these views,
and which as such was eagerly improved. Information
was brought to the Government that certain persons,
obscure members of the Corresponding Society, had
formed a project to assassinate the King by discharging
at him a poisoned missile through an air-tube. The
persons thus accused were taken up and examined
before the Privy Council, but no evidence was found
sufficient to support so heavy a charge. From the first
the story was received with the greatest ridicule. Perhaps it had even been devised with that view. It was
called in derision the 'Pop-gun Plot,' and may be
deemed to have had considerable though indirect influence upon the public mind with regard to the now
impending State Trials.

---

[1] See on this subject the letter of Holcroft to his daughter, dated
Sept. 30, 1794, and inserted in the *Memoirs* by Hazlitt, p. 161.

Of these trials, the first to come on was that of the shoemaker Thomas Hardy. It began on the 28th of October before a Special Jury. Sir John Scott, as Attorney-General, opened the case. His speech, including the papers read, was of nine hours. It may be doubted—let me say in passing—whether speeches of such vast length are ever of service to their cause. Many years afterwards a gentleman who had served on this jury said to Mr. Adolphus, 'Sir, if even the evidence had been much stronger, I should have had great difficulty in convicting men of a crime when it took the Attorney-General nine hours to tell us what it was.'[1]

In this long but able speech Sir John Scott declared that he would show the real object of the Corresponding Society, whose penman Hardy had been. That object was no other than to abolish the Kingly office and to set up a National Convention as in France. For his proofs Sir John relied in the first place on the papers which had been seized. These were for the most part of practical business and in guarded terms. But there were also among them some base and infamous jests. There was, above all, a mock playbill, which announced 'a new and entertaining farce called La Guillotine, or George's Head in a Basket. *Vive la Liberté! Vive la République!*'

Secondly, Sir John relied on numerous witnesses who had once belonged to the Society or been present at its meetings, and who stated what they had heard and seen. There was John Cammage, for example, who could speak as to the preparation of pikes at Sheffield, and who had been shown the model of another spiked instrument called a 'night-cat,' intended to be cast into the streets and there to arrest the progress of the cavalry.[2]

---

[1] Adolphus's *History of England*, vol. vi. p. 75, ed. 1843.

[2] See on these 'night-cats,' similar to the *craw-taes* of Scotland (still, according to Sir Walter Scott, dug up from time to time on the field of Bannockburn), Howell's *State Trials*, vol. xxiv. pp. 595 and 670.

There was George Sanderson, who answered as follows, in reply to Mr. Law:—'Was any piece of good news or anything they called good news announced at that time by one of the members?—Yes, there was some good news, as they termed it, announced that very night. What was it?—A defeat of part of the British Army; I do not recollect what.'[1]

Another witness, Edward Gosling, deposed as to the language addressed to him by Baxter, a most active member of this Society. 'For my own part,' said Baxter, ' I do not wish the King or any of his family to lose their lives, but I think they might go to Hanover. As to other persons, it must be expected that some blood will be shed. Some particular persons have offered such insults to the people, that human nature could not overlook them.'—'Did he,' asked Mr. Garrow, 'name any of those persons?—He named several; I cannot recollect all; Mr. Pitt was one, Mr. Dundas another.'[2]

All these witnesses, however, Mr. Erskine, as Counsel for the prisoner, cross-examined with his usual skill. Some were involved by him in apparent contradictions; of others he blasted the credit by branding them with the name of spies. In the case of George Sanderson, whose evidence I just now cited, he framed one of his questions thus: 'What date have you taken, good Mr. Spy?'—'I do not think,' replied the witness, 'that on such an occasion being a spy is any disgrace.' And here the Lord Chief Justice Eyre interposed : ' Mr. Erskine, these observations will be more proper when you come to address the Jury.'

It is said that up to this time there had been scarce any instance in England of a trial for High Treason that had not been finished in a single day. But here the hour of midnight came before any great progress had been made with the Crown witnesses. It became necessary to adjourn, and the Court sat day by day from

<hr>

[1] Howell's *State Trials*, vol. xxiv. p. 707.
[2] *Ibid*, p. 717.

the Tuesday to the Saturday. On Saturday, the 1st of November, at two in the afternoon, Erskine rose for the defence. He spoke for seven hours, until at the last his own voice, his own strength failed him, and leaning for support on the table, he could only whisper to the Jury. But amidst the breathless silence even his faint whispers could be heard. Never was the public expectation, though high, more fully answered. Never did his admirable talents as an advocate shine forth with brighter lustre. It may be said, indeed, that in these State Trials his great forensic fame attained its culminating point. Besides many collateral issues, all of which he carefully wrought out, the main drift of his argument was to show that the law of High Treason, inflicting as it did such tremendous penalties, required to be most strictly and literally construed. It had been framed for the safety of the Royal life and person, not for the defence of the Royal government. To conspire against the King's lawful authority—supposing for a moment such a conspiracy proved—was a crime of great magnitude which the law was open to punish, but it was not the crime alleged in the indictment—it was not High Treason as defined by the Act of Edward the Third.

On the Monday and the ensuing days the trial was resumed. The Duke of Richmond was summoned as a witness to admit the authenticity of his letter to Colonel Sharman in 1783, from which strong expressions urging a Reform of Parliament had been often and triumphantly quoted in the Corresponding and Constitutional Societies. Lord Lauderdale, Mr. Sheridan, Mr. Philip Francis, and some others bore witness to the peaceable conduct of Hardy and his friends so far as they had observed them. A second speech in behalf of the prisoner was made by his second Counsel, Mr. Gibbs, afterwards Sir Vicary; and the Solicitor-General, Sir John Mitford, in an address of ten hours replied on the part of the Crown. The Lord Chief Justice summed up the case

with strict impartiality, and then on the eighth day of
the trial the Jury, after retiring for three hours, brought
in a verdict of Not Guilty.

It has been usual in State Prosecutions, when several
persons have been sent to prison on the same charge,
and when the trial of the first has resulted in his acquittal, to consider that decision as involving the fate
of the next. But at this most critical period the magnitude of the interests at stake led the Government to
a different course. It was determined to proceed with
the trial of John Horne Tooke on the same charge, and
nearly the same evidence.

The second trial accordingly commenced. Erskine
was again the Counsel for the prisoner, but the prisoner
here took an active part in his own defence. With
great delight did the old opponent of Junius and of
Thurlow renew his intellectual wars. He showed himself as ever, ready, quick-witted, unabashed. Whether
in the cross-examination of witnesses or in repartees
against the Court, he indulged in many humorous
sallies which the authority of the Judges could not
check, and which were rewarded by the laughter of the
audience. Erskine, however, made as before an earnest
and impressive speech for the defence. Then came a
whole host of witnesses, mustered perhaps for show
rather than for use. Mr. Pitt and the Duke of Richmond were summoned to state the part they had
formerly taken in meetings and associations for the
reform of Parliament. Earl Stanhope and the Rev.
Christopher Wyvill gave testimony to the same transactions from a different point of view. Major Cartwright spoke of the foundation and first steps of the
Constitutional Society. Mr. Fox, Mr. Sheridan, Mr.
Philip Francis deposed that they had known Mr. Tooke
for many years, and had never found his opinions upon
politics disloyal, nor even extreme. He was wont, it
seems, to excuse himself for acting with men of much
more vehement views by an ingenious though inconclu-

sive illustration, which, since he first devised it, has grown into common use. ' If,' said Mr. Tooke, ' I and several men are in the Windsor stage-coach, we travel together as long as it may suit us. When I find myself at Hounslow I get out; they who want to go farther may go to Windsor or where they like; but when I get to Hounslow, there I get out; no farther will I go, by —— ;' and here the former clergyman uttered an oath!¹

In this case the Jury, having retired for only eight minutes, came back with a verdict of Not Guilty. Most of the remaining prisoners were now discharged without any evidence being offered against them. But the Crown Lawyers resolved to proceed with a third trial, that of John Thelwall, who had taken a much more active part in the Societies than either Hardy or Horne Tooke. He was vain of his reputation as a lecturer, and it is said that he proved a very troublesome client. At one time he was so much dissatisfied that he wrote on a piece of paper which he threw over to Erskine, ' I'll be hanged if I don't plead my own cause ;' upon which his Counsel returned for answer, ' You'll be hanged if you do!' The result of the Trial, however, was the same. Again was Erskine the chief Counsel, and again did the Jury acquit.

Thus ended these Crown prosecutions. Through the whole course of them the feeling of the multitude ran strongly in favour of the accused. On the last night of the trials there were bonfires and blazing torches through the streets, while the horses of Erskine being taken from his chariot, he was drawn home amidst the loudest acclamations to his house in Serjeants' Inn. There, with Gibbs by his side, he indulged in the pleasure of one more parting speech from the windows. When in after years he was wont to boast of this ovation, some of his friends sought to mortify him by

¹ See the evidence of Major Cartwright (*State Trials*, vol. xxv. p. 330).

asserting—perhaps untruly—that the patriots who took the horses from his carriage had forgotten to return them.

The result of these trials was of course a great triumph to the Opposition and a signal discomfiture to the Government. Judging from their result, most of the later writers have arraigned their policy. Yet it may be doubted whether such language and such acts as were proved against members of both the Societies could under any Government have been left unnoticed. It may be doubted whether even the prosecution of them, ending as it did in failure, was not better for the State than mere silence or neglect would have been. The loyal at heart, some of whom were misled and deceived, had now clear evidence laid before them of the true intent and meaning of one at least of these Societies. The Revolutionary leaders might exult that they had, according to the decision of a Jury, kept within the law, but they must have felt that there were some further limits which they would not be allowed to overstep without imminent peril to themselves. And thus it may perhaps be said of the whole result that though the traitors were unpunished, the treason was prevented.

Mr. Pitt at all events allowed no signs of disappointment or vexation to escape him. He earnestly applied himself on the return of Lord Spencer from Vienna to give new strength to his administration. His brother, placed in 1788 at the head of the naval service, had certainly in no small degree disappointed the public hopes. But he was personally a favourite with the King. Indeed on several points of politics his opinions approached much nearer to those of George the Third than to those of Mr. Pitt. Thus, for example, Lord Chatham was no friend either to the Abolition of the Slave Trade or to the enfranchisement of the Roman Catholics.

In the autumn of 1794, however, a new arrangement was effected. Lord Chatham was transferred to the easy post of Privy Seal, while the direction of the Admiralty was entrusted to Earl Spencer.

Another change of no less importance had been for some weeks in contemplation—a change in the Lord Lieutenancy of Ireland. But as it proceeded this design was fraught with most serious difficulties, and almost a disruption of the new political alliance.

Here, however, some retrospect of Irish affairs will be required.

Ever since the advance of the French Revolution, Ireland had been one of the many sources of anxiety to the English Government. I have already had occasion to show in the trial of Hamilton Rowan how rife the secret societies had grown. But besides these the whole body of Roman Catholics, many of them most loyal subjects, deemed not unjustly the moment favourable for urging their pretensions. They had for their principal agent Mr. Theobald Wolfe Tone, and for their spokesman in the Irish House of Commons Sir Hercules Langrishe. From England they received all the aid that the genius and authority of Burke could give. In January, 1792, he published his celebrated letter to Sir Hercules, pointing out the impolicy of the continued restrictions on the Irish Roman Catholic body. At the same time he sent over his son, Richard Burke, as Secretary to their Committee in Dublin. Great ability was shown by the father, and great zeal by the son.

Thus supported, Sir Hercules Langrishe, even before the same month of January, 1792, had closed, brought in a Bill to remove some, the more prominent, grievances of his Roman Catholic fellow-subjects. He proposed that marriages between Protestants and Papists might be solemnized by Protestant clergymen, and should no longer incapacitate the husband from voting at elections. He proposed that attorneys might, if they pleased, take Roman Catholics for clerks—that schools

might be opened without licence from the Ordinary—
and that other such barbarous restraints upon education
should cease. At the same time he left untouched the
higher question of the Roman Catholic franchise.

The justice of the case was clear. Clearer still, if
possible, was the pressure of the times. The motion of
Sir Hercules was seconded by the Secretary for Ireland,
Mr. Hobart; and in spite of some High Protestant
murmurs, the Bill passed both Houses with ease. In
this result we may readily trace the resolute will of
the Prime Minister of England. To the mind of Pitt,
indeed, the whole system of penal laws was utterly
abhorrent. He had reflected much on the position
of the sister island, and desired to see both islands
closely bound together on the footing of equal laws and
equal rights. It is not too much to say of him, as Lord
Macaulay has not forborne to say, even at the risk of
some implied reflection upon Fox, that ' Pitt was the
first English Minister who formed great designs for the
benefit of Ireland.'

With these convictions, and overruling all whispers
to the contrary, Mr. Pitt urged forward the far from
willing Government of Ireland. The Earl of Westmorland, at that time Lord Lieutenant, was, as through life,
an opponent of the Catholic claims, and leaned for support mainly on the High Protestant families. Yet,
under the influence of the master-spirit in Downing
Street, the Lord Lieutenant opened the Session of 1793
with a speech expressive of the King's desire for ' a general union of sentiment among all classes and descriptions of His Majesty's subjects;' and he added:—
' With these views His Majesty trusts that the situation
of his Catholic subjects will engage your serious attention.' It is worthy of note that the Address of the
House of Commons in answer to this speech was seconded by Mr. Wesley, who was afterwards Sir Arthur
Wellesley, and at a later period the great Duke of
Wellington.

In pursuance of the intentions thus shadowed forth, Mr. Hobart, on the 4th of February, 1793, moved to bring in a Bill for the further relief of the Roman Catholics. Sir Hercules Langrishe, in seconding the motion, used some language worthy the correspondent of Burke, and almost worthy of Burke himself. ' Give them the pride of privilege,' he said, ' and you will give them the principle of attachment ; admit them within the walls of the Constitution, and they will defend them.'

The Bill of Mr. Hobart was of a large and comprehensive kind. It repealed all the penalties and disabilities affecting the education of children or the succession of estates. It admitted the Roman Catholics to vote at elections, taking only the oaths of allegiance and abjuration. It enabled them to hold civil or military offices, with the exception of a certain number that were specified in the Act. That list of exceptions was still too great, comprising as it did, for example, the offices of chief or puisne Judge and of Lord Lieutenant of counties. Still, as compared with the previous system, the progress was immense.

So great, indeed, was this improvement, that it could not pass into law without considerable opposition. Dr. Patrick Duigenan, Professor of Law in the University of Dublin, and a man of considerable learning, exerted himself against it vigorously, but in vain. None, perhaps, were less well pleased with it than some members of the Government itself, and especially the Chancellor, Lord Fitzgibbon, a man of powerful intellect, who had made many friends in his own, and many enemies in the opposite ranks. As, however, Lord Fitzgibbon had no intention of resigning the Great Seal, he could only, for the present, mutter his displeasure and alarm.

In spite of these concessions—or rather, as Dr. Duigenan would have said, on account of them—Ireland was far from tranquil. There, as in England, the

leaven of the French Revolution was at work. Even
the Committee for the Roman Catholic claims which
sat in Dublin, intent upon a common object, did not
remain united. Richard Burke resigned his office of
secretary, and returned to England in disgust. Even
before the Bill of Sir Hercules Langrishe, sixty-four of
the most respectable members, including Lords Fingal
and Kenmare, alarmed at the violence around them,
withdrew from the Committee. Other members, among
whom the Hon. Simon Butler and Mr. Wolfe Tone
were conspicuous, with no more reserve than their own
safety demanded, appear to have aimed at the establishment of a Republic on the model and by the aid of
France.

Besides this schism of the Roman Catholic body,
there were many other sections in Ireland, some within
and some without the law. There was the party of the
Whig Club in Constitutional opposition to the Ministry,
and having for its leaders the Duke of Leinster, the
Earl of Charlemont, and Mr. Grattan. There was the
faction of the ' United Irishmen,' which sought to blend
the Roman Catholics with the Protestant Dissenters,
and to make of the whole an engine against England.
At Dublin there was an active band of agitators, at
its head Mr. Hamilton Rowan and Mr. Napper Tandy,
seeking to wrest the city into their own control, and
with that view attempting the formation, on the French
plan, of a National Guard. At Belfast there were ga-
therings from every part of Ulster to celebrate the
anniversary of the taking of the Bastille. At Dun-
gannon delegates from the province came together, and
concerted measures for a National Convention to meet
in the following September at Athlone.

All this time, in many parts of the open country,
gangs of depredators prowled. These were formed from
the lowest class of the Roman Catholics, complaining
of various grievances, as of hearth-money, county-cesses,
and tithes; and known by divers names, especially

'Peep of Day Boys' and 'Defenders.' The latter, as
their name implies, claimed to act only for their own
protection, and on this plea, assembling at night and
marching in small bodies, they broke into the houses
of Protestants and took their arms.

To these causes of distraction in the sister island
we ought, in fairness, to add the unsoundness of some
parts of the system which England was called on to
defend. It was more easy to abolish the penal laws
than to root out the feelings and tendencies which they
had produced in both the subject and the ruling classes.
There were defects and abuses, many and grievous, in
every department of the State, such as could only be
eradicated in the course of years. Take, for instance,
the case of the Established Church. There the spirit
was as different as possible from that of the present
time. The Duke of Norfolk, himself a convert, though
certainly not a keen one, to the Protestant faith, declared in the House of Lords that in many districts
of the south or west of Ireland the Clergy, far from
seeking to form a congregation, rejoiced in their ex-
emption from any. It was, said the Duke, a common
remark amongst them, 'You have got a good living,
for there is no Church in your parish!' [1]

Under all these difficulties the ruling men in Ireland,
as instructed from Downing Street, sought to blend conciliation with firmness. In the same Session of 1793,
in which they carried the Roman Catholic Relief Bill,
they passed an Act to prevent the importation of arms
or military stores, and another Act to prohibit the appointment of delegates to unlawful assemblies, which
was levelled against the intended Convention at Athlone. Early in 1794, as I have already shown, Mr.
Hamilton Rowan was indicted for a seditious libel, and
found Guilty. In April, the same year, the Rev. William Jackson, who was acting as an emissary of France,
was arrested on a charge of High Treason, and, pending

____

[1] Speech in the House of Lords, May 8, 1793.

his trial, was detained many months a close prisoner in Newgate.

Meanwhile, through the country districts the conduct of the 'Defenders' grew more and more outrageous, and less and less in accordance with their name. In the county of Longford, and some others, the gentlemen and freeholders found it necessary to combine and protect themselves; and they obtained leave to levy a sum of money by subscription, in order to raise and to maintain a troop of horse.

In this anxious state of Ireland it seemed to Mr. Pitt that while avoiding any abrupt changes, great advantage to that country might be derived from the accession to office of the Whig chiefs in the summer of 1794. Such an accession led almost as of course to a concert of measures with Mr. Grattan and his friends. Grattan had unhappily pledged himself not under any circumstances to accept of office, but there might be a new Government of Ireland formed with his approval and receiving his support. With this view it was contemplated to recall the Earl of Westmorland, if some other office could be found for him in England, and to send in his place the newly-made President of the Council, Earl Fitzwilliam. This was a nobleman of excellent character and upright intentions, but whose abilities were estimated far too highly by his friends. It will appear from a Memorandum which I shall presently insert, that in appointing him to Ireland, Mr. Pitt consulted the opinions of others much rather than his own. There was also an idea in some quarters that the son of Burke might go out as Secretary, but the untimely death of that young man in August, 1794, threw the appointment into the hands of Lord Milton, eldest son of the Earl of Dorchester. There was a further idea that Mr. George Ponsonby, as a chief of the Irish Whigs, might, in the event of a vacancy, become Attorney-General of Ireland. In any such case, the Duke of Portland as Home Secretary would be the

Minister in direct communication with his especial friends.

In the month of October, while these arrangements were pending, Mr. Grattan came to London. He met Mr. Pitt for the first time at a dinner-party given by the Duke of Portland. According to Grattan's report, ' Mr. Pitt sat by Sir John Parnell, talked a good deal to him, and seemed to like him much; but the Ponsonbys and the Grenvilles were cold and distant, and looked as if they would cut each other's throats.' There is one remark of Mr. Pitt here recorded which tends to prove that although he desired to enfranchise the Roman Catholics of Ireland, he was not quite at ease as to their future conduct. Sir John Parnell was talking of the Irish Catholics, and rejoicing at their union with the Protestants, when Mr. Pitt said, 'Very true, Sir; but the question is, whose will they be?'[1]

It was soon found, however, that Mr. Grattan, and through him the Whig chiefs, required large concessions. They wished to recall Lord Westmorland at once, whether or not any place could be found for him at home. They wished to remove the Chancellor, Lord Fitzgibbon. They made a set at some other steady supporters of the Government. To these terms Pitt felt that he could not in honour or in justice yield. We find him write as follows to one of his most trusted friends :—

Mr. Pitt to Mr. Dundas.

Downing Street, Tuesday night
(Oct. 14), 1794.

Dear Dundas,— . . . .

Nearer home than Holland everything looks ill. I enclose you a letter which I had from Windham to-day. His letter to Lord Fitzwilliam contained everything that I could have desired him to write; but I have seen him since, and I do not see that any progress is made towards settling the business on terms in which I ought to acquiesce.

[1] *Life and Times of Grattan,* by his son Henry, vol. iv. p. 175.

I am fully determined that I will not give way either to Lord Westmorland's recall without a proper situation for him here, or to Lord Fitzgibbon's removal on any terms. But though I cannot determine otherwise, it is dreadful that anything like personal considerations (though in fact they are not all so) should seem to mix at such a crisis as this.

Yours ever,   W. P.

Lord Grenville in this transaction showed very great generosity and public spirit. He was then at his newly-acquired seat of Dropmore—a domain which in after years was so highly embellished by his taste. Here is a letter sent from thence which Pitt received on the morning of the very day that he wrote, as we have just seen, to Dundas. It will be noticed that in one passage Lord Grenville refers to a rich office for life—as Auditor of the Exchequer—which Mr. Pitt had shortly before bestowed upon him :—

Dropmore, Oct. 13, 1791.

My dear Pitt,—In ruminating over the Irish difficulty in the course of my ride here, and thinking of the various solutions which might be found, it occurred to me that supposing the principal point, that of the change of system, to be settled, as I think it may be, by explanation, the other might be solved by Lord Mansfield's taking my office. He is quite equal to the official business, and has *words enough* at command to take the ostensible lead in the House of Lords. Whatever service I can do there to you or to the cause we are embarked in, you would equally command, and you might depend on my not neglecting that part of the business there which might be necessary in order to keep together *your* party in that House.

I am not ignorant that the plan is liable to some objection, but it is out of all comparison preferable to the infinite mischief of breaking up a system with the maintenance of which the fate of the country seems to me to be in great degree connected.

It would be wasting time to tell you how readily I should make such a sacrifice. You have put me in a situation to be able to do it without bringing distress or even inconvenience of any kind upon myself, or one still dearer to me; and even if you had not, I should not, at least I hope not, have thought that I ought to hesitate. The only thing I should feel in it that required explanation would be just to be able to tell enough of the story to show that I retired for accommodation, and not to avoid the difficulties of the moment; and if I could explain this in the first instance, I could sufficiently show by my public conduct afterwards that I should not be backward in taking my share of the public difficulties, whatever they are or may hereafter be.

Pray consider this seriously. I am confident if you do so, you will think this arrangement much more beneficial to the public interest at this crisis than suffering yourself from any predilection or partiality to me to incur the hazard and certain evil that must attend the breaking up such a system as you have just formed.

Ever most affectionately yours,   G.

The generous offer of Lord Grenville was not accepted, nor even for one moment entertained. It seemed to Mr. Pitt, however, that a personal interview between Grattan and himself would bring matters to a clearer issue. Next morning, therefore, he wrote this note:—

Mr. Pitt presents his compliments to Mr. Grattan. He wishes much, if it is not disagreeable to Mr. Grattan, to have an opportunity of conversing with him confidentially on the subject of an arrangement in Ireland, and for that purpose would take the liberty of requesting to see him, either at four to-day or any time to-morrow morning most convenient to Mr. Grattan.

Downing Street, Wednesday,
    Oct. 15, 1794.

The interview thus proposed took place on the same day. Grattan found Pitt, as he described it, 'very plain and very civil in his manner.' As to the Lord Lieutenancy, Mr. Pitt observed, 'The question is, how shall Lord Westmorland be provided for?' As to measures, and above all the Roman Catholic question, Mr. Pitt is alleged to have stated his resolution as follows:—'Not to bring it forward as a Government measure; but if

Government were pressed, to yield it.'   In the biography of Mr. Grattan, by his son, it is stated that such were 'the identical expressions.'   But I think it certain (although with the fairest intentions on Mr. Grattan's part) that the latter clause must have been either imperfectly heard or imperfectly remembered.   It is quite clear from the other documents upon this question, some of them dated only the next day, that Pitt was fully determined not to pledge himself or his Cabinet positively as to their future course.   It is quite clear, on the best testimonies we can now obtain, that the assurances given to various persons by Mr. Pitt in the winter of 1794 with respect to the Roman Catholic question went only, at the utmost, to his own favourable bias, but reserved in express words to his colleagues and himself full liberty to consider and decide on, as at the time seemed best, any measure that came to them from the Parliament of Ireland.

Indeed I must observe that there is not, nor does there purport to be, any complete report of this important conversation between the Irish patriot and the British Minister.   In the passage referring to it from the biography of Grattan, the statements of the father are greatly intermingled and blended with the reflections of the son.   Now I am bound to say that these two things are to be very differently viewed.   The statements of Henry Grattan the elder deserve our utmost respect.   The reflections of Henry Grattan the younger all through his five volumes are marked beyond all other things by the greatest possible degree of invective and vituperation against all whom he dislikes. Twice in this very passage does Mr. Grattan the younger declare his persuasion that Mr. Pitt intended 'to cheat,' and that he managed the House of Commons only 'by arts and money.'   I hope that it will not be thought incumbent on me, as the biographer of Mr. Pitt, to add to this last passage even a single word of comment or reply.

On the same afternoon, with a most scrupulous sense of honour, Mr. Pitt addressed to Mr. Grattan a second note :—

Mr. Pitt presents his compliments to Mr. Grattan. Having requested that the conversation which Mr. Grattan has had the goodness to allow him might be considered confidential, he does not think himself at liberty to refer to it without being sure that he has Mr. Grattan's permission ; but he rather imagines he will have no objection to Mr. Pitt's doing so as far as may be necessary in any explanation on the subject with the Duke of Portland and any other of his colleagues.

Mr. Pitt's anxiety to avoid any doubt on this point will be his apology for giving Mr. Grattan that additional trouble.

Downing Street, Wednesday, Oct. 15, 1794,
¾ past 5 P.M.

That Pitt was firm in his purpose will fully appear from the secret correspondence which passed next day between Windham and himself :—

Mr. Windham to Mr. Pitt.

(Endorsed Oct. 16, 1794.)

Dear Sir,—*I* have likewise talked with Mr. Grattan since his conversation with you, and I had hoped for some opening of better prospects. A very little would, I am persuaded, content them—I mean Mr. Grattan and his friends, if the matter could be fairly brought as a question of their moderation. What might give an unfavourable appearance to Mr. Grattan's conversation was a suspicion in his mind that more was meant than seemed to be declared ; that there was an objection to the system more than a tenderness about particular persons. I really believe that if the C.[1] could be given up, ——[2] might be saved. But I don't know, nor should I think, that there could be any secret article about that, and any understanding upon the subject would be too delicate and dangerous. If you cannot make up your mind to expose him to the risk, I fear the thing is desperate, and with it, I also fear, any hope of quiet or safety in Ireland. The

[1] The Chancellor (Fitzgibbon).
[2] In the MS. an initial, or perhaps two letters, but illegible.

acquiescence of men in the situation of G. and his friends would be an effort of virtue too great to be long continued.

I ought not to disguise from you either the probable effects here, great or small : it is proper they should be before you. Though I could say nothing positive about myself till the return of Lord Spencer, yet it does not appear to me that it would be possible for me to stay on the grounds on which the D. of P. and Lord F. would go out, nor do I conceive that Lord S. would be, with respect to himself, of a different opinion. How much I deprecate such an extremity on the public account, you will easily conceive. I assure you I should hardly do so less on account of the perfect satisfaction that I have found in the connection as it has hitherto subsisted.

Yours, dear Sir, with great truth,   W. WINDHAM.

Mr. Pitt to Mr. Windham.

Downing Street, Oct. 16, 1794.

Dear Sir,—The more I consider every part of this unfortunate subject, the more I am confirmed in the impossibility either of consenting to the Chancellor's removal or of leaving either him or any of the supporters of Government exposed to the risk of the new system. What you say with respect to yourself, embitters the regret which, even without it, I should feel at the probable consequences of what has passed. My consolation under all the difficulties will be that I have nothing to reproach myself with in what has led to this misunderstanding; but I must struggle as well as I can with a distress which no means are left me to avoid without a sacrifice both of character and duty. Allow me only to add, that before you finally decide on your own line of conduct, I trust you will give me an opportunity of discussing with you without reserve the great public considerations which at this moment are involved in it.

Yours, with great truth and regard,   W. PITT.

Mr. Pitt to Mr. Windham.

Downing Street. Oct. 16, 1794.
½ past 5.

Dear Sir,—Strongly as I stated to you my feelings in my last letter, I fear, on looking at your letter again, that

I have stated them in one respect imperfectly. Besides the impossibility of sacrificing any supporters of Government, or exposing them to the risk of a new system, I ought to add that the very idea of a *new system* (as far as I understand what is meant by that term), and especially one formed without previous communication or concert with the rest of the King's servants here, or with the friends of Government in Ireland, is in itself what I feel it utterly impossible to accede to; and it appears to me to be directly contrary to the general principles on which our union was formed and has hitherto subsisted.

Painful as the whole subject is, I feel nevertheless that it is material to leave no part of it liable to be misunderstood, and I therefore give you this additional trouble.

Yours, &c.,   W. Pitt.

It will be seen that Pitt was fully determined to risk the resignation of his new colleagues rather than act with injustice to his old supporters. To set his determination on the several points beyond doubt, and to make use of in discussion, he drew up the following

Memorandum.

Much the best event of the present discussions would be some arrangement which avoided Lord Fitzwilliam's going to Ireland. But if satisfaction is given on the other points, it is impossible to put a negative on his going. If it were right to do so at all, it could only have been done by forming and notifying that determination as soon as it was fully known what had been the conduct of the party respecting this business. Not having been done at first, there is no tenable ground on which it can be done now. Even if the decision were still in our power, much as I should wish to avoid his going, I do not think it would be wise to break on that ground. If so, it also follows that facility must be given to any reasonable arrangement. But before Lord Fitzwilliam can go, these four things are indispensable :—

1st. A full explanation that all idea of a new system of measures, or of new principles of government in Ireland, as well as of any separate and exclusive right to conduct the

department of Ireland differently from any other in the
King's service, is disclaimed and relinquished.

2nd. Complete security that Lord Fitzgibbon and all
the supporters of Government shall not be displaced on the
change, nor while they continue to act fairly in support of
such a system as shall be approved here.

3rd. That a situation shall previously be found for Lord
Westmorland, such as may show on the face of it that he
quits Ireland with his own free consent. This can only be
from his having a situation in the Cabinet, or one of the
great Court offices, or some respectable office which has
been held by persons quitting those situations.

4th. An adequate and liberal provision for Douglas, if
the office of Secretary of State is not granted to him.

If these points are arranged, and the change of the
Lord Lieutenant is settled, Lord Westmorland must be
prevailed on not to press his recommendations to the Pro-
vostship and Secretary of State.   W. P.

For above a fortnight longer the question continued
in suspense. We find Lord Auckland—who was now
residing at his house of Beckenham, and who, in 1793,
had received an English in addition to his Irish peerage
—express himself with considerable bitterness, and, as I
think, considerable injustice, to his old political friends :

' I have said we are like the man in the nightmare ;
we feel the weight and horror, and yet sleep on. The
scramble of the Portland set is all in that style ; they
look with horror towards Jacobinism, but in the mean
time are absorbed in the old and sleepy game of patronage, in the pursuit of which they are at this instant
risking the convulsion of Ireland.'

These words are taken from a letter to Mr. John
Beresford, dated October 23rd. On the other side of
the question Mr. Grattan wrote as follows to a private
friend :—

Oct. 27, 1794.

My dear M'Can,—Had I anything to write, I should
have written. All I can say is, that nothing is determined
at present. Mr. Pitt don't agree to those extensive powers

which we were taught to believe the Duke of Portland had.
However, I should not be surprised if it were settled well
at last, and that Lord Fitzwilliam went over; nor yet
would the contrary surprise me.   This week will decide.

Desire them not to write from Tinnehinch, for I hope to
leave this on Monday or Tuesday next.

Yours most sincerely,　　　H. GRATTAN.

In this controversy, as finally settled, Mr. Pitt prevailed on every point, the Duke of Portland and his
other Whig colleagues remaining in their places.   The
retirement of Lord Westmorland was delayed until he
could be invested with a high Court office as Master of
the Horse.   Then, and not till then, was Lord Fitzwilliam sworn in before the King as Lord Lieutenant.
The Irish Chancellor was not to be removed, nor yet
any other holder of office in Ireland, unless for any act
of insubordination in office.   It seems, however, probable
that the Duke of Portland, who was always sparing of
words and expressed himself with great difficulty even
in private conversation, may have but very imperfectly
explained this last stipulation to Lord Fitzwilliam.
Certain it is, as we shall find, that Lord Fitzwilliam
on reaching Dublin began to act at once in utter disregard of it.

By the appointment of Earl Fitzwilliam as Lord
Lieutenant there remained the office of Lord President
to fill.   The King was gratified by the selection for that
post of one of his personal friends and followers of the
Coalition period, Lord Stormont, who had recently succeeded as second Earl of Mansfield.   The following
letter will best explain by what arrangement that nomination and Lord Westmorland's were combined.   It is
addressed by Mr. Pitt to the former Lord Graham, now
Duke of Montrose and Master of the Horse :—

Holwood, Nov. 21, 1794.

My dear Duke,—Understanding that you are expected
in town to-day, I take the first opportunity of writing to
mention a proposal which I flatter myself has nothing in it

likely to be unacceptable to you, and I know you will be inclined to give it a favourable consideration when I tell you that it will furnish the only means for relieving Government from an embarrassment of the most serious nature. With a view of Lord Fitzwilliam's going to Ireland, there are circumstances that render it necessary for me to be able to open some situation of distinction for Lord Westmorland. Lord Mansfield would be to succeed Lord Fitzwilliam as President of the Council, and would relinquish his office of Justice General in Scotland. Considering the rank and value of the latter office, I am led to hope that you would not consider a grant of it for life as an unfavourable exchange for the situation which you now hold, and to which Lord Westmorland might succeed. I wish, however, rather to make the proposal to you on the ground of affording me at a very anxious moment a very essential accommodation, which I shall feel as an additional proof of the friendship and kindness which I have always experienced from you.

Believe me yours sincerely,   W. PITT.

Thus reinforced the administration met the Parliament on the 30th of December. The King in his opening speech declared that, notwithstanding the disappointments and reverses of the last campaign, he retained a firm conviction of the necessity of persisting in a vigorous prosecution of the war. He announced his acceptance of the Crown of Corsica, and the conclusion of a treaty for the marriage of the Prince of Wales with the Princess Caroline of Brunswick.

The Addresses in reply gave rise to warm debates with some circumstances not wholly in favour of the Government. Among the Peers, indeed, there were only the usual speakers of Opposition, as Lords Lansdowne and Stanhope, and the usual minority of ten or twelve. But in the Commons several members of great weight had become inclined to peace from the reverses of the last campaign and from the fall of Robespierre. Foremost among these stood Mr. Wilberforce. In spite of the personal friendship which had long connected him with the Prime Minister, and of which he foresaw the too probable severance, he moved an amendment to the Address, advising an endeavour for peace. He was seconded by Mr. Duncombe, his colleague in the representation of Yorkshire, and supported by Mr. Bankes of Dorset. In the division which ensued at four in the morning, the amendment had only 73 votes against 246. But the secession of such men was of itself no inconsiderable aggravation to the troubles of the Ministry, and no light blow to the war party throughout England. Mr. Wilberforce has noted in his journal, 'When first I went to the Levee after moving my Amendment, the King cut me.'[1]

The doubts and misgivings of Mr. Wilberforce had, as was just, far greater weight with the public than the continued denunciations of the war by its original opponents. Thus, on the 6th of January, Earl Stanhope brought forward a motion against any interference in the internal affairs of France, but with so much of ardour and so little of concert, that on dividing the House he was not supported by any other Peer. In consequence of this disappointment Lord Stanhope, though up to that time one of the most active members of the House of Lords, wholly seceded from it during the next five years.[2]

While thus in the House of Commons the war party was enfeebled by the secession of Mr. Wilberforce and his friends, a blow still far more serious, still far more unexpected, was dealt on it in Holland. It was known that the armies had withdrawn to winter quarters. It was thought that the campaign was concluded. But as it chanced, the winter in that region set in with extreme severity, such as had not been felt for many years. The great rivers which form the barrier of Holland to the southward were frozen over, and seemed to invite rather than to guard against invasion. General Pichegru, who

---

[1] *Life of Wilberforce*, by his Sons, vol. ii. p. 73.

[2] See the *Public Characters* of 1800–1801, p. 125. A medal was struck on this occasion in his honour with a motto, 'The Minority of One, 1795.'

was ill at Brussels, hastened back to his post. The French soldiers, displaying their usual alacrity for action, came forth with scanty clothing and rent shoes, but without a murmur, from their comfortable quarters. The ice being strong enough to bear them, they crossed with the greatest ease both the Meuse and the Wael. General Walmoden with the English and Hanoverians fell back towards Deventer to effect their retreat by way of Westphalia. The Prince of Orange with the Dutch fell back towards Utrecht and Amsterdam. He sent to ask for a suspension of hostilities and to offer terms of peace, but both were disdainfully rejected. Then no other resource was left him. The French troops pressed forward in overwhelming numbers; and the French party, which had been struck down in 1787, again raised its head. The Prince relinquished the contest and embarked for England, while Pichegru entered Amsterdam in triumph on the 1st of Pluviose, as he termed it, or the 20th of January.

Nor was this all. The greater part of the Dutch fleet was ice-bound in the Zuyder Zee. Against it some regiments of cavalry and light artillery were at once despatched by Pichegru; and for the first time perhaps in the annals of war did ships surrender to horsemen. Only a small number of armed vessels that lay in the outer ports could sail away to England as adhering to the House of Orange. A new Constitution was then proclaimed throughout the country, abolishing the dignity of Stadtholder, and setting up a democratic Republic under the dictation of the French.

The rapid subjugation of the Dutch afforded two fresh arguments to the friends of peace in England—as evincing the power of the French arms, and as freeing us from the obligations of burthensome allies. Nevertheless, large majorities in both Houses of Parliament continued steady to the Minister. Motions tending to a cessation of the war were brought forward by the Duke of Bedford in the one House and by Mr. Grey in

the other, but without the smallest success. A loan of
18,000,000*l.*, requisite to carry on the war, was cheer-
fully voted, and was negotiated at the rate of less than
five per cent. Another loan of 3,000,000*l.*, for the use
of the Court of Vienna, was assisted by the guarantee
of England. Several new taxes were also imposed ;
one especially of a guinea a year upon every person who
wore hairpowder, an impost which, from the prevalence
at the time of that silly fashion, would, according to
Mr. Pitt's calculation, produce annually the net sum
of 210,000*l.*

In February of this year there was a change in the
Mastership of the Ordnance. It had been decided that
the Duke of Richmond should be removed from it for
the sake of concord in the Cabinet. But His Grace
was continued on the Staff, and continued to give his
general support to the administration.[1] Indeed, notwithstanding their difference from time to time as colleagues, he retained the deepest respect for Mr. Pitt; as
did also Colonel Lennox, his nephew and presumptive
heir. Four years after Pitt's death, we find the then
Duke accept the Presidency of the Pitt Club, and write
as follows to Mr. Rose: 'There is nothing I pride
myself on so much as having been the intimate friend
of such a man.'[2]

The vacant office of the Ordnance with the Cabinet
seat were conferred on a meritorious public servant,
Lord Cornwallis, who had also received some time before
the Garter and a Marquisate. At the same time that
Lord Cornwallis became Master-General of the Ordnance
and a Cabinet Minister, the Duke of York was named
Commander-in-Chief.

[1] The King to Mr. Pitt, Jan. 29, 1795.
[2] *Diaries, &c., of the Right Hon. Geo. Rose,* vol. ii. p. 220, ed.
1860.

CHAPTER XX.

1795.

Precipitate measures of Lord Fitzwilliam—Dismissal of Mr. Beresford and Mr. Cooke—Addresses from Roman Catholics and
Protestant Dissenters—Mr. Grattan's Bill—Recall of Lord Fitzwilliam and appointment of Lord Camden—Riot in Dublin—
Contentions in the Irish House of Commons—Rejection of Mr.
Grattan's Bill—Foundation of Maynooth—Trial of the Rev. W.
Jackson—Brothers the Prophet and his disciples—Marriage of
the Prince of Wales—Acquittal of Warren Hastings—Provision
for Burke—Distress in France and England—Anxiety of Pitt.

WE must now after this brief interval revert to the
Lord Lieutenancy of Ireland. There is no doubt that
the intentions of Lord Fitzwilliam were upright and
high-minded. But some persons, perhaps less disinterested than himself, were busy at his side. Even in
December, 1794, before the new Viceroy had left England, we find Lord Auckland predict that his new supporters would be 'restless to get a larger share of
patronage.' It was again and again represented to
Lord Fitzwilliam that certain persons holding offices in
Ireland had too much power—that they would obstruct
the new administration and overshadow the new Lord
Lieutenant—and that they ought to be removed. The
persons thus aimed at were especially Mr. John Beresford, Chief Commissioner of the Revenue, and directing
several other kinsmen in place, and Mr. Edward Cooke,
the Secretary at War.

Under these circumstances the course for Lord Fitzwilliam to pursue seems clear and plain. He should
have commenced his government and judged for himself. He should have fairly tried whether the gentlemen in question were in truth, or wished to be, obstacles
in his path. If so, he might have laid their conduct
before the Cabinet in England, or even perhaps after
full trial have dismissed them himself. Instead of this,

he chose to rely solely on the representations of others. There really is no answer to the plain statement of this part of the case as made in a private letter from the Chancellor of Ireland. 'One broad fact,' writes Lord Fitzgibbon, 'must damn him on this subject for ever. He landed here on Sunday evening (January 4, 1795), and was confined to his room by indisposition for the whole of the next day. On Wednesday Mr. Bowes Daly was sent to you (Mr. Beresford, with a notice of intended dismissal). So that he had one day only to inquire into the multiplied acts of malversation which he alleges against you as his justification for wishing to remove you.'[1]

In sending notice of dismissal through his Secretary to Mr. Beresford and Mr. Cooke, Lord Fitzwilliam did his best to soften the communication. To the first he offered the full amount of his salary as retiring allowance, and to the latter a pension of 1,200*l.* a year. But both these gentlemen, then in the prime of life, were by no means disposed to retire from active service. Still less were they disposed to brook any imputation, express or implied, upon their public character. Mr. Beresford set out for London, there took counsel with Lord Auckland and his other friends, and earnestly appealed by letter to the justice of Mr. Pitt. 'I hope,' said Mr. Pitt to Rose, 'there may be some mistake in the statement, because it would be an open breach of a most solemn promise.' The Whig friends of Lord Fizwilliam in the Cabinet could by no means approve his conduct. It had been — so Lord Loughborough explained to Mr. Grattan — even apart from the merits of the question — most discourteous to Mr. Pitt. 'Supposing Mr. Pitt merely the First Commissioner of the Treasury, without the influence usually attached to that office, to have removed an officer in his department by a letter from the Lord Lieutenant's Secretary, would not

<hr>

[1] Letter of March 26, 1795, as published in the *Beresford Correspondence*, vol. ii. p. 88.

have been agreeable to that respect which Ministers owe to each other.'[1]

In public measures Lord Fitzwilliam was equally headlong. The state of the Roman Catholics had been the subject of many anxious conversations in England. By the Acts of the two last years they were freed from the Penal Statutes, but there still weighed upon them great political disabilities — above all, as excluding them from Parliament, and restricting their possession of arms. A measure for their complete equality on all points with the Protestants was now desired, though not as yet publicly proposed. Mr. Grattan was especially charged with the conduct of their cause, and had great power either to press forward or delay it. The Prime Minister, though guarded in his language, was friendly and comprehensive in his views. Indeed, it may be doubted whether any one single member of the Cabinet was at this time hostile to the measure on its merits. The difficulty with all was only as to the means and time. But these were not mere details. On the contrary, they were matters of paramount importance. It might be a cause of peril, it would certainly be a cause of alarm, to make such momentous changes in the midst of a critical war. Nor could a measure of complete Roman Catholic emancipation be carried through at that juncture without the assent, or at least the acquiescence, of the main Protestant party. The feelings and wishes of that party if directly expressed could not be set aside at a time when so much treason was astir, when so many Republican conspiracies were brewing, when so much of combined exertion was needed to uphold the Throne.

Under these difficulties Mr. Pitt and the Duke of Portland conferred with Lord Fitzwilliam before he went, and, as I have already in part explained it, came to the following result. The new Viceroy was on no ac-

---

[1] Letter from Lord Loughborough, dated Feb. 28, 1795, and published in the *Memoirs of Grattan*, by his Son (vol. iv. p. 198).

count to bring forward the emancipation of the Roman
Catholics of himself or as a Ministerial measure. It
was highly desirable that this question should be deferred until more tranquil times. If, however, the
Roman Catholics themselves, or Mr. Grattan as their
champion, insisted on pressing it at once, the Ministers
in England would deliberate on the provisions of the
Bill so introduced, and consider how far they could in
prudence or in policy give it their support.

Here again, had Lord Fitzwilliam been a man of
ability, acting from deliberate judgment rather than
from sudden impulse, the course which he should have
taken seems very clear. On arriving in Ireland he
should have felt his way. He ought either to have
shunned any public declarations on the point at issue,
or have expressed in them his desire to reserve himself
until after some personal experience of the country and
of office. Such was the course that he might have
taken; the very reverse was the course that he took.
Almost immediately upon his landing he received addresses from bodies of Roman Catholics and Protestant
Dissenters, and in his answers was understood as inti-
mating his agreement to their wishes. The consequence was that far from allaying he stirred the flame.
Petitions to the Irish House of Commons praying for
the complete emancipation of the Catholics poured in
from every county in Ireland. By the middle of February it was computed that the number of signatures
to these exceeded half a million.[1] Mr. Grattan, even
had he wished it, had no longer the power to hold back.
On the 12th of February he moved to bring in a Bill
enumerating all the exceptions to complete equality
and abolishing them all.

The rash precipitation of Lord Fitzwilliam both in
dismissing statesmen and in deciding measures was not
long in bearing bitter fruits. Resentment and alarm

---

[1] See on this point the letter of Dr. Hussey in *Burke's Correspondence*, vol. iv. p. 277.

took possession of the minds of the Irish Protestants. They looked on the dismissal of their political friends as casting light upon the measure framed for their religious opponents, as revealing its true spirit and design. All hope of their concert or even their acquiescence was gone.   Only two days after the motion of Grattan, the Chancellor wrote to his friend in London declaring that the King could not give his assent to the measure ' without a direct breach of his Coronation Oath. Whenever,' he added, ' Mr. Grattan brings in his Bill and it is printed, I mean to send it over to England with comments in reference to British Statutes, which certainly bind the King upon this subject.' [1]

The King himself, it may be added, conceived from the first the strongest disrelish to the scheme.   In a Private Memorandum drawn up for Mr. Pitt, and dated on the 6th of February, we find him argue at length against it, and call it (but might not that be in truth its praise?) 'a total change of the principles of government which have been followed in that kingdom since the abdication of King James the Second.'

Such scruples were by no means confined to the King alone.   They extended to many of Pitt's most zealous followers.   They extended to many even of those who held office under him.   These gentlemen had from the first viewed with jealousy the accession of the Portland party, and that jealousy was now inflamed to the highest pitch.   As one sample, among several others, of this feeling on their part, I shall here insert a letter which the Solicitor-General, Sir John Mitford, addressed to Mr. Pitt—a letter which evinces, let me say, in passing, the upright and independent spirit of the writer :—

Adelphi. Feb. 14, 1795.

Dear Sir,—It is with much pain that I prevail on myself again to trouble you on a subject which perhaps you wish, if possible, to banish from your thoughts.   But the evident difficulty of your present situation, the solitude in

[1] Letter in the *Beresford Correspondence*, vol. ii. p. 73.

which you seem to be placed amongst a throng of Cabinet
Ministers, the ignorance in which I believe most of your
friends are with respect both to your real situation and your
intentions, and their apparent uncertainty whether you are
not acting upon the impulse of the moment because you are
unwilling to look at the evil in its full extent, give me the
greatest uneasiness. This uneasiness is increased by knowing that your conduct of late has turned some warm friends
into cold friends, or perhaps bitter enemies. I confess too
that I feel not merely on your account, but in some degree
on my own. I have perhaps too much pride, and am not
much disposed to brook disgrace, which I think I see fast
approaching. As long as I shall hold the place I have, I
will endeavour to discharge its duties to the best of my
power; and though conscious perhaps that I ought not to
have taken it, and wishing ardently that I had declined it, I
shall be unwilling to quit it in a manner distressing to you.
But I shall not like to be told that I have kept it too long,
and I perceive that the Attorney-General's mind is labouring under the same difficulties. You must be aware that
almost all your friends feel something of the same uneasiness.
Many of them apprehend that what they long ago foretold
has at length happened; that you are completely surrounded,
that you stand in effect alone, that you are no longer your
own master, and that if you can extricate yourself from the
chains prepared for you, you have not a moment to lose.
What has happened in Ireland seems to be generally considered as a death-blow. I speak in some degree from rumour,
in some degree from conjecture, but not entirely.

  .   .   .   .

In fairly giving you my thoughts, I believe I best prove
myself   Faithfully yours,   JOHN MITFORD.

But let us for a moment waive the scruples of the
King, or of a portion of his servants—scruples which
then were not publicly known. Let us assume (no light
assumption) that the Ministers could have overcome
those scruples, and had been able to give to the Bill of
Mr. Grattan their active aid. Even on that supposition,
considering how the Irish House of Commons was at
that time composed, I do not think it probable that

the Bill could have been carried through.   Carried, at
all events, it could not have been without a tremendous
party battle—without a political conflict shaking Ireland, and perhaps Great Britain also, to the very
centre.   Would it be possible to hazard that political
conflict at a time when there were daily threats to
Ireland at least of a foreign invasion?   Might it not,
on the other hand, be hoped that in such a ferment and
against such obstacles the loyal majority of the Roman
Catholics would themselves feel the propriety of a pause
on the part of the administration—of a desire to abide
for the present by the large concessions of the two last
years?

Moved by considerations such as these, and acting
with entire unanimity, although with great regret,
the Cabinet in England came to the decision that
Lord Fitzwilliam must be at once recalled.   Lord
Fitzwilliam himself had been much chafed even by
the first objections both to the dismissal of Mr. Beresford and to the Bill of Mr. Grattan.   On the 21st of
February Mr. Pitt addressed to him a private letter,
stating courteously but firmly his fixed resolution on
both points.   Receiving that letter, His Excellency on
the 25th summoned the Chancellor to his presence,
and announced his determination to lay down his
government and return to England within a very few
days.   The news was quickly noised on all sides, to the
joy no doubt of the Protestant, but to the sorrow of the
more numerous Roman Catholic party.

Lord Fitzwilliam, however, did not fulfil his threat
of immediate departure; he remained at Dublin until
the 25th of March.   The day of his departure was one
of general gloom: the shops were shut; no business
of any kind was transacted; and the greater part of
the citizens put on mourning, while some of the most
respectable among them drew his coach down to the
water-side.[1]   A corresponding degree of aversion was

[1] See the *Annual Register*, 1795, p. 226.

showed a few days afterwards when the new Viceroy, Lord Camden, arrived. Yet, as Mr. Grattan owned, Lord Camden had considerable claims to public regard from the exalted character of his father, and he brought with him a living sign of moderation in the person of his Secretary, Thomas Pelham, a gentleman who had been bred in Whig principles, and who had filled the same office during the administration of the Duke of Portland.

Such considerations have no weight in troubled times. When the new Lord Lieutenant was sworn in at Dublin Castle there was a formidable riot — which, however, the populace directed against their own countrymen in office. They assailed the coaches of the Chancellor and Primate with volleys of stones; one stone striking the Chancellor on the forehead, and slightly wounding him over the left eye. Another party attacked the new Custom-House, but without success, desirous, as they phrased it, 'to extinguish' Mr. Beresford. Their cry was 'Liberty, Equality, and no Lord Lieutentent!' and they were decked with green cockades.

In the Irish House of Commons there were fierce contentions. The course of Lord Fitzwilliam was eagerly discussed; and Mr. Grattan spoke with ardour in defence of his absent friend. Yet he quickly found that the majority was by no means upon his side. When at last on the 4th of May there came on the Second Reading of his Bill, it was, after long debate, rejected; 84 members voting in its favour, but against it 155. Some writers, not well versed in the practical working of our Parliamentary system, have assumed that a complete change had come over the Irish House of Commons, since, as they observe, on the 12th of February no more than three members spoke against the first introduction of the Bill, and since they did not call for a division. These writers have overlooked the fact that the motion for leave to introduce a Bill often gives rise to hostile speeches, but very seldom to a hostile division; least of all when that motion proceeds from a man of eminent fame.

In England, Lord Fitzwilliam, appealing to the judgment of the nation, published two letters of great length which he had addressed to Lord Carlisle. There were also two motions in Parliament on the subject of his recall, one by the Duke of Norfolk in which Lord Fitzwilliam himself spoke, the other by Mr. Jekyll, backed by Mr. Fox. Lord Grenville conducted the defence of the Government in the House of Peers, and Mr. Pitt of course in the House of Commons. Both declined a discussion of the circumstances as injurious at that time to the public service, and took their stand on the undoubted prerogative of the King to appoint or to dismiss his confidential servants.

It seemed probable at one time that this controversy would have been continued with even sharper weapons than the tongue or pen. A passage of Lord Fitzwilliam's published letters applied to Mr. Beresford the words 'imputed malversation;' Mr. Beresford gave his Lordship the lie direct; a challenge ensued; and it was only by the quick interposition of magistrates that a duel was prevented, when the parties had already met with pistols in hand.[1] Lord Fitzwilliam, after the duel was prevented, said he need no longer scruple to make an apology, and made it in generous terms. Many pamphlets also came forth in confutation or corroboration of Lord Fitzwilliam's, and charges of ill-faith and treachery were freely levelled at the Government. But when calmly viewed the ground for these charges is so slight that they do not seem to require any more detailed examination. A single fact may suffice in answer to them. The Duke of Portland, Lord Spencer, and Mr. Windham were men of high feeling and unblemished honour. They had long been friends and allies of Lord Fitzwilliam. Yet they,

[1] See Mr. Beresford's own account of this affair in his *Correspondence*, vol. ii. p. 115.

with whatever reluctance, concurred in the necessity of his recall, and remained in office as the colleagues of Mr. Pitt.

Thus was the prospect of equal laws in Ireland marred by precipitation on the one side and by prejudice on the other. Thus did the hopes of a better system vanish like an airy dream. In one respect, and one respect only, were the schemes of Lord Fitzwilliam's Government fulfilled in Lord Camden's—in the establishment, namely, of a College for the education of the Roman Catholic priesthood. A Bill for that purpose was brought into the Irish House of Commons on the part of the Government during the month of April, and it passed with little opposition. The result was the foundation of Maynooth.

Up to this time, and under the harsh repression of the Penal Laws, the young men designed for Holy Orders in the Roman Catholic Church had been brought up in foreign colleges. Some few, who attained great eminence in after years, had gone to Portugal and Spain. Thus for example, Bishop Doyle (best known as J. K. L., from the signature which he adopted in his political writings) had been trained at Coimbra, and Archbishop Curtis at Salamanca. But by far the greater number went to Douay, St. Omer, and other colleges in France. The Revolutionary torrent had swept these colleges away, and no others nearly as convenient could be found. Under these circumstances Archbishop Troy, on behalf of himself and the other Roman Catholic prelates, had presented, in 1794, a Memorial to the Earl of Westmorland as Lord Lieutenant, representing the absolute necessity of some place of education for the Roman Catholic Clergy, and praying a Royal Licence for the endowment of an ecclesiastical academy in Ireland. The Memorial was favourably entertained, and the College of Maynooth was instituted in the spring of the following year.

The founders of this College, besides the manifest necessity of the case to the Roman Catholics, looked forward to great national benefits. They hoped that the Irish priests, if trained within the confines of the kingdom, would be the more certainly imbued with attachment to the King and Constitution. They hoped that this establishment, voted by Protestants for the sake of their Roman Catholic fellow-subjects, would be a pledge of peace and good will between the two communions. Certainly, at least considering the general assent with which the measure passed, they could not foresee that in after years it would be so bitterly denounced.

But among the many who have thus on abstract principles denounced it, there are some, at least, who have paid regard in a spirit of candour to the special circumstances of the case. They have been willing to consider how far in this transaction the national faith might be engaged. They have found that it was proffered as a boon to the Roman Catholics of Ireland at the very time when their hope of equal rights derived from Mr. Grattan's Bill was dashed to the ground—at the very time when they were called on to make common cause with their Protestant brethren and join in measures of resistance to the threatened French invasion. Passed at such a time, and received in such a spirit, I believe that the foundation of Maynooth does bear many features of a compromise or compact. I am sure that it could not be cancelled without some breach of the English honour and some disparagement to the English name.

In the midst of this political agitation of Ireland there came on at Dublin, after long delay, the trial for High Treason of the Rev. William Jackson. He was a native of Ireland and a clergyman of the Established Church, but for several years past a resident at Paris. It was his object to establish a concert of measures between the rulers of France and the malcontents of Ireland.   But in his negotiations he had relied on an attorney of ill repute, named Cockayne, who betrayed him to the British Government.   When he was brought to trial at Dublin Curran stood forth as his Counsel, but Cockayne appeared against him as a witness, and he was found Guilty.   When, on a subsequent day, he was again brought up to receive judgment, the unhappy man, who had swallowed poison that same morning, sank down in the agonies of death and expired in the presence of his judges.

A similar condemnation might have probably awaited his confederate Wolfe Tone, had he not, in June this year, anticipated an arrest by a timely escape to America.

It is worthy of note how often we find the tidings of state revolution go side by side with tales of supernatural power.   The former seem to have a tendency to stir up in the human mind a craving or a credulity for the last.   Thus, at the very height of the Reign of Terror, the cold heart of Robespierre warmed to the prophecies of a female enthusiast, Catherine Theot. And thus in England, at nearly the same momentous period, the public attention was seriously attracted by a male fanatic.   This was Richard Brothers, a native of Newfoundland, and at one time a Lieutenant in the Navy.   His imagination had become disordered by pondering over some dark books on the Apocalyptic prophecies.   Supposing himself to have received a Divine Commission, he assumed some lofty titles— 'Nephew of God,' and 'Prince of the Hebrews.'   He predicted the speedy and complete destruction of London ; but on the other hand he promised to establish his kingdom in Jerusalem before the close of the year 1798.   For the support of these views he relied on divers signs, visions, and portents.   Thus, for example, he declared that on one occasion he plainly saw the Devil sauntering in London streets.   Here are his own words : 'After this I was in a vision, having the angel of God near me, and saw Satan walking leisurely into London.'[1]

Strange though it may seem, it is yet a common case, that pretensions even so wild as these found some ready believers among educated and accomplished men. Thus one of the greatest artists of that age presented to the world a fine print of Brothers, with these words beneath:—'Fully believing this to be the man whom God has appointed, I engrave his likeness—William Sharp.'

Thus again, Mr. Nathaniel Brassey Halhed, a gentleman who had filled an office of trust in India, who had published a translation of the Gentoo Code of Laws, and who was now Member of Parliament for Lymington, avowed himself a follower of the new prophet. Twice in the Session of 1795 he brought the claims and the sufferings of Mr. Brothers before the House of Commons; but, having no seconder, his motions fell of course to the ground.

So long as the visions of Mr. Brothers were confined to the world of spirits or to the land of Judaea, they might be disregarded by the Government; but the case was altered when they took the form of a printed notice to His Majesty in the following terms:—

'The Lord God commands me to say to you, George the Third, King of England, that, immediately upon my being revealed in London to the Hebrews as their Prince and to all nations as their Governor, your Crown must be delivered up to me, that all your power and authority may cease.'

On the 3rd of March the Prophet was brought before the Privy Council under a warrant from the Secretary of State. Subsequently a commission was issued to inquire into the state of his mind; and the verdict of a Jury having declared him a lunatic, he was sent to Bedlam. In 1806 he was released by an order from

[1] *Brothers's Prophecies*, part i. p. 41, as quoted in a note to Southey's *Poems*, vol. iii. p. 90, ed. 1838.

Lord Chancellor Erskine, and he survived till 1824, not even then wholly destitute of followers. One of the last of these, John Finlayson by name, published, so lately as 1848, a tract entitled 'The Last Trumpet and Flying Angel;' and in this tract we find him write as follows: 'God gave me a dream and a vision of Mr. Brothers, who told me that he approved of all I had done, and lifting his two hands high over his head, he rejoiced mightily at all I had written and published.'

On the 8th of April the marriage of the Prince of Wales with the Princess Caroline was solemnized at the Chapel Royal, St. James's. Some months before Lord Malmesbury had been despatched to Brunswick to ask in due form the hand of the Princess and bring her over to England. He found the Duchess, a sister of George the Third, not a little elated at her daughter's prospects. All the young German Princesses, she said, had learnt English in hopes of becoming Princess of Wales.[1] The bride herself, then twenty-six years of age, made no very favourable impression on the experienced diplomatist. He thought that she had naturally in some degree both good temper and good sense, but was spoiled by ill examples and a faulty education. ·

On the other side the prospect was quite as far from satisfactory. The Prince, in his conversation with the King, which decided the proposal of marriage, had expressed his desire to lead a moral and regular life.[2] But he had little constancy in his good resolutions even if they were sincerely formed. It was rumoured by the public that a lady of high rank held over him at this time a paramount influence. With signal want of propriety in any point of view, the Prince selected this very lady to meet his bride at Greenwich on her first landing, and to attend Her Royal Highness in the same coach to St. James's.

<hr>

[1] Lord Malmesbury's *Diary*, Nov. 22, 1794.
[2] The King to Mr. Pitt, Aug. 24, 1794.

His own first interview with the Princess was by no means such as could be wished. Lord Malmesbury, the only other person present, has described it. He says that the Princess, according to the established form, attempted to kneel before the Prince when he came in, that he raised her gracefully enough and embraced her. But immediately afterwards he turned round, retired to a distant part of the apartment, and calling Lord Malmesbury to him said, ' Harris, I am not well; pray get me a glass of brandy.'

Such then was the unpromising outset of this most unhappy marriage.

In April Pitt was confined by an attack of gout, which however in his own letters is treated very lightly :—

Wimbledon, Monday, April 20, 1795.

My dear Mother,—Your letter, which I received on Saturday, found me recovering from a very moderate and regular gout, and able on that day to remove hither. Two days of quiet and country air have completed my cure, with the exception only of being probably obliged to wear rather a larger shoe for some days to come. This last circumstance will perhaps exempt me from the crowded drawing-rooms and balls which are to be repeated in the course of this week. If it has this effect in addition to having already made me much better in general health, I shall have no reason to quarrel with my confinement. I have nothing very new to tell exactly at the present moment, and so many interesting occurrences of different sorts have been crowded into the last four or five months, that one should be at a loss where to begin or end the reflections they lead to. I look forward with much impatience to an interval of leisure sufficient to have the comfort of talking over with you the long history of this short period. It is too early yet to say whether I can promise myself that satisfaction in the course of this summer. I trust, however, it is not impossible, especially if the weakness and distraction of France, which seems likely to lead to the best solution of all our difficulties, goes on increasing as rapidly as it has done lately. . . . . . .

Ever, my dear Mother, &c.,   W. Pitt.

On the 23rd of April the House of Lords brought to
a conclusion the long-pending trial of Hastings. The
Indian topics which it involved had wholly ceased to
attract the public interest. There was only some stir
from time to time at the able speeches made by the
Managers of the Impeachment, and by Mr. Law, the
chief Counsel for the defence. There had grown to be
a general feeling that the Charges against Hastings
were not sufficiently proved, or that even if they were,
the length of the trial was of itself no inconsiderable
penalty. Burke indeed retained against the culprit,
for so he deemed him, all his early zeal. He depre-
cated with the greatest warmth all idea of concession
or of clemency. So early as the spring of 1794 we find
him urge Mr. Pitt ' not to suffer the House of Commons to be dishonoured by the Indian faction.'[1]   But
almost everyone else was weary of the trial and impatient for its close. No more than twenty-nine Lords
had of late attended to hear the evidence. It was,
indeed, as Burke in his letter calls it, 'a miserable
remnant of the Peers.' No more than twenty-nine
Lords therefore thought themselves entitled to appear
and vote when summoned in due state to give sentence
in Westminster Hall. Of these, only six pronounced
Hastings guilty on the Charges relative to Cheyte Sing
and to the Begums of Oude. On some points the majority in his favour was greater still. On some others
his acquittal was unanimous. Upon this the prisoner
(for so in legal phrase he continued to be called) was
directed to come into court. He came, and as on the
first day of his trial, he knelt down. Then the Lord
Chancellor Loughborough desired him to rise, and addressed him in these words: ' Warren Hastings, you are
acquitted of all the Charges of Impeachment brought
against you by the Commons and of all the matters
contained therein. You and your bail therefore are
discharged.' Mr. Hastings then bowed and withdrew.

[1] Letter of Mr. Burke, dated March 14, 1794 (Pitt Papers).

Thus did Hastings prevail at last over his accusers. But from the length of his trial his victory bore along with it nearly all the concomitants of a defeat. It was not only that his mind had been harassed and soured—that his fair hopes of some high office had been dashed—that the Coronet once rising in near prospect had wholly faded from his view. His own private fortune and the hoards, as they were termed, of Mrs. Hastings, had become exhausted by his lawyers' bills and the other charges of his long defence. When he left the Bar of the House of Lords acquitted and set free, he was almost a ruined man. Then it was that the Directors of the East India Company displayed the generous spirit which has seldom, if ever, been found wanting to any of their great public servants. They proposed to repay to Hastings all the legal costs of his trial, and to settle on him moreover a pension of 5,000*l.* a-year. Dundas, however, as President of the Board of Control, refused to give his consent. It could not be expected that a statesman who had taken a forward part in pressing the accusation of Hastings should readily agree to schemes for his reward. There was a long controversy and a final compromise. The Company was permitted to grant Hastings an annuity of 4,000*l.*, and to advance to him a sum of money without interest. The retired Governor-General had, however, contracted in India some habits of expense and carelessness. On several subsequent occasions he found it necessary to apply to the Company for further assistance, which was on each occasion cheerfully afforded. Books and gardening gave him all the solace that they can to an ambitious mind. He lived almost entirely at Daylesford, and survived to the great age of eighty-five, dying in August, 1818, of a gradual and gentle decay.

In this Session Mr. Pitt did not, as he had designed, bring down a Message from the King for a grant to Mr. Burke. He desired, if he could, to spare to the retired statesman the uneasiness of an angry debate. And the means were, he found, in his power. Certain West India Duties called the Four-and-a-Half per Cents.—the same on which Lady Chatham's pension stood—were still so far at the disposal of the Crown that a further annuity of 2,500*l.* to Mr. Burke could be assigned upon them without the need of any vote from the House of Commons.[1] There was no delay in the payments, although the necessary forms were not completed until October in this year. Then did Burke write again to the Prime Minister, both to express his thanks and to convey his counsels, and both in his ever admirable style :—

Beaconsfield, October 28, 1795.

Dear Sir,—I send you with this a letter of acknowledgment through you to the King for his extraordinary goodness to me. It is ostensible, if you think it of any use that it should be so.

You have signally obliged me. I am a person incapable of any active return for the services I receive, but I make some sort of amends for the inefficiency of a feeble body and an exhausted mind by the sentiments of a grateful heart.

You have provided for me all I am capable of receiving in the last stage of my declining life—that is, Repose. I have only to wish you all those good things which you can or ought to look for in the vigour of your years and in the great place you fill—much manly exertion and much glory attendant on your labours. Indeed you have the prospect of a long and laborious day before you. Everything is arduous about you. But you are called to that situation, and you have abilities for it. I hope in God that you will not distrust your faculties, or your cause, or your country. Our people have more in them than they exactly know of themselves. They act on the condition of our nature. We cannot lead, but we will follow if we are well led, and the spirit that is really in us is properly and powerfully exercised. There is one thing I pray for in your favour (for in you is our last human hope)—that you may not fall into the one great error from whence there is no return. I trust in the mercy of God to you, and to us all, that you may never be

---

[1] *Life of Burke*, by Prior. p. 409, ed. 1854.

led to think that this war is, in its principles or in anything that belongs to it, the least resembling any other war; or that what is called a peace with the robbery of France can by any plan of policy be rendered reconcileable with the inward repose, or with the external strength, power, or influence of this kingdom. This, to me, is as clear as the light under the meridian sun; and this conviction, for these five years past and in the midst of other deep and piercing griefs, has cost me many an anxious hour at midday and at midnight.

I trust you are too discerning and too generous not to distinguish the faults of too earnest a zeal from an unbecoming presumption, though both seem to take the same course. My anxiety has led me from the depth of this melancholy retreat (which, however, the King's goodness and yours renders more quiet to me) to interfere by obtruding my poor opinions on a person whom I confess and must feel to be, no less by nature than by situation, much more capable of judging than I am.

I have the honour to be, with the most perfect respect and attachment, &c.,　　　　　　　Edm. Burke.

Both France and England in this year were enduring great distress, even apart from the war which they waged against each other. There was the crash of paper credit in France. There was the pressure of heavy taxes in England. But moreover both nations at this time suffered grievously from dearth. The havoc of war had laid waste great part of the corn districts on the Vistula and Rhine, and the harvest of 1794 had proved scanty in other parts of Europe. Thus at Paris 'Bread, Bread!' became the favourite watch-word both of the poorer classes and of all who desired to overthrow the existing Government. In England the price of provisions continued to rise; there was severe distress through the winter, and in the spring many a dangerous riot. Thus at Birmingham in the month of June a mob of a thousand people gathered before a bakehouse and mill, which they proceeded to break open and plunder, crying, 'A large loaf! Are we to be starved to death?' It was necessary to call in the military force, and the disturbance could not be quelled without the lamentable loss of one life. Other disturbances, similar in kind, though less in degree, took place in Coventry, Nottingham, and other towns, and there was one upon the Sussex coast where the Oxfordshire Militia was stationed, and in which men from that regiment joined.

In July there were tumults in London arising from another provocation, or at least putting forth another plea. There was the cry of illegal detention at the recruiting, or as they were called, the crimping houses, and two of these were on two separate evenings attacked by a large mob. The doors were burst open and the furniture was burnt in the streets, while another band seized the opportunity to break, as the newspapers reported, the windows of Mr. Pitt in Downing Street; but further mischief was prevented by the timely arrival of the City Associations and the Lambeth volunteers, besides a party of the Royal Horse Guards. No lives were lost, but several persons were wounded and others trampled down.

The newspaper paragraphs of the attack in Downing Street gave some alarm to Lady Chatham at Burton. She addressed to her son an anxious inquiry, and he wrote at once to re-assure her:—

Holwood, July 18, 1795.

My dear Mother,—I have this moment received your letter just in time to save the post by the return of the messenger. I take shame to myself for not reflecting how much a mob is magnified by report; but that which visited my window with a single pebble was really so young and so little versed in its business, that it hardly merited the notice of a newspaper. The ceremony has not been repeated since, and when I left town yesterday afternoon there was reason to believe that the disposition to disturbance which has appeared in some parts of the town was over, at least for the present. If it should revive, the precautions taken will, I am sure, prevent any serious mischief.

This wind must soon bring accounts from Brittany, for

which one must wait with anxious impatience, though with
every reason to hope that they will be good. When I parted
with my brother yesterday afternoon, he had not quite fixed
his day of setting out. I wish I could see a nearer prospect
of fixing mine. In great haste, as you well see,

Your dutiful and affectionate   W. PITT.

It is plain that the real roots at this time of the
popular dissatisfaction were first the high price of provisions, and secondly the unprosperous conduct of the
war. But the flame which had sprung from high prices
was industriously fanned by the friends of French principles in England. The Corresponding Society again
reared its head. The London press again poured forth
a volley of publications—from pamphlets down to broad-
sheets or placards—levelled at the Government in
Church and State, and arraigning it as the cause of the
distress. In fairness it should be acknowledged that
the great majority which took part in these publications, or in the subsequent proceedings, desired to assail
only what they had been taught to consider as abuses
of the system. They had no wish to strike at the root
either of the social order or of the Christain faith.
Nevertheless there were some among them, and those
not very few, willing and eager to go the extremest length.
There was, above all, Thomas Paine, who had now
returned to England, having been cast into prison and
most narrowly escaped the Guillotine during the sway
of Robespierre. His own danger had not sobered him,
nor yet all the scenes of woe which he had beheld.
On the contrary, his great object seemed to be to bring
England into the same condition, civil and religious, as
under the Reign of Terror in France. The worst and
most unbridled of all his publications—the ' Age of
Reason'—was sent forth at this critical time.

On the 29th of June, in the midst of the riots
through the kingdom, a public meeting was convened
by the Corresponding Society, and held in St. George's
Fields. There many thousands assembled. A vehe-

ment declaimer, Mr. John Gale Jones, was placed in the Chair. As a kind of symbol, biscuits were distributed, embossed on one side with the words 'Freedom and Plenty, or Slavery and Want.' Addresses to the nation and to the King were moved and carried, as also a string of Resolutions. In these they predicted, very much in the style of Barère, that 'the voice of Reason, like the roaring of the Nemean Lion, shall issue even from the cavern's mouth.' They demanded annual Parliaments and universal suffrage as the undoubted rights of the people. They deplored the high price of provisions, which they ascribed entirely to the present cruel and unnecessary war; the only remedy for this and other ills being immediately ' to acknowledge the brave French Republic, and to obtain a speedy and lasting peace.' They voted thanks to Citizens Erskine and Gibbs for their eloquent defence of the prisoners in the recent trials, and thanks also to Citizen Earl Stanhope and Citizen Sheridan for showing them that they had ' one honest man in each House of Parliament.' It is clear from this last vote that Sheridan was at this time considered to go much greater lengths in his politics than did his coadjutors Fox and Grey.[1]

Up nearly to this time it had been hoped that a plentiful harvest might remove the main cause of suffering and distress. But notwithstanding the midsummer season, we are assured that intense cold set in on the 18th of June. This in the first place destroyed the sheep and lambs, more especially on the open plains. It was computed that in Wiltshire not less than one-fourth of the flocks had perished.[2]

But this was not all. The inclement weather continued, and exerted its influence on the arable as on the pasture lands. The inferior kinds of grain were indeed not deficient, and barley, above all, was reaped in abun-

<hr>

[1] A full account of these proceedings, and of the later ones on the same side, is to be found in the *History of Two Acts*, &c., as published in 1796. See especially pp. 90–108.

[2] *Ann. Register*, 1795: Chronicle, p. 27.

dance ; but as regards wheat there was a second scanty
harvest.   The price of wheat, which in February had
been at the high rate for those times of 58s. a quarter,
rose in August to the famine price of 108s., and in
September was still at 78s.

Notwithstanding the alarms of this period, Pitt was
enabled in the course of September to pass a few days
with his mother at Burton Pynsent.   He addressed a
lively letter to her on the very day of his return :—

Downing Street, Sept. 30, 1795.

My dear Mother,—The engagements I found on my arrival leave me just time for one line to say that I brought
the spoils of the Commerce table safe last night to Bagshot,
and reached town this morning as I intended, after a journey
very successful, and rendered very pleasant by the recollection of all the comfort and satisfaction of the few days preceding it.   Accounts from Burton will, I hope, soon give me
the pleasure of knowing that you remain at least as well as
I left you.   You will probably have received by this time a
full account of the naval campaign from Lord Bridport,
whom I met on the road, and found disposed to complain a
little of the length of his cruise, but looking, as I thought,
much the better for it.   Pray remember me kindly to all
your companions, among whom Eliot, I reckon, is by this
time one.   Ever, my dear Mother, &c.,   W. Pitt.

At nearly the same time Pitt wrote a letter to his
friend the Speaker, which closed with the following
words :—

Sunday, Oct. 4, 1795.

. . . . I am still sanguine that the line we
talked over will bring us speedily to a prosperous issue.

I am going next Thursday for a week or ten days to Walmer, and hope to return with my Budget prepared to be
opened before Christmas ; and if that goes off tolerably well,
it will give us peace before Easter.

Ever yours,   W. P.

But although Mr. Pitt desired to calm his mother's
anxieties, and although he might look hopefully to the

prospects of the foreign conflict—expecting to awe France into peace by the magnitude of his preparations—he viewed in truth the internal state of England at this time with deep anxiety. It was his opinion that unless a strong arm were extended, the people might be hurried by a temporary frenzy to excesses not far unlike or those of France. Only a few weeks from this time, as he was supping at his own house in company with two close friends—Mornington and Wilberforce—he let fall this expression: 'My head would be off in six months were I to resign.'[1]

In this anxious and perturbed condition of the labouring classes, it seemed to Mr. Pitt and to his colleagues that Parliament should be called together at an early period to consider every practicable measure of relief. The Recess had only begun on the 27th of June, and was allowed to continue no longer than the 29th of October.

On the 26th, three days before the intended opening of the Session, another Meeting, under the direction of the Corresponding Society, was held in a wide open space with a tavern and tea-garden called Copenhagen House. It was said, though no doubt with much exaggeration, that no less than one hundred and fifty thousand persons flocked together.[2] Mr. Thelwall, Mr. Gale Jones, and other orators made inflammatory speeches; and divers Resolutions, calling for 'execration' on the present Ministers, and demanding Universal Suffrage with Annual Parliaments, were declared to be passed.

[1] *Diary* of Wilberforce, Nov. 16, 1795.
[2] See the *History of Two Acts*, &c , p. 98.

CHAPTER XXI.

1795.

Congress at Basle—French advantages in the West Indies—The
Maroon war—English conquests in Asia and Africa—Projected
descent on the western shores of France—The Chouans—De
Puisaye—Landing at Quiberon—Fatal inaction—Rout and distress of the Royalists—Executions—Comte d'Artois—New Constitution proclaimed in France—Insurrection in Paris—Campaign
upon the Rhine—Depreciation of Assignats—Meeting of Parliament—Attack upon the King—Debates on the Address—
Measures to alleviate scarcity and to repress sedition—The Duke
of Bedford and Lord Lauderdale—Pitt's desire for peace.

DURING the spring and summer of 1795 there was for
the most part a lull in the military operations. The
French rulers seemed to be satisfied with the rapid conquest of Holland and the formal annexation of the
Belgic provinces. They listened to overtures of peace
from several Powers, and opened a Congress for further
negotiations at Basle. At home they were mainly
intent on framing a new and less democratic Constitution—on pacifying La Vendée—and on crushing the
insurrectionary movements of the Jacobins.

Of all the Princes who had declared war against the
French Republic, the first to conclude peace was the
Grand Duke of Tuscany. The treaty between them
was signed at Paris on the 9th of February. On the
5th of April there followed the signature at Basle of a
peace with Prussia. By that treaty, far from honourable to the Court of Berlin, the French remained in
full possession of their conquests to the left of the
Rhine. Another compact, also signed at Basle, a few
weeks afterwards, stipulated the neutrality of the north
of Germany. On the 12th of June the King of Sweden
acceded to the Peace of Basle, and the same city on the
22nd of July beheld the conclusion of a separate treaty
with the King of Spain. By this last the French Republic agreed to restore all its conquests beyond the

Pyrenees, while the Court of Madrid in return gave up its rights to the Spanish portion of the isle of St. Domingo.

On the other hand the English diplomacy was not inactive. The Court of Vienna was certainly gratified, and perhaps stimulated, by a new Convention of Subsidy, and great efforts were made to obtain the active co-operation of the Court of Petersburg. There was even signed a Triple Alliance, less, however, for use than for show.

The nominal cession of the Spanish half of St. Domingo was by no means the only advantage gained by the French this year in the West Indies. Victor Hugues at Guadeloupe displayed a true Jacobin energy. Turning his views of conquest to the English islands, he succeeded in kindling the flame of revolt among the negroes, the Maroons, and the Caribs. With their aid the French gained possession of St. Lucia and St. Vincent's. In Grenada and Dominica their attacks, though at first successful, were finally repulsed. We might almost fancy that the scene lay in Western Europe during the days of Robespierre, as we read of the butchery of defenceless prisoners, and the violation of enemies' graves—of red caps and tricoloured cockades —of flags inscribed with 'Liberty, Equality, or Death,' —and of proclamations against 'the vile satellites of George—those infamous promoters of every kind of robbery! For rob they must,' adds the discerning Victor Hugues; 'that is the very principle of the English military service. In such a corrupt government no preferment can be obtained but for money, and money must be had, no matter by what means.' The Declaration of Victor Hugues and his two colleagues at Guadeloupe, from which I extract this passage, is dated as follows: 'Port of Liberty, the 3rd day of Ventose, or 21st of February according to the style of slaves, in the third year of the French Republic, One and Indivisible.'

Jamaica at the same period was exposed to constant alarm from the desultory but destructive skirmishes of the Maroons. These, the descendants of the early settlers in the Spanish times, were no slaves, but on the contrary had maintained their freedom in the mountain fastnesses towards the centre of the island, their chief settlement being called Trelawney Town. There were now some grievances on the part of the English, and some lures on the part of the French. On these the Maroons had at once recourse to arms. In vain did the Earl of Balcarres, as Governor of Jamaica, make every effort to reduce them. He was foiled again and again by their nimble escape and rapid re-appearance. Then, in concert with the local Legislature, he adopted a resource which the precedent of the Spaniards is wholly insufficient to excuse. They sent over to Cuba and imported a hundred blood-hounds with thirty huntsmen to trace and pursue the fugitive Maroons. It does not seem, however, that this savage expedient, though resolved on and prepared, was actually employed. Some reinforcements from England arriving at this very period, the Maroons grew inclined to peace, and a treaty was concluded.

In Asia and in Africa during the course of this year our arms were also felt. The subjugation of Holland by the French led the English to reduce the ancient colonies of that Republic. Ceylon, the Moluccas, and some others surrendered without a blow. To the Cape of Good Hope we sent a small expedition, the ships commanded by Sir George Elphinstone, and the troops by Sir Alured Clarke. No more than sixteen hundred men of all arms could be set on shore, and the Dutch forces were much larger, but consisting in great part of burgher guards and Hottentots. Their irregular resistance was quickly overpowered, and so this important colony was gained.

But the hopes of Mr. Pitt at this time principally turned to a projected descent on the western shores of

France. In La Vendée, ever since the fatal rout of Savenay, the civil war had smouldered rather than burned, and the Republic had lately concluded terms of pacification first with Charette and afterwards with Stofflet. It was believed, however, that a new insurrection would readily burst forth, including even the reconciled chiefs, as soon as a British fleet with a body of land forces on board should appear in sight of the French coasts. And meanwhile the civil war had spread on the north of the Loire. There had been to some extent a popular rising in Brittany. The insurgents of that province were known by the name of *les Chouans*, a word of doubtful origin, but said to be corrupted from *chat-huant*, the night owl, to denote their secret signal in their nightly expeditions.

The name was not the only difference between the insurgents of La Bretagne and those of La Vendée. In the latter it had been the revolt of a brave and loyal peasantry stirred beyond endurance by the cruel wrongs of their priesthood and their King. In the former the peasants were no less brave and no less loyal. But with these there was a large admixture of outlaws and marauders, ever ready for some deed of rapine or of private vengeance. Upon the whole then the insurgents north of the Loire did not muster *en masse*, to form an army, but prowled about in small bands for some special object. It was not so much a province which had risen as a province which was ready to rise.

In the ranks of Les Chouans the leading influence belonged to Comte Joseph de Puisaye. He had been at one time a member of the National Assembly, and was distinguished both for conduct and courage. Soon discerning that the bands of Brittany could not of themselves achieve any great Royalist end, he had fixed his hopes on the co-operation of England, and with that view, bidding his friends bide their time, himself repaired to London in the autumn of 1794. Mr. Pitt, who has been accused of coldness and distrust to the

Emigrants in general, showed to the Comte de Puisaye
both esteem and confidence. De Puisaye became the
ruling spirit of the intended enterprise, and his papers
even now afford the best materials for its history.
Having been bequeathed by him to the British Museum,
they were received by that institution in the year 1829.
They form no less than one hundred and eighteen
volumes, comprising some few letters of Mr. Pitt.

The plan of M. de Puisaye was to conduct an English
squadron to the coast of Brittany—that squadron to
have on board some French Royalist troops, and at
their head a French Prince of the Blood. In furtherance of these views the English Government had taken
into its pay several bodies of French Emigrants—now
grievously reduced in numbers—that had lately been
serving on the Rhine. An active officer, M. d'Hervilly,
enlisted some more from among the fugitives of Toulon
and the Breton prisoners of war. On the whole there
were ready to embark upwards of three thousand men,
besides a second division of about twelve hundred which
had not yet arrived from Germany. The English Government, in addition to its earlier advances, supplied
ten thousand guineas in gold for the military chest, and
there had been fabricated by order of M. de Puisaye a
large number of Assignats, distinguished by a private
mark and designed for a ready circulation.

To obtain a Prince of the Blood might seem a much
easier, but was in truth a more difficult task. The exiled
Royal Family of France was at this time much divided.
Monsieur had retired from the Rhine as the Republican
armies advanced, and had fixed his residence in the
states of Venice, at Verona. He continued to take the
title of Regent during the minority and the captivity
of his nephew, Louis the Seventeenth; and he sent
forth as his Envoys to the various capitals men of the
highest rank among the Emigrant nobility, as the Duke
d'Harcourt to London, and the Duke d'Havré to Madrid. With divers malcontents at Paris he carried on

an active correspondence, and they had formed themselves into a secret Committee for the management of
his affairs. The Comte d'Artois, on the other hand,
was ever moving from Court to Court or from camp to
camp. Thus, for instance, he had travelled to Petersburg, where the Empress Catherine showed him great
marks of honour, but gave him no substantial aid.
He did not by any means hold the same opinions nor
yet correspond with the same persons as his brother.
Detached from both of these, the Prince of Condé had
still under his command some three thousand Emigrants
in arms, and continued to wage war upon the Rhine
with more spirit than success.

It was the wish both of Mr. Pitt and of M. de Puisaye
that the Comte d'Artois should lead the projected expedition. The Prince did not refuse, but made difficulties, and hung back. Many of the officers around
him wished to land in La Vendée rather than in Brittany, and seemed to think it beneath them to go night-
owling—*de chouanner*—as they said.

It was also wished that, except as regarding the
Comte d'Artois, the strictest secrecy might be observed.
But this secrecy, though absolutely essential to success,
gave great umbrage to the other chief Emigrants. Still
more did it offend the manifold intriguers who undertook to manage the Royalist cause at Paris. As for
these last, indeed, they appeared far less intent to
achieve a Restoration than to prevent its being
achieved by any other hands except their own. The
directions which they sent to the chief men in Brittany,
both before the landing of the armament and after it,
were designed to thwart, and did thwart, its objects in
the highest degree.

The English squadron for this enterprise was in-
trusted to Sir John Borlase Warren, a tried and excellent
seaman. There were put on board large supplies of
all kinds, not merely every requisite for the Royalist
troops embarked, but eighteen thousand uniforms and

stands of arms for the insurgents who were expected to join them. Before the middle of June the preparations in England were complete. The second division of the Emigrant regiments, commanded by De Sombreuil, had not yet arrived; still less His Royal Highness of Artois. But any further delay, in order to await them, would have forfeited all prospect of surprise and success. The armament accordingly set sail, M. de Puisaye having the supreme direction, and M. d'Hervilly the immediate command of the troops. There were also a Breton prelate, the Bishop of Dol, and about forty gentlemen of rank, who served as volunteers.

The place for landing which had been selected, but which had been kept most carefully secret, was the peninsula of Quiberon, in front of the bay of the same name. That bay, it was thought, would afford to the English ships a secure anchorage, and that peninsula to the French troops a commanding station. The expedition began well. Nearly off Brest it was joined by the squadron of Lord Bridport, and fell in with the enemy's fleet under Villaret Joyeuse, when Lord Bridport, by superior manœuvring, cut off and captured Le Formidable and Le Tigre, each of eighty guns, and L'Alexandre of seventy-four.

On the 27th of June the Emigrant chiefs with their soldiers were safely disembarked near the Druid stones of Carnac, and within the bay of Quiberon. They stepped on shore full of exultation, rejoicing at their return to their native land, and not foreboding the dismal fate which impended over them. The news of their landing flew like wildfire on every side, and the Chouans eagerly flocked in to swell their ranks. Within three days they were joined by ten thousand men. It was desired by M. de Puisaye to lose no time, to seize the favourable moment, to advance rapidly upon Vannes and Rennes, and to raise the whole of Brittany in arms. Here, if ever, was a case in which boldness was the truest wisdom.

But more timid counsels prevailed. Though the commission of the British Government to D'Hervilly had been limited to the period of the voyage, that officer continued to claim the direction of the troops. He refused to obey the superior orders of Puisaye, and rendered necessary an appeal to the Ministers in London. Meanwhile no advance was made. After some days, however, Puisaye prevailed upon his colleague to attack the small fort Penthièvre, which commanded the entrance to the peninsula of Quiberon. The garrison of a few hundred men surrendered after a slight resistance. M. de Puisaye then brought over his troops to the peninsula, and landed his stores from the ships, occupying in this manner a strong position of defence, while the Chouans took up a forward line beyond the fort on the main land.

The injury of the inaction thus enforced upon Puisaye was not merely to be measured by the loss of time to himself, or by the gain of time to his enemies. It gave leisure for discord and jealousy to spring up in his own ranks. The Emigrant officers could not always conceal their scorn of the peasant chiefs, nor the peasant chiefs their suspicion of the Emigrant officers. 'Where,' said the Chouans, 'is that Prince of the Blood who had been promised us? Where is that rapid advance of which M. de Puisaye spoke? Is it possible that the English are striving only for some conquest to themselves?'

The command for the Republic in this province had been vested in General Hoche, a young and most able officer, the same who was designed as head of the projected expedition to Ireland. At the time when the Royalists landed he had under him only some five thousand troops, but, through the leisure left him, he found means gradually to double his numbers; and he acted throughout with singular spirit and vigour. Suddenly assailing the advanced position of the Chouans, he put them to the rout, driving them in utter confusion beyond Fort Penthièvre into the peninsula of Quiberon.

There they found themselves cooped up side by side with the Emigrant troops in a narrow space, and with scanty food.

Puisaye and D'Hervilly, however, made a vigorous effort to retrieve this check. On the 16th of July, at daybreak, they marched out from Fort Penthièvre, and in their turn assailed the troops of Hoche. But they did not succeed. D'Hervilly himself was mortally wounded; the signals were misunderstood; a body of Chouans, which had been sent round to the enemy's rear, failed to arrive; and valour was in vain. Great numbers of the Royalists were slain; the rest, protected by a sharp fire from the English gun-boats, were driven back to the tongue of land.

Meanwhile there had come from England a second smaller squadron, bringing M. de Sombreuil and his division of eleven hundred men, and bringing also a full confirmation of the superior powers which had been vested in M. de Puisaye. These succours, these powers, all arrived too late. M. de Sombreuil at once disembarked his men, eager as they were for action, but they were only in time to be partakers of the final disaster which ensued.

On the first taking of Fort Penthièvre, M. d'Hervilly had induced the Republican garrison to enlist in his own regiment. The consequences of this imprudent step may be readily guessed. No sooner had Fortune seemed to declare against M. de Puisaye than these new-made Royalists went over to General Hoche. In concert with them the General, during the night of tht 20th of July, made a sudden attack upon the fort and carried it sword in hand. Next morning, the 21st, he pursued his advantage against the remaining Emigrant troops, now scattered along the tongue of land. Inferior as they were in numbers, harassed as they had been by the night assault, they could offer no effectual resistance; and as it chanced, the sea was rolling high, and greatly impeded the English boats and ships in their efforts to aid them.

Grievous indeed was the scene that now displayed itself. There was some of the best blood of France—the descendants of its Knights and Barons in the olden time, of the men full of chivalrous daring, of the men who had marched to free the Holy Sepulchre beneath the banner of Godfrey de Bouillon, or who, in Poitou and in Picardy, had striven face to face and hand to hand with Edward the Black Prince—pressed together on the desolate beach of Quiberon, with stormy waves behind and implacable bayonets before them—with no choice but between the pitiless sea and their still more pitiless foe! Many of the officers in despair threw themselves upon their own swords. Many others were seen to plunge into the raging surf breast-high, or even neck-high, as they sought to gain the already over-burdened boats. Yet even thus their heads above the water afforded a sure mark to the musketry of Hoche, while many more were swept down for ever by the angry seas. Some few, on the contrary, succeeded and caught hold of one or other of the fishing barks that continued to hover off the coast. But their fate was, if possible, more dreadful still. The boatmen were dismayed at the number of the barks which, as loaded with many of the fugitives, they had lately seen to sink; and acting, as they thought, in self-preservation, they hewed off with their cutlasses the hands of the drowning wretches that clung to them. Seldom in any war has there been a scene of more unmingled horror and distress.

It is painful to find, two days after this total rout of the Royalists, Mr. Pitt wholly unsuspicious of it, and, on the contrary, writing to congratulate M. de Puisaye upon their success. I will here insert his letter, as derived from the Puisaye papers, mainly for the sake of showing the correctness of his French :—

Downning Street, le 23 Juillet, 1795.

Monsieur,—J'ai appris avec la plus vive satisfaction par vos différents rapports (dont le dernier nous a été remis hier par le Capitaine Bertie) tout ce que vous et vos braves compatriotes ont fait depuis votre arrivée en Bretagne pour la cause que vous soutenez avec tant de gloire. J'espère que vous aurez lieu d'être content du zèle et de l'activité qu'on ne cessera d'employer ici pour seconder vos efforts. A moins que le vent n'a contrarié l'expédition, un renfort de trois mille troupes Britanniques et des secours qui pourront suppléer à vos plus pressants besoins doivent être déjà près de vos côtes. Nous faisons tout ce qui dépend de nous d'accélérer l'envoi de Milord Moira avec une force beaucoup plus considérable. Soyez persuadé, Monsieur, que nous sentons toute l'importance de la crise actuelle, et que nous regardons la réussite de votre entreprise comme le grand moyen de terminer les malheurs de la France, et de rétablir la sûreté et la tranquillité de l'Europe.

Croyez toujours, Monsieur, aux sentimens d'attachement et de considération avec lesquels je ne cesserai d'être,

Monsieur, &c.,   W. Pitt.

J'ai donné l'ordre de fournir les fonds pour l'achat des chevaux que vous demanderez.

But let me hasten to the close. Some of the chiefs, as M. de Puisaye, did find means to reach the English squadron; many more, as M. de Sombreuil, were compelled to remain on that fatal shore. These, with about a thousand Emigrants, laid down their arms. It is said that there was some kind of capitulation with General Humbert—that a verbal promise was made to them that their lives should be spared on their surrender. This was most earnestly asserted by Sombreuil even in his dying moments, but was no less earnestly denied by Hoche.

It cannot be said, however, that the young General-in-Chief for the Republic took any part in the matter of the prisoners which misbecame so brave a man. If he made no effort to save them at this period, he is quite clear of any step to precipitate their fate. In truth he considered that fate as beyond his sphere, and he did no more than refer it to the decision of the Government at Paris.

Many considerations might have disposed that Government to mercy. It had overthrown Robespierre, and ought not to tread in his steps. Unhappily, for some time past, it had been seeking to conciliate the Men of Blood. It was afraid of being denounced as favourable in secret to the Bourbons. It was afraid, according to the felicitous phrase of that era, lest it should be *soupçonné d'être suspect*. It often happens in Revolutionary times, that men are supposed to show a ferocious energy who in truth have become cruel only because they were not courageous. Under these circumstances, the ruling men of the Ninth of Thermidor resolved to put in force one of the most sanguinary Decrees of the Reign of Terror—that every Emigrant taken with arms in his hands should be put to death without further trial. They sent orders into Brittany to execute this law upon all who had surrendered, excepting only the recent Republican prisoners, who were supposed to be enlisted against their will.

The just horror inspired by this sentence was by no means confined to its victims. Many of the common soldiers in the Republican army showed a far more humane and civilised spirit than did their political chiefs. They assisted, or connived at, the escape of as many single prisoners as they could. Still upon the whole the orders of the Convention had to be obeyed. A band of captives was led forth, drawn out in order, and shot; at their head M. de Sombreuil and the Bishop of Dol. Next day the same execution was repeated, and next day again. There was no intermission until fifteen days had passed, and upwards of seven hundred prisoners had perished. In vain did Hoche write word more than once to the Convention that his soldiers were weary of being used as butchers.[1]

[1] ' Hoche et le Conventionnel Mathieu écrivirent plusieurs fois

No sign of mercy came until after the executions were completed.

To this day the scene of these executions is still pointed out to the passing traveller—a meadow near the small town of Auray; and to this day the peasants call it *le champ des martyrs*. It is marked at present by a Grecian temple as a monument, the first stone of which was laid by the Duchess of Angoulême in 1823.[1]

At the very time when this ill-fated expedition had been ready to set out from the ports of England, there died at Paris the young Prince in whose name it was prepared. The nominal King, Louis the Seventeenth, expired on the 8th of June, 1795. He was only eleven years of age, brought down to his early grave by a course of systematic ill-usage, sure as the musketry of Quiberon; by bodily privations, and by anguish of mind. At the news of his decease Monsieur assumed the title of Louis the Eighteenth, King of France and of Navarre—an empty title, only to be realised after nineteen years.

On retiring from the bay of Quiberon, the wretched survivors of the expedition took shelter in the storm-beaten islet of Houat. There, when all was over, they were joined by His Royal Highness le Comte d'Artois. But Puisaye, chafed by his disaster, and harassed by the recriminations of his comrades, threw himself almost alone upon the coast of Brittany, there to rejoin the Chouan bands. Had His Royal Highness followed the example—had he landed without delay on some point of the French coast—the name and the presence of a French Prince might still have wrought wonders for his cause.

que les soldats se lassaient de faire le métier de bourreaux.' (De Barante, *Hist. de la Convention*, vol. v. p. 63, ed. 1853.)

[1] Mr. Mounteney Jephson, in his lively and entertaining *Walking Tour*, describes this temple as 'a dreadfully ugly building' (p. 198, ed. 1859). On the architrave is carved: *Gallia moerens posuit*.

Instead of such wise temerity, the Comte d'Artois, on receiving further succours from England, took possession of the island of Belleisle, and there remained at gaze for upwards of six weeks. He received divers deputations from both Brittany and La Vendée, and employed himself in discussing a great variety of plans. Even the worst of these, if at once adopted, would have been far preferable to the best so long delayed. Certainly Charles Comte d'Artois bore but little resemblance to Prince Charles Edward Stuart; and although with adherents equally devoted, ' the Ninety-five ' of France can never be ranked with ' the Forty-five ' of Scotland.

General Hoche during this whole period had been unremitting in his exertions. He had drawn together no less than forty-four thousand troops for the protection of La Vendée. When therefore at last, towards the middle of October, the Comte d'Artois showed some readiness to land on the Vendéan coast, and to join with his Emigrants the peasantry under Charette, there were obstacles that might have daunted even a much more enterprising chief. In the face of such obstacles the most prudent course seemed to be to do nothing at all. Much against the wish of the officers, both Emigrant and English, the Prince relinquished all idea of a landing, and sailed back with the squadron to England.

The chief result of this abortive enterprise was to draw down ruin on the principal Royalist chiefs. Charette had risen once again in arms on the project of co-operation from the French Prince and the English squadron, but being left alone, was quickly overpowered and taken prisoner. Nearly the same was the fate of Stofflet in another district. Both being brought to rapid trial were condemned and executed, the one at Nantes, the other at Angers.

Thus ended this most unfortunate expedition. Complete as had been the failure, the causes of that failure seemed plain and open to view. Not so, however, have they seemed to all writers. Several, and above all Frenchmen from the most opposite parties, differing on every other point, have alleged an occult cause as the true one. They trace the whole to the fiendish malignity of the English Minister. They declare that Pitt secretly wished the expedition to fail, and contrived it accordingly. He hated all Frenchmen, Republicans and Royalists alike, and desired nothing so much as to see them destroy each other with their own hands. For this purpose he had sought and found a fitting instrument in M. de Puisaye, who was in reality a traitor bought by the gold of perfidious Albion.[1] It is of course unnecessary to waste a single word in refutation of these charges. It may seem as unnecessary to record them. Yet they deserve to find a place in History as a striking instance how far, under certain circumstances of party hatred, the noblest minds may be traduced.

The news of the disaster at Quiberon reached Mr. Pitt on the 1st of August, as did other ill tidings two days afterwards. On both occasions we find him write as follows to Lord Chatham.

Downing Street, August 1, 1795.

My dear Brother,—I have wished to write to you every day these three days, but have not been able to find time. In the mean time you will have had the mortification of seeing the unexpected bad accounts from Brittany, the public reports of which, though somewhat exaggerated, are in substance but too true. The Gazette of to-day (which I have desired to be sent to you) contains a short statement of the result of our information, as far as relates to this unfortunate event. We have, on the other hand, reason to believe that everything has been going on as well as could be wished in the interior; and although their spirits must for a time be damped by this misfortune, there is the greatest reason to hope that if we can establish some other

---

[1] See for instance the *Mémoires de l'Abbé Georgel*, vol. v. p. 362; and the *Règne de Frédéric Guillaume*, par Ségur, vol. iii. pp. 79 and 225.

point of communication, our disappointment may soon be repaired.

Lord Moira remains eager for the enterprise, and I hope will be enabled to make a fresh attempt with a very considerable force in a very short time.

By Paris papers, it appears from an official report to the Convention, that on the 13th of last month the French fleet of eighteen sail of the line fell in with ours of twenty-three, south of Hières: by their own account they got away as fast [as] they could, and seem very proud of having reached Fréjus Bay, though not without the loss of the Alcide, which they represent to have been burnt. I hope you have found all well at Burton. Pray give my duty to my mother, and love to Lady Chatham.   Ever affectionately yours,

W. PITT.

Downing Street, August 3, 1795.

My dear Brother,—In addition to the bad news which was the subject of my last letter, I am very sorry to have to tell you that we have received from Paris accounts of peace being concluded with Spain at Basle on the 22nd of July: the terms are the restitution of all conquests, made on Spain in Europe, in exchange for the cession to France of the Spanish part of St. Domingo. This varies so much the whole state [of] things, both from setting at liberty so large an additional French force, and from the impression which it may produce on other Powers, that it makes it a new question whether any British force can, without too great a risk, be hazarded on the Continent of France. I incline to think that our plan must now be changed, and that the only great part must be in the West Indies, where I trust enough may yet be gained to counterbalance the French successes in Europe.   Ever affectionately yours,

W. PITT.

The Government of France at this time underwent an entire change. A new Constitution was proclaimed, called 'the Constitution of the Year Three,' from its date in the Republican calendar. Instead of a single Chamber as heretofore, two were instituted, the one designed as a Senate to be called 'the Council of

Ancients,' and the other 'the Council of Five Hundred.' The executive power was entrusted to a Council of Five, with the title of Directors, one of them to retire every year. These chiefs took up their residence in the palace of the Luxembourg, gave audiences seated on gilt chairs, and affected on all occasions a kind of semi-regal state. There were then or shortly afterwards among them men of most undoubted ability and patriotism, such as Carnot. But in general it may be said of this new Government that it showed the vices of the old Monarchy far more than those of the recent Republic. The civilians in office at this period were not Men of Blood; they did not seek to revive the Reign of Terror, but they were for the most part corrupt, dissolute, and slothful; either ill-qualified for public affairs, or intent upon personal objects.

In framing this new system, the members of the Convention had by no means forgotten their own special interests. They had passed a decree that in the new Legislature two-thirds should consist of men who had already sat in the Convention, and that only one-third should be new. That measure, though it might spring from selfish motives, had strong grounds of public utility to recommend it. There was little opposition to it in the greater part of France. But at Paris it was most fiercely resented, both by the old Republicans and the secret Royalists; and at the beginning of October these parties combining rose in open insurrection.

The Government and the Convention had been long forewarned, and were in some degree at least prepared. They had brought into Paris a body of five thousand chosen troops, and as their chief they relied on General Menou. But Menou at the decisive hour showed himself feeble, faltering, and unequal to his post. There seemed some prospect that the insurgents might prevail. Several of the newly-named Directors began to turn pale and look aghast. Barras, who took the lead amongst them at this juncture, bid them fear nothing.

' I have the very man we want,' he cried, ' a little
Corsican officer whom I knew at Toulon.' And with
these words he introduced to them the future Emperor
Napoleon.

General Bonaparte, on being invested with the chief
command under Barras, justified the choice by his
promptitude and skill. He dealt with the insurgents of
Paris as with the insurgents of Toulon. He had forty
pieces of artillery, rescued only just in time, and he
well knew how to dispose them. As the ' Sections,' for
so they called themselves, advanced to invest the hall of
the Convention, a tremendous fire both of musketry and
grape-shot was opened on their long and dense columns
in the narrow streets. After a sharp conflict they were
put to flight, utterly dispersed, and successively dis-
armed. This victory, which secured the power of the
newly-named Directory, took place on the 5th of
October, and is commonly known from its date in the
Republican calendar as the ' Treize Vendémiaire.' [1]

The campaign upon the Rhine had not opened till
the month of September. Then General Jourdan
crossed the river near Dusseldorf, and General Pichegru
near Mannheim. But the former chief was soon repulsed by General Clerfait, and the latter by General
Wurmser. Both with some disadvantage found it
necessary to repass the Rhine, while Clerfait by a
brilliant manœuvre made himself master of the lines
before Mayence, and raised the blockade of that important city. All this while there was a latent hope of
a far more considerable gain. The Prince of Condé had
made some secret overtures to Pichegru by means of
Fauche Borel, a bookseller from Neuchâtel; and the
General, after some coy demur, was found well inclined
to the Royalist cause. He was willing, if possible, to
engage his army with him, to assume the white cockade,

[1] A clear and excellent account of this insurrection is given by
Napoleon himself in the *Memoirs dictated to Comte Montholon.* See
vol. iii. pp. 65–75, ed. 1823.

and to march back upon Paris; but he would by no means give up in the first instance the fort of Huningen, as Condé required. So there was no actual agreement concluded, and still less any active co-operation begun.

A less secret source of hope to the enemies of the French Republic was at this time afforded. Her finances seemed on the very brink of ruin. So enormous was the depreciation of the Assignats she had issued, that in October 1795, it was computed as seventy to one.[1] Indeed this national bankruptcy (for so in truth it may be termed) is ranked among the causes of the intended defection of Pichegru. He was fond of pleasure and expense, and his pay, when given in Assignats, amounted, even before the lowest point of depression, to less than two guineas a week.[2]

In England, as we have seen, the meeting of Parliament had been fixed for an early day—the 29th of October. On that day the combined effect of popular distress with democratic agitation was soon apparent. As the King went down in State to deliver his opening Speech, he found the loyal shouts which were wont to greet him exchanged for hootings and hisses. The cries were 'Bread!' 'Peace!' 'No War!' 'No Famine!' 'No Pitt!' Some voices were even heard to utter 'Down with George!' When His Majesty's coach came opposite the Ordnance, a pebble or bullet, proceeding as was supposed from an air-gun, struck the window glass, through which a small hole was broken. It was not improbably the realisation of that very conspiracy in the preceding year which the Opposition had derided under the nick-name of the 'Pop-gun Plot.'

Throughout this trying scene the King showed perfect composure and serenity. On entering the House of Peers he calmly said to the Chancellor, 'My Lord, I have been shot at;' and he proceeded to read the Royal Speech in his usual clear and deliberate tones.

---

[1] *Parl. Hist.*, vol. xxxii. p. 190.
[2] Thiers, *Hist. Rév. Fran.*, vol. iv. p. 408.

On his way back there was a renewal of the former cries, and more than a renewal of the former violence. Stones were thrown, breaking the panels and another window of the coach. And when the King quitted that State coach at St. James's Palace, and proceeded to Buckingham House in his private carriage, His Majesty being then almost without guards, found himself most closely beset by exasperated numbers. It was fortunate that some of the Horse Guards, who had been dismissed from duty, returned of their own accord and lent their timely aid.

With much good sense the King gave a speedy token that, notwithstanding such excesses, he felt that he could rely on the attachment of the great body of the people. On the very next evening he went to Covent Garden Theatre accompanied by the Queen and three of the Princesses. The Royal party was received with a loud burst of applause, and the air of 'God save the King' three times repeated.

In the House of Lords the insult to the Royal Person was considered before any of the topics in the Royal Speech. Some witnesses to the fact were examined, and an Address moved by Lord Grenville, and afterwards concurred in by the Commons, expressed the indignation of both Houses at this 'daring outrage.' But so high had party-spirit risen at this time, that Lord Lansdowne in his place was heard to declare that this alleged attack was only 'the alarm-bell to terrify the people into weak compliances. He thought it was a scheme planned and executed by Ministers themselves for the purpose of continuing their power!' [1]

On account of the new topic thus unexpectedly brought forward, the Peers postponed until the next night their consideration of the Speech from the Throne; but pending the Message from that House on the other subject, the Commons made the Royal Speech as usual their first matter of debate.

[1] *Parl. Hist.*, vol. xxxii. p. 155.

The Royal Speech on this occasion had expressed
the King's satisfaction at the recent successes of the
Austrians in Germany and Italy, but adding his hopes
that there might soon arise in France a disposition to
negotiate for general peace on just and suitable terms.
It further stated that His Majesty had viewed with the
greatest anxiety the very high price of grain, and the
strong probability of an insufficient harvest. In the
Commons the Address was seconded by a young Member speaking for the first time in that Assembly which
at a later period he was to lead: this was the Hon.
Robert Stewart, soon afterwards Lord Castlereagh.
'Pitt spoke capitally and as distinct as possible on
the main point'—that is a wish for peace—so writes
Wilberforce. On the other side both Sheridan and Fox
inveighed with their usual eloquence against the whole
conduct of the war. With great force did Sheridan
contrast the former proposal of Mr. Jenkinson for 'a
march to Paris' with our actual achievements on the
coasts of Brittany and Poitou, 'where,' he said, 'British
blood indeed has not flowed, but British honour has bled
at every pore!' And Fox, at the conclusion of his
powerful invective, moved an amendment entreating,
among other things, His Majesty 'to reflect upon the
evident impracticability of attaining in the present contest what have hitherto been considered as the objects
of it.' Pitt was more brief but not less masterly in
the speech replying to both the Opposition chiefs, and
on a division the amendment was rejected by a majority
of four to one—240 votes against 59.

Next day in the House of Lords the same amendment which Fox had offered was moved, but with quite
as little success, by Francis, Duke of Bedford. His
Grace was grandson of the Minister who had signed the
Peace of Paris, and having recently come of age after
a long minority, began public life with much zeal as a
follower of Fox. He spoke often, and with considerable weight, in the House of Lords.

The attention of the Legislature was now directed upon two subjects of paramount importance—the measures to alleviate scarcity, and the measures to repress sedition.

As regards the former, Mr. Pitt brought forward the question so early as the 3rd of November. He proposed the appointment of a Select Committee to inquire into the causes of the high price of corn, and he gave at the same time an outline of the divers steps that he desired to take. He proposed to amend the law on the Assize of Bread, which up to that time was governed by the depositions periodically laid before the Lord Mayor of London. He proposed to prohibit the use of wheat flour in the manufacture of starch, and to clear away all obstructions in the transit of grain. He proposed that bakers should be no longer bound by law to make bread from wheat of the first quality, but should be authorised to use an admixture of inferior grain, as also perhaps of Indian corn and potatoes. Several experiments, said Mr. Pitt, had been already made, giving hopes that a mixed bread of this kind would be both nutritious and palatable. There had been an Act in the last Session prohibiting for a limited time the use of wheat in the distilleries, and this Act, at whatever loss to the revenue, might be renewed for another year. In like manner the King had been empowered last Session, for a limited time, to prohibit the exportation and allow the import duty-free of various kinds of food; and this prerogative also might be again enacted. But as afterwards appeared, the Minister was prepared to go even farther, and to grant a bounty on the import of these much needed supplies.

The Report of the Committee when presented expressed a general concurrence in these views; and Acts of Parliament were passed accordingly. Mr. Fox stated some doubts whether the bread from these mixed materials would prove sufficiently nutritious, but owned that he had nothing better to suggest, and indeed was but little at home on these financial or commercial topics. A bounty of twenty shillings was granted on the import of each quarter of wheat, and there were bounties in proportion on other articles of food.[1] But the Report of the Committee showed, that in addition to legislative measures, great advantage might ensue from private and voluntary efforts. An agreement which it recommended became of general adoption, pledging the persons who adopted it to reduce the consumption of wheat in their families by the use of mixed bread and the disuse of fine pastry.

Nor were pecuniary sacrifices wanting for the same benevolent object. The East India Company imported and disposed of greatly under cost several cargoes of rice, and the City of London gave bounties for the sale in Billingsgate Market of cod and haddock at twopence a pound. It is gratifying to add that by this timely combination of measures the object in view appears to have been fully attained. The advance of public distress was arrested, and the price of wheat was restrained within moderate bounds.

The next most pressing subject was how sedition might be punished or prevented. A Royal Proclamation had been issued on the 31st of October, in pursuance of the wish expressed by both Houses in their joint Address, offering 1,000l. as a reward to discover the perpetrators of any act by which the Royal Person was endangered. But no such discovery ensued. It was never known by whom the air-gun was discharged, or the missile flung. Only one person, a journeyman printer named Kyd Wake, was tried before Lord Kenyon, and convicted of having hissed and hooted round the King's state carriage, and having cried 'Down with George!' He was sentenced to stand an hour in the pillory, and to be imprisoned for five years.

[1] See the scale, with an account of the other measures adopted on this subject, in Macpherson's *History of Commerce*, vol. iv. pp. 359–363.

On the 4th of November there came forth a second Proclamation referring to the recent meetings in the open air—denouncing both the harangues and the publications which had tended to disturb the public peace—and calling on the magistrates to exert themselves to bring to justice any persons who might again offend. Expressions like these did not pass without comment from both sides. It was warmly maintained by Mr. Fox and by his friends that there was not the smallest connection between the outrageous acts at the opening of Parliament and the violent language in Copenhagen Fields. But far otherwise thought the nation at large. They considered the seditious language and the seditious acts to stand to each other in the precise relation of cause and effect; and they expected from the King's Servants some more stringent measures for the public peace. Such also, in the eyes of Mr. Pitt and of his colleagues, was their own opinion of their duty. ' It is notorious,' said Lord Grenville, ' that the evil we are seeking to correct has attained an alarming height—the most seditious papers circulated and the most inflammatory discourses delivered to public assemblies. To this is to be ascribed the outrage that has lately taken place. It is no longer the flimsy allegation of some imaginary grievance, or the slight pretext of a wish for Parliamentary Reform, that can be set up as the motive for such meetings. That thin veil has been lately torn away, and in the face of broad daylight an attempt has been made directly on the person of the Sovereign.'

Such were the words of Lord Grenville when, on the 6th of November, he presented to the House of Lords a Bill defining and extending the Law of Treason. The old Statute of Edward the Third had looked mainly to attacks intending the King's death, but here were penalties also on attacks intending any bodily harm. It was further declared that any person who, by writing, preaching, or speaking, should stir up the people to hatred of His Majesty's Person, and of the established Government and Constitution, should be liable to the penalties of a high misdemeanor, and on a second conviction might be transported for seven years.

Nor was this all. On the 10th of the same month Mr. Pitt laid before the House of Commons a Bill against seditious meetings. A summary power was given to the magistrates to disperse such meetings, even by force if necessary, and a licence was required for houses, rooms, or fields where money was taken for admission to hear lectures or discourses. The duration of this Bill—as also of the last clauses in the former—was afterwards in Committee restricted to three years.

In common parlance these two measures were known as the 'Treason' and the 'Sedition' Bills. Taking them together, and laying aside what was no real matter of dispute, the increased security to the Royal Person, they were, no doubt, as the Opposition called them, an alarming infringement of the public liberties. The question is only how far such an infringement might be justified by a peril to the State more alarming still. 'Say at once'—cried Mr. Fox, in a strain of most fervid eloquence, and on the very first night of the Sedition Bill—'say at once, that a free Constitution is no longer suitable to us; say at once, in a manly manner, that upon an ample review of the state of the world, a free Constitution is not fit for you; conduct yourselves at once as the senators of Denmark did; lay down your freedom, and acknowledge and accept of despotism. But do not mock the understandings and the feelings of mankind by telling the world that you are free—by telling me that if out of this House, for the purpose of expressing my sense of the public administration of this country, of the calamities which this war has occasioned, I state a grievance by petition, or make any declaration of my sentiments in a manner that a magistrate may think seditious, I am to be sub-

jected to penalties hitherto unknown to the laws of
England.   .   .   .   .   Did ever a free people meet so?
Did ever a free state exist so?   Good God Almighty!
Sir, is it possible that the feelings of the people of this
country should be thus insulted?'

These words were full of ardour, and no pains were
spared to arouse an equal ardour in the people.   The
Whig Club met and protested with the Duke of Bedford
in the Chair.   The Corresponding Society met and did
their best to dissemble their Republican tendencies,
reprobating in strong terms the recent insults ' offered
to the person of the Chief Magistrate.'   There was a
meeting of the inhabitants of Westminster in Palace
Yard, with Mr. Fox as their Member presiding over
them ; it produced some angry speeches, and a petition
to the House of Commons.   There were meetings of
the same kind at divers places both in England and in
Scotland.   At Edinburgh several vehement Resolutions
were moved by Henry Erskine, the Dean of Faculty,
and like his brother Thomas, of the highest forensic
renown.   In consequence of this step on his part, his
brother advocates dispossessed him of the office of Dean
at their ensuing annual election ; and they were themselves denounced as persecutors by all the Whig speakers
and writers of the day.

Notwithstanding all the pains that were taken, it
may be questioned if there was much effect produced.
Within three weeks after the printing of the second
Bill, Mr. Abbot might observe in the House of
Commons that of all the English counties only four
had met and petitioned against the measure, namely
Middlesex and Northumberland, Surrey and Hamp-
shire ; and in the two last there were counter-petitions
on the other side.[1]   Subsequently there were a few more
county meetings and petitions ; one, above all, of some
contest and importance, in the county of Kent.   In
these, as was usual, the Sheriff or presiding officer

---

[1] *Parl. Hist.* vol. xxxii. p. 417.

signed in behalf of the whole assemblage.   But in other
cases, where individual signatures are required, the total
numbers may be ascertained.   It appears, then, on a
recapitulation of the whole, that against the two Bills
there were presented ninety-four petitions, and that the
number of signatures was 131,284.[1]   So small a frag-
ment of the entire population as opposing, seems to
indicate that the great mass did not disapprove.   It
is scarcely too much to say that in ordinary times even
the tithe of such rigorous enactments would have aroused
ten times more clamour.

Not far dissimilar was the result within the walls of
Parliament.   There the debates were purposely protracted by the Opposition, to give time for the exertions
out of doors.   Fox again put forth his great talents in
several spirit-stirring speeches.   He was seconded in
the Peers by the Duke of Bedford and the Earl of
Lauderdale, and (a new ally) Lord Thurlow; in the
Commons by Erskine and Whitbread, by Sheridan and
Grey.   Yet the highest minority among the Peers was
only 21.   In the Commons the minority did not, on
most occasions, much exceed double that number, and
only once, on an amendment for delay moved by Mr.
Curwen—rose to 70; there being even then, however,
267 arrayed on the other side.   Thus both the Bills
were carried through before Christmas; it may be said
with a high hand.

In the course of these debates there were some slips
of expression on both sides.   Dr. Horsley, Bishop of
Rochester, speaking in support of the first Bill, declared
that he 'did not know what the mass of the people
in any country had to do with the laws but to obey
them.'—'If I had been in Turkey,' began Lord Lauderdale, 'and had heard such a declaration from the mouth
of a Mufti——'   On another day the Bishop explained
away the phrase by the largest reserves in favour of
petitions and elections; still, however, the phrase, as

[1] See the recapitulation in the *History of Two Acts, &c.,* p. 827.

he had first used it, became a kind of watchword on the Opposition side.

Thus, again, in the Commons Mr. Windham was hurried on by the ardour of debate into declaring that 'the Right Hon. gentleman (Mr. Fox) would find that Ministers were determined to exert a vigour beyond the law.' Here he was interrupted by loud cries of 'Hear' and 'Take down his words.' It was only after some delay that he could complete his sentence— 'as exercised in ordinary times and under ordinary circumstances.' But here again the first words were frequently alleged, without their context, to inflame the public mind.

On the other side, Mr. Fox laid himself open to attack. 'If,' he cried, 'Ministers are determined, by means of the corrupt influence they possess in the two Houses of Parliament, to pass the Bills in direct opposition to the declared sense of a great majority of the people, and if they should be put in force with all their rigorous provisions—then, if my opinion were asked by the people as to their obedience, I should tell them that it was no longer a question of moral obligation and duty, but of prudence.' The Minister at once saw and seized the advantage afforded him by these hasty words. He started up and in his loftiest tone denounced them, 'with horror,' he said, 'and indignation,' —'as openly advising an appeal to the sword.' Mr. Fox rose again and declared that he should retract nothing. Yet, in explanation, he certainly qualified very much. 'The case I put was that these Bills might be passed by a corrupt majority of Parliament contrary to the opinion and sentiments of the great body of the nation. If the majority of the people approve of these Bills, I will not be the person to inflame their minds and stir them to rebellion.'

The mortification which Mr. Fox and his friends must have felt at seeing the two Bills carried through in spite of all their eloquence and exertions was, perhaps, in some degree allayed by the steps which they were able to take against Mr. John Reeves. In the autumn of 1792, as we have seen, that gentleman had founded the Association 'against Republicans and Levellers.' In the autumn of 1795 he came forth with a pamphlet designed in like manner for the support of the Government, but most foolishly exalting the monarchical branch of the Constitution at the expense of every other. 'The Parliament and the Juries,' so he wrote, 'were mere adjuncts, subsidiary and occasional powers.' 'Here,' said Mr. Fox, 'is a worse libel than any alleged against the Corresponding Society.' 'Here,' said Mr. Sheridan, 'is a case for the most solemn interposition of the House of Commons.' Consequently he proposed that Mr. Reeves should be dismissed from all his employments— that his pamphlet should be burned before the Royal Exchange by the common hangman—and that the Attorney-General should be directed to commence a prosecution against it. Of these three not quite coherent proposals, the Government resisted the two former, but not the last. The trial came on before Lord Kenyon early in the ensuing year, when the Jury declared that they thought Mr. Reeves's pamphlet a very improper publication, but that not deeming his motives such as were alleged, they found him 'Not Guilty.'

In the same spirit, and as seeking to oppose vehemence of one kind to vehemence of another, the Duke of Bedford took occasion in one of the debates upon the Treason Bill to assail Burke, or rather to assail the Ministers for having granted Burke a pension. In these observations he was seconded by Lord Lauderdale, and answered by Lord Grenville. The debate in itself seems little worthy of commemoration. But the genius of Burke has made it immortal. His pamphlet in reply, entitled, 'A Letter to a Noble Lord,' though not free from some defects, will ever be ranked among the master-pieces of the English language. With wondrous fertility of illustration he defends the cause of the British Constitution, while seeming only to plead his own; and he retaliates still more powerfully than he replies.

It is much to Fox's honour that these puny attacks on a great man were in no degree countenanced by him. The expressions of Lord Lauderdale and the Duke of Bedford, as applied to Burke in November, 1795, stand forth in strong contrast to those of Fox himself in May, 1796.

In this short but most active Session before Christmas there was still other business. On the 7th of December Mr. Pitt brought forward his Budget. He proposed a second loan of 18,000,000*l.*, and several new taxes, one above all upon Legacies, whether of money or of land. The loan was at once negotiated, but the new taxes were reserved for subsequent debates.

Next day, and no doubt with a view to the public credit, Mr. Pitt brought down to the House of Commons a Message from the King referring to the newly-settled form of Government in France, and expressing his 'earnest desire to conclude a treaty for general peace, whenever it can be effected on just and suitable terms for himself and his allies.' This announcement in the King's name appears to have produced a highly favourable impression on the public. Yet, in truth, the King was as keen as ever for the prosecution of the war; and his feelings on this subject were among the principal difficulties with which his Ministers had to contend.

CHAPTER XXII.

1796.

Birth of the Princess Charlotte—Separation of the Prince and Princess of Wales—Legacy Duties—Dog Tax: Mr. Dent—Failure of attempt to negotiate with the French Directory—Pitt's anxiety for peace—Dissolution of Parliament—Austrian Subsidy—Victories of General Bonaparte in Italy—English troops withdrawn from Corsica—Capture of Sir Sidney Smith—Treaty between France and Spain—English conquests in the West Indies—Lord Chatham President of the Council—Lord Malmesbury's Embassy to Paris—Projected invasion of Ireland—Pitt's measures of defence—Loyalty Loan—Debates on the Budget—Pitt's Poor-Law Bill—Experiments in Steam Navigation—Failure of the negotiation at Paris—Death of the Empress of Russia.

ON the 7th of January in the ensuing year the Princess of Wales was delivered of a daughter, who received the names of Charlotte Augusta. The people rejoiced at the appearance of an heiress to the Throne. But their joy was dashed by the tidings which speedily followed it of the complete estrangement of the Prince of Wales from his consort. He wrote her a letter in civil but cold and unfeeling terms to announce their final separation. Leaving her husband's house, the Princess with her infant daughter went to reside at Blackheath. The King showed a strong disposition to pity and protect her, and thus did dissensions break forth anew between the father and son.

The Session of Parliament which was resumed in February continued until May; and several matters of high importance were discussed. General MacLeod brought forward the employment of blood-hounds against the Maroons; when Mr. Dundas owned that such an order had been given in Jamaica, but intimated that it was no sooner made known in England than it was disapproved by the Government and countermanded. Under these circumstances the motion was no further pressed.

On the Legacy Duties the discussion was eagerly

resumed. To frame any new tax at such a juncture had been no mean trial of Pitt's financial skill. How impose further imposts on a people already staggering under the heavy burdens of war, and moreover in that year the famine price of corn? Yet how maintain the public credit if there were to be a vast increase of debt, and no corresponding effort to add to the revenue? A tax upon successions seemed to steer between these opposite difficulties. It was not in any case a pressure upon poverty, but rather a deduction from much larger sums to be received. Not merely the widow, but the children were to be exempted from any payment at all; while with regard to others, the tax was graduated from two per cent. on brothers or sisters, to six per cent. on strangers in blood; thus maintaining, it was hoped, a just distinction between natural and fortuitous claims.

It was difficult, nay almost impossible, to estimate what this new impost might produce; by Pitt, however, it was taken at only 250,000*l.* a-year. He had declared his intention to include all kinds of property in a single comprehensive measure. But the reception of his Budget enabled him to appreciate more justly the strong repugnance of the landed gentlemen. Thus when he pursued his project in the spring, he found it expedient to bring it forward in two Bills, the one for personal and the other for real property.

Both the Bills were stoutly opposed by Fox and Fox's friends. As regarding the legacies on personal property they had nothing of much weight to urge. Their principal argument turned on the alleged hardship to illegitimate children, who would have to pay the highest rate as strangers, though entitled to indulgence as objects of natural affection. But in the division the minority was only 16 against 64.

The second Bill, touching the legacies on real estates, was met by much stronger arguments. So at least they seemed in the apprehension of the country gentlemen. The greater part appear to have stayed away, unwilling either to support the Bill or to oppose the Minister. But the Members who remained were most equally divided. After two other neck and neck votes the same evening, the final numbers were 54 against 54. The Speaker gave his casting vote to the Yeas; but Pitt declared that seeing so many gentlemen unfriendly to the Bill, he would move to postpone it for three months. In other words, he resigned it altogether. Nor was this inequality in the law redressed until the Budget of Mr. Gladstone in 1853.

The ill-success of this proposal, and the pressure of public expense, compelled Pitt to have recourse to a further loan of seven millions and a half. The other points of his Budget—as an increase of the duties on tobacco, and on horses kept for pleasure, and a regulation of the duties on sugar and salt—appear to have passed with little difficulty. But the House of Commons was amused by an unexpected coadjutor to the Minister in the cause of taxation. This was one of their Members, John Dent by name. He availed himself of a petition which came from Leicestershire complaining of the great number of dogs kept in kennels for the recreation of the rich. On this foundation Mr. Dent proposed a duty of half-a-crown on every dog kept either by rich or poor, excepting only those dogs which served as guides to the blind.

Pitt, well pleased to see his Exchequer supplied, declared that he saw nothing improper in laying some tax on the keeping of dogs, provided a distinction were drawn between the opulent and the indigent classes. Thus the proposal of Mr. Dent became the ground-work of a measure which was carried in a subsequent Session. But at the time the principal result was ridicule. Mr. Dent—ever afterwards surnamed ' Dog Dent '—appears to have argued against the entire canine race with most extraordinary passion. We are told in the reports of his speech, that he ' proceeded to state, from documents in his possession, the ravages which were committed by dogs—the quantity of provisions consumed by them—and the increase of hydrophobia.'[1] 'We might have imagined,' cried Mr. Windham, 'that Actæon had revived !'

If such were the jests even of the Ministers to whom Mr. Dent gave his general support, it may be imagined how much keener were the shafts of Opposition. 'I know not,' said Sheridan, 'whether the Hon. Mover is stimulated upon Pythagorean principles to pursue at present those resentments or antipathies which he may have conceived in a former state of existence against a race of animals so long distinguished as the friends of men. . . . . But will not the charge of ingratitude lie against us for such a decree of massacre against these useful animals at the very time when we acknowledge them as allies of the Combined Powers, and when their brethren form part of that army in Jamaica which is fighting successfully against the Maroons, and supporting the cause of social order, humanity, and religion ? '

In the same strain did Mr. Courtenay follow. He derided the alarms expressed by Mr. Dent at the increase of hydrophobia. 'To alleviate that horror,' said he, ' I beg leave to suggest the great advantages which sometimes result from a state of insanity. The late Lord Chesterfield laid it down as a maxim that the only possible process by which a Dutchman could become a wit was by being bit by a mad dog ; and so ambitious was a late Burgo-master at Amsterdam of being distinguished by this shining accomplishment, that he had submitted to the operation. Here, then, is encouragement for the Hon. gentleman ! '

The prospect of negotiation which Pitt had opened in the King's Message of the 8th of December, was sought by him to be carried out in the ensuing month of March. Mr. Wickham, our Minister in Switzerland, applied in writing, as instructed, to M. Barthélemy, the

[1] *Parl. Hist.* vol. xxxii. p. 995.

French ambassador at Basle. He inquired whether France was favourable to a Congress of the Belligerent Powers for the conclusion of a general peace; and what were the grounds of the pacification which France would be willing to propose? The answer of M. Barthélemy was delayed a fortnight to consult the Government at Paris. It proved most ungracious and cold. The Directors stated their doubts of the sincerity of England —were not inclined to a Congress—and would not alienate those of the conquered territories which their Legislature had already annexed to the French Republic. This, in other words, was to declare that they must retain the Belgian provinces. And this was also to forbid the negotiation, since England had bound herself by treaty at the commencement of the war to make no peace without the assent of the Austrian Government, or without maintaining the integrity of the Austrian dominions.

It is probable, indeed, on considering the terms of this answer, and of another answer to the same effect returned to an agent of the Court of Vienna, that the Directors did not at this period desire peace. They might seek to establish their newly-founded power by a victorious campaign. Even now they were busily planning the conquest of Italy and the invasion of Ireland.

The failure of the overtures at Basle, and the publication by England of the documents containing them, gave Fox the ground for an attack in the House of Commons on the 10th of May. In a speech of nearly four hours—one of the greatest of his many great Parliamentary efforts—he reviewed and arraigned the entire conduct of the war, and moved an Address to the Crown in its condemnation. With equal ability did Pitt hurl back the charges made. No speaker beyond these two took part in the debate; and it was thus, as the public said, an intellectual duel between them. Considering how many other able and aspiring men were at that period in the House of Commons, we may wonder at their silence upon such a theme. But the wonder ceases when the two great speeches are perused—each so full, so cogent, and so luminous as to leave apparently little to answer and nothing to supply.

A division ensued, when Fox could muster only 42 votes against 216.

There is no doubt, however, that at this juncture Pitt was most earnestly intent on peace. In the course of the past year he had seen at Basle the Confederacy of the Great Powers melt away. He had seen at Quiberon the best blood of France poured out like water, and all in vain. He had seen with still more poignant feelings of concern the increasing strain of the war on the finances and commerce of England. Therefore, though for the present baffled in his overtures of peace, he was determined to renew them at the first favourable moment. But in this course he had great difficulties to contend with. The King was extremely adverse. Windham and some others were much under the influence of Burke. And Burke on this question had heated instead of cooled. He came forth at this period with the last of his great productions, the ' Letters on a Regicide Peace,' of which the very title shows the tendency ; a piece of surpassing eloquence, but extreme and impracticable views. He speaks even of the wish to treat as of something ' that threatened to fail within. To a people,' he adds, ' who have once been great and proud, and great because they were proud, a change in the national spirit is the most terrible of all revolutions.'

The Parliament had now approached its Septennial period, and on its prorogation in May it was dissolved. In the elections which ensued, the main interest centered at Westminster ; Fox, in his address to his late constituents, describing the recent legislature with much graphic force, as ' having taken more from the liberties and added more to the burdens of the people than any

other Parliament which has ever sat.'   He expected to
be returned without opposition, together with his late
Ministerial colleague, a gallant Admiral and one of
Lord Howe's fleet, Sir Alan Gardner.   Nor indeed (as
in pursuance of the late agreement) did any opposition
arise from the Government side.   But the extreme
section of his own party brought forward Horne Tooke ;
and the polling was continued for the full period of
fifteen days.   Fox and Sir Alan were returned by large
majorities, but the contest gave Horne Tooke opportunity—and this was probably his main inducement for
embarking in it—to deliver from the hustings many
scurrilous personalities and quick retorts.

Other cities were not so favourable to Fox's friends.
Indeed, if we examine in detail their last division in
the Commons on the 10th of May, we shall find that of
the forty-four Members, including Tellers, who voted on
Fox's side, no less than twenty-three sat for Nomination
Boroughs, such as Camelford and Calne.   It was to
these that they again recurred at the Dissolution which
ensued.   The largest and most popular constituent
bodies throughout the country showed in general a firm
determination in such difficult times to support the
Government.   Their good humour was enhanced by the
favourable prospect, soon afterwards fulfilled, of an
abundant harvest.   Thus the new elections made little
or no change in the strength of political parties, and
the great majority of Pitt was not at all impaired.

Notwithstanding the pressure upon our own Exchequer, the Ministers did not refuse, by a further
subsidy, to aid the Austrian.   It was represented by the
Court of Vienna that without some succour they should
be wholly unable to continue the arduous contest which
the French were waging against them both in Germany
and Italy. So urgent was the case that—Parliament not
then sitting—Pitt consented to send, on his own responsibility, the sum of 1,200,000*l.*, to be legalised by a
subsequent vote of the House of Commons.

In Germany there was a change of Generals.   Clerfait had been recalled, notwithstanding his brilliant successes at the close of the last campaign ; and in his place was sent the Emperor's brother, the Archduke Charles, a young prince who had already given signal proofs of his genius for war.   In like manner the French Government had superseded General Pichegru on a vague suspicion of his Royalist intrigues.   Moreau now commanded on the Upper, and Jourdan on the Lower Rhine.   The first crossed the river at Strasburg, and the second near Neuwied.   In August we find Jourdan advanced to Wurzburg and Bamberg, and Moreau beyond the Lech.   Several of the earlier engagements had been greatly in favour of the French.   But the Archduke giving battle to Jourdan in the direction of Wurzburg, gained over him an important advantage, and Moreau was in consequence reduced to a retreat. That retreat across the Black Forest, and with foes on every side, has been often extolled as a master-piece of military skill.   Finally at the close of the campaign the French were again beyond the Rhine, and compelled to relinquish their blockades of Mayence and Ehrenbreitstein.

Italy, however, was the scene of by far the greatest achievements.   There at the beginning of this year the command of the French army had been entrusted to Napoleon Bonaparte, not yet twenty-seven years of age. Within a few weeks the young General astonished the world by a succession of brilliant victories.   Ascending from the coast at Savona, and gaining his two first battles in the gorges of the Maritime Alps, he compelled the King of Sardinia to sue for peace, entered in triumph both Milan and Bologna, and drove the Austrians from the entire plain of Northern Italy, while their remaining stronghold of Mantua was invested before the close of July.   I rapidly pass over this campaign as not in truth belonging to the Life of Pitt, nor even to the History of England.   Yet how hard to com-

press in a single sentence the notice of exploits upon
which whole volumes might be worthily employed!

For the relief of Mantua the Austrians made strenuous exertions. Marshal Wurmser with a new body of
forces was detached from the scene of war in Germany,
and sanguine hopes were entertained of his prevailing
against General Bonaparte. 'I will give a good account
of that young man!' said Wurmser, a veteran of four-
score, despising an adversary not yet one-third of his
own age. But on the contrary in several encounters—
as at Lonato, at Castiglione, and on the Brenta—he
was routed with heavy loss, and he had no resource but
to throw himself into the beleaguered city and take part
in its defence. Meanwhile the French were forming
the territories of Modena and Bologna into a new state,
with the title of the Cispadane Republic; and to the
South the King of Naples was led by their successes to
offer his submission, and conclude a treaty of peace.

Nor were the victories of Bonaparte without great
influence on his native island. Proud of his fame, the
Corsicans began to incline to his party. For some time
past, moreover, there had been a growing alienation
between them and the Viceroy of George the Third.
Faults may perhaps be imputed to each side; some
degree of fickleness to the Corsicans, and some degree
of misrule to the English. Sir Gilbert Elliot had conceived an impolitic jealousy of General Paoli, and had
visited with his displeasure one of his own best officers,
Colonel John Moore, for his friendly communications
with that eminent man. It was natural that the partisans of General Paoli should cease to be very warm
partisans of England. To this it may be added that
the new Constitution, framed in some measure on the
model of ours, was not found to accord with the wants
and wishes of the people. There were already some
partial risings, and it became quite clear that the Corsicans, far from opposing, would most probably welcome
the invasion which was then preparing by the exiles at

Leghorn.   Why then run the chance of a doubtful conflict for no good end, and why not rather at once withdraw the British troops?   In October orders came accordingly, but too late to prevent all collision, since a portion of the French invaders had already landed. By the aid of Commodore Nelson, however, and his squadron, the British troops, about three thousand in number, were safely embarked at Bastia, and departed from the island after an inglorious occupation of two years.   With them went General Paoli, who found in London a secure and honoured retreat for the remainder of his life.

At sea there was no action of importance in the course of this year; but in April the French might boast that they had captured one of the boldest of the English captains.   Sir Sidney Smith, already celebrated for several feats of valour, and who had in his character much of the Knights Errant of the olden time, was then in command of the Diamond frigate off the coast of Normandy.   Seeing in Havre Roads a French privateer of great speed, Le Vengeur, which had been several times chased in vain, he resolved to attempt its capture, and this object he accomplished by means of his boats. The French coast, however, was alarmed; and a number of small craft filled with troops speedily surrounded Sir Sidney in his prize, where, after a gallant defence protracted as long as possible, he found himself compelled to surrender.   The Directory maintained that his object had been to excite an insurrection on the territory of the Republic; and on this flimsy plea they treated him as a prisoner not of war, but of state.   He was sent with John Wright, one of his midshipmen and fellow captives, to the Tour du Temple at Paris, where they were confined in separate cells.

At the time when the head of Louis the Sixteenth rolled upon the block, it was certainly not foreseen that the chief of the still reigning Bourbon Princes would be the first to conclude a treaty of alliance with the

'Regicide Republic.' Such was now the case with Spain. There a weak-minded monarch, Charles the Fourth, was wholly governed by his Queen, Louisa of Parma, and she in her turn by her favourite, Don Manuel Godoy, created Prince of the Peace. Moved partly by dread of the French arms, and partly by inducements still less worthy, a treaty of alliance with France was signed at St. Ildefonso on the 19th of August; and in pursuance of this concert of measures a Manifesto declaring war against England was issued on the 5th of October,—a Manifesto truly described in the English reply as grounded only upon 'frivolous pretexts and pretended wrongs.'

Nor was there any brighter gleam in the diplomatic tidings from Berlin. On the 5th of August the King of Prussia had concluded with the French Republic two Conventions, not indeed of alliance, but of amity. By the second, which was for some time kept secret, His Majesty engaged, on due compensations to himself and others at a general peace, not to oppose the full cession to France of the territories to the left of the Rhine. In vain did Pitt remonstrate; in vain did he send Mr. Hammond on a special mission to Berlin, and endeavour to draw the King of Prussia to a juster sense of his duties to the German empire.

On the whole, the events of the war in Europe, so far as England was concerned, might almost justify the fine metaphor of Burke, where he calls them 'the disastrous events which have followed one another in a long unbroken funereal train, moving in a procession that seemed to have no end.' It was only from beyond the bounds of Europe that good tidings came. The Duke of York and Mr. Dundas had hastened to repair the injustice done by Sir Gilbert Elliot to Colonel John Moore. They sent him to the West Indies with the rank of Brigadier-General, and as second in command to Sir Ralph Abercromby. The arrival of these good officers and of a large body of English troops entirely altered the aspect of affairs in that quarter. The tide of conquest was turned at once against the French. Grenada, St. Lucia, and St. Vincent's were successively wrested from them after a stout resistance; and Demerara and Berbice more easily from their Dutch allies. And although no impression could be made on St. Domingo, yet it might be said that of all the Sugar Islands Guadeloupe alone remained in the enemy's hands.

Early in September Mr. Pitt travelled to Weymouth, desiring to speak to His Majesty on several points of public business. From Weymouth he wrote to his brother, and from London on his return to his mother, in letters that will speak for themselves.

Weymouth, Sunday, Sept. 4, 1796.

My dear Brother,—I arrived here yesterday afternoon, in consequence of several occurrences which made me anxious to see the King; and I am so pressed to return to town, that I cannot find the necessary time either to take Burton in my way, or to wait till to-morrow for the chance of seeing you here. Among many things which I have to mention to you, one relates to yourself. You will of course have seen the account of Lord Mansfield's death, and you will probably receive from the King himself the proposal (which he suggested to me before I could mention it) that you should succeed as President. The difference between the income of that and your present situation is not as considerable as I wish it was; but as far as it goes, it is on the right side, and enough so to be some object in point of convenience. In the way in which it is proposed, it will also, I trust, be not unpleasant to you as a mark of the King's sentiments towards you, and I am sure the arrangement will be very agreeable to every body. What will be in that case the best way of disposing of the Privy Seal will require some consideration. Be so good as to let me hear from you on this subject as soon as you conveniently can. The other subjects I wanted to speak of are too large for a letter written in haste, but I conclude we shall meet soon in town. Hammond's mission has produced nothing effectual at

Berlin. We therefore see nothing left (in order to bring the question of peace and war to a point) but to send directly to Paris. The step of applying for a passport will be taken immediately, but the instructions to the person sent will not be finally resolved on till next week, by which time you will probably be in town. An immediate Spanish war, though not yet formally announced, seems certain, but this does not come unexpectedly; and (if we can satisfy the country that we have done enough towards general peace) it will not, I trust, produce much embarrassment. Our great apparent difficulty is finance, which can only be removed by bringing people to a temper for very unusual exertions. My love to Lady Chatham. Ever affectionately yours,

W. PITT.

Downing Street, Sept. 6, 1796.

My dear Mother,—I entertained till within these very few days the hope that my visit to Weymouth would have afforded me the opportunity of taking Burton in my way back. But it has happened very unluckily that a number of very pressing points of business arose just at the moment of my setting out, and made it impossible for me to extend my absence from London longer than from Friday afternoon, when I set out, till yesterday, when I returned. I am afraid too, that as things now stand, I can hardly flatter myself with the possibility of finding a moment for any distant excursion between this time and the meeting of Parliament, which will probably take place on the 27th; or if it is postponed at all, it will only be for a very short time. I must, therefore, very reluctantly give up the prospect of seeing you till after our Session, which I trust will not be very long, and will I hope prove a very useful one. The apparent difficulties of the present moment will, I am persuaded, when they are discussed prove much less than many persons seem now disposed to think them; and I am in great hopes of being able to come to you before the end of the year, leaving everything in a more promising train than it has appeared to be lately. The state of France, as described in the last message of the Directory, is of itself very encouraging; and we have to-day accounts (through Berlin) of a recent victory of the Archduke, which, if they should

be confirmed in their full extent, will materially improve
the picture.

You will, I am sure, be pleased to hear that on my
arrival at Weymouth it was immediately proposed to me
that my brother should succeed, on the present vacancy, to
the Presidentship of the Council. I could not wait for his
arrival, though he was expected Monday; but left a letter
for him to mention the arrangement, which I think he
cannot but like, as very flattering in the way in which it
comes, and it is also materially better in point of income
than his present office. I shall probably have his answer
to-morrow. I hope the Bishop of Lincoln may be able to
find an opportunity of making the provision Mr. Graves
applies for.   Ever, my dear Mother, &c.,
                                             W. PITT.

Lord Chatham in his reply readily accepted the
Presidency of the Council, and the office of Privy Seal
was left vacant for some time. Not till February,
1798, was it conferred upon Lord Westmoreland.

In proceeding to Weymouth, the main object of the
Prime Minister was to lay before the King a project of
negotiation. The reduction of the French settlements
in the West Indies had given Pitt strong hopes of peace.
By offering to restore them to France, France on her
part might be induced to restore the Low Countries to
the Emperor. With these views the English Minister
resolved to attempt a direct negotiation. Subsequently he and Lord Grenville proposed that Lord
Malmesbury should be the person to proceed on a
special embassy to Paris; and to this nomination they
obtained, though not given without some reluctance,
the assent of George the Third. The Directory sent
the requisite passports, and thus, on opening the new
Parliament on the 6th of October, the King's Speech
might complacently announce the renewal of negotiation. The ambassador himself arrived at Paris a fortnight afterwards.

But while the Directors thus expressed their willingness to treat, they were actively pursuing a project for the invasion of our shores. Ireland, above all, was the object. A large fleet had been equipped at Brest, to which was now expected the accession of some Spanish vessels. Considerable land forces were collected, and General Hoche was appointed to the chief command. Earlier in the year a man of no common ability and ardour, Theobald Wolfe Tone, had hastened over from America to take part in the expected enterprise. He received the rank of Adjutant-General and Chef de Brigade in the French service under the assumed name of Smith, and held conferences both with M. Carnot and General Clarke. The latter, described by Tone in 1796 as 'a handsome, smooth-faced young man,' was better known in after years under the title of Duke de Feltre, and as Minister of War both to Napoleon and Louis the Eighteenth. At this time he stood high in the favour of the Directory. Being born of Irish parents—nay, as he used to boast, of the blood of the Irish Kings— and having once travelled for a few weeks in Ireland, he claimed to have an intimate knowledge of Irish affairs. Yet, according to Tone, he exhibited the most astounding ignorance upon them. One day he asked Tone whether, in the event of a French invasion, the invaders might not hope for the aid of the Lord Chancellor. 'Any one who knows Ireland,' writes Tone in his journal, 'will readily believe that I did not find it easy to make a serious answer to this question. Yes—Fitzgibbon would be very likely, from his situation, his principles, his hopes and his fears, his property and the general tenor of his conduct, to begin a revolution in Ireland!'[1]

To this project of invasion the King's Speech at the opening of the new Parliament adverted—'at a time,' said His Majesty, 'when the enemy has openly manifested the intention of attempting a descent on these

---

[1] *Diary*, March 14, 1796. This publication (which should be read in the American edition of 1826, as better and more complete than the English) here becomes of great historical interest and value.

kingdoms.'   And the Ministers lost no time in bringing forward their measures of defence.   'Our navy,'
said Pitt, 'is the natural defence of this kingdom in
case of invasion : in this department, however, little
remains to be done, our fleet at this moment being
more formidable than at any former period of our
history. . . . But I would propose in the first place a
levy of fifteen thousand men from the different parishes
for the sea service and for recruiting the regiments of
the line. . . . Of all the modes to obtain a further force
there is none so expeditious, so effectual, and attended
with so little expense as that of raising a supplementary
body of Militia to be grafted upon the present establishment.   I would propose that this supplement shall consist of sixty thousand men, not to be immediately called
out, but to be enrolled, officered, and gradually trained,
so as to be fit for service at a time of danger. . . . Another
measure which I would suggest to the committee is to
provide a considerable force of irregular cavalry.   With
a view to repelling an invasion, the more this species of
force is extended the greater advantage is likely to
accrue from it, as an invading enemy, who must be destitute of horses, can have no means to meet it upon
equal terms. . . . By the produce of the recent tax we
find that the number of horses kept for pleasure in
England, Scotland, and Wales, is about two hundred
thousand.   It certainly would not be a very severe regulation, when compared with the object to be accomplished, to require one-tenth of these horses for the
public service.   Thus might we raise a cavalry force
of twenty thousand. . . . There is still another resource
which ought not to be neglected.   The licences to shoot
game taken out by gamekeepers are no fewer than
seven thousand. Upon the supposition of an invasion, it
would be of no small importance to form bodies of men
who, from their dexterity in using firearms, might be
highly useful in harassing the operations of the enemy.'[1]

[1] Speech in the House of Commons, Oct. 18, 1796.

Against these measures of defence—which are here most briefly sketched—both Sheridan and Fox inveighed with great warmth, though but little success. ' I believe,' said Fox, ' that the French have no intention to invade us. They have a Government too well informed of the disposition of the people and the situation of the country to hope for success in such an enterprise. Supposing they do make that desperate attempt, I have no doubt as to the issue. But what ought we to do in the mean time? What is the duty of this House at this moment? To cherish the spirit of freedom in the people; to restore to them that for which their ancestors have bled; to make the Ministers really responsible. Not to be confiding in the servants of the Crown, but watchful and jealous of the exercise of their power. . . . Then will you have no occasion for adding to your internal military force, for then even an invasion would never be formidable.'

Such was the advice that Fox—at a moment of great public danger, and when the very existence of the kingdom might be at stake—deemed it consistent with his duty to address to the House of Commons. Such was the spirit with which on subsequent days he continued to carp at the Ministerial measures for defence. No wonder if the spleen of independent Members was aroused. ' I will not,' said Mr. Wilberforce, ' charge these gentlemen with desiring an invasion; but I cannot help thinking that they would rejoice to see just so much mischief befall their country as would bring themselves into office.' These words in the debate were resented, with much fierceness by Sheridan, with much good temper by Fox. ' I fear,' says Wilberforce in his Diary, ' that I went too far.' ' No,' wrote to him his friend Dr. Cookson, ' you did not go too far. What you said is what everybody thinks, but what nobody else had the courage to speak out.'[1]

Mr. Wilberforce had, however, another grievance of

---

[1] *Life of Wilberforce*, by his Sons, vol. ii. p. 181.

his own.   In one of the new Bills it was provided that the supplemental corps of Militia should be trained on Sunday afternoons. Against this clause the member for Yorkshire protested, and finally prevailed.   In his Diary he writes as follows: 'Dundas is now clear that it would shock the general morals of Scotland to exercise their volunteers on Sunday; but I can scarce persuade Pitt that in England it would even in serious people excite any disgust.'

Next in order came the financial measures.   Here was ample scope for the most gloomy apprehensions. The National Debt had now risen to upwards of four hundred millions, and the strain upon the public resources was indicated by the progressive decline in the price of Stocks.   In January of this year the lowest point of the Three per Cents. had been 67 ; in the September following they fell at one time to 53. Nevertheless a new loan of at least eighteen millions was required by the pressing exigencies of the public service. Pitt, in the course of the autumn, held long and anxious consultations with the Bank Directors.   They agreed that to attempt to raise the new loan in the ordinary manner would be an operation of exceeding cost and very doubtful success.   Under these circumstances, Pitt, it may justly be said, evinced his own public spirit when he relied on and appealed to the public spirit of the people.   He announced a loan of 18,000,000*l.* at five per cent., to be taken at 112*l.* 10*s.* for every 100*l.* Stock, and with an option to the proprietors to be paid off at par within two years after a treaty of peace.   These terms, which in our own day would seem exorbitant, were but scanty at that time of danger and distress.   From the very first,' says a highly competent judge, 'the undertaking was a source of loss to the subscribers, so far as the market value was concerned.'[1]   This statement I derive from an excellent Essay by Mr. Newmarch, on the Loans

[1] *Essay* by W. Newmarch, Esq., June, 1855, p. 120.

raised by Mr. Pitt—an Essay to which in my review of his financial policy I shall have more ample occasion to refer.

Under these circumstances, then, the Subscription List for the Loan of 1796 could never have been filled had not Pitt in proposing it addressed himself to higher motives than the love of gain. It was by no means as a profitable speculation that he urged it, but as a patriotic duty. And hence it was called 'the Loyalty Loan.'

Not every government would thus appeal to the people. Not every people, I add with pride, would thus respond to the government. For nothing could be more enthusiastic than the manner in which that response was made. Here are the very words of a contemporary writer:—' On the first day of the new loan (Thursday, the 1st of December), before the close of the books, 5,000,000*l.* were subscribed by merchants and others. At ten o'clock this morning, Monday, the 5th of December, the parlour doors of the Bank were opened; before which time the lobby was crowded. Numbers could not get near the books at all, while others, to testify their zeal, called to the persons at the books then signing to put down their names for them, as they were fearful of being shut out. At about twenty minutes past eleven the subscription was declared to be completely full, and hundreds in the room were reluctantly compelled to go away. By the post innumerable orders came from the country for subscriptions to be put down, scarcely one of which could be executed ; and long after the subscription-list was closed persons continued coming, and were obliged to depart disappointed. It is a curious fact, and well worth stating, that the subscription was completely filled in fifteen hours and twenty minutes, namely, two hours on Thursday, six on Friday, six on Saturday, and one hour and twenty minutes on Monday. The Duke of Bridgewater actually tendered a Draft at sight on his banker for 100,000*l.*.

which he subscribed to the new loan, but which of course could not be accepted, since the Act is not yet passed.'[1] It may be added that another man of princely fortune, namely, the Duke of Bedford, though in strenuous opposition to the Government, subscribed in due time an equal sum.

The tokens of such a spirit—a spirit which raises and dignifies and well-nigh hallows the common-place arithmetic of the Stock Exchange—may make the heart of any Englishman thrill. Had the French been duly apprised of all these circumstances, they would surely have abated of their eagerness for projects to invade us. The clangour of their equipments at Brest would have died away; and the sails already swelling to the East wind would have been furled. They would have acknowledged that a people with such a spirit, unshaken in the most trying times, could never be subdued.

Great as was the triumph of Pitt, he could not indulge it. A most painful, but, as he deemed, a bounden duty was before him. Even with that pressure on the resources of the people, he was resolved to lay on new imposts providing for the payment of the interest of the new loan, and for the operation of the Sinking Fund. His own feelings at that period are best portrayed in the words of his principal colleague. Reviewing this whole question thirty-two years afterwards, Lord Grenville adverts to Mr. Pitt as follows : ' With an ardent and generous spirit, devoting all his energies to the national prosperity, he risked, and in no small degree surrendered, his highly-valued popularity to the necessity of a large additional taxation which that measure (the Sinking Fund) compelled him to establish and maintain. This was no light sacrifice, nor did he feel it such ; but he anticipated in return with unspeakable delight the full tide of wealth which, in some distant but auspicious moment, the results of these disinterested exertions were

---

[1] *Ann. Regist.*, 1796, part ii. p. 44.

to pour upon the country. What he so ardently wished he willingly believed.'[1]

On the 7th of December, the day but one after the subscriptions to the Loyalty Loan had closed, Pitt brought forward his Budget in the House of Commons. He proposed new taxes amounting to upwards of 2,000,000*l.*, derived from a great variety of sources, as higher rates on the fine kinds of tea, on sales by auction, on British and foreign spirits, on sugar, on houses, on stage-coaches, and on postage. He also announced the subsidy of 1,200,000*l.* which, during the Recess, he had remitted to the Emperor without consent of Parliament.

Against this expenditure, against this subsidy, against all the ' false and deceitful statements ' (for so Mr. Grey termed them) of the Minister, both Grey and Fox most bitterly inveighed. Nor did Fox forbear from exalting by comparison the financial credit of the country of Assignats. ' Only last year,' he said, ' the Minister had spoken of France as " on the verge, nay in the gulf of bankruptcy." These had been his very words. Now,' said Fox, ' I should like to know whether the French have yet passed the gulf of bankruptcy ? I hope they have, for certainly while they were in it they were most dreadful enemies to this country ! '

The conduct of Pitt in having granted a subsidy to Austria without the consent of Parliament excited some displeasure both in the City and the House of Commons. The citizens, assembling in their Common Hall, called upon their Members to support a vote of censure. That same evening, the 13th of December, the censure was moved by Fox in the Lower House. Without any more particular narration we may readily conceive how in the debate, the one party maintained that the Constitution had been violated, and the other that the public interests had been served. In the division Fox well nigh doubled

---

[1] *Essay on the supposed Advantages of a Sinking Fund*, by Lord Grenville, March 15, 1828.

his customary numbers, mustering 81 against 285. However, when a few days afterwards Pitt brought down a Message from His Majesty, stating the necessity of further advances to the Emperor, and when the Minister proposed the vote of another half million for that purpose, the vote passed, with great objection indeed, but little difficulty.

Another motion that touched the Court of Vienna was brought forward by General Fitzpatrick. He renewed the proposal which he had made almost three years before, that the King should be entreated to intercede with his ally for the deliverance of General La Fayette and his companions in captivity. In his speech he drew a most touching picture, not only of the rigours inflicted on the General in the dungeons of Olmütz, but of the merits and sufferings of Madame de La Fayette, whom he justly termed an admirable pattern of female virtue. 'I readily admit, Sir,' thus Pitt began, 'that a more striking and pathetic appeal was never made to the feelings of the House. . . . . . Nevertheless, however much our humanity may be interested, yet, considered as a question of political relations, it is not one which comes at all within our cognizance. . . . . . No instance of such interference as is now proposed has ever taken place at any former period, ... nor could such interference be attempted without establishing a principle of the most unwarrantable kind—a principle inconsistent with the internal policy and independent rights of Foreign States.'

A long debate ensued, which even at the present day has by no means lost its interest. Wilberforce, after much doubt in his own mind, declared himself favourable to the object of the motion. We find in his journal: 'Never did I rise to speak with more reluctance. I expected all the ridicule which followed; and when Dundas, with a happy peculiarity of expression, talked of my Amendment as designed to catch the *straggling* humanity of the House, there was a perfect roar of laughter.' [1]

Fox, Grey, and Sheridan all spoke eloquently in support of the motion. Then Windham rose to resist it. But the ground which he took was wholly different from Pitt's. He made his stand altogether upon Burke's. For the objections which he urged against the motion rested in great measure on the principles and proceedings of La Fayette in France. 'As the mere suffering of an individual,' said he, 'the case of La Fayette must certainly excite pity. There is no case of calamity whatever, which if abstracted from other considerations, but must awaken the feelings of every one deserving the name of man. . . . . But if La Fayette has fallen into misery, he has fallen a victim to his own acts and his own principles. He has betrayed and ruined his country and his King, and taken refuge for his character and conscience in his own defeat; claiming merit for stopping just at that point beyond which it was out of his power to go, and when he became the enemy of those whom he had made the instruments of his designs upon the King. . . . . Mankind are not formed to pity at once the oppressed and the oppressor.'

In the division which ensued, the minority, notwithstanding the aid of Wilberforce, could muster no more than fifty votes.

In December, 1795, Mr. Samuel Whitbread, the active and able Member for Bedford, and the head of a flourishing brewery, had brought in a Bill to regulate the wages of labourers in husbandry. His plan was to give the Justices of the Peace power to fix the *minimum* rate at the Easter Quarter Sessions. When in the February following the Bill came on for a second reading, it was opposed by Pitt. He declared that he had most carefully considered the subject, and endeavoured to obtain the best information upon it. But he took his stand on the unanswerable grounds, as

[1] *Diary*, Dec. 16, 1796.

we now acknowledge them to be, of Adam Smith. 'Will it not be wiser for the House,' he said, ' to consider the operation of general principles, and rely upon the effect of their unconfined exercise ? I conceive that to promote the free circulation of labour, to remove the obstacles by which industry is prohibited from availing itself of its resources, would go far to remedy the evils and diminish the necessity of applying for relief to the poor-rate. But,' Mr. Pitt continued, ' I should wish that an opportunity were given of restoring the original purity of the Poor Laws, and of removing those corruptions by which they have been obscured. . . . . These great points of granting relief according to the number of children, preventing removals at the caprice of the parish officer, and making them subscribe to friendly societies, would tend in a very great degree to remove every ground of complaint. . . . . . All this, however, I will confess is not enough, if we do not engraft upon it Resolutions to discourage relief where it is not wanted. . . . . . The extension of schools of industry is also an object of material importance. The suggestion of these schools was originally drawn from Lord Hale and Mr. Locke, and upon such authority I have no hesitation in recommending the plan to the encouragement of the Legislature. . . . . Such a plan would convert the relief granted to the poor into an encouragement for industry, instead of being, as it is by the present Poor Laws, a premium for idleness and a school for sloth. There are also a number of subordinate circumstances to which it is necessary to attend. The law which prohibits giving relief where any visible property remains should be abolished. That degrading condition should be withdrawn. No temporary occasion should force a British subject to part with the last shilling of his little capital, and to descend to a state of wretchedness from which he could never recover, merely that he might be entitled to a casual supply.'

The outline of the Bill which Mr. Pitt drew on this

occasion seemed to meet with decided approbation. Accordingly, in the course of the summer and autumn, he applied himself to frame a Bill on the principles which he had announced. On the 22nd of December he laid it before the House of Commons. It was drawn up with great care, and consisted of sixty-eight clauses. A copy of it is still preserved in the Library of the House of Lords. An abstract of it, clause by clause, as derived from that source, was given in the *Times* of March 19, 1838.

The object of Mr. Pitt in laying his Bill upon the Table before Christmas was, ' that during the interval of Parliament it might be circulated in the country, and undergo the most serious and mature investigation.' But the result was not favourable. So many objections were started, and so much repugnance shown by the Members of the House of Commons, that there was no encouragement to press the measure farther and no hope to pass it into law.

In 1796, as in the preceding year, there were some experiments in Steam Navigation set on foot by Earl Stanhope, and sanctioned by the Lords of the Admiralty. He had induced them to construct a ship in the Thames, and had signed a bond dated June 30, 1794, with a penalty to himself of 9,000*l.*, ' to indemnify the public in case the said ship should not answer the purpose of Government.' The subject must be owned to be a curious one, as tending to throw some light on the first steps of a gigantic change in the British navy ; and the origin of the scheme is summed up as follows in a letter which Earl Stanhope addressed to the Lords of the Admiralty.

Chevening. Dec. 22, 1795.

My Lords,—Your Lordships no doubt are all of you informed that an *Ambi-Navigator* ship (called the *Kent*) has been constructed by Government for the purpose of ascertaining the efficacy of the important plan, invented by me, of navigating ships of the largest size without any wind, and even against wind and waves; and that on the 30th day of June in the year 1794 I gave a bond to His Majesty relative to that ship and plan. The steam-engine apparatus constructed under my direction, and intended for moving that vessel, is now on board her in Greenland Dock. For several months past I have been making detached experiments in the ship on various parts of the apparatus: for I do not intend to content myself with merely producing a result, but my series of experiments is such as to be intended to establish every part of the subject on clear and irrefragable proofs, and to ascertain demonstratively what is the best possible plan.

The subject being a new one, the workmen have had everything to learn, and it has taken more time to complete the work than was at first expected. The time mentioned in my bond to be allowed for the making of the experiments is nearly expired. I therefore request your Lordships to add a few more months (such as eight, ten, or twelve) for that purpose, as I take for granted that your Lordships would not deem it either proper or expedient to stop experiments of such consequence in their progress, and at the eve of their conclusion.   I have the honour to be, &c.,

STANHOPE.

In reply, on the part of the Board of Admiralty (Dec. 28, 1795), the Secretary, Mr. Evan Nepean, in a liberal spirit, granted the longest period of extension that had been suggested, namely twelve months. The correspondence which I here select and subjoin took place, as will be seen, near the close of that further term.

Earl Spencer to Earl Stanhope.

Admiralty, Nov. 5, 1796.

My Lord,—The delay which I alluded to in my former letter arose from some doubt whether the experiment which has already been made was sufficient to ascertain the properties of the Kent. In order therefore to remove any doubt upon that subject, the Board of Admiralty have determined on trying another experiment for that express purpose; for which (if your Lordship has no objection to it) directions will be immediately given.

I have the honour, &c.,   SPENCER.

Earl Stanhope to Earl Spencer.

London, Nov. 8, 1796.

My Lord,—The *Kent* is at present (whatever it may be hereafter) a Government vessel. The Board of Admiralty therefore have a right, and will do right, to make with her such experiments as they shall deem proper. My consent is not necessary, nor should I refuse it if it were.

Two things no doubt your Lordship will think it expedient to do. First, that the necessary directions may be immediately given for making those experiments respecting which I shall not interfere. Secondly, that they may be made within a short space of time, inasmuch as your Lordship must be sensible that whilst the vessel is out, no adjustment can be made in the steam apparatus, in order to make the intended experiments with steam.

That subject is of *far* more importance than the Board of Admiralty seems to be aware of.

I have the honour, &c.,   STANHOPE.

Earl Spencer to Earl Stanhope.

Admiralty, May 17, 1797.

My Lord,—. . . . . . . The Report of the Navy Board (dated the 6th of this month), to which the Admiralty must pay some attention, is positively against your Lordship's proposal of renewing your bond; but I believe the fairest way will be to transmit to you a copy of it, that your Lordship may have an opportunity of explaining some points which it is possible they may have misconceived.

You may depend upon my not feeling the most distant intention of trifling with you on this or any other subject, though I certainly do not yet see any reason to alter the opinion I have already expressed, that the method you have imagined of moving ships, independent of wind and tide, will not be found to answer the very great expectations your Lordship appears to have formed of it.

I have the honour, &c.,   SPENCER.

The experiments made by the *Kent* were satisfactory to Lord Stanhope; not so to the Navy Board. On the whole the Lords of the Admiralty deemed this trial of Steam Navigation to be conclusive against it, and they required of Lord Stanhope the penalty stipulated in his bond. Their correspondence with him from first to last was conducted in a most honourable spirit, and with perfect fairness of intention. But I think that we may deduce from it their early distrust and disrelish of the scheme. We may, I think, infer that the trial was not freely accepted, but was rather by some extraneous cause imposed upon them. If so, the question arises, who imposed it? Considering the political hostility of the projector to the administration, and his personal estrangement from Mr. Pitt, no party and no family influence are here to be imagined. No other alternative, so far as I can see, remains, than that the Prime Minister, when consulted, urged the trial of the scheme from his own impression of its possible merits. There is, therefore, as I conceive, a strong probability that Mr. Pitt was the earliest of all our statesmen in office who discerned, however dimly in the distance, the coming importance of steam to navigation, and who desired to bring it to the test; and this at the very time when his own First Lord of the Admiralty, in other respects a most judicious administrator, looked down upon the project as an empty dream.

The more heavily, at this juncture, did the cares of finance and state press on Pitt, the more anxiously did he turn his eyes to the prospects of the new negotiation which the King had sanctioned, and which the Ministers had already commenced.

If the negotiation thus commenced did not end in success, it was certainly from no want of ability in those who conducted it on the part of England. Pitt himself gave assiduous attention to each step in this great matter. Lord Grenville continued to be Secretary for Foreign Affairs. As Under Secretary the Prime Minister had in the course of this very year appointed a young man of the highest Parliamentary promise fulfilled by his subsequent renown. This was George Canning, who, born in 1770, and entering the House of Commons under the Minister's auspices in 1793, had already won laurels in debate. To Pitt the young orator attached himself, not merely with party zeal, but with all the warmth of personal regard. 'In his grave,' he said long afterwards, 'my political allegiance lies buried.'

For the foreign part of the negotiation Pitt at first designed that Mr. Jackson, who had commenced, should still pursue it. But Mr. Jackson, though an able public servant, did not fill a sufficient space in the public eye. 'Everybody feels it,' writes Wilberforce, 'but few dare tell Pitt any such thing. People will not so much believe him in earnest in the treaty as if a more important character were employed.' Pitt yielded at last to these representations, obtained also the assent of the King, and, as I have shown in a preceding passage, entrusted this high commission to Lord Malmesbury, then beyond all doubt at the head of our diplomatic service.

Yet the inherent difficulties of the task were in truth insuperable. So long as they remained in general terms—so long as 'equivalents and restitutions' were vaguely talked of—there might be hopes of a favourable issue. But when it came to close quarters—when Lord Grenville in plain terms sent instructions as follows—'On this point therefore of suffering the Netherlands to remain a part of France, your Lordship must not give the smallest hope that His Majesty will be induced to relax[1]'—it became clear at once that the French Government were wholly averse to such a sacrifice. They were also much displeased at the frequent references for orders and instructions made by the English Ambassador to his Court; and at last, in a sally of ill-humour, they put an end to the whole negotiation. On the 19th of December M. Charles Delacroix, as Minister for Foreign Affairs, wrote to

[1] To Lord Malmesbury, Dec. 11, 1796. *Malmesbury Corresp.* vol. iii. p. 341.

Lord Malmesbury requiring him and his suite to depart from Paris within forty-eight hours, and to lose no time in quitting the territory of the French Republic. The Directors, he said, would listen to no proposal contrary to the edicts which had fixed the limits of that territory. If, added M. Delacroix, the English Government really wished for peace, the French was ready to conclude it on such a basis and by the mere interchange of couriers.

On the rupture of this negotiation, the papers relating to it were immediately laid before Parliament. Pitt in the one House, and Lord Grenville in the other (each on the 30th of December), moved an Address pledging them to support His Majesty in the necessary prosecution of the war. 'In fact,' said Pitt as he concluded a most able speech of three hours, 'the question is not how much you will give for peace, but how much disgrace you will suffer at the outset of your negotiations for it. In these circumstances, then, are we to persevere in the war with a spirit and energy worthy of the British name and of the British character? Or are we, by sending couriers to Paris, to prostrate ourselves at the feet of a stubborn and supercilious Government?'

No sooner had Pitt concluded than Erskine started up, eager to assail the negotiation, the Ministers, and everything appertaining to them. But after a few sentences, he faltered, broke down, and resumed his seat in confusion. Then Fox with his usual readiness stood forward in the place of his friend. 'Sorry indeed am I'—thus he began—'on account of my Hon. and Learned friend, whose indisposition has suddenly compelled him to sit down; sorry for the sake of the House, whose information has been thus unpleasantly interrupted; and sorry for the cause of peace and Great Britain, which Ministers seem determined to push to the last verge of ruin.' Fox then proceeded to charge upon the Government a long succession of 'little tricks and artifices.' He said that they had not desired peace, but only to obtain the credit of pacific intentions. Their deliberate object had been, by unreasonable proposals and vexatious delays, to rouse the pride of the Directory, and compel them to break off the negotiation. Such were the statements of Mr. Fox; but is there at the present day even one man willing to endorse them? Or are there many instances on record of misrepresentations so extreme?

On this occasion, however, Fox was not followed into the lobby by a numerous train. The amendment which he moved obtained but thirty-seven votes; and the same amendment, moved by the Earl of Guilford in the Peers, no more than eight.

In this abrupt dismissal of the British Minister, and, as Pitt declared it, 'this studied insult' to the British people, it was the opinion of Lord Malmesbury that the French Government had been partly swayed by the tidings from Petersburg. On the 17th of November the Empress Catherine died. There had been no sign of illness till she was found stretched upon the floor, and she had been in good spirits till the very morning of that day.[1] It may be observed that the circumstances of her death bear a great resemblance to those of George the Second's.

On the same night that the news had reached him, Pitt announced it to Dundas as follows:—

Downing Street, Sunday, ½ past 11, P.M.
(December, 1796.)

Dear Dundas,—A new scene is opened on the Continent by an event of which the account is just come—the death of the Empress of Russia on the 17th of last month. The despatches are not yet come to the Office. We cannot therefore yet tell in what state our treaty was left, but I am afraid much good is not in any case to be expected from the new Emperor. It is difficult to say whether one ought

[1] *Histoire de Catherine II.,* par Castera, vol. iii. p. 171.

to regret the most that she had not died sooner or lived longer.
　　　　　　　　　　　　　　　　　Yours ever,
　　　　　　　　　　　　　　　　　　　W. P.

At Petersburg the only son of the late Empress was at once proclaimed her successor, under the title of Paul the First. As may be inferred from the preceeding letter, the new Sovereign was not thought to incline to the English interest. It was not yet known how weak, nay even disordered, was his intellect; and how little reliance could be placed on any resolution that he formed.

CHAPTER XXIII.

1796–1797.

Rumoured marriage of Mr. Pitt and the Hon. Eleanor Eden — Projected invasion of Ireland — Wolfe Tone — The *Légion Noire* — French armament in Bantry Bay — Colonel Tate's expedition in the Bristol Channel — Landing at Ilfracombe, and at Fishguard — Battle off Cape St. Vincent — Mantua surrenders — The Pope submits — Preliminaries signed at Leoben — Partition of the Venetian States — Suspension of cash payments in England — Proceedings in Parliament upon it — Mutiny of the Fleet at Portsmouth — Appeased by the Government — Second mutiny at Sheerness — Debates in the House of Commons — The sailors return to their duty.

Busy and anxious as was the year 1796, Mr. Pitt had found opportunities to pass some short intervals of leisure at Holwood. There his nearest neighbour was now Lord Auckland at Beckenham. A close intimacy sprang up between them. Lord Auckland would often pass a day or two at Holwood, and Mr. Pitt a day or two at Beckenham.

It was not only the conversation of Lord Auckland in which Mr. Pitt took pleasure. He was much attracted by the grace and beauty as well as the superior mind of Lord Auckland's eldest daughter, the Hon. Eleanor Eden. She was born in July, 1777, and therefore eighteen years younger than Pitt. It would have been a very suitable marriage; and a report of it was not long in arising.

Lord Auckland himself noticed it as follows, in a letter to his friend Mr. John Beresford of Dublin :—

December 22, 1796.

We are all well here, and I will take the occasion to add a few words of a private and confidential kind. You may probably have seen or heard by letters a report of an intended marriage between Mr. Pitt and my eldest daughter. You know me too well to suppose that if it were so I should have remained silent. The truth is she is handsome, and possessed of sense far superior to the ordinary proportion of the world; they see much of each other, they converse much together, and I really believe they have sentiments of mutual esteem; but I have no reason to think that it goes further on the part of either, nor do I suppose it is ever likely to go further.

Mr. Beresford thus replies :—

December 27, 1796.

I certainly heard of the report which you mention, and saw it in the newspapers. Lord Camden has more than once asked me if I knew anything about it. I answered, as I shall continue to do, that I knew nothing about it.[1]

This strong attachment—for such on Pitt's side at least it certainly was—did not, as many persons hoped, proceed to a proposal and a marriage. Shortly afterwards, however, some correspondence did take place between Mr. Pitt and Lord Auckland. The letters remain in the possession of Lord Auckland's family, and there are neither copies nor originals among the manuscripts of Pitt. But I have heard them described by a person entirely to be relied on who has more than once perused them. Mr. Pitt began the subject. In his letter to Lord Auckland he avows in the warmest

---

[1] *Beresford Correspondence*, vol. ii. pp. 141-143.

terms his affection for Miss Eden, but explains that in his circumstances he feels that he cannot presume to make her an offer of marriage. He further says that he finds each of his succeeding visits add so much to his unhappiness, that he thinks it will be best to remit them for the present.

The reply of Lord Auckland, as I am informed, acknowledges as adequate the explanation of Mr. Pitt. He was already, he says, aware in general of the circumstances of pecuniary debt and difficulty in which Mr. Pitt had become involved. He does not deny that the attachment of Mr. Pitt may have been fully appreciated; and he wishes that the marriage should still take place, although he must have seen and felt that his daughter, who, as one of many children, had a very small fortune of her own, might then under some contingencies of office or of life be left wholly unprovided.[1]

There were yet two further letters as to the manner in which the notes of congratulation which had already begun to arrive at Beckenham might best be answered. Pitt desired that the blame, if any, should be borne wholly by himself.

Thus most honourably, and without any breach of friendship on either side, ended this ' love passage '— the only one, as I believe, in the life of Pitt. More than two years afterwards, in June, 1799, Miss Eden became the second wife of Lord Hobart, who succeeded in 1804 as Earl of Buckinghamshire. She had no children, and she died in 1851.

The account which Mr. Pitt in his first letter implies of his circumstances was unhappily but too well founded. It appears from Lord Cranworth's title-deeds that at this very period, namely, in 1797, the minister found it requisite to raise a further mortgage of 7000*l.* on the small Holwood property. Even then he was still deeply

---

[1] See Note A, at the end of the next volume.

in debt, to the extent, it was estimated by Mr. Rose, of at least 30,000*l.*

To this transaction from the private life of Mr. Pitt it may not be inappropriate if I here subjoin an account of his personal character and habits, as given at nearly the same time in the Diary of Mr. Charles Abbot :—

March 17, 1796.

Dined at Butt's with the Solicitor-General and Lord Muncaster. Lord Muncaster was an early political friend of Mr. Pitt, and our conversation turned much upon his habits of life. Pitt transacts the business of all departments except Lord Grenville's and Dundas's. He requires eight or ten hours' sleep. He dines slightly at five o'clock upon days of business, and on other days after the House is up; but if thrown out of his regular dinner of one sort or the other, he becomes completely ill and unfit for business for a day or two. This has happened to him in the present Session. He will not suffer anybody to arrange his papers, and extract the important points for him. In his reception of the merchants, when they wait upon him, he is particularly desirous of satisfying them that his measures are right. Lord Hawkesbury, on the contrary, entertains them with telling them what he knows of their business, instead of hearing what they have to tell him.

But from these personal details, interesting as they are, I must now pass to transactions of the gravest national importance, which marked the ensuing year as the most critical which, since the Revolution at least, England had ever known.

During the whole of the summer and autumn of 1796 General Hoche had been indefatigable in his exertions to prepare the invasion of Ireland. For a long time he was thwarted by the incapacity, perhaps even the ill-will, of the naval commanders employed. But at the beginning of December he had at Brest ready to embark fifteen thousand regular troops, with transports to convey them, escorted by about twenty frigates and seventeen sail of the line. With him were Colonel Shee, and other good officers of the former Irish Brigade in the French service; some of these, however, the less useful as having—two nephews of Colonel Shee amongst others—in great part forgotten their native language. There was also Wolfe Tone, newly raised to military rank, and full of his old ardour against the British Government. He had prepared Addresses and Proclamations to the peasantry of Ireland, and spoke confidently of a popular rising as soon as the invaders appeared.

In these preparations, though tending to all the horrors of civil strife and bloodshed, there was nothing at all repugnant to the rules and usages of war. But the same can scarcely be said of another scheme of the French Government at this time. They had equipped a considerable number of felons and galley-slaves whom they designed to let loose on the shores of England, not with any hope of victory or conquest, but merely for the purpose of havoc and destruction. These wretches were by no means admitted into the French regular service; they formed a body apart, distinguished by black jackets, and called the *Légion Noire*. For commander they had Colonel Tate, an American officer who volunteered his services. Thus writes Wolfe Tone in his Journal of the 10th of November: 'I saw the *Légion Noire* reviewed; about eighteen hundred men. They are the banditti intended for England, and sad blackguards they are. They put me in mind of the Greenboys of Dublin.' And again on the 26th of the same month: 'To-day, by the General's orders, I have made a fair copy of Colonel Tate's instructions, with some alterations, particularly with regard to their first destination, which is now fixed to be Bristol. If he arrives safe, it will be very possible to carry it by a *coup de main*, in which case he is to burn it to the ground. I cannot but observe here that I transcribed with the greatest *sang-froid* the order to reduce to ashes the third city of the British dominions, in which there is perhaps property to the amount of 5,000,000*l.* . . . . . Yet once, again! The conflagration of such a city as Bristol! It is no slight affair; thousands and thousands of families, if the attempt succeeds, will be reduced to beggary. I cannot help it. If it must be, it must; and I will never blame the French for any degree of misery which they may inflict on the people of England. . . . . The truth is, I hate the very name of England; I hated her before my exile; I hate her since, and I will hate her always.'

The Directory had sent their final orders to General Hoche while the negotiation with England was still in progress; and the armament sailed from Brest on the 15th of December, four days before the injunction to depart from Paris was transmitted to Lord Malmesbury. 'We are all in high spirits,' writes Wolfe Tone, 'and the troops are as gay as if they were going to a ball.' As the place of general *rendezvous*, Bantry Bay had been assigned them. The French ships succeeded in avoiding the English fleet which was cruising off the coast of Brittany. But, on the other hand, they were beset by thick fogs and heavy gales, and they came to be dispersed. Only a part of the armament could anchor in Bantry Bay. General Hoche, who had embarked in one of the frigates with his entire staff, found himself driven to another point of the coast. Here was a General without an army, and there an army without a General. The remaining chiefs had at one time resolved to land without him and push forward, but they found that they could muster not one half the original force, and these almost without artillery or stores. In the absence of Hoche, the Admiral refused his sanction to the scheme, and steered back to France. They reached Brest in safety, though not without some loss of ships, as Hoche, on his side, made his way to La Rochelle. All idea of this invasion was now relinquished, and Hoche was appointed to the command of the army of Sambre and Meuse. 'I do not wonder,' writes Wolfe Tone, 'at Xerxes whipping the sea; for I find myself to-night pretty much in the mood to commit some such rational action!'

The disappointment of Wolfe Tone was in proportion to his sanguine hopes in case a landing had been made. In these he most probably deceived himself. Certain it is that the Government of Ireland had taken most vigorous measures. Russell, Neilson, and other friends of Tone, on whose aid he reckoned, had already been arrested for High Treason. We find the Lord Lieutenant report to the Secretary of State that the Volunteers seemed to vie with the regular troops in loyal ardour; and he adds, 'At the time the army was ordered to march, the weather was extremely severe. During their march the utmost attention was paid them by the inhabitants of the towns and villages through which they passed, so that in many places the meat provided by the Commissary was not consumed. . . . . The poor people often shared their potatoes with them, and dressed their meat without demanding payment. . . . . The roads which had in parts been rendered impassable by the snow were cleared by the peasantry. At Carlow a considerable subscription was made for the troops as they passed. . . . . A useful impression was made upon the minds of the lower Catholics by a judicious address from Dr. Moylen, the titular Bishop of Cork.'[1]

There still remained, however, the banditti expedition to England. In the hopes of more favourable weather, it did not set out till the month of February following. Then two French frigates, with a corvette and a lugger, sailed from Brest and entered the Bristol Channel, having on board Colonel Tate and about twelve hundred of his men. They anchored at Ilfracombe, and scuttled several merchantmen, but notwithstanding their instructions attempted no further

<hr>

[1] Lord Camden to the Duke of Portland, January 10, 1797. *Life of Grattan*, by his Son, vol. iv. p. 265.

progress in that quarter, learning that several bodies of
Volunteers were in full march against them. Steering
for the opposite coast of Pembrokeshire, they cast
anchor in Fishguard Bay. Here they landed and
began to plunder. But here again the Volunteers and
Militia were instantly in arms, commanded by Lord
Cawdor. These were only a few hundred strong, but
they were joined by great numbers of the country-
people, armed with implements of husbandry, or with
the first weapons they could find. Another incident of
a ludicrous kind is said to have done good service. A
large crowd of Welsh women had gathered on the
beach, clad in the scarlet cloaks which then and for
many years afterwards were in common use among the
female peasantry of England, and these being seen from
afar impressed the invaders with an idea of regular
troops.

Under these circumstances Colonel Tate, greatly
lowering his tone, sent a flag of truce with an offer of
capitulation. Lord Cawdor answered by requiring the
invaders to surrender themselves as prisoners of war;
they complied; and next day accordingly laid down
their arms without a blow. Both the frigates which
had brought them were captured on their return to
France; and so ingloriously ended the unwarrantable
enterprise.

This enterprise, however, was only designed as the
forerunner of a more important one. To invade England upon a larger scale was now a favourite scheme
with the French Directors. For this object they had
recourse to their new allies at Madrid and at the
Hague. It was designed that the main Spanish and
also the main Dutch fleet should sail forth from their
respective harbours and join the French armament at
Brest. By this union—of perhaps full seventy ships of
the line—they might have strength to command the
British Channel, and to render easy a descent upon the
British shores.

The main Spanish fleet at this time had for Admiral
Don Joseph de Cordova, and lay in Carthagena Bay.
It set sail on the 1st of February, with Cadiz for its
first destination; but it was driven from its course by
contrary winds to off Cape St. Vincent. There, on the
14th, it was encountered by Sir John Jervis with the
British squadron from the Tagus. Cordova had with
him twenty-five sail of the line. One of these, built at
the Havana in 1769, and called the Santisima Trinidad,
had four decks, and mounted one hundred and thirty
guns: it was the largest ship which at that time existed
in the world. But the Spanish crews were for the most
part raw, untrained, and ill-affected to the service;
having been recently raised by a forced conscription of
landsmen.

At this juncture Sir John Jervis had been most
seasonably joined by Admiral Parker from England
and Commodore Nelson from Elba. On board the ship
of Nelson were Sir Gilbert Elliot, the late Viceroy of
Corsica, with Colonel Drinkwater and others of his
suite; and thus did these gentlemen become spectators
of the coming conflict. All together Sir John Jervis
could display but fifteen ships of the line; but by a
bold manœuvre at the beginning of the action, his
fleet passed through the enemy's, cutting off from the
latter a division of six ships.

The main brunt of the battle which followed was
borne by Commodore Nelson and Captain Collingwood.
Nelson most gallantly boarded one of the Spanish eighty-
gun ships, the St. Joseph. 'Victory or Westminster
Abbey!' was his cry, as he rushed forward. Fighting
from deck to deck, and aided by Collingwood, he finally
prevailed. Thus in a private letter does Collingwood
describe the scene:— 'The Commodore, on the quarter-
deck of a Spanish first-rate, received the submission and
the swords of the officers of the two vessels. One of
his sailors (William Fearney by name) bundled up the
swords with as much composure as he would have made

a faggot, though twenty-two sail of their line were still within gun-shot!"[1]

At the close of the action there had struck to our flag, besides the St. Joseph, three Spanish ships of the line, while several others, and among them the Santisima Trinidad, were almost utterly disabled. The Spaniards showed no inclination to renew the battle, but retired during the night to the refuge of Cadiz Bay.

This victory, though not comparable, either in the fierceness of the struggle or the magnitude of the result, to some others at sea that followed it, was yet, so far as regards effect in England, better timed than any. It came as a speck of blue amidst dark clouds— as the one event to cheer us in a season of danger and distress. It was therefore politic as well as just in Pitt to give lustre to the victory, and shower rewards upon the victors. Sir John Jervis was raised not only to the Peerage, but to a high place in it, as Earl St. Vincent, with a pension of 3000*l.* a year. Nelson was knighted and received the Order of the Bath ; and there were numerous other promotions.

By land as by sea this year the hostilities were not interrupted by the winter season. The Archduke Charles succeeded in reducing Kehl and the *tête-de-pont* of Hüningen. But in Italy the star of General Bonaparte never waned. Early in January General Alvinzi, at the head of another Austrian army, had advanced to the relief of Mantua. At Rivoli he was met and utterly defeated by the French commander, and Mantua, in consequence, surrendered on the 2nd of the ensuing month. Bonaparte was then free to turn his arms against Pius the Sixth. First reducing Ancona and the districts to the east of the Apennines, he was preparing to cross that chain of mountains and march upon Rome, when the Pope, despairing of relief,

[1] *Memoirs of Lord Collingwood,* vol. i. p. 51 ; Pettigrew's *Life of Nelson,* vol. i. p. 94. See also, and above all, James's *Naval History,* vol. ii. pp. 35–40.

submitted to the hard terms that were demanded. By the Treaty of Tolentino, on the 19th of February, His Holiness formally ceded the greater part of the territories which the French had already seized, and agreed to pay to them a sum upon the whole of thirty-six millions of livres. An eloquent English writer, describing the result at the time, speaks of it as follows:—'If by a late submission, which the Romans call a treaty, the rotten grant of St. Peter's rich domain is yet saved a while from utter ruin, its seals are all torn off and its ornaments effaced.'[1]

No sooner was the Papal power humbled than the French chief, ever active and ever victorious, again turned his arms to the north. Marching boldly forward, he invaded the hereditary states of the House of Austria. The Archduke Charles was recalled in haste from the Rhine to defend the approaches of the Danube; but on the 16th of March he was overthrown at the battle of Tagliamento. Other reverses to the Austrians followed; the French still pressed onwards; they were at the foot of the Sömmering Pass, and within a few marches of Vienna. Thus threatened in his very capital, the Emperor gave way, and sent plenipotentiaries to treat with the youthful conqueror. Desirous to conciliate his good will, the Austrians proposed to insert as their first article that the Emperor acknowledged the French Republic. But here the lofty spirit of Bonaparte appeared. 'Strike that out!' he cried; 'the French Republic is like the sun; he that does not see it is blind!'

On the 18th of April the Preliminaries of Peace were signed at Leoben. The principal terms were the cession of Belgium to France and the extension of its frontier to the Rhine, on condition that the definitive treaty should provide fitting indemnity for the Emperor elsewhere.

The real meaning of this last condition was levelled

[1] *Anastasius*, by Thomas Hope, vol. iii. p. 373.

at the Republic of Venice. It may seem surprising
that her territories should thus be parcelled out by
France and Austria when neither of these Powers had
as yet declared war against her. But General Bonaparte
was fully resolved upon her overthrow. He had several
grievances, some just, others only colourable, against
the faltering chiefs of that decrepit state. For a long
time they had wavered between their dread and their
dislike of him. But when they saw him far removed
from their own frontiers, and involved, as they thought,
in the fastnesses of the Austrian mountains, they
allowed the latter feeling in some measure to have
sway. They made—or, what in this case amounts to
the same thing, they were accused of making—some
feeble preparations to assail him in the rear. The
news of his victorious return and of his indignant
language made their very souls die within them. They
offered no defence; but, convening an extraordinary
Senate, agreed to a vote that their own government
was unsuited to times and circumstances. Not even a
single sword was drawn in behalf of the long-decayed
Republic. With so much of ignominy ended a career,
in part so glorious, of thirteen hundred years!

The conclusion of the Preliminaries of Leoben left
England to wage the contest single-handed. Not a
single ally of importance or of active co-operation
remained to her upon the Continent. States such as
Holland and Spain, that were ranged upon her side
at the commencement of the war, had now taken part
against her, and become mere instruments in the hands
of that Great Republic, so formidable an adversary even
while it stood alone.

While thus upon the Continent of Europe the cause
of England was in no common measure overcast and
lowering, our prospects at home were, if possible, more
gloomy still. The darkest, the most perilous hour to
us of the entire war had now arrived; the hour when
we were threatened with the loss both of our financial

credit and of our maritime supremacy ; first by a suspension of the Bank, and next by a mutiny of the Fleet.

The drain upon the Bank had been for some time past increasing. There was a large export of bullion in subsidies and loans to Foreign Powers. There were payments for the freights and cargoes of neutral ships which had been seized, and for which compensation was demanded. There were advances to Government amounting at last, with arrears of interest, to ten millions and a half sterling. There was a further advance in contemplation of a million and a half, required for the service of Ireland. Already, so far back as October, 1795, the price of gold had risen from 3$l.$ 17$s.$ 10$d.$, as estimated in the coinage, to 4$l.$ 4$s.$ the ounce.[1] Still, however, so high was the credit of the Bank, and so flourishing the state of its own resources, that it might probably have borne even these accumulated burthens. But at this very period came the alarm of a French invasion. Under this alarm many persons withdrew in haste their deposits from the country banks ; and these—some already insolvent, and many more threatened with insolvency—withdrew in their turn their deposits from the Bank of England. In the last ten days of February the great pressure came. It was found that the demands for cash in the preceding week were far greater than they had ever been in an equal period. Day by day they most rapidly increased. The Directors, in dire perplexity, addressed themselves to Pitt for counsel and guidance. Nothing but a most energetic determination on the part of the Executive Government could have saved the Bank, or, in its train, the State, from insolvency.

Pitt did not hesitate or falter. He applied to the King, and prevailed upon His Majesty to come at once to town, and, considering the emergency, to hold a Council at St. James's on Sunday. This was the 26th of February. Then was framed and issued an Order

---

[1] See Macpherson's *Annals of Commerce*, vol. iv. p. 407.

in Council, of which the opening words declared it to be, by the unanimous opinion of the Board, indispensably necessary for the public service. It prohibited the Directors of the Bank from issuing any cash in payment until the sense of Parliament could be taken and measures be adopted for maintaining the means of circulation.

This bold step—to sacrifice a part, lest the whole should perish—would have been as nothing, or as worse than nothing, had it not been well supported. A meeting of the merchants of London was immediately summoned, and held next day at noon in Guildhall, the Lord Mayor presiding. They resolved unanimously that they would accept bank-notes in any payment which they had to receive, and tender bank-notes in any payment which they had to make. A Resolution to this effect was signed by all the persons present; and so effectual was this measure in supporting public credit, that the Funds, far from falling, rose that afternoon no less than two per cent.

On that same Monday, the 27th, at the Meeting of both Houses, a message from the King was presented, transmitting the Order in Council, and recommending this most important subject to the immediate attention of Parliament. Pitt gave notice that next day he should move for a Secret Committee, chosen by ballot, to investigate the outstanding engagements and resources of the Bank, expressing, at the same time, his firm opinion that the resources would be found most ample, and much more than adequate to meet the engagements. He should also propose to declare, by a vote of the House, that notes instead of cash would, for a limited time, be received in all pecuniary transactions.

It might, perhaps, be expected by some philosopher in his closet, ignorant of this world's affairs, that at this most momentous crisis, when the financial credit of the country hung wavering in the balance, the gentlemen in Opposition should have, though but for a week, though but for a day, suspended their party resentments. It might be expected that they should show themselves still more desirous to sustain the State than to overthrow the Administration. Yet the ardour of political contention is at all times and in every party hard to be relinquished. We can trace that ardour but too clearly in the votes and speeches of this period. We find amendments moved and divisions taken on every possible occasion. We find invectives of Pitt without stint, measure, or reserve. We find denunciations of the course pursued, and at the same time no suggestion of any other. 'This alarming proposition,' said Fox, so early as the 27th, 'might even put an end to our existence as a powerful nation.' 'The Minister,' he added, next day, 'has issued a Proclamation to destroy the public credit of the country. Year by year he has amused us with ideas of the finances of France—as now on the verge, now in the gulf of bankruptcy. But while thus amusing the country, he has led it to the very same verge, ay, into the very same gulf.' Sheridan and some other Members were eager in predicting that, as the *Assignats* in France had now become waste paper, so would, ere long, the bank-notes of England. To the same effect in the other House spoke the Marquis of Lansdowne: 'Mark my prophecy, my Lords,' he said. 'If you attempt to make bank-notes a legal tender, their credit will perish. This is not matter of conjecture, but of experience. A fever is as much a fever in London as in Paris or Amsterdam, and the stoppage of payment must be the same in whatever country it shall happen.'

Happily for England in this emergency, as in many others, the middle classes evinced far more of spirit and of foresight than some of the statesmen by profession. In London, those merchants and bankers who had not attended the meeting at the Mansion House hastened to subscribe the Resolution which was there agreed to, so that in a few days the number of signatures was upwards of three thousand. Their patriotic example was followed by the members of the Privy Council, and of other public bodies; and through the public confidence thus manifested, all the current pecuniary transactions could proceed without disturbance. Still further was the public confidence increased when the Committees appointed by both Houses to examine the affairs of the Bank presented their Reports. It then appeared that on deducting the liabilities, there remained to the Bank, exclusive of their debt from Government of nearly 12,000,000*l.*, a clear surplus of 3,800,000*l.* At the same time it was recommended that the measures already taken should be continued and confirmed.

To establish a currency for smaller sums while the payments in gold were suspended, the Bank issued notes of one and two pounds each. To supply more silver without the delay of coinage, the Directors devised a new expedient. They stamped a miniature impression of the King's head on a large number of Spanish dollars, which they issued at the rate of four shillings and ninepence. But it was not long ere these stamps came to be counterfeited, and it was necessary to withdraw the first issue in the October following, even at considerable loss.[1]

In the Commons, on the 9th of March, Pitt moved to bring in a Bill to indemnify the Governor and Company of the Bank for any acts done by them in pursuance of the Order in Council. By that Bill, which did not pass into a law until the beginning of May, they were formally prohibited from issuing cash in payments except in sums under twenty shillings, and restricted from advancing to the Treasury any sum exceeding 600,000*l.*, until cash payments should be resumed. It was enacted that these restrictions should not extend beyond the 24th of June; but as that day approached an enlargement of time to the next Session was felt to be necessary, and was made. And though statesmen

[1] Macpherson's *Annals of Commerce*, vol. iv. p. 115.

and Parliament continued to flatter themselves with hopes that they were providing only for a short emergency, and that cash payments might be speedily resumed, yet as time elapsed it was found to be more and more difficult to resume them, and in fact they were not resumed for years after the final close of the European war. Their resumption was founded only on Mr. Peel's Committee of 1818 and his Act of the ensuing year—not the least of the many great services rendered to his country by that eminent man.

It was this first cessation of cash payments that gave rise to a clever epigram on Mr. Pitt :—

> Of Augustus and Rome
> The poets still warble,
> How he found it of brick
> And left it of marble.
>
> So of Pitt and of England
> Men may say without vapour,
> That he found it of gold
> And left it of paper.

I may observe, however, that this conceit is not original ; it only puts into verse a note to the *Pursuits of Literature.*[1]

It is worthy of note that the system of inconvertible paper money ceased in France at almost the very period when it began in England. In the course of 1796 the *Assignats* became reduced to the value of waste paper, and the *Mandats*, which were intended to supply their place, quickly shared their fate. Thus of necessity there was a recurrence in all payments to the precious metals; a recurrence first in practice, and soon afterwards in law.

It must be owned, however, that so long as the war continued, the system of inconvertible paper money did good service in England. Expanding precisely in proportion to the exigencies of the public service, and supported by an undeviating reliance on the national good

---

[1] See p. 176, ed. 1808.

faith, it enabled us, as certainly no other system could, to raise year by year loans of unparalleled amount; to transmit repeated subsidies to Foreign Powers in alliance with us; and to bear without sinking beneath it the burthen of accumulated taxes. It was, in short, a gigantic system of paper credit, giving us power to cope with no less gigantic foes.

The temporary strength derived from an expanded currency was manifested during the month of April in this year. Even after so brief an interval since the last, another loan of eighteen millions was then required, including an advance of a million and a half to Ireland, and of three millions and a half to the Emperor. We have seen that in the previous December the same sum could scarcely have been raised at all without a most earnest appeal to the loyal feelings of the people. Now, on the contrary, the money was obtained without difficulty, though according to the dangers of the country on highly unfavourable terms—at the rate, namely, of 6*l*. 17*s*. per cent. To meet the interest, several new taxes were proposed, one especially of three halfpence on every newspaper, with an increased duty on advertisements.

In reserving so large a sum for the service of the Emperor, Pitt had supposed that the Emperor was resolute to maintain the war. The extreme advocates for war in England were never weary at this juncture in vaunting the Emperor's immovable firmness. Nor were there wanting even in the Cabinet some reflections on the lesser zeal of Mr. Pitt. 'One anecdote of the Emperor I cannot forbear mentioning,' writes Windham to Burke. 'When his courtiers were besieging him with demands for peace, and urging that Vienna must fall, he answered by saying, "What then? Is Vienna the Empire?" The Emperor and Thugut, however, are the only persons who stand upon that ground. I believe we also have an Emperor here to do the same; but where is the Thugut?'

The letter of Windham, from which I have here cited, bore date the 25th of April. On that day a week had already elapsed since the immovable Emperor yielded and the Preliminaries of Peace were signed !

In truth, however, Mr. Pitt was not less zealous than the followers of Burke. He was only more clear-sighted. He was more observant of obstacles, and better prepared for ill-success. We find him on the 28th earnestly press a personal friend to return to the House of Commons for this very question: ' It seems very important not to delay for a moment more than is necessary the decision on the Austrian loan. The sending the result to Vienna may be of infinite import-ance.' [1]   The money was voted as Pitt desired on the 4th of May, but on the 5th arrived the tidings that dashed his hopes—the tidings of the separate peace.

Amidst all this pressure on the national resources, the House of Commons was not unmindful on other points also of its duty to the Crown. A marriage having been concluded between the Princess Royal and the Hereditary Prince of Würtemberg, there was cheer-fully voted a marriage-portion of 80,000l.

The mutiny of the Fleet at this very period, and when, as will presently be shown, an invasion from the side of Holland was impending, seemed to threaten not only the well-being and prosperity, but the very exist-ence of England as an independent state. For some time past discontents had prevailed among the seamen. There had been no increase either of their pay or of the Greenwich pensions since the reign of Charles the Second, while the necessaries of life had risen at least 30 per cent. in price, so that the effect upon them was equiva-lent to a large reduction. There were complaints of the unequal distribution of prize-money, which by its rules gave almost everything to the chiefs, and left the merest pittance to the petty officers and crews. There

' Pitt to Wilberforce, April 28, 1797.

were complaints, I fear but too justly founded, of harsh
and tyrannical conduct in some of the Admirals and
Captains.

Of all the naval chiefs at this time, the one who
enjoyed the highest popularity was the veteran Earl
Howe. The seamen were proud of his exploits and
their own on the memorable 'First of June,' and
they talked of him among themselves affectionately as
'Black Dick.' Lord Howe was still nominally at the
head of the Channel Fleet, but he was seventy-two
years of age. Lord Bridport commanded under him,
and Lord Howe himself had gone to Bath to recruit
his health. It was at Bath that, at the beginning of
March, he received four letters, not signed, but pur-
porting to come from the seamen of the four principal
ships at Portsmouth, his own flag-ship, the Queen
Charlotte, among the rest. These letters pointed out
that both the Army and Militia had lately received
an increase of their allowances, and they asked his
Lordship, as 'the seaman's friend,' to intercede at the
Admiralty, and obtain a similar favour for the naval
service. Lord Howe transmitted these four letters
(three of which appeared to be in the same handwriting) to Lord Spencer, and wrote upon the subject
both to Sir Peter Parker, the Admiral at Portsmouth,
and to Lord Bridport, the commander of the Channel
Fleet. Both these chiefs in their replies treated the
matter as of no importance, as probably the work of
some one ill-disposed person. It is not easy on this
occasion to acquit some Admirals in active service from
the charge of either gross ignorance or gross unconcern
as regards the wants and wishes of their men.

No public notice accordingly was taken of these
anonymous communications, and the Lords of the
Admiralty remained in a state of profound security.
But on the 12th of April they were addressed by Sir
Peter Parker in a far different tone. He had received
intelligence, he said, of a concerted scheme for the

crews of the Channel Fleet to seize the ships and supersede the officers until their grievances should be redressed, and that the 16th of the month was fixed upon as the day for the execution of this project. Active service seemed to be the surest antidote for sullen discontent. An order was instantly sent down to Portsmouth by telegraph for the Channel Fleet to put to sea. Judicious as this measure seemed, it did not prevent, it only hastened, the intended outbreak. No sooner had Lord Bridport made the signal to prepare for sailing than the seamen on board his own ship, the Queen Charlotte, ran up the rigging and raised three cheers of defiance. Their example was followed, and their cheer re-echoed from the other ships of war. So unanimous were they, that they carried their purpose into effect with the utmost ease. They took all command from the officers, sending several whom they accused of oppression on shore, and keeping the others on board as hostages and prisoners. Scarce any insult was offered, and not a drop of blood was spilt. For their government, two 'delegates' (for such was the name they bore) were chosen in each ship, and sent on board the Queen Charlotte, where they held their sittings in the Admiral's state cabin.

The delegates, thirty-two in number, sought in the first place to establish their own authority. They required every seaman in their ships to take an oath of fidelity to them and to the fleet in general; and this ceremony was accomplished in two days. Meanwhile they prepared a petition to the Board of Admiralty and to the House of Commons, and framed a list of rules for the government of the ships under their control. Perhaps no men raised to power by a successful mutiny ever showed so much of temper and moderation. Their petition was neither exorbitant in its demands, nor yet disrespectful in its tone. Besides the smallness of their allowances, as contrasted with those of the Army and Militiamen, to whom, as they said, they were not inferior in loyalty and zeal, they complained of the deficient weight and measure of their provisions; of the scanty care of them when sick; of the stoppage of their pay when wounded; and of their prolonged detention on board when in harbour.

In the rules which they framed they did their best to maintain a right discipline. They enjoined proper returns of watch, and strict obedience to command; they prohibited the introduction of spirits in the ships, and the rambling of the sailors on shore.

One rule may perhaps remind the reader of the fable of the Lion's Den : ' No woman shall be permitted to go on shore from any ship, but as many may come in as please.' [1]

By this time, however, the Government in London was thoroughly roused. Lord Spencer, attended by two of the Junior Lords, hastened down to Portsmouth, and there held a Board of Admiralty. There also he conferred with some of our best Admirals on shore. All agreed that both in justice and in policy the demands of the mutineers ought in great part at least to be complied with. By instructions from the Government, accordingly, three of the Admirals, namely, Gardner, Colpoys, and Pole, were sent on board the Queen Charlotte to confer with the delegates. They came fully authorised to offer a large increase both in pay and in provisions, and required the seamen forthwith to return to their duty. But the delegates answered that the crews would agree to nothing unless the offer were sanctioned by Parliament and guaranteed by a Royal Proclamation. Incensed at this reply, Admiral Gardner, a man of hot temper, lost all self-control. He seized one of the delegates by the collar, and swore that he would have them all hanged, with every fifth man throughout the fleet !

---

[1] For these Rules given at length see the Collection of Papers laid before Parliament relating to the Mutiny (*Ann. Regist.* 1797, pp. 238-256).

This ill-timed sally of passion proved nearly fatal to Admiral Gardner himself. It proved nearly fatal also to the entire negotiation. The conferences were at once broken off. Lord Bridport, who had hitherto remained on board the Queen Charlotte, struck his flag and left the ship. Lord Spencer and his colleagues returned to London. On the other hand, the mutineers ordered a regular watch as when at sea, loaded the guns, and hoisted a blood-red flag. It appears that they intended the latter as only a signal among themselves, but the King's officers, who knew it as the common emblem of piracy, looked on it with alarm as the probable forerunner of some dreadful outrages.

Yet in one or two days more the angry feelings subsided. Lord Bridport received authority to renew the late offers with a more conciliatory form and a larger amount of concession. The delegates wrote to the Admiralty, declaring that with hearts full of gratitude and joy they received the bountiful augmentation of pay and provisions which was designed them. They wrote also to Lord Bridport, whom they styled their father and friend. Preliminaries being thus adjusted, Lord Bridport returned to his ship, once more bade his flag be hoisted, and addressed his men with much effect in the tone of an afflicted father, assuring them that he had brought a redress of their grievances. It was found, in fact, that the new proposals of which he was the bearer comprised substantially all that had been asked. One point only remained. The delegates refused to take the promise of the Board for the full pardon, and insisted on seeing it in the King's own name. This point also had to be conceded. His Majesty was applied to for his Sign Manual to a Proclamation, which was sent down to Portsmouth, read aloud in the several ships, and received with applauding cheers. Then, and then only, did the delegates disperse; the ensigns of revolt were struck down; and the crews declared themselves ready to yield due obedience to their officers. The first use made of this recovered authority was to move the greater part of the fleet from Portsmouth to St. Helen's.[1]

Besides the humiliation (certainly in this case no small one), it was no light sacrifice to which the nation here submitted. According to the estimate which Pitt laid before the House of Commons on the 5th of May, it became necessary to provide for the intended augmentation of allowances an annual expense of 536,000*l.*, although for the current year, on account of the months already elapsed, only the sum of 372,000*l.* was required. Pitt rose, he said, with great embarrassment. Explanations might justly be expected, but, from every view of prudence and policy, he should rather rely on and even claim the silent indulgence of the House than enter into any detail.

The appeal was made in vain. Fox and Sheridan would not relinquish, nor even for a day postpone, their invective against the Ministers. 'Conciliation,' said Sheridan, 'would be more effectual if accompanied with a vote of censure on their delay.' When, however, on the 9th Pitt brought in a Bill for increasing the pay and allowances to seamen, it was passed through all its stages at one sitting; and, being transmitted to the Lords, went through their House with equal speed. Next day the vote of censure which had been threatened by Sheridan was actually moved by Whitbread and seconded by Fox, but at the close of the debate they could muster only 63 votes against 237.

During this time, unhappily, the revolt of the Channel Fleet broke forth anew. So easy and so complete had been the triumph of the mutineers, that on looking back to it they could scarcely convince themselves of its reality. They thought that the promises made

---

[1] See the narrative of the Mutiny in the *Annual Register* (not in this case Dodsley's, but Rivington's rival series), part ii. pp. 140–159.

them would not be fulfilled. They misconstrued into grounds of suspicion the most trivial circumstances that arose, and the slightest delays that intervened. Above all, they resented a Circular Order from the Admiralty of the 1st of May, enjoining 'a proper subordination and discipline,' and directing 'that the Captains and Commanders be ready on the first appearance of mutiny to use the most vigorous means to suppress it, and to bring the ringleaders to punishment.' This Order, though designed only for future regulation, might yet to jealous eyes seem to bear a retrospective sense. Under these circumstances, on the 7th of May mutiny broke forth once more in all the ships at St. Helen's. Once more the crews quietly deposed their officers, and named delegates in their stead. At the same time they despatched some of their body to visit the two ships, the London and the Marlborough, which had remained at Portsmouth. Admiral Colpoys, who commanded on board the London, acted in conformity to his last instructions. He refused to admit the delegates, ordering the officers to be armed, the marines to be in readiness, and the ports to be let down. On the other hand, the seamen of the London, having consulted together, determined that the delegates should be received. The officers stood firm, and ordered the men to go below. Some men refused; one man began to unlash a gun. The First Lieutenant, Bover by name, after giving him a caution, which was disregarded, drew out a pistol and shot him dead.

This act was the signal for open mutiny. The seamen rushed upon the officers and overpowered them, while the marines, far from aiding the latter, took part with the mutineers. They were next proceeding to hang Lieutenant Bover upon the rigging, and it was only through the strenuous entreaties of the chaplain and surgeon, together with the interposition of the Admiral, who declared that this officer had merely acted as he was bound in obedience to instructions, that his life

was spared. In like manner the seamen of the Marlborough rose against their Captain, and the two ships,
then weighing anchor, joined the rest of the fleet at
St. Helen's.

Yet even at the height of this successful mutiny
there was one incident to show the moderation and
public spirit of the mutineers. It was believed that the
seamen in one of the ships at St. Helen's talked openly
among themselves of conveying her to France and giving
her over to the enemy. This idea was thought to be
not spontaneous, but rather derived from certain persons on land. But no sooner did the delegates hear of
it than they expressed the highest indignation. They
threatened to fire upon and sink that ship if such language were continued, and they stationed guard-boats
around her both by day and night, so as to prevent any
further communication with the shore.

To quell this second mutiny the Ministers relied on
the prudence and popularity of Earl Howe. On the
11th he went down in all haste to Portsmouth, bearing
with him a full pardon from the King, and the Act of
Parliament which had been passed in a single day. He
had resolved to go on board every one of the revolted
line-of-battle ships, and to confer in person with the delegates and crews. Everywhere he found himself received
with affectionate respect, and heard with deferential attention. So far had he wrought upon them in the space
of two days, that they consented to express in general
terms their contrition for what had passed. They were
willing also that the removal of unpopular officers on
which they had determined should appear, not as a condition to be stipulated, but as a favour to be asked.
On the 13th Earl Howe, on board the Royal William,
received in state the petitions of the men, and having
declared them granted in virtue of his full powers, the
mutiny was concluded and discipline restored. He had
the great mortification to see Admiral Colpoys, four
Post Captains, and nearly one hundred officers of less

rank, displaced from command and consigned to inactivity, at the call of those whom they had ruled, though still retained by the Government on full pay. But on the other hand he beheld with delight the fleet in general resume the King's authority and return to active service. Except a slight affray, caused by four drunken sailors, who went on shore and were apprehended for rape and robbery, there was no renewal of tumult. The men appear to have done their duty with the same exactness as before ; and, soon weighing anchor, the fleet sailed to its appointed station, to cruise off the coast of Brittany.

So far then as regards the Channel Fleet the mutiny seems to have left no ill traces behind. It had dealt only with practical and pressing grievances; it had put forth no mere theoretical pretensions. Yet even thus the precedent of a victorious insurrection could not pass away without considerable danger. It was an evil seed that struck root elsewhere. On the 11th of May, at the very time when Lord Howe was hastening down to quell the mutiny in the ships at St. Helen's, a new mutiny broke out in the ships at Sheerness. Here also, in the course of a few days, the men with perfect ease overpowered and deposed the officers. For the management of each ship they formed a body of twelve, which they termed a Committee of Vigilance, and for the conduct of the whole they appointed a Committee of Delegates.

But this new revolt essentially differed from the former. It had been fomented by seditious handbills —the same as had been lately, though without success, distributed among the soldiers.[1] It looked to speculative rather than practical wrongs. It was tainted by the political spirit of the times. Finally it was made subservient to the personal ambition of one man. This was Richard Parker, a man in no common degree bold

<hr>

[1] See on this point the statement of Mr. Pitt in the *Parl. Hist.* vol. xxxiii. p. 806.

and active, who had received a more careful—let me
not say a better—education than his fellows. He was
a native of Devonshire, and had been a tradesman in
Scotland; but, being imprisoned in Perth gaol for debt,
enlisted as a naval volunteer. In the course of these
vicissitudes he had become deeply imbued with the
levelling principles of France. Being placed at the
head of the delegates, he assumed the title of their
President, sometimes also, as the mutiny proceeded,
being called Rear-Admiral Parker. By his direction
they took, as it were, possession of Sheerness, holding
their deliberations at a tavern, and parading the town
with music and banners and every mark of triumph.
Meanwhile no seaman was permitted to leave his ship
without a passport, which, by a strange perversion of
language, was termed 'a liberty ticket.'

Nor, indeed, did the delegates themselves remain
many days at Sheerness. They deemed it more prudent
both to concentrate their force and to place it beyond
reach of the batteries on shore. With this view they
moved the ships to the Nore. There they held their
meetings in the state-cabin of the Sandwich, of ninety
guns, lately the flag-ship of Vice-Admiral Charles
Buckner, who was the commander of this fleet.

The account of this fresh mutiny was received in
London with equal concern and surprise. It had been
hoped that the late concessions, ratified as they had
been by an Act of Parliament, had not only allayed
sedition, but expelled what Lord Bacon terms the matter
of sedition. It was therefore anxiously inquired what
other terms the new mutineers demanded. At first there
was no clue beyond a paper entitled an Appeal to the
Nation, which was industriously circulated through the
fleet. It purported to come from the sailors in Lord
Bridport's fleet, but, from the style, was plainly the
work of some disaffected landsman, who did not scruple
at the most malicious falsehoods. Thus it asserted as a
positive and undoubted fact, that, notwithstanding the

free pardon granted by the King, it was the intention
of the Ministers, after a brief interval, to select and
send to execution those seamen who had been prominent in the late proceedings. Indeed it was alleged
that the selection was already made.[1]

On the 20th of May the delegates of the new mutiny
spoke for themselves. Sitting in the state-cabin of the
Sandwich, they sent through Admiral Buckner a written
statement of their claims. But here again the very
first article showed under what gross misrepresentations
they had acted. For in that article they asked 'that
every indulgence granted to the fleet at Portsmouth
be granted to His Majesty's subjects serving in the
fleet at the Nore.' Now on this point there had never
been the smallest doubt or hesitation in the Government or in any of those whom it employed; and the
late Act of Parliament had declared in most explicit
terms that these indulgences should extend to all seamen and marines in the Royal Service. It is quite
plain that concealed behind the mutineers and urging
them onwards there were much worse men than themselves.

Unhappily the other articles transmitted from the
Sandwich were not so easy of solution. They were
found to be for the most part extravagant and inadmissible. Thus they required that no officer who had
been turned out of any ship should be employed again
in the same ship without the consent of the ship's company. Thus again they required that of the Articles of
War some should be expunged and all revised. And
it was necessary to consider also the form of these
requests. It was no longer, as from Portsmouth, a
respectful petition. It was an imperious statement of
demands. We find it in conclusion state that they
(the delegates) 'have unanimously agreed that they
will not deliver up their charge until the appearance of

---

[1] See an account of this publication in Mr. Sheridan's fair and
upright speech of the 19th of May. *Parl. Hist.* vol. xxxiii. p. 639.

some of the Lords Commissioners of the Admiralty to ratify the same.'

Under these circumstances, the Lords replied on the 22nd to the effect that ample concessions had been already made—that no further ones could be admitted —and that, although their Lordships had thought proper to go down to Portsmouth, they saw no reason for a similar step on the present occasion. But they offered to the men in mutiny 'His Majesty's most gracious pardon; and their Lordships' order to all officers to bury in oblivion all that has passed.'

This offer of clemency was transmitted through Admiral Buckner. Being unheeded by the mutineers, it was renewed on the 24th. The Admiral went himself on board the Sandwich to bring the delegates to a sense of their duty. He was received without any of the honours beseeming his rank, and he came back without the smallest result from his endeavours. At his departure the mutineers struck his flag, which they had hitherto foreborne to do, and hoisted in all the ships the blood-red flag of piracy. And on the 25th they addressed a written answer to the overtures of the Admiralty. 'The determination of the whole,' says Richard Parker, who signs as President, 'is that they will not come to any accommodation until you appear at the Nore and redress our grievances.'

The mutineers did not confine themselves to emblems or to words alone. They seized or they fired upon several ships which had hitherto remained loyal to the King, and compelled the crews to take part in the revolt. Among these was the San Fiorenzo frigate, which had been made ready to convey the Prince of Würtemberg and his bride to Germany. There was a return of their fire from the fort at Tilbury. There was a commencement of revolt in the artillery at Woolwich. But, worst of all, they were joined by the greater part of Admiral Duncan's fleet. That fleet had been blockading the ports of Holland, in which an invasion of this country was actively preparing. The heart of our Admiral—brave as it was, and long tried—sank within him when he found himself one morning forsaken by his entire armament, except only his own ship and one other, the Venerable and the Adamant. He called his men together on the quarter-deck, and made them a touching address which is still recorded. 'It has often been my pride,' he said, 'with you to look into the Texel and see a foe who dreaded coming out to meet us: my pride is now humbled indeed.'[1] With excellent skill the Admiral caused repeated signals to be made, as if the main body of his fleet were still in the offing. By this device, which was observed from the shore, the Dutch chiefs were completely deceived. They were kept in ignorance of the desertion that Duncan had sustained. But had they known the real truth, or had they been able at that period to set sail and issue forth, they would have found Old England undefended by her wooden walls, and open on every side to her assailants.

Nor was it only of the fleet that fears were entertained. With equal zeal had seditious handbills been disseminated through the army. Wilberforce has noted in his Diary of the 28th of May: 'Daily reports of the soldiery rising; and certainly some progress made (in corrupting them.)'

Still more precise is the statement of Sir Charles Cunningham, a Captain of one of the King's ships. He declares that the inflammatory handbills sent on shore had wrought upon the Invalids, the only force then stationed at Sheerness. When elevated with liquor, 'which,' says Sir Charles, 'generally happened every evening,' they were heard to express their opinion that they also had a right to have delegates.[2]

No crisis so alarming, or nearly so alarming, has ever been known in England since the Revolution of

---

[1] *Ann. Regist.* 1797, part i. p. 211.
[2] *Narrative of the Mutiny*, p. 17, as privately printed, 1829.

1688. One night the Ministers were roused from their slumbers by the booming of the distant cannon, and had to meet in council before daybreak. This we learn from an entry in Mr. Wilberforce's private journal, dated the 26th of May: 'Pitt waked by Woolwich artillery riot, and went out to Cabinet.' Yet, feeling how much at this juncture depended on himself, he allowed no sign of discomposure to escape him; and he maintained throughout, what Lord Macaulay describes at another period as 'his usual majestic self-possession.'[1]

One strong instance of Pitt's calmness, at a time when all around him shook, was wont to be related by the First Lord of the Admiralty at that period. On a subsequent night there had come from the fleet tidings of especial urgency. Lord Spencer thought it requisite to go at once to Downing Street and consult the Prime Minister. Pitt, being roused from his slumbers, sat up in bed, heard the case, and gave his instructions. Lord Spencer took leave and withdrew. But no sooner had he reached the end of the street than he remembered one more point which he had omitted to state. Accordingly he returned to Pitt's house, and desired to be shown up a second time to Pitt's chamber. Thereafter so brief an interval he found Pitt as before, buried in profound repose.

Another slight incident from the same circle of private life will perhaps pourtray more vividly than could any elaborate description, how very far from such calmness and composure was the public mind at that period. When earlier in the month of May Mr. Wilberforce announced his matrimonial engagement to Miss Spooner, 'it was remarked by those who knew him best as an instance of his confidence in God, that at such a time of general apprehension he should have resolved to marry.'[2]

The same feeling of alarm was manifested in all the

---

[1] *Biographies,* p. 225, ed. 1860.
[2] *Life of Wilberforce,* by his Sons, vol. ii. p. 215

public transactions of this period. Thus in the course of May the Three per Cents. fell to the extreme depression of 48.

It was at this most critical period that Fox and his chief friends in the House of Commons deemed it not inconsistent with their sense of right to give a Parliamentary expression to the discontents by announcing in solemn terms their intended retirement from public affairs. The first step was to bring forward on the 26th, through Mr. Grey, a motion for Parliamentary Reform. Both Grey who began, and Fox who concluded the debate, spoke at length and most ably; as did also Sheridan, and a new accession to the House, Sir Francis Burdett. With equal ability was the grave and warning voice of Pitt raised against them. It is striking to observe how little the argument of practical grievance had as yet been urged. Pitt in his speech found himself able to allege that 'it never was contended that the interests of Yorkshire were neglected because it sent only two members to Parliament, or that Birmingham and Manchester have experienced any ill consequences from having no representative.'[1] Perhaps it may be thought that the real and actual grievance had not been long felt before it came to be redressed.

The main points of interest in this debate were, however, the personal declarations of Fox and Grey. Both disclaimed the idea of an entire and absolute secession. Grey said that he should still be ready to vote, but should not probably after that night desire to trouble the House with any observations. And Fox added on his own part: 'I certainly do think that I may devote more of my time to my private pursuits and to the retirement which I love than I have hitherto done. I certainly do think that I need not devote much of it in this House to fruitless exertions and to idle talk.' These announcements were made on the supposition that the motion for Reform of Parliament

---

[1] *Parl. Hist.* vol. xxxiii. p. 681.

would be again, and by a large majority, rejected. And
so it proved. In the division Grey found himself
supported by 91 Members, but opposed by no less
than 256.

Such announcements to forsake the Parliamentary
career as fruitless, and to despair in effect of all beneficial legislation, were, to say the least of them, ill-fitted
to serve the cause of order. Yet that cause was at this
very time in most imminent peril at the Nore. We
have seen that in their letter to the mutineers the Lords
of the Admiralty had declared that they would not go to
Sheerness. In reply the mutineers had insisted that they
should. To give way to this demand was certainly no
slight surrender of rightful dignity. But the Ministers,
seeing that it would be necessary to make a stand on
the essential questions, resolved to avoid all controversy
on points of form. Accordingly on the 29th, Earl
Spencer and two of the Junior Lords having repaired
to Sheerness and held a Board at the house of Commissioner Hartwell, they were met by Richard Parker
with twelve of his brother delegates. The result was
by no means satisfactory. The tone of Parker was rude
and insolent. Thus when Lord Spencer mentioned the
opinion of the Cabinet, Parker told him to go and
' consult the ring-leaders of your gang.'[1] In substance
the delegates were unbending; they would not recede
from the terms they had required, and they spurned
the offer of pardon and oblivion made in pursuance of
a new Royal Proclamation.

Thus failing in their hopes of adjustment, the Lords
of the Admiralty returned to London, and the delegates
on board their ships. It was at this very time that the
mutineers at the Nore were both reinforced and emboldened by the arrival of the greater part of Admiral
Duncan's fleet. That junction raised their force to
twenty-four sail. It also raised their presumption to

[1] ' Narrative of the Mutiny ' in the *Annual Register* (Rivington's),
part ii. p. 143.

such a pitch, that they proceeded to blockade the
mouth of the Thames; for that object mooring four
vessels at equal distances from shore to shore. Fertile
as England has ever been in sinister predictions, was
ever yet so sinister a prediction made? Had it ever
formed part of even the most dismal forebodings that
our wooden walls should be turned as instruments of
siege against us; and that the English capital should
be held in check by English sailors?

Nor was it thought that the mutineers would rest
satisfied with their blockade. Divers attacks were
apprehended. The people of Sheerness, expecting a
bombardment, fled in great numbers from the town,
or at least sent away their wives and families. London
itself was scarcely deemed secure. But the Ministers
were determined at all hazards to stand firm. They
felt that they had already carried concession to its
utmost limits. At Portsmouth they had granted to
the seamen everything that they could rightly grant.
At Sheerness they had shown themselves willing to
waive every question of form, to remit every question
of punishment. Better now perish than further yield,
since to yield would only be to perish in another form.
Troops were summoned in all haste to London. Detach-
ments were sent to Sheerness, and along both banks of
the Thames. The ships that had remained loyal were
made ready. A flotilla of gun-boats was fitted out.
For the manning of these ships and boats both officers
and sailors were invited to present themselves; and
present themselves they did in considerable numbers.
All the buoys and beacons which point out the passes
through the sand-banks at the mouth of the Thames
were most carefully removed. In short, it may be
asserted that every measure was taken for active resistance as though the French invaders were at hand.

Nor was the action of Parliament neglected. On
the 1st of June a message from the King was delivered
to both Houses. His Majesty lamented that the crews

at the Nore were still persisting in their mutiny, and called upon Parliament to make more effectual provision against such treasonable practices. Next day loyal Addresses in reply were moved and carried. Fox and his closest friends were absent, but Sheridan cordially expressed, as he had once already, those sentiments which at such a juncture any statesman of any party might have been expected to hold.[1] Then Pitt brought in two Bills—the one for inflicting severe penalties on all attempts to excite sedition and mutiny in His Majesty's Service—the other for restraining on the pains of felony any intercourse with the ships at that time in revolt. Both these Bills passed rapidly through their several stages and received the Royal Assent. Thus was manifested in the clearest manner the resolute firmness of both the Administration and the Parliament.

The use of the King's name in the Message to both Houses was certainly productive of good effect. Only three days afterwards came the King's birthday, the 4th of June. Then was it plainly seen that the old spirit of loyalty had only slumbered; that it had by no means died away in the hearts of British seamen. On that day every ship engaged in the revolt, except only the Sandwich, lowered the red flag and hoisted the Royal colours, while at the same time they fired a Royal salute. The single exception of the Sandwich was significant as evincing that this burst of affectionate respect took place against the wish and against the orders of the delegates. This was the first symptom, but each succeeding day seemed to lower the authority of these revolutionary chiefs. The seamen began to feel the arbitrary temper and capricious severity of Parker, and were less and less inclined to worship the brazen image that they had made.

<hr>

[1] See the *Parl. Hist.* vol. xxxiii. p. 801. and Moore's *Life*, vol. ii. p. 271, although in the latter the part of Sheridan seems to be a little magnified.

Parker used every effort to keep up the delusion among his men. As one expedient that he hit upon, he exhibited the effigies of Pitt and Dundas at the foreyard arm of several of the ships, as marks to be fired at. This was done as he desired early in the morning of the 7th of June, and produced no small consternation at Sheerness, where the sounds were heard, and where it was commonly believed that some of the officers on board were undergoing a real execution.[1]

Nevertheless at this very time the delegates themselves showed some signs of wavering. They summoned to their state-cabin in the Sandwich one of the Captains, the Earl of Northesk, who at the outbreak of the mutiny had been detained as a prisoner on board his ship. On appearing before them, Parker, as the President, desired him to convey to London a letter to the King, and a renewed statement of the terms on which alone they would consent to give up the ships. Lord Northesk undertook the mission, telling them, however, that he expected no good effect from it. In London he was introduced by Lord Spencer to the King, but was directed to inform the mutineers that no terms with them would be made; that their repentance and unconditional submission were now required.

Besides the discouragement which this reply produced among the sailors, there were also other causes that conduced to the same end. There was an Address to them from the fleet at Plymouth, and another from the fleet at Spithead, calling upon them to return to their duty, and reprobating their recent conduct as 'a scandal to the name of British seamen.' By the denial of all intercourse with the shore, they found themselves, to their grievous mortification, treated by the great body of their countrymen as outcasts and as enemies. And besides their natural feelings at this non-communication, they had another and a more substantial reason

[1] *Narrative of the Mutiny,* by Sir Charles Cunningham, p. 72.

for regret—their want of water and of fresh provisions. Add to this that from their new masters, the delegates, they underwent day after day a tyranny the more oppressive as upstart and unauthorised.

Of all the ships in revolt, the Repulse and the Leopard were the first to return to their duty. Having cut their cables at the height of the tide, the crews let them drift away from the main body, and sought protection beneath the cannon of Sheerness. Before this retreat could be accomplished, the Repulse was exposed to a heavy fire from the Monarch and Director, two other of the ships in mutiny. Yet it was not long before the Monarch and Director followed her example. In vessel after vessel the revolutionary ensign was lowered, and the rightful authority resumed. By the 13th the red flag had ceased to be displayed in every ship except the Sandwich. Even on the Sandwich the crews rose that day against their self-constituted President, and brought their ship, like the others, under the land batteries. Nor was any resistance offered when Admiral Buckner sent on board a guard of soldiers to arrest Richard Parker and carry him as a prisoner to shore.

Thus, through the vigour and determination of the Government, and by the return of good feeling among the men, was this formidable mutiny quelled almost as rapidly as it had arisen. The ships that belonged to Admiral Duncan's station went back to it; and the blockade of the Dutch fleet was resumed upon equal terms. Throughout the navy the old habits of obedience were re-established with as much security as though they had never been disturbed. In fact it may well excite surprise that after so great a movement, and after also so brief an interval, so few and such slight traces of it should remain. Perhaps this may be in part explained by the reluctance of the naval writers to detail them. So unwilling are they to dwell at all upon this painful subject, that the records of the great mutiny—as it really was seen and felt on board the ships—are among the most scanty and meagre of our recent annals.

There still remained, however, the trial of Parker and of the other delegates. In their case the facts were clear, and admitting of no doubt. They had rejected the King's clemency, and were to become examples of his justice. Parker was the first to be dealt with. Being tried by a Court Martial, he was found guilty and condemned to death. On the 30th of June he was, by a signal retribution, hanged at the yard-arm of the Sandwich. He met his fate with the greatest courage and composure, asserting to the last that his intentions were upright, and denying that he had any instigators or abettors on shore. A similar sentence was executed on some more of the ring-leaders; others were publicly whipped through the fleet; but the greater number received a respite, and remained for the present in gaol.

CHAPTER XXIV.

1797.

Death of Burke – Renewed negotiation with France—Lord Malmesbury sent to Lille—Talleyrand Minister for Foreign Affairs—Secret negotiation—*Coup d'état* of the Eighteenth of Fructidor—New demands of the French Government—Lord Malmesbury returns to London—Pitt's zeal for peace - Overture from a secret agent for a pecuniary gift to some of the French rulers—Pitt's reply—Death of Eliot—Decline of Pitt's health—His translation from Horace—Treaty of Campo Formio—Projected invasion of Ireland by the Dutch fleet—Death of Hoche—Battle of Camperdown—Meeting of Parliament—Parliamentary seceders—Mr. Tierney—The Budget—New Peerages—Lord Carrington—The Anti-Jacobin.

In the first stages of this great mutiny among the seamen, one at least of the Ministers recurred to the

counsels of Burke. Declining in health, and broken
in spirits, that great master of politics had early in
the spring repaired to Bath, with but faint hopes—
perhaps also but faint wishes—of recovery. Mr. Windham had gone to Bath to see him, and there was also
Mr. Wilberforce. Let me relate what followed in the
very words of the latter. 'Monday, April 17. Heard
of the Portsmouth mutiny. The only letter which
reached Bath that day by the cross post from Portsmouth was one from Captain Bedford, of the Royal
Sovereign, to Patty More. She brought it me, and I
took it at once to Burke. He could not then see me,
but at his desire I called again at two o'clock. The
whole scene is now before me. Burke was lying on a
sofa, much emaciated ; and Windham, Laurence, and
some other friends were round him. The attention shown
to Burke by all that party was just like the treatment of
Ahithophel of old.   "It was as if one went to inquire of
the oracle of the Lord." I reported to them the account I
had received ; and, Burke being satisfied of its authority,
we held a consultation on the proper course for Government to follow. Windham set off for London the same
night with the result of our deliberations.' From the
comments which Wilberforce adds, and which he illus-
trates at length by another story, we may learn that the
advice of Burke was entirely against those concessions to
the sailors that nevertheless were made.[1] Eight days
later we find Windham write to Burke from London :
'The business of the fleet is as well over as such a thing
can be ; but I am almost inclined to wish the Admiralty
had refused to comply.'[2]

Meanwhile the health of Burke had not improved.
On the 24th of May he left Bath to return to Beaconsfield and die. The last letter from his pen on record
bears date the 23rd. On the 21st we find him write to

[1] 'Minutes of Wilberforce's Conversation,' as published in his
Life, vol. ii. p. 211.
[2] Burke's Correspondence, vol. iv. p. 443.

Mrs. Crewe as follows :—' All hopes of any recovery to me from any thing which art or nature can supply being totally at an end, and the fullest trial having been given to these waters without any sort of effect, it is thought advisable that I should be taken home, where, if I shall live much longer, I shall see an end of all that is worth living for in this world.' Yet Burke did live to be soothed and cheered by the tidings that the mutinies of the seamen were finally quelled. He expired at Beaconsfield on the 9th of July. According to his own directions he was buried in the parish church, in the same grave with his brother and son.[1]

The latter part of this Session (it did not close till the 20th of July) was marked by a patriotic attempt of Wilberforce to enlarge the basis of national defence. As the law then stood, the Roman Catholics were not able to serve in the Militia. They found themselves excluded by the Declaration ' I am a Protestant,' which each new Militia-man was required to make. Wilberforce now brought in a Bill to omit the obnoxious words. In his own county of York at least he knew that the Roman Catholics were not inferior in loyalty to any of their fellow subjects, and he thought it most impolitic to shut out their services. Pitt gave the measure his support, and it passed the House of Commons. But in the Lords the scene was changed : there it became entangled with a clause including in its provisions the Protestant Dissenters. Bishop Horsley, of Rochester, delivered a violent speech against it ; Lord Grenville was not friendly ; and the Bill was thrown out. It is said that this affair had nearly caused a dissolution of the friendship between Pitt and Grenville.[2]

Hopes of a general peace were at this time enter-

---

[1] *Life*, by Prior, p. 458, ed. 1854. Mrs. Burke continued in the same residence, and survived till 1812. Next year the house was by an accident burnt down.

[2] No record of these debates appears in the *Parl. Hist.*; but in this case, as in many others, the notes of Mr. Wilberforce (see his *Life*, vol. ii. p. 222) are of signal service to History.

tained. In his Speech at the close of the Session the
King had mentioned the negotiation as in active progress, but of doubtful issue. So early as the 9th of
April Pitt had most earnestly represented to the King
‘ the gradual and increasing difficulties of finance.’ He
stated it not as his own opinion only, but as the unanimous opinion of the Cabinet, that the first favourable
opportunity should be taken of another overture to
France ; and that if the claims of the Emperor were
once disposed of by his own consent, we should be prepared to leave France in peaceable possession of her
conquests—with Belgium as her dominion, and with
Holland as her dependency. The King, though with
sorrow and reluctance, acquiesced ; [1] and the tidings of
the Treaty of Leoben coming as they did early in May,
added of course a fresh impulse to the pacific wishes of
Pitt and his colleagues.

On the 1st of June, therefore, Lord Grenville addressed a letter to M. Delacroix, suggesting that as
several obstacles had been removed, the time was favourable to a negotiation. The French Minister at
once replied in terms of most ready assent. Subsequently he proposed Lille as the place of negotiation,
and sent a passport, with the name in blank, for the
English negotiator. But here the haughty spirit of
Lord Grenville took deep offence. The passport sent
was indeed in an unusual and objectionable form : it
purported to be for a person ‘ furnished with the full
powers of His Britannic Majesty for concluding and
signing a definitive and separate treaty of peace.’ Thus
it by anticipation seemed to define and limit the objects
of the whole negotiation.

So incensed was Lord Grenville, so positive in putting the worst construction on this point of form, that
at a Cabinet held on the 16th he pressed to break off
the entire negotiation on this ground. But Pitt was no

---

[1] See in the Appendix an extract of the King's reply, dated
April 10, 1797.

less resolute upon the other side. 'I feel it my duty,' he said more than once, 'as an English Minister and a Christian, to use every effort to stop so bloody and wasting a war.'[1] Windham was not present at that meeting, but Pitt was supported by his other colleagues, and Lord Grenville at last gave way. Still, however, he desired that his dissent from the opinion of his colleagues might be intimated to the King.

Here follows the Draft of those deliberations as drawn up in Mr. Pitt's own writing and as transmitted to His Majesty.

Draft of Cabinet, June 16, 1797.

Present,

Lord Chanc^r., Lord President, Duke of Portland, Earl Spencer, Lord Grenville, Marquis Cornwallis, Mr. Sec^y. Dundas, Mr. Pitt.

It is humbly recommended to Your Majesty that an official note conformable to the accompanying Draft should be transmitted to Paris in answer to the last communication from thence.

Lord Grenville desires to express his dissent.

W. P.

The King made no sign in support of Grenville. No letter from His Majesty of that day or upon that subject appears in the Pitt Correspondence. Next morning, therefore, Grenville was under the disagreeable necessity of framing a despatch contrary to his own predilections. In that despatch, addressed to M. Delacroix, he declared the willingness of the English Government to open a negotiation at Lille, and the choice of Lord Malmesbury as the negotiator. He pointed out the objections to the form of the passport, and hoped to receive a new one ; adding, in reference to the idea of 'a separate negotiation,' that the King would be bound to offer terms on behalf of his ally of Portugal.

The reply of M. Delacroix was far from courteous

---

[1] *Malmesbury Papers*, vol. iii. p. 369.

in its tone, though not unsatisfactory in substance.
He said that the Directory consented to receive Lord
Malmesbury on the part of England, but would have
deemed another choice as of happier augury for the
speedy conclusion of peace. He gave such assurances
as explained away the limitations of the passport; and
he added a wish that couriers might not be sent too
frequently, since, as he alleged, this frequent despatch
had been one main cause of the failure of the late
negotiation.

With so ungracious a spirit in M. Delacroix—with
so much of decided repugnance in Lord Grenville—it
was easy to foresee great obstacles in the way of a conclusion. But Pitt was firm for peace, and on Pitt Lord
Malmesbury relied. 'Be assured,' said the Prime
Minister to him as he set out for Lille, 'be assured
that to produce the desired result I will stifle to the
utmost every feeling of pride.'[1]

On the 3rd of July Lord Malmesbury landed at
Calais, and next day proceeded to Lille. There he
found awaiting him three Plenipotentiaries on the part
of France: first, Le Tourneur, who had been one of the
Directors; secondly, Pleville de Pelley, an Admiral in
the French navy; and thirdly, Maret, lately returned
from an embassy at Naples. All three were gentlemen
in mind and manners, frank, and pleasant to deal with.
'It is impossible,' thus writes Lord Malmesbury at the
close of these proceedings, 'for any men to have conducted themselves with more cordiality, good humour,
and good faith than the whole of the French Legation
have done.'[2]

At the second conference between them, on the 8th
of July, the English Minister gave in his project for a
treaty. England was willing to restore all the conquests
which she had made during the war from France and
the allies of France, except only the island of Trinidad

<hr>

[1] *Malmesbury Papers*, vol. iii. p. 369.
[2] To Lord Grenville, Sept. 11, 1797.

from the Spaniards, and the Cape of Good Hope from the Dutch. It was further desired, so far as the Dutch were concerned, to obtain their possessions in Ceylon and at Cochin in exchange for Negapatnam, on the coast of Tanjore. There were also some stipulations with regard to the private property of the Prince of Orange, and against any burthensome condition on the Portuguese.

The French Plenipotentiaries took, as was natural, this project to refer to their Government. Meanwhile, in pursuance of instructions from Paris, they put in three separate demands :—First, that the title of King of France, which had been borne by the English Sovereign ever since Edward the Third, should be expressly renounced ; secondly, that there should be a restitution of, or an equivalent for, the ships taken or destroyed at Toulon ; and thirdly, that there should be a clear renunciation of any mortgage upon Belgium in consequence of the loans made to the Emperor from the King of England.

These three new conditions greatly chafed and exasperated Grenville. But Pitt was inclined to take a less unfavourable view. Thus he writes: 'I own I am not without some hope that, in one way or another, difficulties on these separate points will not long retard the negotiation, if in other respects an agreement is practicable.'[1]

A divergence of the same kind between the two statesmen was shown a few weeks later, when the French Government, in a manner not a little surreptitious, signed a separate peace with the Portuguese Minister at Paris. 'You will see by your public instructions,' writes Pitt to Malmesbury, ' the impression made here by the manner of concluding the Portuguese peace, and still more by the terms. . . . . . The preventing us from the full and free use of the Portuguese ports is in itself a point of the utmost practical im-

[1] To Lord Malmesbury, July 13, 1797.

portance. . . . . . On these grounds I feel strongly the necessity of our making a stand, but I own I do not feel as much discouraged by the circumstance as some others.'[1]

But at Lille no progress was made. During many weeks the French Plenipotentiaries received no further instructions. They could neither discuss the project of Lord Malmesbury, nor yet bring forward, as he asked, a counter-project of their own. It became evident that two adverse parties were in presence at Paris—each preparing to struggle for the mastery, each desirous to cast upon the other the blame of any condescension to the claims of England. The party in favour of the more moderate counsels which had latterly been in the ascendant possessed a majority in both the Chambers, but was opposed by three out of the five Directors. It was difficult, under such circumstances, to foresee how, without a *coup d'état*, either party could prevail.

Even before the end of July there came a change of Ministers. In the place of M. Delacroix, M. Talleyrand, formerly Bishop of Autun, became Minister for Foreign Affairs. In itself the change was of good augury to the friends of peace. M. Delacroix had shown himself formal, captious, and punctilious, with ' very much the air of a Bishop,' as says Wolfe Tone, with no complimentary intention.[2] The true Bishop, on the contrary, had not only great diplomatic abilities, but also moderate and conciliatory views. Besides M. Maret, who was foremost in his confidence, and Lord Malmesbury, there sprung up at once a most secret negotiation, not divulged to the other French diplomatists nor yet to the whole of the Cabinet in England. Some points of difficulty were, if not adjusted, brought

---

[1] To Lord Malmesbury, August 19, 1797, 'alluding to Lord Grenville '—such is Lord Malmesbury's annotation. The Portuguese Minister had far exceeded his instructions, and was subsequently disavowed by his Court.

[2] *Journal*, February 15, 1796.

to the verge of adjustment.   England might be willing
to forego her claim on the Cape if the Dutch would
bind themselves not to yield that colony to France.
France might be willing to exert her influence over
the Court of Madrid and obtain the relinquishment of
Trinidad; but still there remained the original obstacle
of the impending struggle at Paris, and Talleyrand, as
a thorough-paced diplomatist, would not commit himself
too far.

At length the storm did burst.   The long-appre-
hended *coup d'état* took place on the 4th of September,
or, according to the new calendar, the Eighteenth of
Fructidor.   Then the majority of the Directors, themselves directed by Barras, issued an order of arrest
against two of their colleagues, Barthelemy and Carnot.
In like manner they first sent to prison and afterwards
condemned to transportation their leading adversaries
in the Council of the Ancients and in the Assembly
of the Representatives.   An expedient so simple and
easy gave them a majority in both Chambers, and thus
was established in power for the present the semi-
Jacobin and, unhappily, also the non-pacific party.

The results of the Eighteenth of Fructidor were
quickly felt at Lille.   In the first place the former
Plenipotentiaries were recalled, and two patriots of
austerer mould, Messrs. Treilhard and Bonnier, were
appointed in their place.   Yet little or nothing was
left to the discretion of these new negotiators.   They
were compelled to act in mere obedience to peremptory
orders.   They were instructed to demand, and they
did demand, from Lord Malmesbury (requiring also
an answer in the course of the same day) whether he
had sufficient powers for restoring to the French Republic and to its allies all the conquests which, since
the beginning of the war, had passed into the hands
of the English.   Lord Malmesbury replied that he
thought the question of his full powers had been some
time since decided; but that, to avoid all misunder-

standing, he must declare, as he had already declared, that he neither could nor ought to treat upon any other principle than that of compensations. On receiving this communication Messrs. Treilhard and Bonnier immediately wrote again to apprise the English Minister of a decree of the Executive Directory, 'That in case Lord Malmesbury shall declare himself not to have the necessary authority for agreeing to all the restitutions which the laws and the treaties binding the French Republic make indispensable, he shall have to return within four-and-twenty hours to his Court to ask for sufficient powers.' And to this strange communication, almost without a parallel in the annals of diplomacy, Messrs. Treilhard and Bonnier thought fit to add from themselves: 'Lord Malmesbury can see in this determination of the Executive Directory nothing else than the intention to hasten the moment when the negotiation may be followed up with the certainty of a speedy conclusion.'

'It was my wish,' so writes Lord Malmesbury on this occasion, 'to give every opening to the French Plenipotentiaries to recall the violent step they had taken, and, if possible, convince them of its extreme impropriety.'[1] With this object he proposed and they agreed to another interview. He found them conciliatory and earnest in their language, but fast bound by their instructions. No alternative was left him but to go as he was bid. He set out from Lille early on the 18th of September, and the day but one after arrived in London.

Great was the disappointment that ensued, not in London merely, but in Paris also. The Directors found it necessary to excuse themselves. They protested that in the step which they had taken they had all along meant peace; and they ordered their Plenipotentiaries to remain at Lille as though in expectation of Lord Malmesbury's return. Lord Malmes-

______
[1] Despatch to Lord Grenville, September 17, 1797.

bury, however, by direction of the Cabinet, wrote back from London to declare ' That the King could no longer treat in an enemy's country without being certain that the customs established among all civilized nations with regard to public Ministers would be respected for the future in the person of his Plenipotentiary.' [1]

On a calm review of the whole transaction there seems no just ground to impute, as there was imputed, ill faith to either side. But we must deeply deplore that the negotiation at Lille coincided with and was controlled by the *coup d'état* at Paris. The French Directors felt themselves bound to take a rude, nay, insulting course in vindication of their recent party-cry ; and that course could not be otherwise than resented by the English Cabinet. Thus, while the two nations might be sincerely desirous of peace, the continuation of war during several years came to be imposed upon them. Pitt, much as his conduct was misrepresented at the time, had been earnest and consistent in his zeal for peace. He was prepared, had he found any traces of conciliatory spirit in our adversaries, to have contended in the cause of peace with the formidable obstacles that lay in its path at home, with the vehement prejudice of the King, the unbending temper of Lord Grenville, and the warlike ardour of some other of his colleagues. Lord Malmesbury, after a long conversation at this period with Windham, notes of him that ' he still persists in the idea of the *bellum internecinum* and the invading of France.'

But there was yet a sequel, and a strange one, to this story. No sooner had Lord Malmesbury left Lille than Mr. Pitt received a secret overture, on the part of Barras, offering peace on his own terms, if only an enormous sum—no less than two millions sterling—could be provided for Barras and his friends. The whole offer will be found detailed in Mr. Pitt's letter

[1] Note to the French Plenipotentiaries, October 5, 1797.

to the King. Next day, after receiving the King's assent, he replied to the secret agent as follows :—

Holwood, September 23, 1797.

'Tell Mr. —— that I can make no engagement without knowing the conditions ; but that I should not be unwilling to undertake for the payment of 450,000*l.* if the conditions are satisfactory, and supposing the time and mode of payment can be conveniently arranged, and the transaction remain secret. Before I can say more, he must produce the paper to which he has referred, and explain all points specifically. On doing so he will receive a distinct answer.'

Some further particulars may be gathered from Lord Malmesbury's Diary of the same dates. 'Barras confessedly the only one in the secret : he and his expect to persuade Rewbell, and to prevail on him to take his share of the bribe.' In the result, however, the whole of their notable project—I know not under what circumstances, or for what reason—fell to the ground.

At the very time, and almost on the very day, when the Minister to his deep disappointment found the public negotiation at an end, he was shocked by a grievous family misfortune. This was the decease of his dear friend and relative Edward Eliot, at the early age of thirty-nine. The news reached Pitt on the morning of the 20th of September—the morning of the same day on which Lord Malmesbury arrived in London. I do not find in the series of correspondence any letter from Pitt to his mother on this affliction, nor yet for some time afterwards. At this, as at some other places, a few appear to have been lost.

Here, however, are a few lines which Pitt wrote to Addington the same day :

Holwood, September 20, 1797.

'I am grieved indeed to tell you, and you will, I know, be grieved to hear, that a return of Eliot's complaint has ended fatally. The account reached me from Cornwall this morning, at a moment when I was quite unprepared for the event. You will not wonder if I do not write on any other subject. Lord Malmesbury is returned on the grounds I expected. Ever yours,   W. P.

Here also is an extract of another letter which Wilberforce wrote to Lord Muncaster on this sad occasion:—

Bath, September 27, 1797.

I can truly say that I scarcely know any one whose loss I have so much cause to regret. . . . Peace be with him. May my last end be like his. You will not be sorry to hear that, as Rose, who was an eye-witness, informed me, the effect produced on Mr. Pitt by the news, which came in a letter from Lord Eliot by the common post with his others, exceeded conception. Rose says he never saw and never expects to see anything like it. To Pitt the loss of Eliot is a loss indeed—and then his poor little girl!'

It is worthy of note that only a few months before—in February of this same year—Mr. Wilberforce, in common with several others, had warmly pressed the appointment of Mr. Eliot as Governor-General of India. The nomination seemed to be secure, since, as we are told, 'both Mr. Dundas and Lord Cornwallis preferred him to any other person.' But even then a severe attack of illness compelled him to decline the honourable post.[1]

About a fortnight before the calamitous decease of Mr. Eliot we find in Mr. Pitt's correspondence, almost for the first time for many years, some reference to his failure of health. The toils of office and of Parliament at a most arduous crisis told at last severely upon a constitution that was never strong. He suffered greatly, as did Sir Robert Peel in 1846, from head-aches.

Writing to Dundas from Holwood, Pitt gives in the first place some account of Lord Malmesbury's negotiation, and then goes on to say:—

September 6, 1797.

. . . . This of course will prevent my coming to Walmer at present; besides which, my brother and Lady Chatham

[1] *Life of Wilberforce*, vol. ii. p. 192.

are still here, and (which is a less pleasant reason) I have a return of head-ache, which I have not been able to get rid of for several days, and which makes me less inclined to a long journey than even to a long letter. I hope you and Lady Jane have made good use of the return of summer, which, however, I fear is again taking its leave.

Busy as was this year to the Prime Minister, he found in it some intervals, and perhaps at this very juncture, for other studies. Bishop Tomline, at nearly the outset of his biography, thus refers to it : ' I had frequent opportunities of observing Mr. Pitt's accurate knowledge of the Bible, and I may, I trust, be allowed to mention the following anecdote :—In the year 1797 I was reading with him in manuscript my " Exposition of the First of the Thirty-nine Articles," which I afterwards published in the " Elements of Christian Theology." There were several quotations from Scripture, all of which he remembered, and made no observation upon them. At last we came to a quotation at which he stopped, and said, " I do not recollect that passage in the Bible, and it does not sound like Scripture." It was a quotation from the Apocrypha, which he had not read.'

It was also perhaps during the same period of sickness that Pitt sought solace in a translation from one of Horace's Odes. It is the same recreation which in our own day has sometimes pleased both Mr. Gladstone and Lord Derby. There is one version, or rather one paraphrase, as follows, in Pitt's own handwriting, which his last private Secretary has preserved. The manuscript has no date, but the paper bears the water-mark ' Portal & Cº., 1796.'

Hor. Carm., Lib. iii. Ode 2.

How bless'd, how glorious they who bravely fall,
Their lives devoted, at their country's call !
Death too pursues the coward as he flies ;
The dart o'ertakes him, and disgrac'd he dies.

> No mean repulse intrepid Virtue knows;
> Spotless and pure her native splendour glows;
> No gaudy ensigns her's, of borrowed pow'r,
> No fame, dependent on the varying hour;
> Bow'd to no yoke, her honours are her own,
> Nor court the breath of popular renown.
> On wing sublime resistless Virtue soars:
> And, spurning human haunts and earthly shores,
> To those whom godlike deeds forbid to die,
> Unbars the gates of Immortality.

Two events of great importance to our foreign policy occurred upon the Continent before the close of the year. A definitive treaty of peace between the Emperor of Germany and the French Republic was signed at Campo Formio on the 17th of October. The spoils of fallen Venice served to indemnify the Court of Vienna for its cession of Belgium and Lombardy, while the affairs which more especially concerned the Germanic Empire were referred to a future Congress to be held at Rastadt.

On the 16th of November, after a languishing illness, the King of Prussia died. He left the national exchequer empty, and the national reputation impaired; and his son and successor, Frederick William the Third, a young prince animated by the best intentions, but shy and self-diffident, confined himself in the first instance to schemes of internal reform.

In the ensuing month, writing to his friend Addington, from Walmer Castle, on the very day of Camperdown, Mr. Pitt speaks of his health as follows:—

October 11, 1797.

. . . . I am just returned from a very fine lounging ride, which pretended to be called shooting; and I am already so much the better for the continuance of Farquhar's prescription and (what perhaps is more effectual) for the air of Walmer, that I will not despair of having little or no occasion to say anything about myself.

Most signal was the fortune to England which delayed the equipment of the Dutch fleet until the mutiny in our own had passed away. It was not till near the close

of June that the preparations in the ports of Holland
were completed. Then Wolfe Tone and another Irish
exile, Lewines by name, were summoned in all haste to
the Hague. They found there General Hoche, who had
arrived only just before them. 'Good news for you!'
he cried; 'the two Dutch chiefs, the Governor-General
Daendels and the Admiral De Winter, desire to do
something striking that shall rescue their country from
decline. By the most indefatigable pains they have
got together at the Texel sixteen sail of the line, and
eight or ten frigates, all ready for sea, and in the best
condition. The object they have in view is the invasion of Ireland. For this object they will embark
the whole of their national troops, amounting to fifteen
thousand men, besides three thousand stands of arms
and eighty pieces of artillery.'

But there was an obstacle. The French Government
demanded that of the invading force five thousand men
at least should be French, and that General Hoche
should have the supreme command of the whole. On
the other hand the Dutch Government, which had
defrayed the entire expense, wished to have the entire
glory, of the expedition. Finally General Hoche, in
a generous spirit, waived his pretensions, going back to
Paris, and from thence to his army of the Sambre and
Meuse. The French Directors, not a little chafed,
sent orders to prepare another armament of their own
at Brest, for the command of which, when ready, they
intended Hoche. Meanwhile the negotiation at Lille
being now in progress, they did not scruple to keep up
the spirits of the Irish exiles by very positive but very
false assurances. They authorised General Simon to
declare in a letter, which was shown to Lewines and
Wolfe Tone, that 'the Directors would make no peace
with England in which the interests of Ireland should
not be fully discussed agreeably to the wishes of her
people.'[1]

[1] *Journal of Wolfe Tone*, June 21, 1797.

At this point the two Irishmen parted. Lewines set out from Holland to join General Hoche, while Wolfe Tone embarked on board the flag-ship at the Texel. The Dutch fleet was now ready to proceed, and under no unfavourable auspices at its first setting out, since Admiral Duncan off the Texel had at this time only eleven sail of the line. But as it chanced the Dutch ships were kept in port the entire summer by adverse winds. If ever a fair breeze did spring up, it invariably either changed or died away again in the course of a few hours. During this time the favourable season passed by, and the English fleet was reinforced. The journal of Wolfe Tone at this period abounds with dismal entries: 'July 19.—Wind foul still. Horrible! Horrible! Admiral De Winter and I endeavour to pass away the time playing the flute, which he does very well; we have some good duets.' 'July 26.—I am to-day eighteen days aboard, and we have not had eighteen minutes of fair wind. Well—'tis but in vain for soldiers to complain!'

At length, towards the middle of August, the Admiral summoned Wolfe Tone to a private conference. He pointed out that Duncan had increased his fleet to seventeen sail of the line; so that the English at the Texel had now a superiority in force above the Dutch. Moreover the Dutch troops, so long pent up on shipboard, had by this time consumed nearly all the provisions in store, so that even a victory over Duncan would not enable the voyage to proceed. Under such circumstances it would be necessary to relinquish the expedition to Ireland, although a descent on a much smaller scale upon some point of the English coast might still perhaps be attempted. Tone, though most bitterly chagrined, had little to allege against such considerations. Soon afterwards he set out to join General Hoche at his head-quarters of Wetzlar. Here, however, another mortification not less keen awaited him. Hoche, whom Wolfe Tone found in declining health, in a fortnight more expired. The General was not yet thirty years of age, and his illness has been frequently ascribed to poison from his enemies in France. Yet the journal of Wolfe Tone, who had no conceivable bias on this question, clearly shows that a neglected cough and rapid consumption were the sole causes of his death.

With General Hoche died the master spirit of the Irish expeditions. Henceforth the armament at Brest was slowly and languidly pursued. But on breaking off the negotiation at Lille, the French Directory resolved to strike a great blow at the Texel. They exerted their influence over the Government of Holland, and caused orders to be sent to Admiral De Winter to sally forth and give battle to the English fleet. Winter accordingly set sail with the first favourable wind. Duncan, on the other hand, having sustained some damage in the recent gales, had put back to Yarmouth Roads. But he had left behind some armed sloops to watch the enemy's fleet, and no sooner did he learn its advance than he returned with press of sail. He found De Winter's ships not yet out of sight of land; that land the Dutch coast between Camperdown and Egmont. Without delay he interposed between them and the shore, so as to compel an action had they even desired to avoid it. The two fleets might be taken as nearly equal in their ships, since the English had sixteen sail of the line and two frigates, and the Dutch fifteen sail of the line and four frigates; but the English were superior both in the number of men and in the weight of metal. A little after noon on the 11th of October, the English fleet, bearing down in two lines of attack, began the battle. Admiral Onslow in the Monarch led the van. As he went on, his Captain bade him notice that the enemy's ships lay close, and that he would find no passage through them. ‘The Monarch will make a passage,’ answered Onslow; and he still held on his course.

Then the Dutch ship opposite gave way, and he went through, engaging without delay the officer of corresponding rank—the enemy's Vice-Admiral.[1]

A battle commenced in such a spirit boded well for victory. Duncan himself, on board the Venerable and at the head of the second line, brought his vessel alongside the Vryheid (or Liberty), the flag-ship of De Winter. These two rival ships, each of them a seventy-four, sustained a well matched conflict within pistol-shot for upwards of three hours. So keen was the fire, that at last De Winter was, it is said, the only man on his quarter-deck who was not either wounded or killed. Not in the Vryheid alone, but throughout the fleet, the Dutch fought with a courage and perseverance well worthy their ancient renown. But Fortune declared against them. By four o'clock the Dutch Admiral had struck to Duncan, and the Dutch Vice-Admiral to Onslow; and the action ceasing, the English found themselves in possession of nine Dutch ships of the line, besides two of the Dutch frigates. The scanty remnant of De Winter's fleet, favoured by the shallows near the coast, sought refuge in the Texel; while Duncan, amidst a heavy gale, conveyed his prizes to the Nore. The loss in both fleets had been most severe. Of killed and wounded there had been upwards of eleven hundred on the Dutch, and upwards of a thousand on the English side.[2]

It is said that on the evening of this hard-fought day, and in the cabin of the Venerable, Duncan and De Winter sat down to whist together, and the latter, as he lost the game, placidly remarked that it was rather hard to be beaten twice in one day by the same opponent.

The battle of Camperdown (for such is the name it

---

[1] Brenton's *Naval History*, vol. i. p. 354.

[2] James's *Naval History*, vol. ii. p. 81. Duncan himself in his official report declares that 'the carnage on board the two ships that bore the Admirals' flags has been beyond all description.'

has borne) was hailed in England with merited applause. It was felt that the national honour had been worthily maintained against our ancient rivals at sea. It was felt that there was an end to all fears of invasion from that side. Strongest of all, perhaps, was the satisfaction—felt rather than expressed—that the very ships which had been so lately in open revolt, which had sent their own officers on shore, which had helped to blockade the Thames against their own government, had now so signally redeemed their character and done their duty. On the very day of his arrival at the Nore, the victorious Admiral—almost at the close of his active career, since he was now sixty-seven years of age—was raised to the Peerage with the rank of Viscount. Vice-Admiral Onslow was created a Baronet, and two Captains, Trollope and Fairfax, were made Knights Banneret. The thanks of Parliament were voted and a medal was struck to commemorate the victory.

Turning to the events of this year beyond the limits of Europe, we find Admiral Nelson achieve great personal distinction, although no public success. In the month of July he was detached by Earl St. Vincent to attack the fortified town of Santa Cruz, in the island of Teneriffe. He had a squadron of three ships of the line and as many frigates, but not, as he had asked, a body of troops on board. The difficulties of the coast combined with the want of soldiers to defeat this enterprise and the attack of Nelson. Yet in this attack both officers and men showed the most undaunted bravery, Nelson himself being grievously wounded, with the loss of his right arm.

In the West Indies, and earlier in the year, another Spanish colony, Trinidad, had yielded to an English expedition commanded by Sir Ralph Abercromby, and it was this conquest which at Lille the English Government had desired to retain.

Pitt, as we have seen, was on the Kentish coast at

the time of the battle of Camperdown. His letter from thence to Lady Chatham will certainly be read with considerable interest :—

Walmer Castle, October 22, 1797.

My dear Mother,—I need not say how much satisfaction and comfort I received from your most kind and welcome letter, which reached me yesterday, and brought me the best proof of your returning strength. I hope, however, that your desire to give pleasure to others will not make you repeat the effort of writing when it can be attended with inconvenience. You have a secretary[1] who will always have the goodness to let us know how you do, which is the point most essential. My project of visiting the fleet in my way hither failed, as none of our ships or their prizes had reached the Nore when we passed ; but this disappointment is amply repaired by a visit from Lord Duncan, who is now here as well as Lord Hood. The latter came with us from town, and is, to do him justice, as proud and happy in the victory of an Admiral even of Keppel's school as he could be if it were his own. Lord Duncan joined us very opportunely on Friday at Dover Castle, where we had gone the day before to be present at a *feu de joie* in honour of his victory. Our Admirals leave us to-morrow, but we shall probably stay here till the end of the week, and shall probably visit the fleet in our way back to-morrow sennight, when the King intends to go on board. Such a ceremony will be no bad prelude for the opening of the Session.

Ever, my dear Mother, &c.,   W. PITT.

The Earl of Mornington was one of this party. He had recently obtained from Pitt the office of Governor-General of India, together with an English peerage, and was now preparing to commence his most brilliant Eastern career. In a Memorandum, many years later, bearing date November, 1836, he has thus described the scene :—

' In the month of September, 1797, I went to Walmer Castle to meet Mr. Pitt and Mr. Dundas, and to receive my last instructions. I found Mr. Pitt in the highest

<hr>

[1] Her granddaughter, Miss Eliot.

spirits, entertaining officers and country gentlemen with
his usual hospitality.   Amongst others Admiral Duncan
was his constant and favourite guest.   His fleet was
then in the Downs preparing for the memorable victory
of Camperdown.   The Admiral was a lively and jovial
companion, and seemed to be quite delighted with Mr.
Pitt's society.   I embarked for India early in the
month of November, 1797, and I returned to England
in January, 1806.'[1]

Parliament met again on the 2nd of November.
The King in his opening Speech had expressed his great
concern at the failure of the late negotiations, which he
attributed ' solely to the evasive conduct, the unwarrantable pretensions, and the inordinate ambition of
those with whom we have to contend, and, above all,
to their inveterate animosity against these kingdoms.'
Fox, Grey, Sheridan, and their principal friends continued to absent themselves from these discussions ;
but their secession was far from producing the effect
which they had hoped.   In general, so far as we can
gather, it was disapproved by the public.   It was often
and bitterly censured in the House of Commons.   On
the rare occasions when Fox and his friends reappeared
in their places, they found it necessary to defend themselves before they could proceed to inveigh against the
Ministers.

It was perhaps at this period that Erskine expressed
some willingness, had he been invited, to join the
administration.   So at least writes Mr. Rose in 1806 :
—' His political attachment to Mr. Fox has not been
steady and uniform.   I recollect Mr. Pitt telling me
many years ago that on meeting Mr. Erskine at the
Opera the latter took occasion to tell him that he had
no *determined* political attachments.'[2]

It can scarcely on the whole be doubted that in this,
as in nearly all other Parliamentary secessions, the

[1] See the *Quarterly Review*, No. cxiv. p. 190.
[2] *Diaries*, &c., vol. ii. p. 253.

seceders lost instead of gaining ground. Nor was it only because their retreat was denounced as unpatriotic and unwarrantable; nor only because their names were less frequently before the public. The small minority which remained at its post stood forth in an advantageous contrast. Some members of the Opposition who continued to take part in the debates rose at once from a secondary to a prominent place. Such was especially the case with Sir Francis Burdett and with Mr. Tierney.

George Tierney was born at Gibraltar in 1761; the son of a merchant engaged in the Spanish trade. He was educated for the Bar, and first entered Parliament in 1789 as one of the representatives of Colchester. But in 1796, after some contests at Southwark, an Election Committee declared him the sitting Member. The absence of Fox gave for the first time full play to his eminent abilities. With considerable knowledge of finance he combined great power of lucid statement, while for irony and sarcasm he had, as it were, an inborn aptitude. He now attached himself in an especial manner to the Budgets of Pitt, of which he became the constant, the unsparing, and the able critic. Yet he was far from confining his attacks to financial subjects only. Speaking on the 7th of November, he frankly said: 'I am determined to give my negative not only to this, but to every other act of the present administration. I can assure the House that I have a general retainer for the whole Session.' Nor did he fail in this engagement. His conduct exhibited all that undiscriminating opposition which his language promised.

The first Budget that called forth in their full extent the powers of Mr. Tierney was explained to the House of Commons on the 24th of November. It was no doubt of a most stringent kind. There was a deficiency announced of nineteen millions. The Minister proposed to cover this alarming void, partly by a new loan of twelve millions, and partly by a general tax to raise

seven millions within the year. 'I am aware,' said
Mr. Pitt, 'that this sum does far exceed anything
which has been raised in any former period at one time,
but I trust I have stated sufficient reasons to show that
it is a wise and necessary measure.' The plan was to
augment the Assessed Taxes at once to three times,
and progressively to four times, their existing amount,
with, however, some deductions and exceptions in favour
of those least well able to pay. The number of persons
immediately affected by this impost was calculated by
Pitt at about 800,000.

So vast an increase in taxes already looked upon as
inquisitorial and oppressive could not fail to arouse the
public discontent. It might of itself sufficiently explain
the adverse reception of Pitt on his passage to St. Paul's
about three weeks afterwards. Fox as Member for
Westminster, and Sheridan as Member for Stafford,
were requested by their constituents to come back and
oppose the measure. Not sorry, perhaps, of the plea
for again appearing in their places, they stood forth
at the Second Reading and spoke with their wonted
power. 'What is the object of the war?' said Sheridan. 'The war is continued for the sole purpose
of keeping nine worthless Ministers in their places.'
'What will be the results of this Bill?' said Fox.
'It tends to the immediate destruction of our trade,
to the annihilation of our fortunes, and possibly to the
loss of liberty of our persons. . . . . Gentlemen seem
to forget that we affect at least to call ourselves the
representatives of the people. I know that we are no
such thing, but we call ourselves so. Yet up to this
time in this House only fifteen members could be
found to vote against a measure upon which out of this
House there is not merely a majority but an unanimity
of dissent!'[1] But to both these great orators Pitt made
a reply of which it may be said that it lost nothing of
its point and vigour by its superior calmness and dig-

[1] *Parl. Hist.*, vol. xxxiii. p. 1106, 1112, and 1121.

nity of tone. ' I will leave it,' he said, ' to the House
to judge how far those who in principle give the enemy
a right to ask all—who by decrying our resources give
them confidence to advance every pretension—and who
kindly inform them that from our inability to resist
they may extort whatever they demand—whether these,
I say, are the true friends of their country, or the en-
lightened advocates of peace !'

The real necessity of the case was so apparent that,
notwithstanding the popular excitement out of doors,
the minority against the Second Reading was only 50.
In the Committee Pitt made divers alterations and
modifications in the scheme ; but the popular excitement had increased, and at the Third Reading, when
Fox and Sheridan again appeared, the minority rose
to 75.

It had been deemed right to celebrate by a solemn
act of public worship the three great naval victories
achieved by Lords Howe, St. Vincent, and Duncan over
the French, the Spaniards, and the Dutch. The 19th
of December was appointed as the day of Public
Thanksgiving, and there was a special Service at St.
Paul's. To this went in solemn procession the King
and Queen, the Royal Family, the Cabinet and the
Foreign Ministers, the two Houses of Parliament, the
chief naval commanders or their representatives, and
a body of seamen and marines. In general the temper
of the people was in accordance with the purpose of
the day. But Pitt on his way to the Cathedral was
in some places hooted at and otherwise insulted by
the multitude. In consequence of their conduct he
did not return at once in his carriage, but stopped to
dine with the Speaker and some other gentlemen in
Doctors' Commons, and in the evening he was escorted
home by a party of the London Light Horse.[1]

Here is a letter addressed by Pitt to his mother at
the close of this most eventful year.

[1] *Ann. Register*, 1797, p. 80.

Downing Street, Friday, December 29, 1797.

My dear Mother,—An evening's leisure, from there not having been a sufficient number to make a House of Commons to-day, gives me an opportunity, which I have long wanted, of writing to you. I have nothing new to tell as to what is going on here. The Finance measure (which occupies most of our time) proceeds exactly as might be expected with a general admission of its necessity, and with a great disposition in every quarter to object where it will feel the burden. But on the whole I have little doubt that we shall have finished this business very satisfactorily by the end of next week. I remain extremely well, and have holidays enough in the interval of each week to make up completely for the confinement at other times, which, however, has been less than usual during the Session.

You will be very glad to make Mr. Mitchell happy by telling him that I can give him the living of East Mersea in Essex, now vacant, and worth, as I am told, between three and four hundred pounds a-year. Residence will not, I I understand, be required, but a liberal allowance to the curate. It is in the gift of the Crown, and in the diocese of the Bishop of London. If your usual secretary or any other informs me that Mr. Mitchell accepts, the presentation shall be made out immediately. My brother and Lady Chatham are gone, as you probably know, to Apthorp. My brother's return, as well as Lord Westmoreland's, depends on the necessity of attendance in the House of Lords. I rather think they will not be wanted. Pray give my kind remembrances to Mrs. Stapleton, and love to my dear niece, who, I hope, retains her attachment to Burton.

Ever, my dear Mother, &c.,   W. PITT.

In 1796 there were no less than sixteen and in 1797 no less than fourteen British peerages conferred: a vast multiplication of honours, and scarcely even in such times to be defended. Among them were included many of Mr. Pitt's Parliamentary supporters in the House of Commons. Mr. Rolle became Lord Rolle, Mr. Lascelles became Lord Harewood, Sir Gilbert Elliot became Lord Minto, Sir John Rous became Lord Rous.

Mr. Thomas Powys became Lord Lilford, Mr. Robert Smith became Lord Carrington.

On this last name let me for a moment linger. It is not that I would here seek to delineate the character of one very dear to me, as many years since I sought to do.[1] It is not that in this work I am entitled to express my grateful memory of my grandfather's many acts of most generous kindness. It is not merely because I am proud of my descent from one who himself descended from one of the burgesses of Nottingham, and, never claiming to himself any descent beyond them, raised himself by his integrity of character and his thorough mastery of all points of business from a banker's office to the Peerage. It is not merely because I deem him a worthy co-mate of Lord Overstone and the late Lord Ashburton. But there is one circumstance connected with his elevation that I am bound to notice, not as the descendant of Lord Carrington, but as the biographer of Mr. Pitt.

I am bound then, as I think, to notice some Memoirs which Sir Nathaniel Wraxall wrote for posthumous publication, and which in fact did not appear till the year 1836. These Memoirs display in many passages the bitter feelings of a disappointed candidate for Parliamentary and official distinction. It is in such a spirit that he approaches the peerage to Mr. Robert Smith. He ascribes that peerage to corrupt motives on the part of Mr. Pitt as 'in return for pecuniary assistance,' as rendering it probable 'that even his elevated mind could so far bend to circumstances.'

Such a calumny, however, did not remain without contradiction. It was exposed in a letter from Lord Carrington himself, which first appeared in the 'Quarterly Review' of the same year.[2] The writer of that article introduces the letter as follows :—

'Sir Nathaniel no doubt thought that it was not

---

[1] *Ann. Register*, 1838, p. 225.
[2] No. cxiv. p. 456.

likely that Lord Carrington should survive to repel by
his own testimony this slander on his illustrious friend.
Fortunately Lord Carrington still lives,—retaining in
a venerable old age all the clearness of intellect, the
amiability of character, and the nice sense of honour
which recommended him above half a century ago to
the friendship of Mr. Pitt; and we are happy to be able
to lay before our readers a letter written, without any
expectation that it would ever become public, by Lord
Carrington, to the friend and contemporary of himself
and Mr. Pitt, the Right Hon. Thomas Grenville, immediately after the appearance of Wraxall's publication.

> " Wycombe Abbey, August 7, 1836.
>
> " My dear Sir,—A thousand thanks to you for your kind
recollection of me. It brings to my mind the pleasure I
enjoyed in your society in former days. I never recollect
your name without the kindest feelings.
>
> " I should have broke in upon your retirement at Drop-
more, to pay my respects to Lady Grenville, and to see you,
but I have been confined to my couch for the last three
weeks by an accident to my leg, which, being neglected, became very troublesome. As soon as I am able to put it to
the ground, I shall direct my steps to Dropmore.
>
> " Have you seen the recent publication called 'Sir N.
Wraxall's Posthumous Memoirs'? It commences more than
fifty years ago, and contains many of the same sort of calum-
nies with which his former work was chargeable. In the
earliest pages he has thought fit to state that I owed my
peerage to money transactions with Mr. Pitt. You, who
knew our illustrious friend so well, will picture to yourself
the indignation with which such an offer on my part, however disguised and covered, would have been received by
him, and I am sure also that you would think me incapable
of proposing it. Sir N. Wraxall also, in another part,
alludes to Mr. Pitt's 'gratitude' to me and states that, at
his death, a patent was in progress to raise me in the
peerage. Such a thing was never offered by him or desired
by me. The suppression of these charges for forty years
will certainly, as Sir N. Wraxall intended, have the effect of
screening him from personal responsibility, but, I think, no

other. Lord Abercorn is also named, and, I am confident, with equal falsehood, as being concerned in this shameful traffic.

"I can assert, with perfect confidence and truth, that, during the twenty-five years in which I enjoyed Mr. Pitt's friendship, not only no money transactions ever passed between us, but that not a single word of allusion to such a subject was ever spoken by either of us. You may remember towards the close of his life the various offers of assistance which Mr. Pitt received, and rejected; and with what privacy a subscription was entered into by his particular friends (unknown to himself at the time, and I believe ever after) to discharge some pressing demands.

"I owe gratitude to Providence for having extended my life to eighty-four years in health and spirits, but still more for having enabled me to contradict in person a calumny so unmerited. I am, my dear Sir, &c.,   CARRINGTON."[1]

In November, 1797, appeared the first number of the 'Anti-Jacobin.' It came forth periodically, that is twice a-week, till Midsummer the next year, and it certainly produced a strong political effect. It brought excellent humour and ridicule into the service of the Administration. It turned to Pitt's side what hitherto had flowed against him, the current of poetical wit. The chief founder and promoter of the work was Mr. Canning. In the first number since the Introduction he gave in English *Sapphics* his well-known 'Knife-grinder' holding up to derision the false claims of a 'Friend of Humanity' on the new French pattern.

> Tell me, Knife-grinder, how came you to grind knives?
> Did some rich man tyrannically use you?
> Was it the squire? or parson of the parish?
> Or the attorney?

The *Sapphics* which it was here designed to ridicule were those of Mr. Southey, and the 'Friend of Humanity' glanced at was Mr. Tierney.

In prose also Mr. Canning made several home-thrusts. He took off with great spirit the boastful and rambling

---

[1] Lord Carrington died on the 18th of September, 1838.

style of Erskine whenever he had not a jury to address.
Here is in some part the pretended speech to the Whig
Club:—'Mr. Erskine concluded in a strain of agonising
and impressive eloquence. He said he had been a soldier
and a sailor, and had a son at Winchester School. He
had been called by special retainers during the summer
to many different and distant parts of the country—
travelling chiefly in post-chaises. He stood here as a
man—he stood in the eye, indeed in the hand of God—
to whom, in the presence of the company and waiters,
he solemnly appealed. He was of noble, perhaps Royal
blood—he had a house at Hampstead—and he was convinced of a necessity of a thorough and radical reform.'

This is only a caricature; but I may observe in passing that it differs very little from the portraits. Several
grave observers will be found to speak of Erskine in
nearly the same terms. Dr. Somerville, for example,
the Minister of Jedburgh and the historian of Queen
Anne, came up to town in 1791 to promote the repeal
of the Test Act. He attended at Lord Malmesbury's
house a meeting of some Opposition members, and has
described to the very life the scene before him :—

'I remember I was amused with observing that
while Mr. Fox's countenance indicated profound attention to all that was said, his fingers were incessantly
in motion, catching the drops that fell from the wax
candles, and turning and forming them into little pel-
lets. Mr. Erskine once and again rose from his seat,
mentioning the burden of business that was in his
hands, and the necessity he was under of leaving the
company, naming the number of briefs on which he
must be prepared to plead next morning in the Courts
at Westminster. The number I do not now recollect,
but it was so enormous that after he had left the company I could not help expressing my surprise. Mr.
Windham replied, "You are not to believe all that Mr.
Erskine says;" and the other gentlemen smiled.' [1]

[1] *My own Life and Times*, by Dr. Somerville, p. 239, ed. 1861.

Next to Mr. Canning the principal founder of the
'Anti-Jacobin' was Mr. George Ellis, who had now
attached himself to Pitt, but who in earlier years had
been among the writers of the Rolliad. One day at
a Ministerial party he was called on by one of the
guests to give the secret history of the first poem.
Mr. Ellis seemed a little embarrassed, but Pitt, leaning
forward with much good humour, as ready to hear him,
quoted the line—

> Immo age, et a primâ dic hospes origine nobis.[1]

The aptness of the quotation was at the time admired.
How appropriate the word *Hospes* as applied to a recent
convert ; and with how much good taste did Pitt avoid
the *erroresque tuos* of a succeeding line !

Not only French politics or principles were attacked
in the 'Anti-Jacobin.' There was a poem, the 'Loves
of the Triangles,' in ridicule of Dr. Darwin's 'Loves of
the Plants.' There was a play, 'The Rovers,' in ridicule of the early dramas of Kotzebue and Schiller.
In this Mr. Canning introduced with admirable humour
an account of the signature of Magna Charta according
to the style of a modern newspaper. 'Yes, here,' cries
the patriot Beefington, 'here it is, just above the advertisements. And look, there are some further particulars.
—Extract of a letter from Egham.—" My dear friend,
we are all here in high spirits—the interesting event
which took place this morning at Runnymede in the
neighbourhood of this town. . . . . . . Messengers were
instantly despatched to Cardinal Pandulfo ; and their
Majesties, after partaking of a cold collation, returned
to Windsor." '

In the 'Rovers' Mr. Canning also brought in perhaps the most popular piece in the whole collection—
the song of Rogero in prison recalling his youthful days

at the U-
niversity of Göttingen,
niversity of Göttingen.

---

[1] *Æneid*, lib. 1, vers. 753.

It is said that when Mr. Canning showed to Mr. Pitt the first five stanzas of this song, the Minister was so much amused with it that he took up a pen and composed the last stanza on the spot. That stanza is as follows, and probably, as I have heard it called, the best of them all :—

> Sun, moon, and thou vain world adieu,
> That Kings and priests are plotting in ;
> Here doomed to starve on water-gru-
> el, never shall I see the U-
>   niversity of Göttingen,
>   niversity of Göttingen.

It has also been said that in the poem entitled 'New Morality,' and dated July 9, 1798, Mr. Pitt was the author of the fine lines beginning 'So thine own oak.'[1] But I look in vain for any positive or contemporaneous testimony in support of these allegations; and I do not think it clear that Mr. Pitt added even a single line of his own to this famous collection.

The Latin verses in the volume were by Lord Mornington, and the translations from them by Lord Carlisle.

The talent and the acrimony of the 'Anti-Jacobin' could not fail to raise up numerous answers, or rather, indeed, counter-attacks. Most of these were of very inferior merit. There was one, however, an ' Epistle to the Editor of the Anti-Jacobin,' which was written by Lord Melbourne, many years afterwards Prime Minister, then the Hon. William Lamb, a young man of nineteen, fresh from Cambridge. Canning took into his own hands the rejoinder, which thus commences :—

> Bard of the borrowed lyre ! to whom belong
> The shreds and remnants of each hackney song ;
> Whose verse thy friends in vain for wit explore,
> And count but one good line in eighty-four.

It is recorded by tradition from these times that

---

[1] Notes to the *Anti-Jacobin*, by Mr. Charles Edmonds, p. 184 and 241, ed. 1854.

the 'one good line' of Mr. Lamb to which Mr. Canning thus referred was the last of the following couplet :—

> By Morpeth's gait, important, proud, and big—
> By Leveson Gower's crop-imitating wig.

Lord Granville Leveson Gower, afterwards the first Earl Granville, wore a brown wig to resemble the natural hair, which was a novelty in 1798, and which, therefore, drew upon him the notice of a satirist. Thus after many years were the pleasantries of the Rolliad requited.

CHAPTER XXV.

1798.

Dinner in celebration of Fox's birthday—Dismissal of the Duke of Norfolk from his employments—Patriotic subscriptions—Pitt's scheme for increasing the Supplies—The *Armée d'Angleterre* — Correspondence between the United Irishmen and the French Government—State of Ireland—Progress of the Conspiracy against England—Excesses of both parties—The Earl of Moira —Lord Chancellor Clare—Arrest of the Irish emissaries to France, and of conspirators in Dublin—Death of Lord Edward Fitzgerald—The Rebellion—The 'United Army of Wexford'—Slaughter of Protestant prisoners—Marquis Cornwallis appointed Lord Lieutenant—Lord Castlereagh—Trials of the conspirators.

It became necessary for the Houses, contrary to uniform practice, to sit through the first days of January, that the Finance Bills might be passed. Except on rare occasions Fox and his friends continued to absent themselves from Parliament. They deemed that they better fulfilled their public duty by assiduous agitation out of doors. Thus on the 24th of January there was a great public dinner at the Crown and Anchor in celebration of Fox's birthday. At least two thousand persons attended. Fox himself was present, and the Duke of Norfolk took the chair. Three new songs on the occasion were produced by Captain Morris. Horne Tooke,

so recently the opponent of Fox on the Westminster
hustings, now stood forward to say that he approved of
the conduct of Mr. Fox ever since Mr. Fox had fully
declared himself the advocate of Parliamentary Reform.
The toast of the evening was given by the Duke in the
following words :—‘ We are met in a moment of most
serious difficulty to celebrate the birth of a man dear
to the friends of freedom. I shall only recall to your
memory that not twenty years ago the illustrious George
Washington had not more than two thousand men to
rally round him when his country was attacked. America is now free. This day full two thousand men are
assembled in this place : I leave you to make the application. I propose to you the health of Charles Fox !’

Such language might be deemed sufficiently decisive.
But after the Duke's own health had been given, His
Grace, in returning thanks, further said : ‘ Give me
leave, before I sit down, to call on you to drink our
Sovereign's health—The Majesty of the People !’ [1]

Neither of these speeches, as it appears to me, can
be rightly judged without some reference to the time
at which they were spoken. Be it remembered that
the example of Washington was held forth at the very
period when a rebellion was impending in Ireland, and
when aid to that rebellion had been promised from
France. Be it remembered that the Sovereignty of
the People was invoked at the very period when that
principle had become upon the Continent the watchword of more than one victorious insurrection. Sentiments which at one time may be passed over as Utopian,
must at another be resented as seditious. Proceeding
on these views, the Duke of Norfolk was at once dismissed from the two offices which he held under the
Crown—the Lord Lieutenancy of the West Riding, and
the command of a Militia Regiment.

While thus upon the one hand the adversaries of
the Government went further and further in their

[1] *Ann. Register*, 1798, part ii. p. 6.

democratic language, there was upon the other side by a natural reaction an increased zeal in its support. Already in the preceding December—when the financial scheme of Pitt was in Committee —a practical suggestion had been thrown out by the Speaker. He was confident, he said, that many persons of affluent fortune, sensible of the delicacy which forbore from searching too minutely into capital, would be willing to come forward with free contributions beyond the rate of their assessment, and he advised a clause to give such persons the opportunity. The Minister availed himself of the idea, and during the months of February and March, 1798, such contributions rapidly flowed in. To receive them, hustings, as though for an election, had been raised beneath one of the piazzas of the Royal Exchange. There came crowding by hundreds merchants and tradesmen of all ranks, and with divers gifts, varying from one guinea to 3,000*l*. On the first day the subscriptions exceeded 46,000*l*. Nor did that generous spirit decline. Mr. Robert Peel, father of the celebrated statesman, and at that time in partnership with Mr. Yates as a manufacturer of calicoes at Bury in Lancashire, paid in, from a loyal impulse, no less than 10,000*l*.[1] As I have heard the story told, Mr. Peel having subscribed this large sum on the spur of the moment and without consulting his senior partner, travelled back to Bury in some anxiety as to that partner's assent. But Mr. Yates had a spirit as loyal as his own. On being told by Mr. Peel what he had done, he merely turned round and said, ' You might as well have made it 20,000*l*. while you were about it ! '

In relating the fact, Mr. Macpherson adds, ' Is there any other country on the globe that could produce a manufacturer who can spare such a sum ?' Thus spoke Mr. Macpherson, the annalist of Commerce, in 1805 ; but what would he have said had he survived to see the Manchester Exhibition of 1857 ?

[1] Macpherson's *History of Commerce*, vol. iv. p. 440.

Contributions were received from public bodies also. The City of London subscribed 10,000*l.*, and the Bank of England 200,000*l.* On the whole, these free-will offerings, exclusive of 300,000*l.* which subsequently came from India, amounted to no less a sum than two millions sterling.

But great as might be this resource, the public necessities were greater still. On the 2nd of April Pitt found it requisite to bring forward a new scheme for increasing the supplies. This he desired to do by a partial commutation of the Land Tax. Till then the Land Tax had been granted year by year by Acts of Parliament. Its annual rate had long been fixed at four shillings in the pound, and its annual produce was about two millions. Pitt now proposed to make it perpetual, with a power of redemption; the sums thence accruing to be applied to the reduction of the National Debt. By these means not only would the public revenue be to some extent assisted, but a new impulse, it was hoped, would be given to the public credit. The main objection to the proposal lay in this —that it tended to perpetuate the most grievous inequalities. There had been no new assessment since the year 1692. The value of property since that time had completely changed. Many tracts, as in Lancashire and Yorkshire, which were then mere barren moors, and which were assessed accordingly, had since that time been covered by huge factories and flourishing towns. The result was that as a whole the northern counties bore but the smallest fraction of the rate which the southern counties paid. 'But then observe,' said Pitt, 'that during a century which has now elapsed, no proposal for a more equal partition has been ever entertained. Is it more likely, then, looking to the future, that the anomaly would be corrected, even if the tax continued to depend upon a yearly vote?'

In both Houses, however, the Bill was for the most

part resisted on other grounds. To perpetuate this tax
at all or in any form was represented as a most wanton
oppression of the landed interest. 'Take care,' cried
Lord Sheffield in the Commons, 'not to drive gentlemen from the country!' In the Peers, Lord Thurlow
went even further, and taunted the squires with their
readiness to bear whatever burthens might be laid
upon them. He revived a jest which had been current
in the days of Sir Robert Walpole, that the country
gentlemen were like sheep, which quietly suffered themselves to be shorn and re-shorn, but that the moneyed
men were like hogs, which never failed to grunt and
stir if even one bristle was touched![1] Yet in spite of
such arguments, if arguments they must be called, the
Bill passed by overwhelming majorities.

During the time that this Bill was still in progress,
the public necessities, mainly resulting from the threats
and preparations of the enemy, compelled Pitt to bring
forward what he termed his second Budget. In a
Committee of Ways and Means, on the 25th of April,
he announced that there must be an addition of three
millions to his former Estimates. There must be a
new loan to that amount; and to provide for the yearly
interest divers small imposts were proposed—a tax
especially on armorial bearings, and a tax on the higher
qualities of tea. There was little choice, and these
measures passed accordingly. Nor did the Houses
shrink, when the Irish Rebellion arose, from the
painful duty of suspending the Habeas Corpus and
renewing the Alien Acts. But here I must revert in
more detail to the designs of the plotters in Ireland
and of their confederates in France.

On the very day after the proclamation in Paris of
the Peace of Campo Formio, the Directory issued an

---

[1] The debates in the House of Lords upon the Land-Tax are, I
know not for what reason, omitted both in the Parliamentary
History and in Dodsley's *Annual Register*. But they are briefly
given in Rivington's (1798, p. 233).

Order enjoining the formation of an army on the coast to be called *l'Armée d'Angleterre*, and appointing General Bonaparte to its command. 'Bravo!' writes Wolfe Tone: 'this looks as if they were in earnest!'

Bonaparte did indeed at first display his characteristic energy. He paid a visit of inspection to the northern ports, and directed active preparations. But by degrees his mind, and the minds of the Directors, appear to have turned to the superior importance of an expedition against Egypt. That expedition was, though with the greatest secrecy, planned for the spring of 1798. Most especially was it concealed from the Irish emissaries or exiles, who continued to be flattered with the hopes of undivided aid.

Ever since General Hoche had earnestly applied himself to the armament at Brest, there had been frequent communications on the matter between Paris and Dublin. In this perilous correspondence the chiefs of the United Irishmen trusted much rather to agents than to letter. In 1796 they had sent over Lord Edward Fitzgerald and Mr. Arthur O'Connor, and the latter held a secret conference with General Hoche on the frontier of Switzerland.[1] Subsequently they despatched Mr. Edward Lewines to reside as their Minister in France, and later still Dr. Mac Nevin on only a temporary mission. Besides these, as time proceeded there was a large accession at Paris of Irish refugees. Napper Tandy and the younger Tone had fled from Dublin; Lowry, Tennant, and several others from Belfast. But it may be doubted whether these men in their exile added much to the strength of their cause. According to General Kilmaine, who discussed them with Wolfe Tone, 'the conduct of many of the Irish in Paris was such as to reflect credit neither on themselves nor their country. There was nothing to be heard of amongst them but denunciations; and if every

[1] See the details of this expedition in Moore's *Life of Lord Edward Fitzgerald*, vol. i. p. 278.

one of them separately spoke truth, all the rest were rascals!'[1]

Looking to Ireland itself, the prospect was gloomy indeed. Augmented discontents, more unmitigated violence, had followed the recall of Lord Fitzwilliam. Then, as for many years subsequent in Ireland, moderation was of all qualities the very last to be appreciated or even understood. By a frequent and fatal rebound the excesses on the one side produced excesses on the other. The passionate enemies of English connexion—the United Irishmen or Defenders—were confronted by as passionate loyalists, who assumed the name of Orangemen, in honour of King William the Third.

The first conflict between these two exasperated parties took place in the county of Armagh. It was on the 21st of December, 1795. Then a body of Defenders, though much superior in numbers, even, it is said, in the proportion of ten to one, was repulsed and routed, with the loss of forty-eight killed and many more wounded.[2] This conflict was called, from the name of a neighbouring village, the battle of the Diamond. It was celebrated at the time as a great Protestant victory, and even beyond the reigns of the Georges continued—very little to the credit of the persons using it—a favourite political toast in a part of Ireland.[3]

Some important consequences ensued from this random fight. The victors proceeded immediately after the conflict to search the houses of all whom they suspected as allies of the vanquished. Wherever they found arms, or perhaps if even they did not, they proceeded to demolish the furniture and to plunder the goods. In most cases, probably, these outrages should be ascribed not to the Orangemen who fought, but rather to the rabble that followed at their heels. We

---

[1] *Journal of Wolfe Tone*, June 16, 1798.
[2] *Memoirs on the different Rebellions in Ireland*, by Sir Richard Musgrave, vol. i. p. 80.
[3] See the debate in the House of Commons of December 5, 1837.

find an unexceptionable witness, Lord Gosford, at that time Chairman of the Sessions in Armagh, lament the 'ferocious cruelty' which had been perpetrated on unoffending Roman Catholics, and declare that they had been or were at the mercy of 'lawless banditti.'[1] The result was a large emigration of the Roman Catholics from the county of Armagh to the province of Connaught.

Another consequence of the battle of the Diamond was the organisation of the Orange Society. The name had existed some time before, but the first Orange Lodge was formed in commemoration of that victory. Other Lodges grew up in rapid succession; a Grand Master with a Staff of Officers was named; arms were provided; and thus throughout the province of Ulster a large and well-disciplined body was arrayed.

When the Irish Parliament met in the January ensuing, the Attorney-General (Arthur Wolfe) immediately gave notice of two Bills: the one an Insurrection Act, to prohibit the peasantry in disturbed districts from being out of their houses between sunset and sunrise; the other an Indemnity Bill, to absolve the magistrates who, in seeking to preserve the peace, had gone beyond the strict limits of the law. He also proposed to make a conspiracy to murder a felony; for so frequent, he said, were such conspiracies, that the idea of assassination had become as familiar as the idea of fowling.[2] A little later he laid before the House four Resolutions, designed as the basis for legislative measures, and declaring in strong terms both the disturbed state of the country, and the necessity of more effectual power to the magistrates. Not only should they have power to search for and secure arms, ammunition, and weapons of offence, but also in Sessions to send disorderly persons who had no visible means of gaining a subsistence to serve on board the fleet. These measures were carried by an immense majority, notwithstanding

[1] Address of Lord Gosford, December 21, 1795.
[2] See the *Irish Parliamentary Debates* of January 21, 1796.

the exertions of Mr. Grattan, Mr. Ponsonby, Sir Lawrence Parsons, and a few besides.

With these measures passed, the Session ended in April, 1796; and when the next commenced in October of the same year a further step—the suspension of the Habeas Corpus—was proposed. This seemed no unreasonable demand at the very moment when conspiracy was so rife in Ireland, and when a French army of invasion was embarking in the ports of Brittany; yet, like the preceding measures, it was most keenly opposed. On coming to the vote, however, there appeared a large majority, amounting to 137, in favour of the Suspension, while against it was a mere handful—only seven! 'I know not,' cried Grattan, 'where you are leading me —from one strong Bill to another, until I see a gulf before me at whose abyss I recoil!'[1]

Grattan himself was not much more successful in behalf of the Roman Catholics. Three days afterwards he moved the following as an abstract Resolution: 'That the admissibility of persons professing the Roman Catholic Religion to seats in Parliament is consistent with the safety of the Crown, and the connexion of Ireland with Great Britain.' But this proposal, which in the debate was stigmatised as 'dangerous and seditious,' was upon a division rejected by 143 votes against 19.

It seems clear that the members of Opposition, however reduced in numbers, might have done good service in the Irish House of Commons. They might have kept a just mean between the Orangemen and the Defenders. They might have protested against outrage or oppression in whatever quarter it appeared. They might have sought to crush conspiracy in Ireland, and to repel invasion from France, whilst striving to promote a healing and conciliatory system of public policy. But all such considerations seem to have yielded in their minds to the superior importance of following

[1] *Life of Grattan*, by his Son, vol. iv. p. 257.

Mr. Fox. When, in the spring of 1797, the English statesman declared his intention of seceding in great measure from the Parliament of England, Mr. Ponsonby and his few remaining friends could think of no better course than to declare that they also would secede in great measure from the Parliament of Ireland.

Grattan was not exactly of the same section, nor did he pursue exactly the same course. With higher spirit he determined that he would not retain a seat in Parliament if he ceased to fulfil its duties. Therefore, while concurring in the measure of secession, he issued an Address to his constituents, the citizens of Dublin, to announce that at the approaching General Election (it took place in the summer of 1797) he should decline to offer himself again a candidate. That the object of this Address was lofty-minded scarcely need be stated; that its language was imprudent was afterwards acknowledged by himself. 'It was well written,' said he, twenty years later, 'but it tended to inflame.'[1] His colleague in the representation of Dublin, Lord Henry Fitzgerald, took the same course, and refused to stand again.

Nor was it only from Parliament that Grattan retired. Partly because his health had become impaired, and partly because he disapproved the military system pursued by General Lake as Commander of the Northern District, he threw up his post in a Corps of Yeomanry, which, on its recent formation, he had joined. Thus it happened that in the stirring and momentous period which ensued—the most stirring and momentous in the recent history of Ireland—the great patriot, the foremost Irish politician of that period, took no part at all. Scarcely could he have been more secluded from his country's affairs, had he been already laid in his honoured tomb at Westminster Abbey.

The General Election in the summer of 1797 made little alteration in the strength of parties. From the

---

[1] *Memoirs of Grattan*, by his Son. vol. iv. p. 316.

immense majority in favour of the Government measures, and from the continued absence of the Opposition chiefs, the proceedings in Parliament lost greatly of their interest. Public attention began to turn from the speeches within to the events without the walls. There the two hostile colours, Green and Orange, stood as before in fierce array against each other. There a bloody conflict between them was sometimes experienced, and always apprehended. There each party, as though conscious of the coming struggle, was busy in recruiting new adherents.

At this period the confederacy of the United Irishmen was governed by a secret Directory. Like the French, which it took for its model, and with which it sought to act in concert, it consisted of five persons, namely, Mr. Arthur O'Connor, Lord Edward Fitzgerald, Mr. Oliver Bond, Dr. Mac Nevin, and Mr. Thomas Addis Emmett. Of these, in rank and importance, Lord Edward was the foremost. Born in 1763, the fifth son of the Duke of Leinster, he had entered the army at an early age. But going to Paris in the autumn of 1792, he had eagerly imbibed the new Republican doctrines. This appears the less surprising when we find who was his host. He writes of himself as follows, in October : ' I lodge with my friend Paine ; we breakfast, dine, and sup together. The more I see of his interior the more I like and respect him.' [1] Next month he attended a public banquet given by some English at Paris to celebrate the victories achieved by the armies of France. Toasts of a truly fraternising character were then proposed and drunk. In consequence Lord Edward Fitzgerald was, in his own phrase and according, it would seem, to his own expectation, ' scratched out of the army ' in England. About the same time he married Pamela, an adopted daughter of Madame de

---

[1] Letter to his mother, October 30, 1792. *Biography* by Moore, vol. i. p. 170. See also at p. 176 a passage in a subsequent but undated letter.

Genlis, and as was commonly thought not unconnected
in kindred with the Duke of Orleans.   He returned to
Ireland with his young bride early in 1793. As Member
for the county of Kildare he took a zealous part in the
House of Commons against the measures of 'the Castle.'
Yet he was far from concurring heartily with his Opposition friends. Of Conolly, his uncle by marriage, and
of Grattan, he in the course of the ensuing year writes
as follows: 'Conolly's Militia has frightened him; he
swears they are all Republicans, as well as every man
in the north. He concludes all his speeches with
cursing Presbyterians. He means well and honestly,
dear fellow! but his line of proceeding is wrong. Grattan
I can make nothing of. His speech last night on the
Address was very bad, and the worst doctrine ever laid
down. . . . . It is in vain to look to Parliament for
anything, and if the people do not help themselves, why
they must suffer.'[1]

With these views, however, Lord Edward Fitzgerald
did not at once engage with the conspirators. It was
not till after the beginning of the year 1796 that he,
in connexion with Arthur O'Connor, Emmett, and
Mac Nevin, joined the ranks of the United Irishmen.[2]
That junction once effected, he became one of their
leaders at home, and once also, as I have elsewhere
shown, one of their envoys abroad. Of a frank, open
countenance, and with engaging manners, Lord Edward
had many of those generous and imprudent qualities
which mark his countrymen; and his name, especially
as surrounded with the halo of a mournful and untimely fate, is to this day popular in Ireland, even with
those who dissent most widely from the course which
he pursued.

The most leading men in the Irish Government at
this time were not perhaps either the Lord Lieutenant
or the Chief Secretary. Earl Camden and Mr. Thomas

---

[1] To his mother, January 23, 1794.
[2] *Life* by Moore, vol. i. p. 260.

Pelham were both men of excellent intentions and fair official aptitude; but beside them stood a sterner and a bolder spirit—the Chancellor, John Fitzgibbon, now Earl of Clare.

With men of this energy arrayed on opposite sides—in defence of the Government, or in conspiracy against it—the whole of the year 1797 was marked by painful and irritating scenes. There was a newspaper at Belfast, the 'Morning Star,' noted beyond all others in Ireland for its incitements to sedition and its scurrilous abuse of the loyal party. On the suspension of the Habeas Corpus Act the proprietors, Robert and William Simms, had been committed to Newgate. But their imprisonment did not, as was expected, arrest the progress of the paper nor yet mitigate its tone. The justifiable resentment which it provoked was vented in unjustifiable means. By superior orders, a party of soldiers issued one morning from the Barracks at Belfast, attacked the printing office, and demolished every part of it. The mischievous paper was suppressed, but the mischievous spirit remained. Two other papers, the 'Union Star' and the 'Press,' were sent forth on nearly the same principles and by nearly the same persons. Each of these papers was printed only on one side of the sheet, so as to admit of being pasted on the walls by night, and to serve as a placard for the common people. It was in the columns of the 'Press,' of which one Peter Finnerty was nominal editor, that Thomas Moore, as we learn from himself, made his first essay as a writer of prose.

Public prosecutions almost of necessity ensued. In October, 1797, William Orr was hanged at Carrickfergus for having administered treasonable oaths. For an alleged libel, reflecting on that execution, Peter Finnerty was brought to trial at Dublin. He was defended with much eloquence by Mr. Curran; but being found Guilty, was sentenced to stand in the pillory for one hour and to be imprisoned for two years.[1]

With these judicial proceedings were combined military measures. In March, 1797, a Proclamation was issued by General Lake requiring all persons in his district—that is, in the five northern counties—to surrender their arms. As to the weapons that might remain concealed, the Proclamation invited the aid of informers, promising inviolable secrecy and a reward to the full value of the arms that might be seized.

In the May ensuing the same object was enforced upon the entire kingdom in a Proclamation from the Lord Lieutenant. His Excellency here denounced the traitorous conspiracy of the United Irishmen aiming to subvert the authority of both King and Parliament. In furtherance of their purposes, he said, they have frequently assembled in unusual numbers, under the colourable pretence of planting potatoes, attending funerals, and the like; and when thus assembled in large armed bodies, they have—thus the Proclamation continued—plundered of arms the houses of many of the King's loyal subjects; they have cut down and carried away great numbers of trees wherewith to make handles of pikes and other offensive weapons; they have attempted to disarm several Yeomanry corps; they have fired upon several bodies of the King's regular troops. Therefore all persons were strictly charged to give up their pikes and pike-heads, their guns and swords, and to use their best endeavours to discover those in the possession of others; and, since some men might have joined the traitorous societies either in ignorance or from intimidation, a full pardon was promised to all, not themselves guilty of felony, who should by a certain day surrender themselves and take the oaths of allegiance.

There is no reason to believe that in this document or in others of that time Lord Camden exaggerates

---

[1] See Howell's *State Trials*, vol. xxvi. p. 900–1019.

in any manner the outrages of the United Irishmen;
but it is equally certain that outrages might also be
imputed to the other side. It is just to state that,
at this period, there were acts of violence committed
not merely by the peasants against the yeomanry and
soldiers, but also by the yeomanry and soldiers against
the peasants. It is just to remember the excesses of
one party as the only possible palliation to the excesses
of the other.

From time to time, moreover, the Government was
enabled, by the help of informers, to seize seditious
papers and arrest suspected persons. Thus, at Belfast,
the entire managing Committee on the part of the
United Irishmen was at one time apprehended. We
find Wolfe Tone in his journal again and again lament
that some of his trusted and valued friends—those on
whose assistance he had mainly relied in the event of a
French landing—were now shut up in prison.[1] In like
manner Arthur O'Connor also had been arrested, but
after a brief confinement was released.

Thus, at the beginning of 1798, everything in
Ireland was dark and lowering, everything foreshowed
the coming storm. Loyalists upon the one side, conspirators upon the other, growing daily more embit-
tered, seemed equally inclined to spurn all measures
of conciliation. Yet still there was a statesman who
to the last strove against hope to mediate between
them. There was a statesman who, like Fox and
Ponsonby, was a member of the Opposition, but who,
unlike them, did not at a period of public danger
rank secession and retirement in the list of his public
duties. That statesman was the Earl of Moira. As
a soldier, still bearing the title of Lord Rawdon, he
had achieved high distinction in the American war.
On his return he had received an English, and, ten
years later, inherited an Irish peerage. As a Peer and
as a proprietor of Ireland he had soon become popular

[1] See for example the entries of October 29 and November 7, 1796.

in that country. There was even at one time the idea that he might be appointed either its Commander in Chief or its Lord Lieutenant. He seldom took part in the debates, and brought to them no great gift of eloquence, but an Irish warmth of heart, and a weight justly due to his character and services.

But there was one incident which, at this period, gave especial value and importance to Lord Moira's words. He was known to possess the entire confidence of the Prince of Wales; he was known to express the exact sentiments for the time of His Royal Highness. It was probably through his counsels that the Prince had recently offered to the Ministers to undertake, on conciliatory principles, the post of Lord Lieutenant for his father. The offer had been declined, as was natural, from the Prince's circumstances and connexions; but it came to be known, or at least believed, by the public.[1]

It was in this position of affairs that Lord Moira brought the state of Ireland before the British Legislature. He did so with much earnestness and on two occasions, first in March, and then again in November, 1797. 'My Lords,' he said, ' in such a contest as we are engaged in, I am astonished that any part of the kingdom should be suffered to hang like a dead weight upon the rest. . . . . I will not on the present occasion discuss the heart-burnings which have reduced Ireland to her present calamitous condition. I may discuss them elsewhere; but in lamenting them, I will state that, to my conviction, these discontents arose from a mistaken application of severities. I have myself been a witness in Ireland to cases of the most absurd as well as most disgusting tyranny.'

Lord Moira was in both these debates answered by Lord Grenville; and, failing of success in England, next, in February, 1798, renewed the question in the Irish House of Lords. His speech was heard with deep attention, and the House from an early hour was

[1] *History of Ireland*, by Francis Plowden, vol. ii. p. 388, ed. 1809.

thronged. He began by complaining of some misrepresentations of his speeches in the British Parliament. ' But,' he cried, ' according to the remark of some writer, slander is like the mephitic vapour of the *Grotto del Cane* at Naples,—it suffocates an animal who grovels, but cannot reach the man who walks upright!' Next he proceeded to descant on the wrongs of his native country and the oppression of its rulers. Nor did he neglect a slight tribute, in passing, to the rising virtues of the Heir Apparent. ' Were Ireland,' he said, ' but cordially united, I should care little for the most powerful forces that France could send over to invade us; in a fortnight not a man of them would exist, except as a prisoner.' His motion did not propose any specific measures; but in speeches he urged, as the two cardinal points of redress, Catholic Emancipation and Parliamentary Reform.

To answer such a speech and from such a quarter seemed no easy task; yet, hard as it seemed, it was not too hard for Lord Chancellor Clare. In a most able and impressive oration—widely celebrated at the time both in Ireland and England—he not only replied to, but retorted on the Earl of Moira. If, he said, conciliation is to be regarded as a pledge of national tranquillity, no nation in Europe has had so fair a trial as the Irish. For almost twenty years has the system of conciliation been steadily pursued. First there were the commercial concessions of Lord North; then the legislative equality of 1782; then the relaxation of the Penal Code; and then the Roman Catholic franchise. What had been so far the result? The formation of seditious societies; the system of midnight robbery and outrage; the orders from the Jacobin clubs at Dublin and Belfast to levy regiments of National Guards with the French uniform and French pass-words; the league of the United Irishmen; the determination, frankly avowed, to accept no redress from Parliament; the desire, scarcely concealed, to separate from England.

Here, then, was a complete Revolutionary Government organised against the law. Was such a combination to be met and counteracted, much less dissolved, by the slow and technical forms of regular authority? Far, then, from granting, as Lord Moira had contended, that the Proclamation of Lord Camden to disarm the people was illegal, the Chancellor maintained that it was not only called for by the public interest, but strictly within the bounds of law.

But Lord Moira had gone into particular instances. Lord Moira had declared that he could vouch for the loyalty of his own town of Ballinahinch, in Downshire. Yet in this very town of Ballinahinch the people, when summoned by General Lake, refused to give up their arms until he had recourse to threats; the arms were then surrendered, and among them no inconsiderable number of pikes. Were pikes constitutional arguments for Parliamentary Reform? Were they emblems of loyalty? Or were they the dutiful and affectionate offerings of Lord Moira's tenantry to the rising virtues of the Heir Apparent?[1]

It was a great misfortune to Ireland—continued the Chancellor, and in this he spoke with perfect truth— that the people of England knew less of it than perhaps of any nation in Europe. The Irish, on their part, were exceedingly open to seduction; little civilised, he said, and of all others the most dangerous to tamper with or make experiments upon. Nor should any experiments be hazarded at a crisis so awful as was then impending. The first step towards tranquillising Ireland must be to crush rebellion. No measure of conciliation would satisfy the league of the United Irishmen short of a pure democracy established by the influence and guaranteed by the power of the French Republic.

The motion of Lord Moira after a long debate was

[1] On the 'loyal' town of Ballinahinch see the clever song (ascribed to Mr. Canning) in the Poetry of the *Anti-Jacobin* (July 9, 1798).

rejected by a large majority—45 votes against 11. Had it been carried, it is difficult to fancy that any happier result would have ensued. If Lord Moira had spoken truth, so had Lord Clare likewise. If there were long-standing grievances, there was also a rebellion close at hand, and the former could scarcely be redressed in the very presence of the latter. Perhaps it may be thought that in 1798 Ireland had lapsed into such a state as to admit of no measure altogether safe or altogether satisfactory. Cardinal de Retz in one passage of his Memoirs states that he has sometimes noticed those periods of helpless crisis in human affairs, and has always found that they proceeded not from the accidents or mischances of fortune, but rather from the faults and errors of mankind.[1]

At the beginning of 1798, and in the state to which the country had been brought, it became clear to the secret Directory at the head of the United Irishmen that with or without French succour a rising of their body could not be much longer delayed. To press for that succour with as little delay as possible, they determined to send one of their own number to Paris. Arthur O'Connor undertook this perilous task. He travelled in a military disguise, and called himself Colonel Morris. With him went a Roman Catholic priest who had been to France before on the like errand; his real name was O'Coigley, or more commonly Quigley, but for concealment he called himself sometimes Fivey and sometimes Captain Jones. With them there were also John Binns, well known as the agent of the Corresponding Society, and two confederates of meaner rank, who acted as servants. From London they proceeded to Whitstable, and thence to Margate, pretending to be smugglers, and bargaining for a boat across the Channel. But their design had been sus-

[1] '. . . . . les conjonctures dans lesquelles on ne peut plus faire que des fautes. J'ai observé que la fortune ne met jamais les hommes en cet état, . . . et que personne n'y tombe que ceux qui s'y précipitent par leur faute.'—*Mémoires*, vol. i. p. 149, ed. 1817.

pected, and their journey tracked from London. Two active officers, or as they were then termed ' runners ' of Bow Street, with the aid of some local police, succeeded on the 28th of February in arresting all the five. Their papers also were seized, and were found to contain some secret correspondence serving both to reveal their projects and identify their persons. They were first brought to London and examined before the Duke of Portland as Secretary of State, but as having been captured within the county of Kent they were subsequently removed for trial to Maidstone.

In Dublin also a clue was obtained to the chief conspirators. An informer, Thomas Reynolds by name, was found. He gave exact intelligence of a meeting of the leaders to be held at the house of Mr. Oliver Bond on the 12th of March. Major Swan, a magistrate for the county of Dublin, armed with a warrant from the Secretary's office and attended by thirteen sergeants of police in plain clothes, knocked at the door at the time appointed, and they were at once let in by means of the pass-words which they had obtained from Reynolds. Thus were they able to take into custody besides Oliver Bond himself all the persons assembled at his house. They found moreover a great variety of secret papers, chiefly Returns of force from the Officers of the United Irishmen, and lists of revolutionary toasts. Of these last the following was perhaps the most significant: —' Mother Erin, dressed in green ribbons by a French milliner, if she cannot be dressed without her!'

It so chanced that three of the principal leaders, Lord Edward Fitzgerald, Dr. Mac Nevin, and Mr. Emmett, had not gone to the meeting at Bond's. In the first instance, therefore, they remained at large. But separate warrants being issued against them, Mac Nevin and Emmett were in a short time apprehended. Lord Edward alone continued to elude pursuit. During nearly a month he was concealed in the house of a widow lady on the banks of the canal near Dublin. So long as it was possible, there had been every anxiety to spare him. A few days before the arrests of the 12th of March, the Chancellor, Lord Clare, had said to one of Lord Edward's nearest relatives, ' For God's sake get this young man out of the country ; the ports shall be thrown open to you, and no hindrance whatever offered.' [1]

From the house of the widow lady beyond the suburbs, Lord Edward on some suspicion of discovery came back to Dublin. He took refuge at last with a dealer in feathers, named Murphy, in Thomas Street. But he did not always, as would have been prudent, confine himself within doors. Thus on one occasion he went out in woman's clothes, and paid a visit—a parting visit as it proved—to his wife. Meanwhile he was still looked to as a leader. It was whispered that his standard should be raised through the province of Leinster, and the rebellion be commenced at least, if not continued, in his name. Under such circumstances, the Government, on the 11th of May, issued a Proclamation offering a reward of 1000*l.* for his discovery. Some secret information speedily ensued. The magistrates learnt the place of his concealment, and took their measures accordingly. A party was formed, consisting of Major Sirr, Major Swan, Captain Ryan, and eight soldiers. These on the 19th of May suddenly entered the house of Mr. Murphy and surprised Lord Edward still in his dressing-jacket and lying on his bed. Though surprised, he made a desperate resistance with pistols and poniards, both inflicting and receiving several dangerous wounds. Finally he was secured and carried off to prison. But the result proved fatal to one of his assailants as well as to himself ; Captain Ryan died of his wounds, as a few days afterwards did Lord Edward also.

The arrest of the leaders on the 12th of March gave the Government some hopes of crushing in the bud the intended insurrection. Fresh orders were issued by the Commander-in-Chief requiring the people to give up

[1] Moore's *Life of Fitzgerald*, vol. ii. p. 58.

their arms ; and if these were withheld, commanding the troops to make every exertion to discover and seize them. By such exertion a great number of weapons was actually secured—not less than 48,000 guns and 70,000 pikes.[1]   But in obtaining that result a course of great severity and sometimes great cruelty was pursued. Rigour was shown especially to those, the members of the United Irishmen League, who, as a mark of distinction among themselves, had cut short their hair, and who in consequence were usually termed the ' Croppies.' Many of these unhappy men underwent the military punishments of the lash and the picket—this last consisting in being made to stand with one foot upon a pointed stake.   Others, as is alleged, had a rope drawn round their necks and were nearly strangled to extort a confession of their hidden arms.   As some slight, but very far indeed from adequate, palliation of these cruelties, it should be mentioned that several persons who when first taken into custody denied with solemn oaths all knowledge of concealed instruments of war, subsequently under the pressure of bodily pain made disclosures of considerable stores.

Grievous, most grievous, were now the wrongs on either side.   The soldiers were frequently fired at in the dark, or from dykes and hedges.   They were sought to be assailed when single or unarmed.   On the other hand, when allowed to live at free-quarters in the disaffected districts, and when exasperated by what they deemed the cowardly attacks upon them, they perhaps could not be, and certainly they were not, restrained from acts of outrage.   Many cottages were burned to the ground ; many more were exposed to havoc and pillage of property.   Military law, or rather military licence without law, stood forth in all its naked deformity.

At length, in the months of May and June, burst

<hr>

[1] *Report of the Secret Committee of the House of Commons in Ireland* August, 1798, Appendix No. 39.

forth the long-smouldering flames. There were insur-
rections of the peasantry in various parts of the northern,
the eastern, and the southern provinces. Connaught
alone remained quiet. The leaders being in arrest
or in concealment, there was no central guidance, no
military combination. Instead of these there prevailed
—and, unhappily, not on one side alone—the spirit of
revenge and the hope of havoc. To trace in detail
the scenes that now ensued would be a task of no pleasure and small profit. There was little variety in either
the circumstances or the result. In all there was the
same fierce outbreak; in nearly all the same fierce
repression.

Some districts in Leinster were the first to rise. The
mail-coaches in various directions close to Dublin were
stopped and plundered, while no effort was neglected
to assist the conspirators within the city. But these
last were kept down by a strong hand, and the rebels
outside were encountered in the open field. Kildare,
Naas, Hacket's-town, and other places became the
scenes of conflict. But Prosperous was the only place
where the rebels achieved any considerable success.
They surprised the small town in the middle of the
night, and put to the sword almost to a man the few
soldiers by whom it was defended. On this occasion
their leader was John Esmonde, the younger son of Sir
Thomas Esmonde of an old Roman Catholic family.
He was a physician, and also a Lieutenant of the
Clane-town Corps of Yeomanry. He had dined with
his brother officers at the Mess the evening before, and
next morning joined his troop on march as though
nothing had happened, with his dress unsoiled and his
demeanour unembarrassed. But secret intelligence of
the doings at Prosperous had already reached his
Captain. He was immediately arrested, subsequently
brought to trial, found guilty, and hanged.[1]

[1] Musgrave's *History of the Rebellion*, vol. i. p. 288-298. See
also, at vol. ii. p. 303, the affidavit of Thomas Davis of Prosperous.

In Ulster, contrary to the expectation on both sides, the risings were slight and few. Belfast, which had been the very focus of the conspiracy, was almost untouched by the rebellion. Perhaps of all the places in this province the most tainted with treason was the lately vaunted and 'most loyal' town of Ballinahinch. Antrim was surrounded and attacked by a large body of insurgents; and Lord O'Neil, who lived in the immediate neighbourhood, was dragged from his horse and mortally wounded. There were two actions fought; the one at Saintsfield, the other in Lord Moira's own domain; the rebels on both occasions being put to the rout. Several of their chiefs were seized and executed; and the rebellion in this quarter was suppressed within the week.

But the real conflict was in Wexford county. There a large body of peasants had gathered at the bidding of Father John Murphy, curate of Bonvalogue. This man had gained a vast ascendency over the ignorant multitude. He declared to them that by the special favour of Providence he had been made invulnerable, and used after any action to show them bullets which he said that he had caught in his hands. His followers were already four thousand strong, and had taken post along the hill of Oulart on the morning of Whit Sunday the 27th of May. Here Lieutenant Foote, with only one hundred and ten men of the North Cork Militia, imprudently advanced against them. As might have been expected, the militiamen were both defeated and put to the sword, only the commander himself and four privates being spared.

This easy victory added fuel to the flame. The rebels marched in triumph to Ferns, and, with shouts against 'the heretics,' set fire to the Bishop's Palace, from which the Bishop had in time escaped. Thence they turned to Enniscorthy, a town of no inconsiderable commerce on the river Slaney; it was defended by three hundred soldiers with some assistance from the townsmen. On the 28th they were attacked, and there was a conflict of some hours, but, the town being fired by the assailants in several places, the Royalists at last were driven out, and a dreadful scene of conflagration and slaughter ensued.

At these tidings the Royalists in Wexford saw that they could no longer maintain their post. The officer in command, Lietenant-Colonel Maxwell, retired from the town, into which, on the 30th of May, the rebels marched. They threw open the prison gates and set free Mr. Bagenal Harvey, a Protestant gentleman of good family and fortune. He was known to be a favourer of the rebel cause, and as such had been put in arrest by the Government party. So had been, also, two other gentlemen of landed property in that district, Mr. John Colclough and Mr. Edward Fitzgerald, but these last had been released on bail the day before. All three gentlemen now joined the insurgent force, and were proclaimed among its leaders. It was also joined by another Protestant of large property, Mr. Cornelius Grogan, of Johnstown : he was, however, old and timid, and afterwards claimed to have acted from compulsion.

For their command the rebels now appointed no single leader, but a Committee of seven persons, with Mr. Bagenal Harvey as President. Day by day they received large accessions of force from the neighbouring peasantry. They were joined also by several priests. Their principal camp was on some high ground, called Vinegar Hill, which overlooked the town of Enniscorthy, though on the opposite side of the Slaney. Their force, which ere long became fifteen thousand strong, and which was still increasing, took the title of ' United Army of Wexford,' and by the exhortations of some priests of the lower class, was inflamed to fanatic fury against that very faith which their own adopted chief professed.

The fanaticism of this rebel army was evinced above

all by their treatment of the Protestant prisoners.
These were led forth day after day to be put to death
in cold blood, and with every circumstance of savage
cruelty. Where for any reason the execution was deferred until the morrow, the persecutors meanwhile
took possession of the victims, and gratified themselves
by the infliction of the lash. It is impossible to suppose
that the better priests in the rebel camp took any, even
the smallest, share in these atrocities. As little, of course,
can we impute them to the Protestant chiefs. The
truth is, as one of the Committee, Mr. Edward Fitzgerald, subsequently owned to the Under Secretary of
State, that ‘he and the other leaders had but little command; that the mob were furious, and wanting to massacre every Protestant; and that the only means they
had of dissuading them from burning houses was (to
tell them) that they were destroying their own property!’
Fitzgerald added, ‘that at first his men fought well, but
latterly would not stand at all.’ ¹

At this time Sir Ralph Abercromby was no longer
Commander-in-Chief in Ireland. He and Lord Camden
had differed in judgment so often and so strongly, that
the former at last resigned his post. In the opinion of
Lord Cornwallis, Abercromby had been ‘exceedingly
wrong-headed.’ ² His return, however, led the Cabinet
to review with the utmost anxiety the whole question of
the Government of Ireland. It seemed most desirable,
with a rebellion bursting forth, to concentrate all the
powers of the State in a single and that an able hand.
Lord Cornwallis seemed at that time the only person
to fulfil the required conditions. Accordingly he was
pressed in the warmest terms to undertake the arduous
duty. This pressure upon him he had from the first foreseen. ‘I expect to be most violently attacked (to go)’
—thus he writes to his private friend—‘What shall I,

---

¹ See in the Cornwallis Correspondence the letter of Mr. E
Cooke, dated July 24, 1798.

² To General Ross, March 30, 1798.

what can I do?' His own feelings were repugnant to
the task, for, as we find him state a little later, 'the
life of a Lord Lieutenant of Ireland comes up to my
idea of perfect misery.'[1] But his sense of the public
service prevailed. He went to Ireland both as Lord
Lieutenant and Commander-in-Chief, and with the full
confidence of Mr. Pitt and the Duke of Portland. He
was empowered to issue an amnesty as soon as possible,
and instructed to repress by all the means in his power
the spirit of vengeance at the close of the civil war.

It was not until the 20th of June that Lord Cornwallis arrived at Dublin. By that time the arrangements for attacking the rebels in Wexford were completed, and on the very point of execution. In these
arrangements, accordingly, he took no further share.

The Secretary for Ireland at this period was still
nominally Mr. Thomas Pelham. But in consequence
of illness he had been for some time past detained in
England, and the duties of his office had been discharged by Robert Stewart, Lord Castlereagh. This
statesman, who subsequently played so eminent a part
in his country's annals, was the eldest son of the Earl of
Londonderry, and not yet twenty-nine years of age.
'I have every reason'—thus writes Lord Cornwallis to
his confidential friend—'to be highly satisfied with
Lord Castlereagh. He is really a very uncommon young
man, and possesses talents, temper, and judgment suited
to the highest stations.'[2] Indeed so well convinced was
the new Lord Lieutenant of the merits of his Secretary,
that when, a few months later, Mr. Pelham resigned,
Lord Cornwallis at once solicited and obtained the permanent appointment of Lord Castlereagh.

But before I now proceed to the close of the Wexford insurrection and to the measures of the Cornwallis
Vice-Royalty, I must revert to some intervening events
in England. The trial of the Irish prisoners, Arthur

---

[1] To General Ross, March 30 and July 1, 1798.
[2] To General Ross, July 9, 1798.

O'Connor and James O'Coigley, together with their English confederates, commenced at Maidstone on the 21st of May. The Attorney-General, Sir John Scott, and the Solicitor-General, Sir John Mitford, appeared on the part of the Crown. For the prisoners the leading counsel was Mr. Plumer, subsequently Master of the Rolls. By several witnesses their whole progress to Maidstone was accurately traced, and the papers found in their possession were produced. On the other hand, Arthur O'Connor called as witnesses to his character and principles the chiefs of the Opposition in England. Fox, Sheridan, and Erskine, Lord John Russell, the Duke of Norfolk, and the Earl of Thanet appeared in his behalf. But strongest of all was the evidence of Grattan, who came from Ireland expressly for this purpose. He declared that he had been well acquainted with Mr. O'Connor since the year 1792 ; that he had the means of forming a judgment on his political opinions ; and that he had never heard him express any which could lead to the supposition that he would favour an invasion of his country. Considering the notoriety of the course which Arthur O'Connor had pursued in Irish politics, the excessive candour—if it was such—of Mr. Grattan may well excite surprise.

It was natural, however, that such testimony should have great weight with the Maidstone jury. At the conclusion of the trial they found O'Coigley Guilty, but acquitted O'Connor, as also the two other prisoners. Previous to the verdict, O'Connor had been apprised that a police-officer was in court, with a warrant to apprehend him on another charge. Nevertheless, no sooner had the verdict been pronounced, than O'Connor stepped from the box in which he stood with the other prisoners, and attempted to go free. One of his witnesses, Lord Thanet, and one of his counsel, Mr. Robert Ferguson, took his part, and attempted to aid his escape ; but after some scuffle and confusion the officers prevailed, and the prisoner was again secured.

For this offence Lord Thanet and Mr. Ferguson were, in the following year, brought to trial and found Guilty, notwithstanding a most able defence by Mr. Erskine. They were sentenced to fine and imprisonment; the fine upon Lord Thanet of a thousand, and that upon Mr. Ferguson of a hundred pounds; the Earl to be confined for one year in the Tower; the Barrister for the same period in the King's Bench prison.

For Arthur O'Connor, he was detained in custody several months longer, but at last on confession of his guilt was permitted to retire to France. There he obtained a commission in the army, and rose to the rank of Lieutenant-General, but was not employed after 1803. He attained a green old age, surviving till April, 1852. His brother, Roger O'Connor, had been, like himself, arrested for High Treason, but after some delay was also, like himself, released and sent abroad. This gentleman was the father by his second marriage of Feargus O'Connor, well known in our own times by his Chartist opinions and his representation of Nottingham.

On the 7th of June O'Coigley underwent the sentence of the law on Penenden Heath. On being taken from the gaol at Maidstone he was seated upon a hurdle drawn by two horses, and escorted to the place of execution by a body of two hundred volunteers. He was first hanged and then beheaded; and the executioner, holding out the head to the multitude, cried in the appointed form: 'This is the head of a traitor.' But the other more revolting practices enjoined by the ancient law of High Treason had been previously remitted by the King. O'Coigley was attended by a Roman Catholic priest, and maintained to the last great fortitude and calmness.

CHAPTER XXVI.

1798.

Measures of national defence—Fox's speech at the Whig Club—His name struck from the Privy Council—Duel between Pitt and Tierney—Wilberforce's notice of motion against duelling—Dissuaded by Pitt from pressing it—Ill health of Pitt—Bonaparte reduces Malta, and lands in Egypt—Battle of the Nile—Surrender of Minorca—English Militia Regiments sent to Ireland—Action at Vinegar Hill—Execution of rebel leaders—Excesses of Militia and Yeomanry—Conciliatory course of Lord Cornwallis—General Humbert lands at Killala—Attacks General Lake at Castlebar—Surrender of Humbert—Trial of Napper Tandy—Action in Killala Bay—Trial and suicide of Wolfe Tone—His Diaries and Correspondence.

THE British Parliament was at this time busily employed on measures of national defence. A Message from the King on the 20th of April had announced 'considerable and increasing activity in the ports of France, Flanders, and Holland, with the avowed design of attempting the invasion of His Majesty's dominions,' and had called for 'such further measures as may enable His Majesty to defeat the wicked machinations of disaffected persons.' An Alien Bill was at once introduced by the Government, as also a Bill for the suspension of the Habeas Corpus. Both were opposed in the House of Commons, but with very slight result. Thus, on the Suspension Bill, Sheridan, who led the resistance, found on the general principle only six other members willing to divide with him.[1]

Fox took no part in these debates. His familiar letters at this time express the utmost aversion to resume his Parliamentary duties. Thus in March he had written to his nephew: 'I should dislike to a degree I cannot express to attend again myself; indeed, if there is a point upon which I cannot bring myself to give

[1] *Parl. Hist.*, vol. xxxiii. p. 1431.

way, it is this ; but I am far from wishing others to do the same.'[1]   But Fox was by no means equally unwilling to attend the meetings of the Whig Club.   There, at the beginning of May, he made a speech, using some inflammatory language, and repeating the Duke of Norfolk's toast—to the Sovereignty of the People. A great stir ensued.   Many friends and some colleagues of Pitt pressed for a public prosecution or a Parliamentary reprimand.   Pitt, on the other hand, appears to have thought that such steps would be 'giving Mr. Fox too much consequence.'[2]   We find him in a private letter consult Dundas upon the subject :—

Downing Street, Saturday, May 5, 1798.

Dear Dundas,— .   .   .   .
Our friends are very eager for some Parliamentary notice of Fox's speech.   The objection to prosecuting him is certainly very great from the chance of an acquittal and a triumph, but it has been suggested that he might be ordered to attend, and if he avows the speech, might be reprimanded by the Speaker.   If he disavows it, the printer might be prosecuted with success.   If after a reprimand he offers a new insult (as he probably would at the next meeting of the Club), he might be sent to the Tower for the remainder of the Session, which would assert the authority of the House as much as expulsion, and save the inconvenience of a Westminster contest.   Pray let me know in the course of to-morrow what you think.   I shall be here in the morning, but go with Long to Bromley to dinner.

Yours ever,   W. Pitt.

Finally, after full deliberation, it was determined that no steps should be taken against Fox, except to strike his name from the Privy Council.   On the 9th of May, accordingly, a Board of Privy Council being held at St. James's, Mr. Faulkner, as Clerk of the Council, presented the list to the King, when His Ma-

---

[1] *Correspondence*, vol. iii. p. 144.

[2] There is a story upon this subject (but given doubtfully) in a later entry of Lord Malmesbury's Journal (May 8, 1804).

jesty with his own hand drew his pen across the name of Mr. Fox.

Fox himself in his private letters refers to this event with great equanimity. ' I believe,' he says, ' the late Duke of Devonshire is the only instance in this reign of a Privy Councillor being turned out in England; and the more the circumstances of the two cases shall appear exactly similar, the better I shall like it.' Lord John Russell has justly remarked that this sentiment is singular, since the Minister who in 1762 turned out the Duke of Devonshire was Mr. Fox's father.[1] Fox adds : ' I wish I knew whether it is necessary I should go to Court ; I had much rather not, but would do in this as is thought right.'

On Friday, the 25th of May, Pitt brought in a Bill for the more effectual manning of the Navy, and gave reasons why it was expedient that this Bill should pass through all its stages in one day.   Mr. Tierney, not without some warmth, opposed this, as he termed it, precipitate course. ' The Hon. gentleman,' said Pitt in reply, ' would have long notice given of the present motion, and would retard its progress through the House.   He acknowledges that were it not passed in a day, those whom it concerned might elude its effect, thus assigning himself the reason for its immediate adoption.   But if the measure be necessary, and that a notice of it would enable its effect to be eluded, how can the Hon. gentleman's opposition to it be accounted for but from a desire to obstruct the defence of the country ? '

At this point, however, Tierney rose to Order. ' This language,' he said, ' is surely not Parliamentary.   I appeal to the Chair for protection.'

The Speaker, thus appealed to, said that whatever tended to cast a personal imputation for words spoken in debate was certainly disorderly and unparliamentary. It was for the Right Hon. gentleman to explain his

---

[1] Note to *Fox's Correspondence*, vol. iii. p. 289.

meaning. Then Pitt rose again, and haughtily declared that he must adhere to his words, which he repeated. And whilst he would freely submit his arguments to the judgment of the House, 'I must say,' he added, 'that I will neither retract from, nor further explain, my former expressions.'

The result of this haughty determination on the part of Mr. Pitt was a challenge on the morrow, Saturday the 26th, from Mr. Tierney. It was at once accepted. Mr. Pitt apprised the Speaker of it as a personal friend, thus in honour binding him against any public interference, or any attempt to prevent the duel. Here is Lord Sidmouth's own account: 'On the day afterwards, which was Saturday, I was dining with Lord Grosvenor, when a note was brought me from Mr. Pitt stating that he had received a hostile message from Mr. Tierney, and wished me to go to him, which I did as soon as the party at Lord Grosvenor's broke up. Mr. Pitt had just made his will when I arrived. He had sent in the first instance to Mr. Steele to be his second; but finding that he was absent, he sent next to Mr. Ryder. On the following day I went with Pitt and Ryder down the Birdcage Walk, up the steps into Queen Street, where their chaise waited to take them to Wimbledon Common.'[1]

Under these circumstances, then, on Sunday, the 27th, at three o'clock in the afternoon, the two parties met on Putney Heath. Mr. Pitt was attended by Mr. Dudley Ryder, afterwards Lord Harrowby, and Mr. Tierney by Mr. George Walpole. The seconds had some conversation, and endeavoured to prevent further proceedings, but they did not prevail. The principals took their ground at the distance of twelve paces, and fired at the same moment; each without effect. A second case of pistols was produced and fired in the same manner, Mr. Pitt on this last occasion firing his pistol

[1] Communicated by Lord Sidmouth to Dean Pellew, *Life*, vol. i. p. 205.

in the air. Then the seconds jointly interfered, and insisted that the matter should go no further, ' it being their decided opinion that sufficient satisfaction had been given, and that the business was ended with perfect honour to both parties.'

Meanwhile the Speaker, unable to rest, mounted his horse and rode that way. He took his stand at some distance on a small hill where was a gibbet, upon which a felon named Abershaw had been lately hanged. ' When I arrived on the hill,' he says, ' I knew from seeing a crowd looking down into the valley that the duel was then proceeding. After a time I saw the same chaise which had conveyed Pitt to the spot mounting the ascent, and riding up to it I found him safe, when he said, " You must dine with me to-day." '

In a note written the same evening we find Pitt in a few lines relate the event to Dundas, as in a letter next day he did also to his mother from Holwood.

Downing Street, Sunday. 9 P.M.

Dear Dundas,—You will perhaps hear that I had occasion to visit your neighbourhood this morning, in order to meet Mr. Tierney, in consequence of what passed between us in the House on Friday. We exchanged two shots on each side ; and by the interposition of the seconds the affair ended in a way with which, I think, neither party had any reason to be dissatisfied. I am going to Long's this evening, and will dine with you to-morrow.

Yours ever,   W. Pitt.

Holwood, Monday, May 28, 1798.

My dear Mother,—You will be glad, I know, to hear from myself on a subject in which I know how much you will feel interested, and I am very happy that I have nothing to tell that is not perfectly agreeable. The newspapers of to-day contain a short but correct account of a meeting which I found it necessary to have with Mr. Tierney yesterday, on Putney Heath, in consequence of some words which I had used in the House of Commons, and which I did not think it became me to retract or explain. The business terminated without anything unpleasant to either party, and in a way which left me perfectly satisfied both with myself and my antagonist, who behaved with great propriety. You will, I know, hear from my brother on the subject, but I could not be contented without sending these few lines from myself.

Ever, my dear Mother, &c.,   W. Pitt.

At that period, and even down to a much later, the practice of duelling on any political or private wrong was in conformity with the public opinion and temper of the times. But in 1798, when everything depended on the life of the Prime Minister, there was a common thrill of horror at the risk which Mr. Pitt had run. Nor were there wanting some few more serious men who strongly condemned the practice on moral and religious grounds. Chief among these few was Mr. Wilberforce. In his Diary he writes as follows:—
'May 28. Ashley came in at my dressing-time, and brought word of Pitt and Tierney's duel yesterday. I more shocked than almost ever. I resolved to do something if possible.—May 30. To town. Found people much alive about duel, and disposed to take it up. I gave notice of a motion in the House of Commons against the principle of duels.'

But on the very same evening Wilberforce received a letter from Pitt, already published in the Life of the former, but which I shall here produce again.

Downing Street, Wednesday, May 30, 1798.

My dear Wilberforce,—I am not the person to argue with you on a subject in which I am a good deal concerned. I hope, too, that I am incapable of doubting your kindness to me, however mistaken I may think it, if you let any sentiment of that sort actuate you on the present occasion. I must suppose that some such feeling has inadvertently operated upon you, because, whatever may be your *general* sentiments on subjects of this nature, they can have acquired no new tone or additional argument from anything that has passed in this transaction. You must be supposed to bring this forward in reference to the individual case.

In doing so, you will be accessory in loading one of the parties with unfair and unmerited obloquy. With respect to the other party, myself, I feel it a real duty to say to you frankly that your motion is one for my removal. If any step on the subject is proposed in Parliament and agreed to, I shall feel from that moment that I can be of more use out of office than in it; for in it, according to the feelings I entertain, I could be of none. I state to you as I think I ought distinctly and explicitly what I feel. I hope I need not repeat what I always feel personally to yourself.

Yours ever,　　　　W. PITT.

It was natural that a communication so distinct and so momentous should have caused Wilberforce to waver in his purpose. We find him write :—' June 1, 1798, To town to-day and yesterday, and back in the evening. Much discussion about duel motion. Saw Pitt and others—all pressed me to give it up. Consulted Grant and Henry Thornton, and at length agreed to give it up, as not more than five or six would support me, and not more than one or two speak, and I could only have carried it so far as for preventing *Ministers* fighting duels.'

On announcing his decision to the Minister, Wilberforce received in reply a few cordial lines.

Downing Street, Saturday, 6 P.M.

My dear Wilberforce,—I cannot say to you how much I am relieved by your determination, which I am sincerely convinced is right on your own principles, as much as on those of persons who think differently. Much less can I tell you how sincerely I feel your cordial friendship and kindness on all occasions, as well where we differ as where we agree.

Ever affectionately yours,　　　　W. PITT.

Two days subsequently we find in the same journal : ' June 4. Stayed away from Court on account of motion impending. The King asked the Speaker if I persevered. Pitt told me the King approved of his conduct.' [1]

During the short remainder of this session—it closed

---

[1] Yet the King's first impressions were certainly of at least a chequered kind. See in the Appendix his letter of the 30th of May.

on the 29th of June—the affairs of Ireland took up, as
was natural, the largest portion of the time.   In the
Lords there were three separate motions on the state of
the sister kingdom—from the Duke of Leinster, the
Earl of Bessborough, and the Duke of Bedford.   But
at the desire of Lord Sydney, the Standing Order for
the exclusion of strangers, which is usually allowed to
lie dormant, was put in force, so that no record of these
debates was preserved.   If therefore there were members
of the Opposition who hoped at that critical juncture to
inflame the public mind by their Parliamentary harangues,
that hope was altogether disappointed.   And for the
same reason the exclusion of strangers was equally
enforced in the corresponding debates in the House of
Commons.   First came a motion from Mr. Sheridan,
calling for a Committee on the state of Ireland.   Next
there was a string of Resolutions from Lord George
Cavendish.   On this last occasion Fox emerged from his
retirement, and delivered a speech of some length,
which, though wholly unreported, was beyond all doubt
fraught as usual with admirable eloquence.   Later in
the evening he moved, though without success, a separate Resolution of his own.   Lord George was also supported, and most ably, by both Sheridan and Grey, but
with all their exertions could muster no higher minority
than sixty-six.

In the Diary of Wilberforce under the date of
June 2—the same day on which Pitt addressed to him
a note of thanks—there are these words, 'He (Pitt)
seriously ill.'   The news of this illness spread quickly
and with much exaggeration.   It was even alleged that
the Prime Minister had become insane.   Towards the
end of July, Lord Muncaster, from his house in Cumberland, wrote to Wilberforce upon the subject.   'You ask
me,' replied Wilberforce, 'concerning the report about
Pitt.   Altogether without foundation is my answer.   Yet
the Opposition papers go on with it.'

Just before this answer the two friends had passed a

day alone together. Here again I recur to Wilberforce's Diary. 'July 16. After breakfast to Auckland ;
and then on to Pitt at Holwood. *Tête à tête* with Pitt,
and much political talk. He much better—improved
in habits also—beautifying his place with great taste—
marks of ingenuousness and integrity. Resenting and
spurning the bigoted fury of Irish Protestants.'

The ' habits ' to which Wilberforce here refers as
admitting of improvement were probably in the first
place as to the system of hours. No longer break-
fasting at nine o'clock as in his first years of office, Pitt
had become the very reverse of early in the forenoon.
The Speaker, Mr. Addington, describing his life about
this time, says of him that he never rose before eleven,
and then generally took a short ride in the Park. Any
change which he made in this respect, as Wilberforce
notes, was not of long continuance, and for the rest of
his life Pitt was very late in his morning hours. Some
have thought that the time which he passed in bed was
compelled by his delicate health ; others have supposed
that he employed it in revolving the details of his
speeches or his measures.

Secondly, it is probable that Wilberforce alludes to
the large potations of port wine. These, as we have
seen, were in the first instance prescribed to Mr. Pitt
as a medicine, and they gave strength to his youthful
constitution. But amidst the labour of Parliament
and office he certainly in some cases carried them beyond what his health could require, or could even without injury bear. Not that they had any effect on his
mental powers or mental self-command. Two bottles
of port, as Lord Macaulay says, were little more to him
than two dishes of tea. Nothing could be rarer in his
public life than any trace of excitement in his after-
dinner speeches.

Here, again, the authority of the Speaker is quite
decisive. When in long subsequent years Lord Sidmouth was questioned on the subject, he said that

Mr. Pitt loved a glass of port wine very well, and a bottle still better ; but that he had never known him to take too much if he had anything to do, except upon one occasion, when he was unexpectedly called up to answer a personal attack made upon him by Mr. William Lambton, father of the first Lord Durham. He had left the House with Mr. Dundas in the hour between two election ballots, for the purpose of dining, and when on his return he replied to Mr. Lambton, it was evident to his friends that he had taken too much wine.　The next morning, Mr. Ley, the Clerk Assistant of the House of Commons told the Speaker that he had felt quite ill ever since Mr. Pitt's exhibition on the preceding evening.　'It gave me,' he added, 'a violent headache.'　On this being repeated to Mr. Pitt—'I think,' said the Minister, 'that is an excellent arrangement—that I should have the wine and the Clerk the headache!''

It is not to be supposed that even a single instance of the kind would be left unimproved by the wits at Brooks's. The *Morning Chronicle* came out with a long array of epigrams upon this tempting subject.　Here is one in which the Prime Minister is supposed to address his colleague—

> 'I cannot see the Speaker, Hal ; can you ?'—
> 'Not see the Speaker !—hang it, I see two !'

In July of this year we find Mr. Pitt give his mother an account, probably far too favourable, of his health.

Holwood, July 9, 1798.

To-day's post has brought me your kind and welcome letter, and I have just time to thank you for it by the return of a messenger to town, and to assure you that I am growing stronger and stronger every day, and am as well as ever I was.　I do not want to be better ; but to be the more sure of continuing as well as I am, I mean soon to take a few weeks of sea air, and still more complete idleness than I

---

¹ *Life of Lord Sidmouth*, by Dean Pellew, vol. i. p. 153.

have had here, at Walmer, which, next to the possibility, if it could arrive, of a visit at Burton, I shall enjoy more than any other excursion.

On the other hand we find Lord Auckland give to Mr. Beresford a very different account.

Eden Farm, August 1, 1798.

Yesterday I passed the day quietly at Holwood with Mr. Pitt, who set out this morning for Walmer. I trust that the sea-air will do good to him ; he is greatly recovered, but is much shaken in his constitution, and must be very attentive as to diet, exercise, and hours. His spirits are as good and his mind as active as ever. We have many and long discussions as to Ireland : it seems hardly justifiable to return merely to the old system.

On the 2nd of August, accordingly, Pitt proceeded to Walmer Castle, where he remained about a fortnight. Then he paid a visit of some days in the opposite direction, going to Burton Pynsent, but was obliged by the end of the month to return to his official post. Thus he writes to his mother from Downing Street, August 30 :—' Favourable as the prospect is, I must not allow myself to regret the sacrifice I made in coming here, as it is material to be on the spot to expedite any measures which might become necessary for increasing Lord Cornwallis's force.'

Next month he writes again :

Holwood, September 16, 1798.

I write for to-morrow's post, meaning in the morning to set out from hence to Walmer. Our good news from Ireland reached me at such a time that I could not give you the satisfaction of knowing it sooner than it was conveyed by the newspaper. The conclusion of the struggle, or rather of the pursuit, is most satisfactory, and promises the best effect in various ways. On the side of the Mediterranean our expectation, which had been almost extinguished where it was most alive by the account of Nelson's disappointment, is now suddenly awakened by reports of great armies formed, and, as some say, victories obtained over Bonaparte by the Arabs. Something of the fabulous is perhaps mixed in the

relation, but if it is only true that there is resistance enough
to retard his progress, the great object of his expedition will
be defeated.

I shall now proceed first to the events in the Mediterranean, and next to those in Ireland.

General Bonaparte, having on his way reduced the
island of Malta, appeared off the coast of Egypt, and
began to disembark his troops on the 1st of July. He
was encountered by the Mamalukes, both on his landing
and on his march to Cairo, and a report of their victory
came, as we have seen, to England. But so far from
defeating the French army, they were not even able,
as Mr. Pitt had hoped, to retard its progress. General
Bonaparte established his head-quarters at Cairo, and
ruled the country with undisputed sway. Meanwhile
he had left his fleet, commanded by Admiral Brueys, in
the Bay of Aboukir, about twenty miles north-east of
Alexandria. On that fleet entirely depended his power
of communication and his prospect of return.

On the other side, Admiral Nelson had learnt the
departure of the French armament from Toulon, but,
like the rest of the world, was altogether ignorant of its
destination. He had therefore pursued it at hap-hazard
and in vain. He could neither prevent the capture of
Malta, nor yet the landing in Egypt. He had rightly
conjectured the latter as perhaps the probable object,
but when he appeared off Alexandria on the 28th of
June the enemy was not there, and he tried them in
another direction. On the 19th of July, much in need
of water and provisions, he stood towards Syracuse. It
was no easy matter to obtain any supplies at that place,
since the Court of Naples had bound itself to a strict
neutrality. But Emma, Lady Hamilton, wife of Sir
William, the English Minister at that Court, was a
personal favourite with the Queen, and obtained from
Her Majesty a secret order to the Sicilian Governors.
' Thanks to your exertions'—thus writes Nelson to the

Hamiltons—'we have victualled and watered; and surely, watering at the fountain of Arethusa, we must have victory. We shall sail with the first breeze; and be assured I will return either crowned with laurel or covered with cypress.' To his chief, Earl St. Vincent, he wrote also, and bade him be convinced that if the French were above water he would find them out.

From Syracuse Nelson sailed to the Morea, where he hoped to obtain some positive tidings. There he learnt that the French had been seen from Candia about four weeks before, steering to the south-east. Nelson at once decided to sail back to Alexandria. About ten in the morning of the 1st of August he came in sight of that port. To his great joy he saw that it was crowded with masts, and that the French tricolour was flying from the walls. Here, then, was the enemy at last!

Nelson's fleet was thirteen sail of the line, and the French had exactly the same number. But yet there was on their side a considerable superiority. In the first place, they had four frigates, and the English none, but only one fifty-gun ship. Next, the English ships of the line were all seventy-fours, while the French had two of eighty guns, and one—their Admiral's ship, the Orient—among the largest in any service, of a hundred and twenty guns.

The plan which Nelson formed, on reconnoitring the position at Aboukir, was to make his attack by doubling on the enemy's ships. His own could not be brought within range, or in line, till late that afternoon, and the French fully expected that the battle would be delayed till the next day. But Nelson, with his characteristic ardour, commenced it a little before sunset. It continued through several hours of darkness, lit up only in flashes by the fire on each side.

From the beginning of the action the huge Orient was hotly engaged, first with the Bellerophon, and then with the Swiftsure. Within the first hour Brueys was three times wounded: the third time mortally. Still he desired not to be carried below. ' A French Admiral,' he said, ' should die on his deck.' Thus calmly did this brave man breathe his last. Had he even been unwounded, he would only have perished by another mode of death. The Orient had just been painted, and the oil-jars and paint-buckets had been carelessly left on the poop. On a sudden the ship caught fire ; it was soon enveloped in flames ; and about ten in the evening it blew up with a most tremendous explosion. In its ruin it caused nearly as much havoc as it ever had by its active strength. The vibration shook the neighbouring vessels to their very keels, and opened many of their seams, while fragments of the blazing mass flew far and wide, and whenever they fell on decks and rigging set them in a flame not easy to extinguish. Of the many hundred men on board the Orient, by far the greater number were blown up or drowned ; only some few were saved on board the British ships. The second in command, Admiral Ganteaume, found means to throw himself into a boat and to reach the shore.

After an awe-struck pause, which continued full ten minutes, and during which not a gun was fired on either side, the conflict again commenced. Nelson, on board the Vanguard, and engaging both the Spartiate and the Aquilon, had been severely wounded. A splinter had struck him above the eye and cut the flesh from the forehead. When he was carried down to the cockpit, the surgeon, who was just then dressing the wound of a common sailor, quitted it to attend the Admiral. ' No,' said Nelson; ' I will take my turn with my brave fellows ; '—an answer which may well deserve to stand side by side with that of Sir Philip Sidney at Zutphen.

Before daybreak the victory of the English was complete. Never was any battle more decisive than that which the French call ' *le combat d'Aboukir*,' but which is known to the victors as the battle of the Nile.

Of the thirteen French ships of the line, one, as we have seen, perished in the flames, eight surrendered, and two, as half wrecks, were stranded on the shore. Of these, the Timoleon was set on fire and destroyed by her crew, and the Tonnant struck her flag to the English. Only two of the thirteen escaped. Thus was one of the best French armies wholly cut off from France. Thus did their recent conquest of Egypt become to them as it were a prison, from which there was no return.

In England the people knew the character of Nelson. All through the summer they had been expecting some great successes on his part. Once, in July, Lady Chatham saw or heard of the Falmouth mail-coach passing through Taunton bedecked with laurels, and bearing, it was said, the tidings of such a victory. Pitt could not confirm the rumour; but he added, in his letter dated July 25 :—

As far as we can judge by comparing dates and circumstances, there is very good ground to hope that if Bonaparte has ventured out of Malta and has not got into Toulon, Nelson will have come up with him. If this should have been the case, the triumph will, I have little doubt, be only premature, and the coaches will in due time have a right to their laurels.

And again, August 30 :—

The reports of Nelson's success are again revived from various quarters, and will, I really believe, somehow or other, prove true at last.

When at last the authentic tidings (the first being diluted through French channels) came of the great battle of the Nile, the public joy—and not in England only—knew no bounds. Honours and rewards were showered upon Nelson by other Sovereigns besides his own. By King George he was created Baron Nelson of the Nile, with a pension of 2,000*l.* a year for three lives. The well-selected motto, *Palmam qui meruit* *ferat*, was chosen by Lord Grenville, from an ode of Dr. Jortin. It was commonly felt that a higher degree of rank ought to have been conferred upon him, since there had been an Earldom for the less conspicuous victory of Cape St. Vincent. When, in the November following, the grant was moved in the House of Commons, General Walpole expressed his opinion accordingly, that a Barony was not enough for Nelson. 'It is unnecessary,' said Pitt, 'to enter into that question. Admiral Nelson's fame will be co-equal with the British name. It will be remembered that he has obtained the greatest naval victory on record, when no man will thing of asking whether he had been created a Baron, or Viscount, or an Earl.'[1]

Nelson never, in fact, did attain any higher rank than that of Viscount, which was afterwards awarded him for his victory at Copenhagen. It is singular, however, that the unequal distribution of honours as between Jervis and himself has been redressed, and, as it were, reversed, by the accidents of their succession. The heir of Jervis is now a Viscount; the heir of Nelson is now an Earl.

Before the close of the same year there was another conquest in the Mediterranean, of some importance in its result, though of none in its achievement. The island of Minorca being undefended by the Spaniards, was given up to a British force under General Charles Stuart, without the loss on his part of a single man.

The rebellion in Ireland had roused the energy of the Militia in England. On the 16th of June Mr. Secretary Dundas brought down to the House of Commons a message from the King announcing that several regiments had freely tendered an extension of their services to Ireland. Mr. Dundas moved an Address in reply, which, though resisted by many members of the Opposition, as Mr. Sheridan and Lord William Russell, and

---

[1] I derive this passage from the *Life* by Southey, p. 163, ed. 1857. It has been omitted in the *Parliamentary History*.

even by one or two friends of Government, as Mr. Bankes, was carried by a large majority. Several Militia regiments went over accordingly. It was hoped that they would do more than assist in quelling the rebellion; it was hoped that, having no personal injuries to avenge, they might check the excesses of the Militia from the sister kingdom. In many cases this result may really have ensued; in many others it is to be feared that the English Militiamen caught for the time and in some degree the contagion of the violence around them.

In Wexford my narrative left the King's troops preparing to engage the rebels almost at the very time that the new Viceroy was arriving. Lord Cornwallis landed on the 20th of June. On the same day General Moore routed one body of the armed peasants at Goff's Bridge. On the 21st at daybreak General Lake attacked their principal encampment upon Vinegar Hill. He had under him about thirteen thousand men in four separate columns, with which it was intended to assail the position simultaneously on four different sides. But the accidental delay of one of these left to the rebels a loophole for escape. For that very reason perhaps they made but a faint resistance, the whole loss of the Royal army being only one man killed and four wounded. Later in the same day the town of Wexford, which had been in the insurgents' hands ever since the 30th of last month, was re-entered by General Moore. There was no difficulty in the trial and no doubt as to the execution of the principal chiefs taken with arms in their hands. Among them Mr. Bagenal Harvey, Mr. Colclough, and Mr. Grogan, one of the Fathers Murphy, and another Roman Catholic priest named Redmond, met the doom which they had dared.

Even after the victories of Generals Moore and Lake, the civil war was not completely at an end. There remained some thousands of the runaways from Vinegar Hill, who, armed with pikes, took shelter in the Wicklow mountains. There remained in a few other districts, as Lord Cornwallis states it (to the Duke of Portland, June 28), 'deluded wretches who are wandering about in considerable bodies, and are committing still greater cruelties than they themselves suffer.' These men Lord Cornwallis made every effort to reclaim. He authorised the General Officers in the several districts to issue proclamations inviting those who were still assembled to surrender themselves and forsake their leaders within fourteen days, and in that case promising certificates for their protection.

In this step, and in every other which pointed in the same direction, Lord Cornwallis found himself thwarted and withstood by the leading Irishmen around him. Here are his own words on the 8th of July to the Duke of Portland:—'The principal persons of this country and the members of both Houses of Parliament are in general averse to all acts of clemency. . . . The words *Papists* and *Priests* are for ever in their mouths, and by their unaccountable policy they would drive four-fifths of the community into irreconcilable rebellion.'

To such counsels of violence—counsels in part excused by deeds of violence upon the other side—there were, however, two signal exceptions. These it is the more necessary to state, since they have seldom in Ireland received the meed of common justice, even from that party which at the time benefited by them. The one exception was the Earl of Clare, Lord Chancellor. 'My sentiments,' says Lord Cornwallis in speaking of his measures of amnesty, 'have coincided with those of the Chancellor, whose character has been much misrepresented in England.' The other exception was Lord Castlereagh, the acting Irish Secretary. 'I should be very ungrateful,' says Lord Cornwallis, 'if I did not acknowledge the obligations which I owe to Lord Castlereagh, whose abilities, temper, and judgment have been of the greatest use to me.'

With this humane determination on the part of Lord
Cornwallis, nothing could be more precise than the in-
junctions which in his name Lord Castlereagh had from
the first conveyed.   Here are his very words to Lieut.-
General Stuart on the 25th of June:—'His Excellency the Lord Lieutenant highly approves of your
issuing the most positive orders against the infliction
of punishment under any pretence whatever not authorized by the orders of a General Officer in pursuance of
the sentence of a General Court-martial.'   But in too
many cases the Militia and Yeomanry were not to be
restrained.   Free quarters were freely indulged in;
flogging to extort confession was often inflicted; nay,
even death itself was sometimes not withheld.   'These
men,' says Lord Cornwallis on the 24th of July, 'have
saved the country, but they now take the lead in rapine
and murder.'   And in a still earlier letter he bears a
still more emphatic testimony:—'The accounts that
you see of the numbers of the enemy destroyed in every
action are, I conclude, greatly exaggerated.   From my
own knowledge of military affairs, I am sure that a very
small proportion of them only could be killed in battle;
and I am much afraid that any man in a brown coat
who is found within several miles of the field of action
is butchered without discrimination.   It shall be one of
my first objects to soften the ferocity of our troops,
which I am afraid, in the Irish corps at least, is not confined to the private soldiers.'

The conciliatory course of Lord Cornwallis was exactly conformable to the instructions of the Ministers in
England.   On the 4th of July the Duke of Portland in
the name of the Cabinet suggested to his consideration
the further propriety of passing an Act of Grace extending to all cases of sedition, but guarded by many
reserves.   Lord Cornwallis accordingly sent messages
to both Houses at Dublin announcing that a Bill with
the Royal Sign Manual would shortly be presented,
granting, with certain exceptions, a general pardon to

the rebels. The exceptions proved to be numerous, but they were in name rather than reality; for in practice, exclusive of the leaders, an individual pardon on certain terms was seldom refused to any person who desired to surrender or submit.

There remained, however, to the Government two objects of pressing importance: first, the disposal of the remaining State prisoners; and, secondly, the resistance to a French invasion.

As to the former, the gaols of Newgate and Kilmainham were crowded. There were in custody the principal planners of the late revolutionary movement, as John Mac Cann, the two Sheares, John and Henry, Thomas Emmett, Samuel Neilson, Dr. Mac Nevin, Michael Byrne, and Oliver Bond. There were some scores also of their most active partisans. The two Sheares, being brought to trial and found guilty, were executed on the 14th of July. So on the 19th was John Mac Cann. The trials of Michael Byrne and Oliver Bond had also been gone through, and had ended in a verdict of Guilty. At this point the greater part of the remaining prisoners, in number sixty-four, drew up and sent a proposal to the Government. They engaged to give important information, and to reveal all they knew, provided they were not called upon to implicate any other person by name or description. On these terms they asked that their lives should be spared, and their sentences be commuted into banishment for life. They stipulated also for the lives of Byrne and Bond.

On receiving this proposal, Lord Cornwallis saw its great importance, and was well inclined to accept it; so also was Lord Castlereagh. But they doubted whether it would be possible to find in Dublin a third man of their party who would agree with them. Here again let me quote the words of Lord Cornwallis in writing to the Duke of Portland:—'The Chancellor, who, notwithstanding all that is said of him, is by far the most moderate and right-headed man amongst us, was gone for a week to his country house for the recovery of his health, and I knew of no other of our political friends who was likely to have temper to bear even the statement of the question.' But Lord Cornwallis hoped to find more temper in the heads of the law. These he sent for, and in confidence consulted. To his great disappointment he found both the Chief Justices, Lord Carleton and Lord Kilwarden, as also the Attorney-General, Mr. Toler, strongly advise the rejection of the offer, pressing as usual for the utmost rigour against their countrymen. Lord Cornwallis, though with much reluctance, was obliged to yield to their representations. 'The minds of people,' he says, 'are now in such a state that nothing but blood will satisfy them.' Michael Byrne accordingly was executed the same day.

Next morning, the 26th of July, the State prisoners, finding their first offer rejected, and dismayed at the fate of Byrne, sent in a second proposal of a more extensive nature as to confession and information, and signed by seventy-eight persons instead of sixty-four. Moreover the return of the Chancellor to Dublin entirely changed the scene. The other legal gentlemen on learning his opinion modified their own. They gave in their adhesion, and the Government thus supported determined to brave the displeasure of its general adherents. The terms of the State prisoners were accepted; all their lives were to be spared. Oliver Bond received a respite the same day, and would have been sent abroad with his fellow-captives not yet brought to trial, had he not shortly afterwards (after playing ball all the evening in prison) died suddenly of an attack of apoplexy. The other chiefs, as Emmett, Mac Nevin, and O'Connor, were examined on oath before Secret Committees of both Houses of Parliament. They gave much important information, which they afterwards showed a strong desire to disavow. But they made no mystery of their real objects. Emmett, above

all, boldly avowed the aim which he had set before him
—to dissolve the connexion with Great Britain, to accept
France as only an ally, and to establish Ireland as an
independent Republic.

On reviewing these transactions as authentic documents disclose them, the reader may for himself determine whether the Irish Government of that day can be
justly accused, as it often has been, of rigour and revenge
in the punishments which it did inflict. He may determine whether, on the contrary, it is not entitled to high
praise for risking in the cause of humanity the resentment and alienation of its friends. He may determine
whether it was indeed a light and easy task to stem in
such a matter the furious temper of those times. 'Even
at my table,' so writes Lord Cornwallis, on the 24th of
July, 'even at my table, where you will suppose I do all
I can to prevent it, the conversation always turns on
hanging, shooting, burning, and so forth; and if a
priest has been put to death, the greatest joy is expressed
by the whole company. So much for Ireland and my
wretched situation!'

The witnesses at this time before the Secret Committee of the House of Lords—which was far the most
important, since there they were examined upon oath—
did not altogether spare the character of Mr. Grattan.
The direct charge was indeed of small account. There
was only some hearsay evidence of no legal value that
he had been sworn in an United Irishman by Neilson
and Oliver Bond. This allegation was, I have no doubt
at all, untrue. But his own testimony at the Maidstone trials in behalf of Arthur O'Connor, with whose
designs it was argued that he must have been well
acquainted, and the character of some other of his
associates, seemed to many persons to cast a shade
upon his loyalty. So far had these suspicions wrought
upon the Irish Government that Lord Cornwallis wrote
to recommend his dismissal from the Irish Privy
Council. The assent of the Cabinet having been ob-

tained, the name of Henry Grattan was accordingly struck out of the list by the Lord Lieutenant on the 6th of October.

During the progress of the insurrection, and even after its close, the Irish chiefs looked at first with eager hope, and at last with lingering agony, to the promises of support from France. The expedition of Egypt had drawn to another quarter the troops and the chief that they expected for themselves. Still there were other armaments preparing for their aid, but these were so small and so tardy, that, in fact, they only injured the cause they were designed to serve. One division of three frigates and some transports sailed from La Rochelle. It was commanded by General Humbert, with about eleven hundred men. He had with him a considerable number of spare muskets, and three of the Irish exiles, Matthew Tone, Sullivan, and Teeling. On the 22nd of August they landed at Killala, in the county of Mayo. There General Humbert took up his abode in the Bishop's palace, and began to gather the peasants to his standard.

On receiving this intelligence Lord Cornwallis at once sent General Lake across the Shannon, intending himself to follow in two days. General Lake accordingly took the command of several regiments of the Irish Militia encamped at Castlebar. They very much outnumbered the French of General Humbert, who nevertheless, having pushed forward from the sea coast, boldly attacked them on the morning of the 27th. The Irish regiments, for the most part, behaved as ill as possible; they fled almost without firing a shot. An officer present, the Secretary of General Lake, declared that so shameful a rout he never saw. Two of the Colonels, Lord Ormond and Lord Granard, exerted themselves with great spirit, but in vain. It is probable, however, that many of the Militiamen may have run through disaffection quite as much as through panic, since immediately afterwards several hundreds of them joined the French. This engagement, if so it can be termed—

   'Si rixa est, ubi tu pulsas, ego vapulo tantum'—

used to go in Ireland by the name of 'the Castlebar Races.'

The Prime Minister showed on this occasion his characteristic energy. Thus writes Lord Auckland to his friend John Beresford: 'I passed the morning yesterday at Holwood. . . . Mr. Pitt, within four hours after the arrival of the news (of the rout at Castlebar), had given orders for great reinforcements to be sent to you, and they will embark immediately.' [1]

But the triumph of the French was of short duration. Lord Cornwallis appeared at the head of some regular forces, and superior numbers. General Humbert, after losing two or three hundred men in action, was compelled to surrender with the rest at Ballynamuck. Of the insurgents who had joined him, about four hundred were killed in conflict, about one hundred and eighty suffered by sentence of Court Martial. Of the exiles who had landed with him, Sullivan escaped in the disguise of a Frenchman. Matthew Tone and Teeling were conveyed in irons to Dublin, there tried, and executed.

At the same time a single French brig from Dunkirk, the Anacreon, with Napper Tandy, appeared off the coast of Donegal. In his usual vapouring and vain-glorious strain he had boasted that land where he pleased, he would be joined by thirty thousand men. But no signs of any, not even the smallest junction, appeared; and on learning the fate of Humbert, Tandy re-embarked with great precipitation, and sailed off to Norway. In November of the following year he was given up by the Senate of Hamburg to the Government of England, and he was sent back as a prisoner to Dublin. 'Napper Tandy,' so at that time wrote Lord Cornwallis to the Duke of Portland, 'is a fellow

---

[1] See the *Beresford Correspondence*, vol. ii. p. 180.

of so very contemptible a character, that no person in this country seems to care in the smallest degree about him.'[1] He was treated accordingly as a person of no sort of importance. Upon his pleading guilty when brought up again for trial, he was respited, and after a short interval allowed to retire to the Continent.

When the Anacreon appeared off the coast of Donegal, the principal French squadron for the invasion of Ireland was yet behind. It had been for some time past preparing at Brest. There was the Hoche, a seventy-four gun ship, and there were eight frigates, with about three thousand men on board. The ships were commanded by Admiral Bompart, and the troops by General Hardy. Only four of the Irish exiles accompanied this expedition; but amongst them the ablest of all, Wolfe Tone, who bore the commission of a French officer, and took the name of Smith. On the 11th of October they entered the bay of Killala. But they were followed by a superior squadron under Commodore Sir John Borlase Warren. On the 12th the Hoche was engaged in furious action side by side with a ship of the same size, the Robust. After a well-matched fight of some hours, and a most brave resistance, the French tricolour went down. Six of the French frigates were either taken then or subsequently; only two of the number made good their escape to France.

Wolfe Tone, who in the sea-fight had shown great intrepidity, was taken prisoner with the French officers, and wearing their uniform was not at first distinguished from the rest. But on shore an intimate friend of former years—such a friend as La Rochefoucauld describes—recognised his features, and revealed his name. He was conveyed to Dublin, where, on the 10th of November, a Court Martial was convened. Before this tribunal he appeared in his French uniform, and pleaded his French commission as his privilege. Finding this, as

[1] *Cornwallis Correspondence*, vol. iii. p. 112. See also p. 338.

he expected, overruled, and being condemned to death,
he anticipated the sentence of the law by a self-inflicted
wound, and after lingering several days in agony expired.

The Diaries and Correspondence of Tone were published at Washington by his son in 1826. Being
written with entire unreserve, they are of great historical interest and value, and as such I have constantly
consulted them. The son by whom they were published
received, like his father, a commission in the French
service, and has appended to the Diaries an account of
the campaign of Leipzig, in which as a mere stripling
he served. It is one of the best and most entertaining
military memoirs that I have ever read in any language.
It gave me an interest, notwithstanding the constant
hatred of England which he expresses, in the subsequent
fate of the author, and I addressed an inquiry upon the
subject to an American friend. Here is the answer,
dated in April 1860: ‘When at Washington attending
the Supreme Court last week, I found one gentleman
who remembers him, and who determines the date of
his death by reference to his tombstone in the George-
town cemetery, October 11, 1828. He is described as a
highly intelligent and eccentric person, whose domestic
life was not very tranquil, and made him very much a
recluse from society. He held, I believe, a subordinate
clerkship in the War Office.’

CHAPTER XXVII.

1798—1799.

Pitt's design of an Act of Union with Ireland—Conferences of the Irish Chancellor and Speaker with the Ministers in London—Heads of the intended measure—Opening of the British Parliament—The Income-Tax—Voluntary contributions in aid—Opposition to the Union in Ireland—Meeting of the Irish Parliament—Equal division—Debates in the British Parliament—Impressive Speech by Pitt upon the Irish question—Its powerful effect—Resolutions carried in both Houses—Change of opinion in Ireland—Compensations—Renewal of war on the Continent—Congress of Rastadt dissolved—Russian army under Suwarrow sent into Italy—Bill for partial Abolition of the Slave Trade thrown out by the Lords—Letter from Lady Chatham.

FROM the outset of the troubles in Ireland Mr. Pitt had fully considered and finally determined the course he should pursue. He thought that to put down the insurrection by force of arms was only the first part of his duty. He thought that to revert to the old system would be a most shallow policy. A new, and comprehensive, and healing measure must be tried—an Act of Union, which should raise the minds of Irishmen from local to imperial aims,—which should blend the two Legislatures, and if possible, also the two nations into one.

To this design Mr. Pitt obtained the full assent of his colleagues. It was also entirely conformable to the opinions of the King. Before Lord Cornwallis set out for Ireland, it was confidentially imparted to him, and he was instructed to regard it as the great point of ultimate settlement. One month after his landing we find him write as follows to Mr. Pitt:—'The two or three people whom I have ventured in the most cautious manner to sound, say that it must not be mentioned now—that this is a time of too much danger to agitate such a question. . . . . . Convinced as I am that it is the only measure which can long preserve this country, I will never lose sight of it.'

When, however, the Irish insurgents had been defeated and the French troops made prisoners, the communications of Lord Cornwallis on this subject became more open and direct. On the 25th of September he reports to Mr. Pitt: 'The principal people here are so frightened, that they would, I believe, readily consent to an Union; but then it must be a Protestant Union; and even the Chancellor, who is the most right-headed politician in the country, will not hear of the Roman Catholics sitting in the United Parliament.

Lord Cornwallis, on the contrary, would have preferred their immediate admission as a part of the Act of Union. Till they were admitted, he said, there would be no peace or safety in Ireland. But it is plain—as the subsequent letters of Lord Cornwallis most clearly show—that at this time he greatly underrated the immense obstacles in the way of an Union, even on high Protestant terms. 'Our great measure I should think would be carried here without much difficulty.' Such are his words to General Ross on the 8th of November. A few months later, and we find the same man almost despairing of success!

Both the Chancellor, and the Speaker, John Foster, a man of great weight and ability, went to England about this time, and conferred with several of the Ministers in London. The result as to Mr. Foster is related as follows.

Mr. Pitt to Lord Cornwallis.

Downing Street, Nov. 17, 1798.

My dear Lord,—I have had a great deal of conversation with the Speaker, who arrived here on Wednesday. I found him in his manner perfectly cordial and communicative, and though in his own general opinion strongly against the measure of an Union (particularly at the present moment), yet perfectly ready to discuss the point fairly. . . . . On the whole, I think I may venture to say that he will not obstruct the measure; and I rather hope, if it can be made palatable to him personally, which I believe it may, that he will give it fair support.

. . . . In the interval previous to your Session there will, I trust, be full opportunity for communication and arrangement with individuals on whom I am inclined to believe the success of the measure will wholly depend. You will observe that in what relates to the oaths to be taken by Members of the United Parliament, the plan which we have sent copies the precedent I mentioned in a former letter of the Scotch Union; and on the grounds I before mentioned, I own I think this leaves the Catholic question on the only footing on which it can safely be placed. Mr. Elliot, when he brought me your letter, stated very strongly all the arguments which he thought might induce us to admit the Catholics to Parliament and office, but I confess he did not satisfy me of the practicability of such a measure at this time, or of the propriety of attempting it. With respect to a provision for the Catholic clergy, and some arrangement respecting tithes, I am happy to find an uniform opinion in favour of the proposal among all the Irish I have seen; and I am more and more convinced that those measures, with some effectual mode to enforce the residence of *all* ranks of the Protestant clergy, offer the best chance of gradually putting an end to the evils most felt in Ireland.

Believe me, my dear Lord, &c.,   W. PITT.

P.S.—You may be assured that I shall omit no opportunity of obviating any false impression of the transaction with the State prisoners; but I believe the benefits derived from their discovery are now generally felt and admitted in both countries.

The hopes entertained of the Speaker were by no means fulfilled. His letters from England to his friends at home were, as Lord Castlereagh learnt, very adverse; and on his return he became of all born Irishmen the most powerful opponent, as Lords Clare and Castlereagh were the most powerful promoters, of the Union.

On the 12th of November the heads of the intended measure were transmitted by the Duke of Portland to Lord Cornwallis. They differed in several main points from the Act which subsequently passed. There was no limitation on the prerogative of creating Irish Peers. There was no entire disfranchisement of any Irish county or borough, but either a reduction or an alternation of the members elected to the Imperial Parliament, so that the entire number should on no account exceed one hundred. There was power reserved to alter the oaths taken by members of both Houses; a power manifestly designed for the future admission of the Roman Catholics. Such was the measure which, when further digested and matured by communications between Dublin and London, was to be brought before the Irish Parliament immediately on its meeting at the close of January next.

Meanwhile the British Parliament had already met. It was opened by the King in person on the 20th of November. There were debates, but no amendment moved in either House.

So early as the 3rd of December Pitt brought forward his financial plan in one of the greatest of his great financial speeches. He stated, in the first place, the necessary expenditure for the year at 29,272,000*l.* Land and Malt, the Lottery, the Consolidated Fund, and the tax laid in the last Session upon exports and imports, would produce altogether little more than six millions, so that there remained upwards of twenty-three millions. In the debates of the preceding Session on the Assessed Taxes he had laid down, and the House seemed to have adopted, two fundamental principles. First, to reduce the total amount to be at present raised by a loan; and next, as far as it was not reducible, to bring it within such a limit that no more loan should be raised than a temporary tax would defray within a limited time. On these principles the increased assessment of last year had been made; but it had proved less productive than was then expected. 'It now appears,' said Pitt, 'that not by any error in the calculation of our resources, not by any exaggeration of our wealth,

but by the general facility of modification, by the
anxiety to render the measure as little oppressive as
possible, a defalcation has arisen which ought not to
have taken place. Yet under the disadvantage and
imperfections of an unequal and inadequate scale of
application, the effects of the measure have tended to
confirm our estimate of its benefits. Every circumstance in our situation, every event in our retrospect,
demonstrates the advantage of the system of raising a
considerable part of the supplies within the year, and
ought to induce us to enforce it with a more effectual
provision against frauds. . . . . In these sentiments our
leading principle should be to guard against all evasion,
and to endeavour, by a fair and strict application, to
realize that full tenth which it was the original purpose
of the measure of the Assessed Taxes to obtain. . . . .
For this purpose it is my intention to propose that the
presumption founded upon the Assessed Taxes shall be
laid aside, and that a general tax shall be imposed upon
all the leading branches of income. No scale of income,
indeed, which can be devised will be perfectly free from
the objection of inequality, or entirely cut off the power
of evasion. All that can be attempted is to approach
as near as circumstances will permit to a fair and equal
contribution.'

Mr. Pitt then proceeded to unfold the very elaborate
plan which he had formed. The power of fixing the
rate of assessment in each case was to be given to Commissioners appointed for the purpose. They were to be
men of independent position, removed as far as possible
from any suspicion of partiality; and with that view
a qualification of 300*l.* was proposed. In fixing the
assessment upon any person, they were to have not only
a legal power, but a large discretion allowed them.
From calculations which Pitt gave in full detail, he
estimated the annual rents of lands and houses, tithes
and mines, the profits of trades or professions, the payments of the Fund, and all other sources of income, at

the total amount of one hundred and two millions, so
that a tax of ten per cent., if fully carried out, would
produce ten millions. Pitt now proposed that, in lieu
of the former Assessed Taxes to be at once repealed,
there should be a new assessment on all the various
kinds of income. The scale was to begin at 65*l.* a year,
at which point one hundred and twentieth part was to
be taken. It was to proceed by minute advances up to
200*l.* a year, on which and all exceeding incomes ten
per cent. was imposed. English subjects residing out
of England were not to be exempted, nor yet any bodies
politic or corporate. Nor yet was there any distinction
between fixed and fluctuating incomes—as between the
rents of land, for instance, and the profits of professions.

The scheme of a general tax on all kinds of income
was by no means a new one. It had several times been
suggested to the Minister by speculative financiers and
writers of pamphlets. Thus Bishop Watson of Llandaff
had, earlier in the year, published an able essay entitled
'Hints towards an improved System of Taxation, extending to all persons in exact proportion to their property.' The Bishop states that, so early as December,
1797, he sent in the substance of these hints to Mr.
Pitt, who, however, took no notice of it, probably, adds
the Bishop, 'throwing it aside among the numerous
schemes with which he must frequently be pestered.'
But although the idea was far from new, the whole
merit of the execution—of the skilful and prudent
framework by which a design so bold and comprehensive was for the first time carried out—belongs undoubtedly to Mr. Pitt.

In opposing the idea of an income-tax, Mr. Tierney
appears to have contended that it pressed unduly on
the land and was too favourable to the moneyed interest. Here is his argument: 'The Chancellor of
the Exchequer says that this plan will cause the Funds
to rise; so that, if any gentleman has 20,000*l.* in the
Funds, his fortune may improve by this duty. If you

raise the Funds, for example, two per cent., he will make a large sum of money by his capital; whereas your plan, to be worth anything, should compel the moneyed men to take at least their share of the public burthens.'

Another opponent of the measure, Mr. William Smith, took up the very contrary ground. He thought that the land was unduly favoured. He considered the country gentlemen drones, as distinguished from the manufacturing bees, and he called for some distinction in the payment between the useful and the useless class. These remarks, however, drew upon him a severe retort from Mr. Pitt. 'In the class of useless the Hon. gentleman has thought proper to rank all the proprietors of land, those men who form the line which binds and knits society together; those men on whom in a great measure the administration of justice and the internal police of the country depend; those men from whom the poor receive employment, from whom agriculture derives its improvement and support, and to whom, of course, commerce itself is indebted for the foundation on which it rests. Yet this class the Hon. gentleman has thought fit to stigmatise as useless drones, of no estimation in the eyes of society. A light and flippant theory, the offspring of mere temporary, unthinking policy!'

Notwithstanding the arguments of Mr. Tierney and Mr. William Smith, which might be taken as answering each other, the Minister prevailed by a very large majority. The progress of the Bill was affirmed by 183 votes against 17, and it was read a third time on the last day of the year.

The Diary and Letters of Mr. Wilberforce give some account of the Minister at this time. 'Nov. 27. Walked in the morning with Pitt and Grenville; much talk about income-tax.' 'Dec. 6. Pitt's plan of income-tax seems well received upon the whole.' 'Dec. 14. Supped with Pitt *tête-à-tête*. Much talk about Europe,

Ireland, income-tax, Lord Cornwallis, Union.   He is, of course, in high spirits, and, what is better, his health, which had seemed to be again declining a few weeks ago, is now, I am assured, more radically improved than one could almost have hoped.'   'Dec. 17. With Cookson and Gott (from Leeds) at Pitt's all morning.   We hit off a plan for commercial commission.   Walker says the manufacturers can't and won't pay.'—But they could pay, and they did.

Before Christmas Mr. Pitt deemed it his duty, in view of the recent rebellion and still existing conspiracies, to bring in a Bill continuing from the last Session the suspension of the Habeas Corpus.   It led to some debate, and also to several complaints of the treatment of the prisoners arrested under the suspension, amongst others of Colonel Despard; yet, in the sole division that was taken against the measure, the minority, exclusive of the tellers, mustered only six.

In the first days of January, 1799, the Income-Tax Bill came before the House of Peers.   It was assailed by Lords Suffolk and Holland and by the Duke of Bedford, and defended by Lords Liverpool, Auckland, and Loughborough; but it passed without any division.

On the measure becoming law, it was thought most desirable to assist and enhance its effect by further voluntary contributions.   Men in high places set the example.   Mr. Pitt and Mr. Dundas subscribed each 2000*l.* a year in lieu of their legal assessments; to endure, if they remained in office, so long as the war continued. So did also to the same amount the Speaker, and each of the two Chief Justices, and so did also, though he held no office, Lord Romney.   The King subscribed no less than one-third of his Privy Purse, or 20,000*l.* a year.[1]

At the beginning of 1799 the news that came from Ireland was not inspiriting.   Lord Cornwallis and Lord Castlereagh had done their utmost to promote the

---

[1] See two notes of Mr. Pitt upon this subject in *Rose's Correspondence,* vol. i. p. 240.

intended Union. By putting forward in its behalf the whole weight and authority of the Government, they gained it a great many—some very unwilling—supporters. Thus, on the 7th of January, we find the Earl of Ely, in a private letter, denounce 'this mad scheme,' for which, he says, he has not heard a single argument adduced. Yet, in the following year, we find the scheme supported not only by his Lordship, but by his Lordship's six members in the House of Commons. The result to his Lordship was that, on the passing of the Bill, the noble Earl received a Marquisate and also an English peerage.

Mr. Beresford, though with some reluctance, agreed to support the measure; but, sooner than take that course, his second son, Mr. John Claudius Beresford, threw up his sinecure office as Inspector General of Exports. In other cases where gentlemen in office were found obdurate, the Government informed them that there was no further occasion for their services. Thus, in the course of January, both the Chancellor of the Exchequer, Sir John Parnell, and the Prime Serjeant, Mr. James Fitzgerald, were dismissed. In place of the former, Mr. Isaac Corry, the son of a considerable merchant at Newry and himself the member for that town, was appointed Chancellor of the Exchequer.

On the other hand the Speaker, who now assumed in a very decided manner the character of partisan, Mr. George Ponsonby, Sir John Parnell, and several others, were no less active in the opposite direction. In some cases they sought to alarm selfish interests; in others they appealed to patriotic feeling. Thus prepared on both sides of the question, the two Houses met on the 22nd of January, and the speech of the Lord Lieutenant announced in general terms the project to be laid before them. In the Commons there ensued a debate of perhaps unprecedented length, extending from four in the afternoon of that day till one in the afternoon of the next. Finally, an amendment pledging the House to maintain an ' independent Legislature as established in 1782,' was rejected by only one vote, the numbers being 106 and 105.

With such a neck and neck division, it was plain that the measure could be for the time no further pressed. But at the very time when this heavy blow was dealt on it in Dublin, it received the aid of a most powerful lever in London. On the same day that the Irish Parliament was opened, the King sent a Message to both Houses in England recommending, in the same words which the Lord Lieutenant had used, the consideration of the best means of consolidating the strength, the power, and the resources of the British empire. Next day Dundas laid upon the table, sealed up, papers relative to the proceedings of persons and societies engaged in a treasonable conspiracy to effect the separation of the two kingdoms. Little discussion was expected, since only an Address of Thanks was moved. But on the sudden Sheridan moved an amendment levelled at the project of Union. Pitt, though he had not been prepared to open the whole case on this occasion, met the arguments of Sheridan by a most able and convincing reply. We find it on the morrow transmitted as in triumph from the Home Office to the Lord Lieutenant of Ireland. Thus writes the Under-Secretary: ' I now send your Lordship, by the Duke of Portland's direction, a dozen impressions of the " Morning Post," which is the paper that appears to me, upon the whole, to contain the best report of Mr. Pitt's speech last night. It is, however, after all, but a miserable sketch of the most impressive and one of the most judicious speeches I ever heard. It has, I think, completely decided the question on this side of the water, where people's minds were much afloat.'

Two days later the news came of the ill success in the Irish House of Commons, and Pitt himself wrote to the Lord Lieutenant, but without the smallest reference to his own exertions.

Downing Street, Jan. 26, 1799.

My dear Lord,—You will receive from the Duke of Portland an official despatch, in answer to the accounts which came this morning of the proceedings of the first day of your Session. I am certainly much disappointed and grieved to find that a measure so essential is frustrated for the time by the effect of prejudice and cabal. But I have no doubt that a steady and temperate perseverance on our part will, at no distant period, produce a more just sense of what the real interest of every man who has a stake in Ireland requires—at least as much as duty to the country and the empire at large.

You will, I hope, approve our own determination to proceed here on Thursday in opening the Resolutions stating the general outline and principles of the plan. It may, I think, be done in such a manner as to show how much Ireland is dependent on us for every benefit she now enjoys, and to lay the strongest ground for resuming the subject in the Irish Parliament with better prospects, either in the course of the present Session (when the real merits of the question shall have been more fully stated to the public) or in the next; and, at all events, the measure is one which we cannot lose sight of, but must make the grand and primary object of all our policy with respect to Ireland. In this view it seems very desirable, if Government is strong enough to do it without too much immediate hazard, to mark by dismissal the sense entertained of the conduct of those persons in office who opposed. In particular it strikes me as essential not to make an exception to this line in the instance of the Speaker's son. No Government can stand on a safe and respectable ground which does not show that it feels itself independent of him. With respect to persons of less note, or those who have been only neutral, more lenity may perhaps be advisable. On the precise extent of the line, however, your Lordship can alone judge on the spot; but I thought you would like to know from me directly the best view I can form of the subject.

We shall be impatient to hear what further may have passed in Ireland on Thursday; but whatever may have been the result, it will make no difference in our intention of proceeding here in the manner I have mentioned. . . . .

Believe me, &c.,   W. Pitt.

According to the intention expressed in this letter, Pitt, on the Thursday following—that is on the 31st of January—brought forward in the House of Commons some Resolutions affirming the principles of an Union with Ireland. On this occasion, in a speech of very considerable length, he achieved one of the highest of his many oratorical triumphs. Lord Auckland, writing to Mr. Beresford the day but one after, describes it as follows: 'Mr. Pitt's speech on the Irish business surpassed even the most sanguine expectations of friends, and perhaps even any former exhibition of Parliamentary eloquence. It will be published next week, and shall be forwarded to you for the fullest and most extensive circulation through Ireland.'

A few years later Mr. Pitt stated in conversation to my father that there were only three speeches (these three being published as pamphlets) that he had ever revised for the press. First, the speech 'on finance before the commencement of the war:' this was, as I conceive, the speech of February 17, 1792, proposing both a repeal of certain taxes and an increase of the Sinking Fund;[1] secondly, the speech on the Union (January 31, 1799); and, thirdly, the speech on the overtures from France (January 22, 1800). From the authenticity of this speech on the Union, and from the important views of policy which it discloses, I shall, contrary to my usual practice, proceed to give some considerable extracts :—

'Suppose, for instance, that the present war, which the Parliament of Great Britain considers to be just and necessary, had been voted by the Irish Parliament to be unjust, unnecessary, extravagant, and hostile to the principle of humanity and freedom. Would that Parliament have been bound by this country? If not,

---

[1] Lord Grenville, in conversation, mentioned as corrected by Pitt the speech 'on the Sinking Fund.' This has led the editor of Mr. Rogers's notes to conclude, but I think erroneously, that the speech in question was on the first proposal of that Fund, March 29, 1786. See Rogers's *Recollections* (p. 188, ed. 1859).

what security have we, at a moment the most important
to our common interest and common salvation, that the
two kingdoms should have but one friend and one
foe? . . . . . This country is at this time engaged in
the most important and momentous conflict that ever
occurred in the history of the world—a conflict in
which Great Britain is distinguished for having made
the only manly and successful stand against the common
enemy of civilized society. We see the point in which
that enemy thinks us the most assailable. Are we not
then bound in policy and prudence to strengthen that
vulnerable point, involved as we are in a contest of
liberty against despotism—of property against plunder
and rapine—of religion and order against impiety and
anarchy? There was a time when this would have
been termed declamation; but, unfortunately, long and
bitter experience has taught us to feel that it is only
the feeble and imperfect representation of those calamities, the result of French principles and French arms,
which are every day attested by the wounds of a bleed-
ing world.'

'I am well aware that the subject of religious distinction is a dangerous and delicate topic, especially
when applied to Ireland. The situation of Ireland is
different in this respect from the situation of every
other country. Where the established religion of a
state is the same as the general religion of the empire,
and where the property of the country is in the hands
of a comparatively small number of persons professing
that established religion, while the religion of the great
majority of the people is different, it is not easy to say
on general principles what system of Church Establishment in such a country would be free from difficulty and
inconvenience. . . . . . . No man can say that in the
present state of things, and while Ireland remains a
separate kingdom, full concessions could be made to the
Catholics without endangering the state and shaking
the constitution of Ireland to its centre.'

' On the other hand, without anticipating the discussion, or the propriety of discussing the question, or saying how soon or how late it may be fit to discuss it, two propositions are indisputable: first, when the conduct of the Catholics shall be such as to make it safe for the Government to admit them to the participation of the privileges granted to those of the established religion, and when the temper of the times shall be favourable to such a measure—when these events take place, it is obvious that such a question may be agitated in an united, imperial Parliament, with much greater safety than it could be in a separate legislature. In the second place, I think it certain that, even for whatever period it may be thought necessary, after the Union to withhold from the Catholics the enjoyment of those advantages, many of the objections which at present arise out of their situation would be removed if the Protestant legislature were no longer separate and local, but general and imperial; and the Catholics themselves would at once feel a mitigation of the most goading and irritating of their present causes of complaint.

' How far, in addition to this great and leading consideration, it may also be wise and practicable to accompany the measure by some mode of relieving the lower orders from the pressure of tithes, which, in many instances, operate at present as a great practical evil, or to make, under proper regulations, and without breaking in on the security of the present Protestant establishment, an effectual and adequate provision for the Catholic clergy, it is not now necessary to discuss. It is sufficient to say that these and all other subordinate points connected with the same subject are more likely to be permanently and satisfactorily settled by an united legislature than by any local arrangements.

' But, Sir, if, on the other hand, it should happen that there be a country which against the greatest of all dangers that threaten its peace and security has not

adequate means of protecting itself without the aid of
another nation; if that other be a neighbouring and
kindred nation, speaking the same language, whose
laws, whose customs, and habits are the same in principle, but carried to a greater degree of perfection,
with a more extensive commerce and more abundant
means of acquiring and diffusing national wealth—the
stability of whose Government, the excellence of whose
constitution is more than ever the admiration and envy
of Europe, and of which the very country of which we
are speaking can only boast an inadequate and imperfect resemblance—under such circumstances, I would
ask, what conduct would be prescribed by every rational
principle of dignity, of honour, or of interest?   I would
ask whether this is not a faithful description of the
circumstances which ought to dispose Ireland to an
union?—whether Great Britain is not precisely the
nation with which, on these principles, a country situ-
ated as Ireland is would desire to unite?   Does an
union under such circumstances, by free consent, and
on just and equal terms, deserve to be branded as a
proposal for subjecting Ireland to a foreign yoke?   Is
it not rather the free and voluntary association of two
great countries, which join, for their common benefit,
in one empire, where each will retain its proportional
weight and importance, under the security of equal laws,
reciprocal affection, and inseparable interests, and which
want nothing but that indissoluble connexion to render
both invincible?

> ' Non ego nec Teucris Italos parere jubebo,
>   Nec nova regna peto ; paribus se legibus ambæ
>   Invictæ gentes æterna in fœdem mittant.' [1]

The eloquence of Pitt on this occasion produced
a most powerful effect.   We find, for example, just
before it, Wilberforce in great doubt as to his vote;
almost immediately afterwards his mind was made up

[1] _Æn._, lib. xii. ver. 189. In the second line Pitt put _nora_ instead
of _mihi_, which would have been inapplicable.

to support the measure. The fame of that great speech reached Lady Chatham in her retirement, and she could not refrain from congratulations to her son. Here is his reply:—

Downing Street, Saturday,
Feb. 9, 1799.

My dear Mother,—I have to give you a thousand thanks for your kind letter. I am very far from having suffered by the labours which gave occasion to it. The report which has reached you is, I fear, much too partial; but I shall have great reason to be satisfied if I have at all done justice to the question I had to bring forward. We are not likely to encounter any serious difficulty here, and the discussion in the House of Commons will probably be finished in the course of the next week. In Ireland the progress of conviction cannot be expected to be very rapid; but I see enough to entertain a strong persuasion that it will probably work its way sooner than is now expected.

Ever, my dear Mother, &c.,   W. Pitt.

The project of Union as mooted on the 23rd of January, and the Resolutions as moved on the 31st, gave rise to several keen debates. Fox continued absent, and did not declare his opinion. But the project was opposed with great eloquence by Sheridan and Grey, and not less ably supported by Dundas and Canning. The Speaker delivered a weighty and impressive speech in its favour, while another personal friend of the Prime Minister, Henry Bankes, declared against it. Yet, though the palm of eloquence might perhaps be disputed, there could be no doubt as to the predominance of numbers. An amendment moved by Sheridan was rejected by a majority of almost ten to one—140 to 15; and on a subsequent day the numbers were 149 and 24.

The Resolutions, when carried in the Commons, were transmitted to the other House for its concurrence. They were agreed to without a division, though after a long debate. Lord Grenville and Lord Auckland, now joint Postmaster-General, greatly distinguished themselves in support of the measure, while Lord Lansdowne and Lord Moira spoke with effect upon the other side.

The King also was much in favour of the scheme. 'I only hope,' he said to Dundas about this time, 'Government is not pledged to anything in favour of the Roman Catholics.' 'No,' the Minister answered; 'it will be a matter for future consideration; and on the King going on to allege his scruples upon the Coronation Oath, he endeavoured to explain that this Oath applied to His Majesty only in his executive capacity, and not as part of the Legislature. But George the Third angrily rejoined, 'None of your Scotch metaphysics, Mr. Dundas! None of your Scotch metaphysics!' [1]

It had been hoped by the English Ministers that the scheme of Union might still be resumed in the Irish Parliament before the close of the Session. But Lord Cornwallis represented the attempt as impracticable, and the question was postponed till the commencement of the ensuing year. Meanwhile the Irish people became better informed as to the project, and the strong arguments in its support began in various quarters to prevail. 'From everything that I can learn,' so writes Lord Cornwallis on the 28th of March, 'the opinion of the loyal part of the public is changing fast in favour of the Union.' And again on the 13th of August he reports of the South : 'In general, good disposition towards the Government, and cordial approbation of the measure of Union. This sentiment,' he adds, ' is confined to no particular class of men, but equally pervades both the Catholic and Protestant bodies.'

Great advantage also was derived from the recent

---

[1] *Life of Sir James Mackintosh,* by his Son, vol. i. p. 170, ed. 1835. This conversation was related to Mackintosh by Dundas himself.

debates in the Irish Parliament. Lord Castlereagh pointed out various changes in the project to meet the objections that had been or that might be urged. If only one member was left to each county, the primary interests would still prevail, but the secondary interests would be swept away. Lord Castlereagh recommended that each county should be allowed two members as before, and that on the other hand there should be a considerable disfranchisement of nomination boroughs, the proprietors to receive a liberal price in money. There should be liberal compensation also to the holders of office in Dublin, and to all other persons whose interests might be unfavourably affected by the measure. Lord Castlereagh calculated that a million and a half in money would be required to effect all these compensations, but that without them the Union would not be carried. Most of his suggestions were in consequence adopted.

It will be observed that the system of compensation here proposed was not of a party character, or such as applied to friends alone. Thus a proprietor of borough influence, on the passing of the Union would receive exactly the same sum, whether he had voted for the measure or against it. But the remark cannot be extended to other compensations or rewards tendered on condition of support to the members of both Houses. There were many promises of a Marquisate, or some other step in the Irish Peerage. There were many promises of a Barony in the English Peerage. There were many promises of an office, a pension, or a favour of some other kind. And before the actual promise there was a great deal of bargaining and chaffering as to terms. Nothing but the national necessity of carrying the measure could have reconciled the English statesmen to such a course. Lord Cornwallis most especially speaks of it with deep disgust. To a confidential friend he wrote as follows on the 20th of May : 'The political jobbing of this country gets the better of me.

It has been the wish of my life to avoid all this dirty
business; and I am now involved in it beyond all bearing. . . . . How I long to kick those whom my public
duty obliges me to court!'

It has been alleged that at this time there were also
large payments of money, or, in plain words, the purchase of votes. To any large extent the allegation does
not seem true. There were certainly some payments of
money on both sides. There was a stock-purse of the
Opposition chiefs, furnished by subscription. There was
a demand from time to time of secret supplies from the
Treasury in England. But these secret supplies, as confidential notes have since disclosed them, were on no
considerable scale. Thus we find in January, 1800, after
much and earnest pressing, the despatch of only 5,000*l*.
from London, with some hopes of 'a still further sum,
though not immediately.'[1]   And as to the application of
these sums on the Government side, it must be remembered that the Union was not only the subject, nor
Members of Parliament the only persons, with which they
had to deal. They had conspiracies to trace as well as
opposition to encounter; and in a lower class they had
runners and informers in their pay.

Meanwhile the sealed papers which Mr Dundas presented to the English House of Commons on the 23rd of
January had been referred to a Select Committee. On
the 15th of March the Committee gave in their Report.
They stated that they had found the clearest proofs of
a systematic design, formed by conspirators at home in
conjunction with France, and pursued during several
years, to overturn the laws and constitution both in Great
Britain and Ireland. They explained in detail the means
which had been used for that object; the system of the
Society of the ' United Irishmen,' and other societies
in Great Britain; the attempts to form National Conventions in England and Scotland, and the proceedings
subsequent to the arrests of 1794. They expressed

[1] *Cornwallis Correspondence*, vol. iii. p. 156.

their firm belief that treasonable plans were now more than ever in progress, and that agents from Ireland were concerting with the French a fresh and general insurrection.

On the 19th of April Mr. Pitt rose to call the attention of the House to this Report. It was so full, he said, of convincing proofs as to render any comments useless. He proposed that whoever should continue, after a day to be named, to be a member of the 'Corresponding Society,' the 'United Irishmen,' or 'United Englishmen,' should be liable to a punishment varying, according to the circumstances of the case, from a fine to imprisonment or transportation. The same penalties should attach to the members of any other societies which, like those he had mentioned, were bound together by secret oaths. The necessity for a licence and the restrictions already applied to lecture-rooms should be extended to debating societies. The proprietors of printing-presses were to obtain certificates from the Clerks of the Peace; and the name and abode of the printer were to appear on every copy of every book or paper printed, under a penalty for each omission of 20*l.* Mr. Tierney stated his entire dissent: nevertheless the Bill, prepared according to the views and on the motion of Mr. Pitt, passed both Houses with but little opposition.

Next month we obtain a glimpse of Pitt in private life from a visit of Wilberforce, which his Diary describes: 'May 18, 1799. To Holwood by half-past four. Pitt riding out. Lord Camden and J. Villiers came, with whom walked. Pitt, Canning, and Pepper Arden came in late to dinner. . . . . Evening: Canning and Pitt reading classics.'

In the spring of this year there was a renewal of the war upon the Continent. The Congress of Rastadt, after long and wearisome sittings, had failed to effect its objects. It was formally dissolved in April, not without considerable animosity in its last discussions. But that animosity was much farther inflamed by a mysterious crime, which has never yet been clearly explained, the murder of the French plenipotentiaries on their journey homeward. They had set out on a dark night for Strasburg, when just beyond the gates of Rastadt their carriages were attacked by a body of horsemen in the dress of Austrian hussars. Two of the plenipotentiaries were dragged out and slain in cold blood; the third, Jean Debry, though struck down by two of the men with their sabres, and left for dead upon the road, was able to creep into the neighbouring wood, and to escape with little harm.

Even before this atrocious act, which the press at Paris of the time did not fail to ascribe to the villany of Mr. Pitt, the French and Austrians had taken the field. To recover Italy was now the great object of the latter. They had upon the Adige a well-appointed and numerous army, commanded by the Baron de Melas, an excellent soldier, but greatly past his prime. Their principal reliance, however, was upon their allies. They obtained the aid of the Emperor Paul of Russia, whose fickle and eccentric mind was at this time vehemently turned against France. He engaged to support the Court of Vienna in its designs upon Italy with an army of fifty thousand men, which accordingly he sent to the Adige under the command of the most renowned of his generals, the queller of the Turks, and surnamed Rimniksky from the battle of Rimnik,[1] the half-savage but hitherto unconquered Marshal Suwarrow.

In pursuance of the same object the English Cabinet had concluded a treaty of subsidy with Russia. It was agreed that the Emperor should employ an army of forty-five thousand men, and that England should assign to him the sum of 225,000*l.* as preparation money, and 75,000*l.* monthly, besides a further payment at the conclusion of a peace made by common assent. Thus we were no longer without allies,—but we had to pay for them!

[1] Castera, *Vie de Catherine II.*, vol. iii. p. 76.

This treaty was communicated to Parliament by a Royal Message in the month of June. Pitt, in moving for a grant of 825,000*l.* to make good His Majesty's engagements, expressed his hope that, notwithstanding, the English people would mainly rely on their own exertions. 'Even if,' he said, 'the common cause were to be again abandoned by your allies, you will never forget that in the moment of difficulty and danger you found safety where only it is to be found—in your own resolution, firmness, and conduct.' Tierney, though without dividing the House, opposed the grant, and Pitt replied. 'The Hon. gentleman persists in saying that we have an intention to wage war against opinion. It is not so. We are not in arms against the opinions of the closet nor the speculations of the school. We are at war with armed opinions. . . . . . Their appearance in arms changed their character; and we will not leave the monster to prowl the world unopposed.'

In this year, as in the preceding ones, Wilberforce brought in a motion to abolish the Slave Trade at a limited time. It was again supported by Pitt, and also with great eloquence by Canning, but on the other hand opposed by Dundas and Windham, and again rejected by 84 votes against 54.

Yet the question was not laid aside. A Bill was introduced by Mr. Henry Thornton for a much smaller object—to confine the trade within certain limits upon the coast of Africa. This Bill passed the Commons, and was sent to the House of Lords. There, however, it was exposed to great hazards, some of a very peculiar and mortifying kind. They will be found explained in the following letter, which Lord Chatham received from Mr. Pitt.

Downing Street, May 29, 1799.

My dear Brother,—There is a Bill depending in the House of Lords, which will probably not be decided before your return, for restraining the Slave Trade on that part of the African coast where the Sierra Leone Company has its establishment. It is a measure which really seems to be liable to no one of the objections which have weighed against the general abolition of the trade, and, without even any alleged inconvenience to the West India Islands, might be productive of very beneficial consequences to that part of Africa. An opposition, however, has been raised to it, ostensibly by the Duke of Clarence, but in fact, I am sorry to say, by some of the members of the administration, who are supported by a great appearance of Court influence. This leads to very unpleasant consequences, not merely with a view to the measure itself, but from the general effect of an attempt openly to employ the weight and influence of Government against the sentiments of those in whose favour it ought to operate; and I have therefore found myself under the necessity of calling in all the strength I can in support of the measure.

On the general question of the Slave Trade I am afraid your sentiments may not exactly coincide with my own; but I am persuaded, when you come to consider the measure, you will see there is no pretence for this opposition except a blind determination to encourage, for its own sake and without the shadow of advantage, a trade which no one pretends to justify; and I am sure you will feel the force of the other considerations I have mentioned to you. My chief motive, however, in troubling you just now is only to beg earnestly that you will have the goodness to keep your decision open upon the subject till we have an opportunity of talking it over fully, which will probably be in a few days. I have little doubt that upon the whole the Bill will be carried, but not without a great contest.

We are still without the news so impatiently looked for from the fleet.

Ever, my dear Brother, affectionately yours,

W. PITT.

On the 5th July came the debate upon the Second Reading. Wilberforce, in his Diary, gives of it a pithy account. 'The Bishops' proxies all in favour of the Bill. Thurlow profane balderdash. Westmorland coarse. Bishop of Rochester (Dr. Horsley), ill-judged application of Scripture. Grenville spoke well.' Lord Grenville, it should be noted, was warmly in favour of the Bill, which, on the other hand, was opposed by the Duke of Clarence, Lord Thurlow, and Lord Liverpool. A division being called for, the proxies were found to be exactly equal, 36 on each side, while of the Peers in the House there were only 27 Contents to 32 Not Contents. So, to Pitt's great mortification, the Bill was lost.

The vote on the 5th of July was one of the last of this Session; it was closed by the King in person on the 12th.

It gives me pleasure at this place to be able to lay before the reader one letter at least from Lady Chatham to her son. As I have mentioned elsewhere, there are none left among Mr. Pitt's papers. But three, which refer to applications for offices, remained in the hands of his last Private Secretary; and that gentleman has most kindly presented them to me.

Lady Chatham to Mr. Pitt.

Burton Pynsent, July 27, 1799.

Very bad weather, my dear son, for me to use my pen to-day; but, however, I must just write three lines to you. The folly of poor Croft's addled, wild head has been sufficiently punished, for, as I have been informed, what small place remained to him has been taken from him, and he is really left destitute. Mr. Rose promised me that a place should be found for him in a way which would be least talked about, as the offended gentlemen were angry with his impertinence. Notwithstanding the oddity of his character, his unceasing, and, indeed, his extraordinary attachment and zeal for your ever-loved father, entitles him to be forgiven and provided for; for, though often absurd in his manner, his merit is very great. Your brother Chatham, I know, and Lady Chatham also, are equally anxious for him, and his wife, in their hard situation. I need, I am sure, add nothing further on the subject, so shall finish my letter with a thousand congratulations for our various successes.

God bless you.

Ever your most affectionate Mother,

HESTER CHATHAM.

CHAPTER XXVIII.

1799—1800.

Invasion of Mysore—Seringapatam taken by assault—Bonaparte advances into Syria—Siege of Acre—Sir Sidney Smith—Retreat of the French—The Turks defeated at Aboukir—Victories of Suwarrow in Italy—His retreat in Switzerland—Landing of the Duke of York in Holland—Surrender of the Dutch fleet—British army re-embarks—Return to France of Bonaparte—Revolution of the Eighteenth of Brumaire—Bonaparte First Consul—His letter to George the Third—Projected secret expedition—Meeting of Parliament—Debate on the expedition to Holland—Treaties with the Emperor and the German Princes—Petition from the City of London—Pitt's financial measures—Deficient harvest—Union with Ireland.

The year 1799 was marked by a wide extension of hostilities. Beginning with the quarter most remote from England, we find ourselves for the second time arrayed against Tippoo. By his peace with Lord Cornwallis the Sultan of Mysore had been compelled to yield a considerable portion of his territory, and his two sons as hostages; and although they had received every token of kindness, and been restored to him with all honour and respect, his animosity continued unabated. The French conquest of Egypt wrought upon his fancy and flattered him with the view of approaching succour, while the French agents on their part were indefatigable in courting his alliance. Some of them, in their eagerness to give what they deemed the most honourable title, addressed him as ‘ Citizen Sultan !’

At the beginning of 1799 Lord Mornington still entertained the hope that peace might be maintained. He came from Calcutta to Madras to conduct in person from a nearer point the negotiation with Tippoo. But he soon became convinced that the only object upon the other side was to gain time until French succour, already stipulated by a secret treaty, might arrive. Assured of this fact, and accomplished in administration as in diplomacy, he took his measures with promptitude and skill. Early in March a well-appointed army of more than thirty thousand men invaded the kingdom of Mysore. General Harris held the chief command. By his side, with the rank of Colonel, was a young officer as yet unknown to fame, but destined ere long to fill one of the brightest pages in his country's annals— th Hon. Arthur Wellesley, a younger brother of Lord Mornington.

Advancing from the coast, the British army defeated Tippoo in several encounters, and besieged him in Seringapatam. On the 4th of May, after a hard contested struggle, the city was taken by assault. The Sultan himself showed a courage worthy of a better fate; he fell fighting in one of the gateways, where General Baird, the officer in command, subsequently discovered his body pierced with four wounds and buried beneath a heap of slain. With his death ended the war. The whole kingdom of Mysore was now in the gift of the Governor-General, who resolved to divide it between the Company, the Nizam, and the Peishwah.

It is interesting to trace in the papers now before me how close was the intimacy that had grown up in England between Lord Mornington and Mr. Pitt. The letters of the Governor-General to the Prime Minister are all in the most familiar strain. Here are some chief passages of one written after the reduction of Mysore :—

Fort St. George, Aug. 8, 1799.

My dear Pitt,—I refer you to the despatches and printed papers which I now transmit for the state of affairs in this quarter, and for the detail of the late glorious and happy events. . . . . With respect to myself, I continue very well, although occasionally much fatigued with business. However splendid our successes have been, however bright are our prospects, and whatever may be the delight of being toad-eated by all India from Cabul to Assam, I dislike this throne, and wish most ardently for the moment when I may return *functus officio*. With these sentiments I may be allowed to say that I suppose you will either hang me or magnificently honour me for my deeds (mine they are, be they good or bad). In either case I shall be gratified, for an English gallows is better than an Indian throne; but these words must be buried in your own breast, for here I pretend to be very happy and humble.

I think you will enjoy *Le Citoyen Tipou* and *Citoyen Sultan* in the papers found at Seringapatam.

I admire your conduct with respect to the Union. I hope you will persevere, but *I trust you* will *not trust* Ireland to my old friend Hobart. He used to be a good humoured fellow, but from what I have heard of his reign here he is utterly unfit to govern anywhere.

Ever yours most affectionately,   M.

I take this opportunity to remind you of your kind intention to make my brother Gerald a fat pluralist: he is at present a meagre singularist; and singularity nearly approaches to the crime of heresy and schism.

I send you by Henry a pair of pistols found in the palace at Seringapatam. They are mounted in gold, and were given by the late King of France to the Citizen Sultan. They will, I hope, answer better for your next Jacobin duel than those you used under Abershaw's gibbet.

I do not know what has become of the pistols to which Lord Mornington refers; but one of the commanding officers at Seringapatam transmitted to Mr. Pitt another of the spoils—a small powder-flask of solid gold which Tippoo had worn on his last day, suspended on his side by a silken cord. That memorial is now in my possession, having been presented by Mr. Pitt to his niece, Lady Hester Stanhope.

In the course of the same year the services of Lord Mornington were acknowledged by a step in the Peerage. He took the title of Marquis Wellesley; having about the same period changed to this the family name. 'Arthur Wesley'—such in his earlier letters was the signature of the Duke of Wellington.

In Egypt General Bonaparte, cut off from all intercourse with Europe by the destruction of his fleet, had planned another conquest for his army. Early in the year he marched into Syria with the flower of his forces. The smaller places on his route were reduced without obstacle; and the Turks were as easily routed in the open field. Djezzar Pacha shut himself up in his fortress of Acre and awaited a siege. In this beyond all doubt the French would have prevailed, if the Pacha had relied only on his Asiatic levies. Happily for him, at this juncture he obtained the zealous co-operation of a British chief. This was Sir Sidney Smith.

Sir Sidney, whom we left a captive in the prisons of the Temple at Paris, had some time before, with great enterprise and boldness, effected his escape. In England he obtained the command of the naval force appointed to cruise off the coast of Egypt. Landing with some of his boats' crews, he showed, as they did under his direction, a most unremitting gallantry in the defence of Acre. In vain did General Bonaparte try all the resources of his skill; in vain did the French, with their customary ardour, rush up again and again to the assault, and pour forth their blood with prodigal courage. On the sixty-first day of the siege they found it necessary to desist from their enterprise and commence in all haste their retreat to Egypt. Until that time, and for many years afterwards, this was Napoleon's sole reverse in his campaigns.

The Turks, however, presumed too far on this case of ill-success. Intent on the re-conquest of Egypt, they set on shore, with little precaution, a large but undisciplined army at Aboukir. General Bonaparte from Cairo watched and seized the favourable opportunity. Darting as by a sudden spring on these barbarous hordes, he inflicted on them a signal defeat on the 26th of July, putting to the sword a great number, and scattering the rest far and wide, with the total loss of their artillery, tents, and baggage.

Italy was at this time the theatre of some strange vicissitudes. Towards the close of 1798 the King of

Naples, emboldened both by the absence of Bonaparte and by the presence of Nelson, had imprudently declared war against the French. His troops, commanded by the Austrian General Mack, had advanced in triumph to Rome, where they proclaimed the old forms and commenced a system of reaction. But ere long they were routed utterly and irretrievably by the French General Championnet. The King and Royal Family found themselves compelled to embark for Palermo, while Championnet, entering Naples, proclaimed a new commonwealth, under the name of the Parthenopeian Republic.

In the spring of 1799 the alliance of the two Emperors entirely changed the scene. The Austrians and the Russians appeared in force on the Adige. The King of Naples returned from Sicily under the protection of Lord Nelson and the British fleet. The French in the south fell back from Naples to Rome, and from Rome to Florence. In the north, Marshal Suwarrow, at the head of the Allied forces, achieved a series of splendid victories. At the battle of the Trebbia, General Macdonald was defeated. At the battle of Novi, General Joubert was defeated and slain. Milan and Turin opened their gates to the Allies. Mantua surrendered after a period of blockade. By the autumn, no part of Italy, except the state of Genoa, remained in possession of the French.

In Germany the French chiefs also underwent reverses, and were compelled to recross the Rhine. It was only in Switzerland that the ascendency of the French arms was during this year maintained. There had been sent another body of Russians, under General Korsakow, to the aid of the Archduke Charles. It was defeated by General Massena in a great battle near Zurich; and Marshal Suwarrow was summoned in all haste from Italy to repair the faults of his lieutenant. But he found them irreparable. He found it necessary to retreat, which it was his boast to have never done in a military service of forty years. Even in this retreat, however, he evinced his energy and skill. He led his troops over mountain passes hitherto trodden only by the goat-herd and the chamois-hunter. By such means alone could he rescue his army from its dangerous position, and bring it back within its frontiers at the close of the campaign.

It was the anxious wish of Mr. Pitt to take an effective part in the warlike movements of this year. Holland, or as now termed, the Batavian Republic, was his object. He was flattered with positive assurances that the Dutch were weary of the French dominion, and would rally in large numbers around the Orange banner, if once unfurled. With this hope, and in concert with Mr. Dundas, he planned a joint expedition. It was to consist of about thirty thousand British troops and half as many Russians. It was to effect a landing on some point in the province of North Holland, and march forward to Amsterdam. The Duke of York was to have the honour and the difficulties of the chief command; and as one of the Major-Generals, Lord Chatham was to serve.

An excellent officer, Sir Ralph Abercromby, commanded the first division of the British forces, amounting to twelve thousand men. They had been encamped on Barham Downs, and they embarked from Ramsgate and Deal. Arriving off the Dutch coast, they found the enemy already apprised of their design. Yet, could they have pushed forward at once, they might not improbably have succeeded in their enterprise. But when the troops were ready to go on shore, a violent storm arose, and drove the ships again to sea. In a fortnight, when they re-appeared, the state of affairs was no longer the same. The Dutch General, Daendels, had with great activity and vigour collected all the troops in the province, and formed them in lines of defence from the Helder to Haerlem. Nevertheless, on the 27th of August the British chiefs effected a landing, repulsed the Dutch forces, and reduced the Helder fort. A further and considerable success ensued. The remainder of the Dutch fleet was now in the Texel, and still amounted to thirteen ships of war, besides some smaller frigates. Deprived of support from the land side, and blockaded from the sea by Admiral Mitchell, these ships surrendered by capitulation. In the naval contest which we had then to wage such a capture was of the highest importance, and had been one main object with Pitt and Dundas when they planned this expedition.

Sir Ralph Abercromby now made a movement in advance, and having successfully repulsed some attacks from the Dutch General Daendels and the French General Brune, intrenched his position at the Zype to await the coming of the Duke of York. His Royal Highness arrived towards the middle of September, bringing with him the main division of the Russians from the Baltic, and three more brigades of British troops. The whole united body numbered three and thirty thousand effective men; a larger force than the enemy could muster; but on the other hand the enemy had the great advantage of neighbouring supplies and of daily reinforcements; while the partisans of the late Stadtholder, though probably most numerous, as in 1813, gave no signs of the enthusiasm which in that year and to the cry of 'Orange Boven' they so triumphantly displayed. Certainly there was no appearance of any popular rising, and the Duke of York perceived that he must rely on his own forces alone.

Hoping by activity and enterprise to retrieve the want of native aid, the Duke, on the 19th of September, advanced with the army in four columns. Here, however, was made manifest the want of military concert between the Allies. One column of Russians, in neglect of their instructions, pushed forward too far and beyond the village of Bergen, until their ammunition became exhausted, and they were driven back with some loss and in great disorder. They communicated that disorder to another column composed partly of their countrymen, so that the complete success of the other two columns proved of no avail.

On the 2nd of October the attack upon the enemy's positions was renewed. Then the Russians reversed their former fault, and could not be brought to advance in sufficient time. The English, however, gained the victory, but it was heavily purchased by the loss of above two thousand killed and wounded. On the 6th there was another action, attended with fresh losses and marked by no decisive result.

During this time we find Mr. Pitt anxious to spare both the Ladies Chatham all uneasiness, and sending to each the earliest accounts of the safety of her son or of her husband. Here is one of his letters:—

Downing Street, Sunday, Oct. 12, 1799.

I am most happy, my dear mother, to be able to begin by telling you that my brother is *safe and well*, after another severe and honourable action, in which he bore a very considerable part. We have to be thankful for a very narrow escape, as he was struck in the shoulder by a spent ball, which his epaulette prevented from entering. We have this information from an officer who writes, having seen and conversed with him the next day, and who kindly sends this account, thinking, as was the case, that my brother from his position would not have been able to send his letter to head-quarters in time for this messenger.

The action took place on the 6th, in consequence of an attack made by us, which ended highly to the honour of our troops and left us masters of the field of battle; but the advantage was not decisive enough to promise much further progress at such a season in so difficult a country, and our army therefore afterwards retired to its former position. I write in haste and in the first moment, lest by accident any false or exaggerated report should reach you.

Ever, my dear Mother, &c.,   W. PITT.

How frail, how very frail the thread on which the government of England at that time depended! Any chance bullet which had closed the life of Lord Chatham must also have closed the administration of Mr. Pitt, so far at least as its main point, the leadership of the House of Commons, was concerned.

On the action of the 6th of October Sir Ralph Abercromby and the other General Officers delivered a representation to the Duke of York, urging the reduced state of the army, less by nearly ten thousand men than at its landing, and opposed to the daily increasing forces of the French. They pointed out the many other difficulties in the way of their enterprise from the unwillingness of the Dutch to rise, and from the approach of the winter season, and they recommended an immediate retreat of the army to its late position at the Zype. In compliance with this counsel a retreat was at once effected, only fifty wounded English and Russians being left behind.

But even at the Zype His Royal Highness was sorely perplexed. He had before him only a choice of evils and of difficulties. To advance was now admitted as impossible; to maintain his position was to sacrifice his troops to marsh-fevers without attaining any useful end. To re-embark them in the face of a vigilant enemy would cost him, as he calculated, at least three thousand men. Under these circumstances he determined to try the issue of negotiation. Several conferences took place at the outposts, and finally a convention was signed. It was agreed that the Allied troops should re-embark without molestation by the end of November. On the other hand the fortress of the Helder was to be given up entire with all the artillery upon the works, and eight thousand Dutch or French prisoners, to be selected by agents from those nations, were to be freely restored. Thus ingloriously ended an enterprise on which such large sums had been expended, and of which such high hopes had been formed.

At the close of this expedition Mr. Pitt wound up as follows his correspondence with his sister-in-law :—

Holwood, Sunday, Oct. 21, 1799, 4 P.M.

My dear Lady Chatham,—We have just received accounts from Holland, by which I find my brother is perfectly well, and all further suspense and anxiety is happily removed, as an agreement has been concluded, by which our army is to evacuate Holland within a limited time, and is ensured from all molestation in doing so. It is certainly no small disappointment to be coming away by compromise, instead of driving the enemy completely before us, as we once had reason to hope; but under all the difficulties which the season and circumstances have produced, it ought to be a great satisfaction to us to know that our valuable army will be restored to us safe and entire. The private relief it will be to your mind as well as to my own is of itself no small additional consolation. Huskisson does not mention in sending me these accounts whether there is any letter to you from my brother. If there is not, I have desired him to send on to you my brother's letter to me; but if there is one to yourself, I have desired him to send my brother's to Dundas, which I wish him to see, because it gives a fuller account than the official letters of the reasons for the arrangement, and leaves no doubt of its propriety.

Ever affectionately yours,   W. Pitt.

In the early part of this expedition to Holland the English Parliament was sitting. The King's Speech on the opening of the Session was delivered on the 24th of September. His Majesty stated that he had convoked the Lords and Commons at that unusual season that they might consider the propriety of enabling him without delay to avail himself of the voluntary services of the Militia. Immediately afterwards Mr. Dundas brought in a Bill giving new facilities for this purpose; a Bill which passed the Commons with no opposition, and the Lords with very little. This business having been concluded so early as the 12th of October, Parliament was adjourned over the Christmas holidays for a period of more than three months.

But the opening Speech of the King had been by no means confined to this single topic. It had been marked by a tone of high exultation, expressing the sanguine hopes which the progress of the war inspired. The north of Italy might be looked upon as already rescued from the French. Naples had thrown off their dominion; in Syria their arms had been repulsed, and in India their interests counteracted. And on our part, added His Majesty, there was every reason to expect that the attempt to deliver the United Provinces would be successful. With words such as these last placed in the mouth of the Sovereign and delivered in state from the Throne, it must have been doubly painful only a fortnight afterwards to confess the utter disappointment of that brilliant aspiration.

Notwithstanding, however, the retreat of the Duke of York from the Dutch plains, as of Marshal Suwarrow from the Swiss mountains, the general results of this campaign were certainly most adverse to the French. During many months General Bonaparte had been without any tidings of Europe. At length—through the courtesy, it is said, of the commander of the English squadron—he received a packet of newspapers up to the month of June. There he learnt for the first time the great disasters which the feeble government of the Directors had sustained. 'The wretches!' he cried to Murat, as he tossed the papers to him, 'they have lost me Italy!' He took at once the resolution to quit his army and return to France. This he felt that he could do with honour and with no loss of fame, since his own recent victory over the Turks at Aboukir.

The design was, however, as policy required, kept strictly secret till the very moment for its execution. General Bonaparte had already given orders to Admiral Ganteaume to keep his two remaining frigates ready for sea, and without any previous announcement to his army he went on board at midnight on the 22nd of August. He took with him a few of his most devoted followers, as Murat, Berthier. Lannes, and left the chief command in Egypt to General Kleber, a brave soldier of Alsace. His voyage was protracted to an unusual length by adverse winds, but he succeeded in keeping clear of the British fleet. At length on the forty-fifth day he neared the coast of France at Fréjus. The people of that town, on learning that the conqueror of Italy had returned, set no bounds to their joy and exultation; they broke through the laws of quarantine, and bore him in triumph to the shore.

Proceeding to Paris, the young General was greeted with like expressions of the popular feeling in his favour. With this support, though not without the aid of a military force, he was enabled to effect the Revolution known in French history by its date in the Republican calendar, the eighteenth of Brumaire, or in ours the ninth of November. The Directory was overthrown, and a new Constitution was framed, vesting the executive government in three Consuls. These, though colleagues in name, were by no means equal in authority. The First Consul, no other than General Bonaparte, centred in himself, full as much as the Sovereign in a limited monarchy, the principal powers of the State.

Grasping these powers with a vigorous hand, the First Consul at once by various means reduced all parties to his sway. He took measures to conciliate La Vendée and to close the civil war; he took measures to crush the still busy conspiracies of the remaining Jacobins; he applied himself to retrieve the ruined finances; he strove both to recruit and to animate with a spirit like his own the diminished and disheartened armies. But while earnestly preparing for war, and bent on reconquering Italy, he made to England at least an offer of negotiation. Whether, as some assert, he really desired peace with this country, or whether, as others have thought, his object was rather to gain in France the reputation of a moderate and pacific policy, he took the unusual step of a letter which contained a proposal to treat addressed directly from himself to George the Third.

The letter thus written was despatched by a messenger to London, with a short note from M. Talleyrand to Lord Grenville, requesting its transmission to His Britannic Majesty. At that period the Prime Minister in England was deeply intent on another secret expedition, which he designed for the coast of France. But his views at this time will best be gathered from his own most confidential letters to the War Secretary, who had gone for a few weeks to Scotland.

Mr. Pitt to Mr. Dundas.

> Downing Street, Thursday,
> Dec. 12, 1799.

Dear Dundas,—We have had a Cabinet to-day, and agreed on sending immediate orders to our officers in the Mediterranean to disregard any convention for suffering the French to return from Egypt, and to act accordingly, giving notice of their intentions by a flag of truce to the French commander. It was, however, generally felt that as we determine to prevent the Turks from getting rid of these troublesome visitors, we are bound to make some effort for enabling the Turkish force to act against them with effect. Lord Spencer seemed to think that you had had it at all events in contemplation to propose an expedition from India up the Red Sea; and if such a plan can be made practicable with an adequate force, it would certainly have much to recommend it. Finding your departure is deferred till to-morrow, I write to you, not for the purpose of proposing to you to delay it any longer, which seems quite unnecessary, but only to beg that either before you set out, or from any resting-place on the road, you will send me your ideas on this subject, as it might be very material, to prevent either disheartening or offending the Porte, that Lord Elgin should be instructed, when he announces our disapprobation of the convention, to accompany that unwelcome communication with some encouraging assurance of our intentions to take effectual steps for co-operating against the enemy, and preventing the consequences of his remaining in Egypt from being attended with danger.

> Ever yours,   W. P.

Bromley Hill, Sunday,
Dec. 22, 1799.

Dear Dundas,— . . . .

I have already stated that I conceive the support to be given to the Royalists may be advantageously combined with our views upon Brest. In the course of our conversations, though I entirely avoided anything which could bring that plan into question, I found both Monsieur and De la Rosière repeatedly bringing it forward; and the latter particularly stated that the Royalist army when in force might easily take such a position as might effectually cut off all communication between Paris and Brest, and intercept all supplies of provision or money by land, while we might maintain a blockade by sea. This alone he considered as very likely to produce a mutiny in the garrison and the crews, and to induce them to give up the place. But at all events such a force in addition to our own would certainly furnish a sufficient covering army, in addition to that which would be necessary to besiege the place. Monsieur de la Rosière was himself employed in the care of the fortifications, and seems positive that it may be easily taken.

On considering these circumstances, I thought a full communication on the subject would certainly procure better information than we could any other way obtain, and might also furnish additional means for the execution of the plan; and at the same time the taking Monsieur confidentially into consultation upon it on a strict promise of secrecy seemed to furnish the best chance of preventing its being made a subject of general conversation in his circle. I therefore yesterday conversed with him upon it as an idea which his conversation and De la Rosière's had led me to entertain, and on which I wished further information, but represented to him the necessity of absolute secrecy, and obtained his promise that he would never mention it to any one but De la Rosière and the Bishop of Arras (who is his chief adviser), and that he would obtain a similar promise from them. I explained to him that we should be willing to hold both the place (as long as we retained it) and the French ships in trust for the King, but should consider the Spanish ships as prize. He entered most cordially into the whole of our ideas, and undertook to direct De la Rosière to put us in possession of all his information on the subject,

which of course I should likewise immediately communicate
to Lord St. Vincent and Sir Charles Grey.

Yours ever,   W. P.

Downing Street, Tuesday,
Dec. 31, 1799.

Dear Dundas,— .   .   .   .
Having said all that is material for the present with respect
to means of war, I have now to tell you (what does not in
any degree supersede the former consideration) that to-day
has brought us the overture from the Consul in the shape of
a letter to the King, a copy of which I enclose. It is, as
you will see, very civil in its terms; and seems, by the
phrase which describes the two countries as being both more
powerful than their security requires, to point at their being
willing to give up at least a part of the French conquests
if we do the same as to ours. It is, however, very little
material, in my opinion, to speculate on the probable terms,
as I think we can have nothing to do but to decline all
negotiation at the present moment, on the ground that the
actual situation of France does not as yet hold out any solid
security to be derived from negotiation, taking care, at the
same time, to express strongly the eagerness with which we
should embrace any opening for general peace whenever such
solid security shall appear attainable. This may, I think,
be so expressed as to convey to the people of France that the
shortest road to peace is by effecting the restoration of
Royalty, and thereby to increase the chance of that most
desirable of all issues to the war; but at the same time so
as in no degree to preclude us from treating even with the
present Government, if it should prevail and be able to
establish itself firmly, in spite of Jacobins on the one hand
and Royalists on the other. This is my present view of the
subject, and is very conformable to what seemed Grenville's
opinion, in a conversation which I had with him yesterday
before the letter had arrived, as well as to that of Lord
Spencer and Windham, who are the only members of
Government whom I have seen since. I am afraid we
must return some answer before I can hear from you, but I
think you will not see anything to object to in this line.

Yours ever,   W. P.

Holwood, Saturday,
Jan. 11, 1800.

Dear Dundas,—I was in hopes long before this time to have been able to write to you fully on the project relative to the French coast; but Sir Charles Grey has continued so much indisposed that I have not been able to see him again, and have not received from him anything like a full and deliberate opinion. I find, however, that both he and Colonel Twiss entertain at present a very unfavourable opinion of the strength of the post proposed to be occupied, and Sir Charles seems also to entertain (as it was very probable he would) a very strong and obstinate prejudice against the Chouans and every description of French, which makes him apparently unwilling to estimate impartially their real strength. Under these circumstances I see no prospect of our having at present any such report as would justify encouraging the scheme, and I shall therefore endeavour to keep the whole subject in suspense till your return, when the whole plan of campaign must be an immediate object of full discussion. I am afraid we shall find great difficulty in arranging any scheme which will be attended with advantages as important as ought to result from the employment of so large and expensive a force as that which we possess or are bringing forward; and operations on a small scale and in quarters not decisive, though better than absolute inactivity, are not suited to the present crisis, in which I feel, as you do, that we must make our impression in the course of the ensuing campaign, or we shall find our means fail us.

Belleisle is certainly for one operation very advantageous, if upon further examination it proves to be attended with no insurmountable obstacles from additional works and defences since the former expedition; but that once accomplished, I see nothing that remains but mere demonstrations, or at most flying and predatory expeditions (which may alarm and distract, and be of some benefit as a diversion both to the Austrians and the Royalists, but will be of no real consequence in themselves), unless, upon full consideration, we think our force sufficient to justify risking a great army either in Brittany, with the view of taking Brest with the aid of the Royalists, or between the Seine and the Somme for the purpose of occupying at least the district between the two rivers and carrying terror to the capital, even if we do not advance thither. Either of these enterprises, if prosperous, will decide the fate of the war in our favour; but it must be confessed that the failure of either would be nearly as decisive against us. In these circumstances I do not feel that the attempt can be justified unless, on full examination, and with the best military opinions we can procure, the chances in favour of success strongly preponderate; but if that should be the case, some unavoidable risk from the contrary chances ought not, I think, to deter us, and you will, I believe, be of the same opinion.

I hope the answer to Bonaparte has appeared to you conformable to the general ideas I had stated to you, and in which I was glad to find you so entirely concurred. I hope, too, that you have not been disappointed in your expectation of getting rid of your sore throat on such easy terms, and that we shall see you quite well by the end of the week in which Parliament meets. We must, of course, lay the letter from Bonaparte and our answer before the House on the Tuesday or Wednesday; but I mean to put off all discussion upon them till the Monday following, which will be the 27th, in order to give you full time without breaking in on your original plan. We must determine, in the mean time, exactly what line to hold respecting the production of any papers or information on the subject of the expedition to Holland. There will be some difficulty in the selection, but I continue to think we must give enough to clear away all possible doubts about the sufficiency of supplies, medical assistance, and transport for bringing the troops back. Pray let me know your ideas, as some questions will probably be asked, though perhaps no motion made, before you return.

Yours ever,   W. P.

Yet after all, eagerly as this expedition was pressed forward by Mr. Pitt, so many obstacles and causes of delay arose that the design was finally abandoned.

The offer of negotiation on the part of the French Government had been considered with great care by the members of the Cabinet in London. There seems to have been no difference nor wavering of opinion. It was agreed that the answer ought not to come from the King, nor yet go to the First Consul. It should be addressed in due form by the Secretary of State for Foreign Affairs to the Minister of the same rank in the other country—by Lord Grenville to M. Talleyrand. In this well-weighed reply, which bears the date of the 4th of January, Lord Grenville stated that His Majesty saw no reason to depart from the forms long established in Europe for transacting business with foreign States. The King had never had any other view in this contest than to maintain against all aggression the rights and happiness of his subjects. He could not hope that the necessity of contending for these objects would be removed by entering at the present moment into negotiation with those whom a fresh Revolution had so recently placed in power, until it should appear that the danger had really ceased, and that the restless schemes of destruction which had endangered the very existence of civil society were at length finally relinquished.

This answer of Lord Grenville was intended to close the correspondence, but it had not that effect. A rejoinder came from M. Talleyrand. He still pressed the opening of a negotiation between France and England, declaring that France had been all through the Revolution animated by a love of peace, and had been driven to war by the unprovoked hostility of other European powers. In another reply, dated the 20th of January, Lord Grenville declined to debate the latter question or to proceed with the former; and he lightly touched on the important fact that the overtures of France on this occasion were addressed to England only, and did not extend to her allies. Whenever, he said, the attainment of peace could be sufficiently provided for, His Majesty would eagerly concert with his allies the means of immediate and joint negotiation.

On the next day after this despatch, on the 21st of January, the two houses met again after their long adjournment. The correspondence which had passed

on the overtures from France was immediately laid
before them, introduced by a message from the King.
On the 28th there was moved in the Lords an Address
in reply, expressive of concurrence in the course which
the English Government had taken.

Lord Grenville himself moved the Address in the
House of Peers. His speech, elaborate and eloquent,
was answered also with ability by the Duke of Bedford
and Lord Holland. In the division which ensued the
Address was carried by an immense majority—92
against 6. One name among these six may have
caused some surprise: it was the name of Lord
Camelford, the head of the Pitt family and the brother
of Lady Grenville.

In the Commons a week afterwards there was a
longer and a fiercer fight. There the corresponding
Address was moved by Dundas. Whitbread was the
first to oppose it in (as usual with him) a pithy and
a pungent speech. This afforded scope to Canning
for an admirable display of both wit and eloquence.
Erskine continued the debate in a speech very far
superior to his customary speeches in the House of
Commons, and bearing some faint likeness to his
great achievements at the Bar. After him the Prime
Minister rose, and in a luminous argument explained
and defended the whole conduct of the Government.
'As a sincere lover of peace,' he said, 'I cannot
be content with its nominal attainment; I must be
desirous of pursuing that system which promises to
attain in the end the permanent enjoyment of its
blessings for this country and for Europe. As a sincere lover of peace I will not sacrifice it by grasping
at the shadow when the reality is not in truth within
my reach.—" Cur igitur pacem nolo ? Quia infida est,
quia periculosa, quia esse non potest." ' [1]

---

[1] These words are from the seventh Philippic of Cicero (cap. 3).
But the first epithet in the original is *turpis*; for which Mr. Pitt,
no doubt by design, has substituted *infida*.

The Prime Minister was followed by Mr. Fox, who for this day only had re-appeared in his place. He owned that he could not justify the French Government in many of its proceedings, but he summed up his own main argument as follows :—' I think you ought to have given a civil, clear, and explicit answer to the overture which was fairly and honourably made. If you were desirous that the negotiation should have included all your allies as the means of bringing about a general peace, you should have told Bonaparte so ; but I believe you were afraid of his agreeing to the proposal. You took that method before. Ay, but you say, the people were anxious for peace in 1797. I say they are friends to peace now, and I am confident that you will one day own it; but by the laws which you have made restraining the expression of the sense of the people, their opinion cannot now be heard as loudly and unequivocally as before.'

Notwithstanding the return of the seceders for that day, the result of the division was greatly in favour of the Government. The Address as moved by Mr. Dundas was carried by 265 votes against 64.

From these numbers it appears that the arguments of the Opposition had not produced much effect upon either of the Houses. Nor yet do they appear to have produced much effect upon the public. There can be no stronger instance than that of Mr. Wilberforce. He had early professed his zeal for peace ; he had on that account publicly dissevered himself from Mr. Pitt; yet when Mr. Pitt showed him the official correspondence previous to its publication, and explained to him the reasons for it, we may observe the effect upon his mind : —' January 24. I wrote to Pitt, and he sent for me to town. I saw him. Till then I was strongly disposed to condemn the rejection of Bonaparte's offer to treat ; greatly shocked at it : he shook me.—January 27. Slowly came over to approve of the rejection of Bonaparte's offer, though not of Lord Grenville's letter.' It must also be acknowledged that Mr. Fox, and those who thought with him, descanted too much in their speeches on what they deemed the exhausted state of England, and the buoyant resources of France—that they seemed to think no conditions hard which the enemy demanded, and that they gave some handle to the popular reproach at that time applied to them, as clamorous for ' peace upon any terms.'

A few days afterwards Mr. Sheridan in the one House, and Lord Holland in the other, discussed the late expedition to Holland, and moved for a Committee of the whole House to inquire into the causes of its failure. The objects and the measures of the Government were unsparingly criticised, but the Opposition, with much prudence, far from censuring the conduct of the Duke of York, concurred with the Ministers in eulogies upon him. In vindication of himself and of his colleagues, Mr. Dundas contended that the expedition was not in truth the failure which it had been described. In the attempt to rescue the United Provinces from the yoke of France, we had certainly not succeeded. But we had taken between six and seven thousand seamen who might have been employed in the French service, and forty thousand tons of shipping which might have annoyed the British trade. We had withdrawn from the general operations of the war during this campaign forty thousand French troops, and by the capture of the fleet we had put an end to all further prospect of invading Great Britain.

On this occasion the minority in the House of Lords mustered only 6, and in the Commons only 45.

On the 13th of February a message from the King informed both Houses that he was concerting arrangements with the Emperor, the Elector of Bavaria, and other German Princes, to strengthen the common cause, and appealed to Parliament for the means of making such pecuniary advances as might be needed. When Mr. Pitt, four days later, moved an Address in reply, he explained that for the present half a million would be required, with two millions more in prospect on the completion of the treaties.

Mr. Tierney, who in Fox's absence was considered as the leader of the scanty Opposition ranks, rose to resist the Address and the subsidies which it involved. With great earnestness, and with some effect, he inveighed against the whole course of Mr. Pitt. Notwithstanding, he cried, the 'ifs and buts,' and the diplomatic special pleading which the Ministers always introduce on the subject, he was persuaded they would never be satisfied with any terms of peace short of the restoration of the Bourbons. Why else was the war continued? It had for some time been defended as just and necessary; but these words had died a natural death. Jacobinism was an indescribable phantom; its power and influence in France were by recent events almost annihilated. 'I would demand of the Minister,' he added, 'to state in one sentence what is the object of the war.'

The speech of Pitt, thus suddenly called upon to rise, may deserve to rank among the most successful instances of a ready reply. 'The Hon. gentleman,' he began, 'defies me to state in a single sentence the object of the war. Sir, I will do so in a single word. The object, I tell him, is Security! Security against the greatest danger that ever threatened the world— a danger such as never existed in any past period of society. . . . . But how long is it since the Hon. gentleman and his friends discovered that the dangers of Jacobinism have ceased to exist? How long is it since they have found that the cause of the French Revolution is not the cause of liberty? How or where did the Hon. gentleman discover that the Jacobinism of Robespierre, of Barère, of the five Directors, of the Triumvirate, has all disappeared because it has all been centred in one man, who was reared and nursed in its bosom, whose celebrity was gained under its auspices, and who was at once the child and the champion of all its atrocities?'

Proceeding next to vindicate at length the alliance with Germany, Pitt then applied himself to the often repeated, and as often contradicted, assertion of Mr. Tierney, that the war was carried on for the restoration of the House of Bourbon. 'Here the Hon. gentleman,' he said, 'has assumed the foundation of the argument, and has left no ground for controverting it or for explanation, because he says that any attempt at explanation is the mere ambiguous language of *Ifs* and *Buts*, and of special pleading. Now, I never had much liking for special pleading, and if ever I had any it is by this time almost entirely gone. He has besides so abridged me in the use of particles, that, although I am not particularly attached to the sound of an *If* or a *But*, I should be much obliged to him if he would give me some others to supply their places. The restoration of the French Monarchy I consider a most desirable object, because I think that it would afford the best security to this country and to Europe. *But* this object may not be attainable, and, *if* it be not attainable, we must be satisfied with the best security we can find independent of it. Peace is most desirable to this country, *but* negotiation may be attended with greater evils than could be counterbalanced by any resulting benefits. And *if* this is found to be the case; *if* it affords no prospect of security ; *if* it threatens all the evils which we have been struggling to avert ; *if*, on the contrary, the prosecution of the war affords the prospect of attaining complete security ; and *if* it may be prosecuted with increasing commerce, increasing means, and increasing prosperity, except what may result from the visitation of the seasons ; then I say that it is prudent in us not to negotiate at the present moment. These are my *Buts* and my *Ifs*. This is my plea, and on no other do I wish to be tried by God and my country.'

When Pitt sat down the argument was ably continued by Wilberforce and Sheridan, and closed, on the part of Ministers, by Windham. Then, the House dividing, the Address to the Crown was carried by 162 votes against 19. Many years afterwards I have heard divers persons congratulate themselves on their good fortune at being present as spectators in the Gallery or as members of the House that evening, more especially as regarded the speech of Mr. Pitt. They spoke in the highest terms of the great impression which that speech produced. Certainly one of its phrases, ' the child and champion of Jacobinism,' became for many months a popular watchword in England, until the Anti-Jacobin energy shown by the First Consul and his firm hold of the Sovereign Power had belied its application.

The minority in the House of Commons received, however, some support from the citizens of London. A meeting was held at Common Hall, attended by at least two thousand persons, and there a large majority voted and signed a petition praying for an immediate negotiation with France. This step was followed by further proceedings in both Houses. In the Lords Earl Stanhope, emerging from his retirement of five years, moved an Address imploring the House most earnestly, and, as he said, upon his knees, to put an end to the calamities of this cruel war. Acting, as was his usual fault, without concert, his motion had little effect. After a very few and very slighting words from the Lord Chancellor, the House divided, when only one other Peer (it was Lord Camelford) stood forth on Earl Stanhope's side.

In the Commons Mr. Tierney had more support. He took the course of an abstract Resolution, declaring that it was not just or necessary to carry on war for the purpose of restoring the monarchy of France. This was met by John Eliot, next brother of Pitt's friend, who moved the Orders of the day, and an animated debate ensued, but in the division Tierney was followed into the lobby by a force of thirty-four.

At nearly the same time Mr. Pitt unfolded his financial measures in the House of Commons. He had

renewed the Bank Charter for twenty-one years on the
Company advancing to the public 3,000,000*l.* without
interest for six years. This was bitterly opposed by
Mr. Tierney, though with much more, so far as we
can trace them, of invective than of argument. ' I
really think,' he said, ' that the country is dealing in
assignats, in flimsy paper, and that a mean plan of
state juggling is carried on between Government and
the Bank: Ministers courting the Bank, and the Bank
courting Ministers.' Mr. Tierney does not seem to
have quite made up his mind which it was of the two
parties to the contract that had gained the unfair
advantage.

Mr. Pitt had also contracted a loan for eighteen
millions and a half, which would be required for the
public service of the year, the terms evincing a most
prosperous state of public credit, since it had been
readily subscribed at an interest of less than four and
three-quarters per cent. No additional taxes were
proposed, except a small augmentation of the duties
upon spirits, and five per cent. on all teas valued at
more than two shillings and sixpence the pound. The
principal critic of Mr. Pitt's financial schemes was still
Mr. Tierney, yet even Mr. Tierney acknowledged that
the Minister's Budget had exceeded his most sanguine
expectations.

The prosperous state of the public credit was the
more remarkable, since the people were at this time
suffering great scarcity and distress from the late deficient harvest. To mitigate the evil many measures
were proposed and some adopted. In the House of
Lords a form of agreement, prepared by the Archbishop
of Canterbury, was carried as a Resolution. Every
subscriber to that agreement bound himself to limit the
quantity of wheaten bread consumed in his family to
one quartern loaf a week for each person. In the
Commons a Committee was appointed to consider the
laws which regulated the ' Assize of Bread.' The

Committee in their first Report recommended the self-denying system, as already sanctioned by the House of Lords. They further recommended a law which should prohibit bakers from selling bread until it had been baked twenty-four hours, and a law to this effect was passed accordingly. The Committee also expressed their full approval of the policy which Mr. Pitt had steadily pursued, on the principles of Adam Smith, and in spite of much pressure to the contrary—of abstaining, as a Government, from all interference in the purchase of corn in foreign markets, conceiving that the speculations of private individuals gave the most likely prospect of producing a sufficient supply.

This, the first Report of the Committee, was presented in February. A month later the second followed. The Committee proposed a bounty, to serve as an indemnity, to importers of grain from the Mediterranean and America before the end of October, if, in consequence of a good harvest, it should decline in price. This recommendation and some others in the same Report were adopted. On the other hand, Mr. Whitbread egregiously failed in a renewed attempt to regulate by legislation the wages of agricultural labourers.

Sir John Mitford, who was now Attorney-General—for Sir John Scott had by this time become Chief Justice of the Common Pleas, with a Peerage as Lord Eldon—brought in a Bill during this Session to continue the suspension of the Habeas Corpus. There were debates and divisions in both Houses, but in each the minority against the measure was extremely small.

In the midst of these Parliamentary proceedings the public was startled by the news that the King's life had been attempted. On the evening of the 15th of May His Majesty, accompanied by the Queen and the Princesses, went to Drury Lane Theatre. As he entered his box a man in the pit raised himself upon one of the benches and fired at the King a horse-pistol, happily without effect. The King showed great courage and

composure, advancing firmly to the front of the box,
and calmly, through his opera-glass, looking round the
house.   Meanwhile the offender had been seized and
conveyed across the orchestra to a private room, where
he was examined by several magistrates.   It appeared
that his name was James Hadfield ; that he had served
in the army in Flanders under the Duke of York ; and
that he had there received some dangerous wounds in
the head.   Being subsequently brought to trial in the
Court of King's Bench, the mental malady resulting
from those wounds was clearly proved by several witnesses.   He was sent to Bedlam, and he survived his
sentence forty years.

But the main and leading event of this year, and
on this side the Straits of Calais, was the Union with
Ireland.   I do not propose to relate in any detail the
final passage of the Act through the Houses of Parliament at Dublin.   It was marked on both sides by great
eloquence and great asperity.   Mr. Grattan desired to
re-enter the House of Commons for the express purpose
of opposing the measure.   He obtained, accordingly,
a seat by purchase for the close borough of Wicklow,
paying, as is alleged, the sum of 2,400*l*.[1]   Suffering
from recent illness, and supported to his place by two
friends, he rose, nevertheless, to speak on the first night
of the meeting, the 15th of January, when an Anti-
Union amendment had been moved by Sir Lawrence
Parsons.   It was a striking and a solemn sight to
behold the eminent patriot, the author of the Act of
Legislative Equality in 1782, raising his voice once
more to vindicate and maintain his past achievement.
He spoke on this subject, as might be expected, with
extraordinary weight and force ; and he levelled his
declamation more especially against the published speech
of Mr. Pitt. 'In all that is advanced,' he said, ' the
Minister does not argue, but foretell. Now, you cannot
answer a prophet ; you can only disbelieve him. The

[1] See the *Cornwallis Papers*, vol. iii. p. 161.

thing which he proposes to buy is what cannot be sold —Liberty. For it he has nothing to give. Everything of value which you possess you obtained under a free Constitution; if you resign this, you must not only be slaves, but fools.' The Chancellor of the Exchequer, Mr. Isaac Corry, replied to Mr. Grattan with great ability; and, after a debate of eighteen hours, the House divided late on the morning of the 16th. In that great and, as it proved, decisive trial of strength, the Anti-Union amendment was rejected by a majority of 42, the numbers being 96 and 138.

A week later the Lord Lieutenant, writing in confidence to his brother the Bishop, sums up as follows his general impressions of the public feeling: 'In Dublin and its vicinity the people are all outrageous against Union. In the other parts of the Kingdom the general sense is undoubtedly in its favour. It is, however, easy for men of influence to obtain Addresses and Resolutions on either side.'

As the principal spokesman at this time of the administration in the Irish House of Commons, Lord Castlereagh evinced that clear sagacity, that constant readiness, and that resolute courage, which, combined with his high gentlemanly bearing, supplied in him the place of eloquence, and subsequently raised him to the highest offices in England. On the 5th of February he moved preliminary Resolutions, giving an outline of the intended scheme. As to representation, he said, the object should be to take it in the combined ratio of numbers and of wealth. Now, the population of Great Britain was supposed to exceed ten millions, and that of Ireland to be between three millions and a half and four millions. Here was a proportion of more than two to one. On the other hand, the contributions of Great Britain were to the contributions of Ireland, as intended to be fixed, about as seven and a half to one.[1] These

[1] These calculations, probably from some error of the printers, are very incorrectly given in Mr. Adolphus's *History*, vol. vii. p. 362. See also Coote's *History of the Union*, p. 358.

two proportions taken together would produce a mean proportion of about five and a half to one. If, therefore, to the British House of Commons, consisting of five hundred and fifty-eight members, Ireland should send 'one hundred, ' I am of opinion,' said Lord Castlereagh, ' she will be fairly and adequately represented.'

With respect to the Irish House of Lords, it was intended that there should go to England as its representatives four spiritual Peers, chosen by a system of rotation, and twenty-eight temporal Peers, elected, not as in Scotland, for the Parliament, but for their lives. In two other particulars, likewise, there was a favourable deviation from the precedent of the Scottish Peerage. Any English Commoner who had received an Irish Peerage might still sit as a Commoner for any but an Irish seat in the House of Commons, on waiving for the time his privileges as a Peer of Ireland. Nor was the Royal Prerogative of creating Peers of Ireland entirely abolished; it was limited to one for every three extinctions until the number of Peers should be finally reduced to one hundred, exclusive of such as were also English Peers.

The circumstances of the time, said Lord Castlereagh, did not allow, as he desired, a complete incorporation of commercial interests. As obstacles, there were first the protecting duties required by some branches of the Irish manufactures, and secondly, the heavier taxation to be borne by the British people. But it was proposed in a liberal spirit to Ireland that articles exported to Great Britain should pay a duty equal to that which for the same articles was imposed on British subjects.

To the position of the Established Church Lord Castlereagh next adverted. 'So long as the separation shall continue, the Church of Ireland will ever be liable to be impeached upon local grounds. Nor will it be able to maintain itself effectually against the argument of physical force. But when once completely incorporated with the Church of England, it will be placed upon such a strong and natural foundation as to be above all apprehensions or alarms.' With this view it was proposed to declare the continuance and preservation of that United Church an essential and fundamental article of the Union.

'It had been said,' so continued Lord Castlereagh, 'that the Catholic Clergy had been *bribed* to the support of this measure. This is an illiberal imputation, and one devoid of truth; for it is known that an arrangement for the Clergy, both Catholic and Protestant Dissenters, has long been in the contemplation of His Majesty's Ministers.'

On concluding his statement and laying before the House his Resolutions, Lord Castlereagh was followed by Mr. George Ponsonby in an able and bitter speech. A most keen debate ensued, but on dividing, the propriety of considering the King's Message in favour of an Union was affirmed by 158 against 115. On the 17th, when the debate was again renewed, there was a sharp personal altercation between Mr. Grattan and the Chancellor of the Exchequer, Mr. Corry. Nor was the quarrel between the two orators confined to words. There was a duel even before the adjournment of the House; and the Chancellor of the Exchequer was wounded in the arm.

In the Irish House of Lords, the debate which ensued on the 10th of February was especially distinguished by a luminous speech from the Chancellor, the Earl of Clare. It was a speech of four hours; and the most remarkable, next to that of Mr. Grattan, which was delivered in Ireland through the whole course of that year. 'It produced,' says Lord Cornwallis, 'the greatest surprise and effect on the Lords and on the audience, which was uncommonly numerous.' The division, at half-past three in the morning, gave to the Government, including proxies, a majority of 75 against 26.

The more favourable reception of the projected Union in both the Irish Houses was greatly promoted by a change since last year in the measure itself. The Ministers in England had determined to grant a compensation in money for the boroughs to be disfranchised. No less a sum than a million and a quarter was assigned for this purpose, and each proprietor or patron of a borough was to receive for each seat 7,500*l*. The two largest shares by far fell to Lord Downshire and Lord Ely. The former, who had seven seats, received 52,500*l*.; the latter, who had six seats, 45,000*l*. This compensation was, I need scarcely say, quite independent of the course in Parliament which might be taken on the Union. Lord Downshire, for example, voted in opposition, and Lord Ely in favour of the measure. But peerages, both Irish and English, and other preferments or favours in both countries, were freely, nay, it may be said, lavishly promised to those wavering politicians whose minds, or at least whose votes, hung suspended in the balance.

The Resolutions, comprising the outline of the Union, being passed by both the Houses in Dublin, and accompanied by a joint Address, were transmitted to the King. On the 2nd of April His Majesty sent them to both the Houses in London, with a Message declaring his 'most sincere satisfaction,' and urging 'the speedy execution of a work so happily begun.'

It was designed that in the British Parliament there should be passed corresponding Resolutions and a corresponding Address; and on the 21st of April, Mr. Pitt in the Commons, and Lord Grenville in the Peers, moved that the House should go into Committee on the question. Mr. Pitt, in the course of his comprehensive and masterly speech, took occasion to review his own opinions on Reform.

'As I do not wish,' he said, 'to have the least reserve with the House, I must say that if anything could throw a doubt upon the question of Union—if anything could in my mind counterbalance the advantages that must result from the Union, it would be the necessity of disturbing the representation of England; but that necessity fortunately does not exist. In stating this, I have not forgotten what I have myself formerly said and sincerely felt upon this subject; but I know that all opinions must inevitably be subservient to times and circumstances; and that man who talks of his consistency merely because he holds the same opinion for ten or fifteen years, when the circumstances under which it was originally formed are totally changed, is a slave to the most idle vanity. Seeing all that I have seen since the period to which I allude; considering how little chance there is of that species of reform to which alone I looked, and which is as different from the modern schemes of reform as the latter are from the Constitution; seeing that where the greatest changes have taken place the most dreadful consequences have ensued, and which have not been confined to that country where the change was exercised, but have spread their malignant influence in almost every quarter of the globe, and shaken the fabric of every government; seeing that, in this general shock, the Constitution of Great Britain has alone remained pure and untouched in its vital principles; when I see that it has resisted all the efforts of Jacobinism, sheltering itself under the pretence of a love of liberty; when I see that it has supported itself against the open attacks of its enemies, and against the more dangerous reforms of its professed friends; that it has defeated the unwearied machinations of France, and the no less persevering efforts of Jacobins in England; and that, during the whole of the contest, it has uniformly maintained the confidence of the people:—I say, when I consider all these circumstances, I should be ashamed of myself if any former opinions of mine could now induce me to think that the form of representation which, in such times as the present, has been found amply sufficient to protect the interests and secure the happiness of the people, should be idly and wantonly disturbed from any love of experiment, or any predilection for theory. Upon this subject I think it right to state the inmost thoughts of my mind; I think it right to declare my most decided opinion that, even if the times were proper for experiments, any, even the slightest change in such a Constitution must be considered an evil.'

These words at first sight appear decisive against all future projects of Reform. Yet it should be observed that Mr. Pitt lays down the evil of making ' any, even the slightest change ' in the constitution of the House of Commons as dependent on the condition, among others, of that House in troubled times retaining the ' confidence of the people in England.' If this confidence should cease, that constitution ought not to endure. With this limitation in view Lord Macaulay states as follows, but perhaps a little too strongly, the general conclusion to be drawn : ' Though Pitt thought that such a Reform could not be made while the passions excited by the French Revolution were raging, he never uttered a word indicating that he should not be prepared at a more convenient season to bring the question forward a fourth time.' [1]

We learn from Mr. Fox's private correspondence that he was hostile to the scheme of Irish Union. He thought it ' one of the most unequivocal attempts at establishing the principles as well as the practice of despotism.' [2] Yet, so thinking, he would not leave his retirement at St. Ann's to oppose it. He left his place to be supplied by Grey, Sheridan, and Tierney. These gentlemen, with all their great ability, had but small success upon the question. An amendment, moved by Mr. Grey, against the entire scheme, pending an appeal to the Irish people, was rejected by 236

[1] *Biographies*, p. 231, ed. 1860.
[2] Letter of Feb. 4, 1799, as published in the *Life of Grattan*, vol. iv. p. 435.

to 30, while in the other House only three Peers—Lords Holland, King, and Derby—recorded their votes against it.

The Resolutions affirming the plan of Union, having passed in England as in Ireland, a Bill founded upon them was introduced and carried through in both countries. The English Bill received the Royal Assent on the 2nd of July. It was enacted that the election for the representative Peers of Ireland should be forthwith made, and that the members already representing the counties and the boroughs that were to be retained should be declared to be still the members for them in the United Parliament. With these accessions the United—or, as it was now termed, the 'Imperial'—Parliament might meet for its first session on any day appointed by his Majesty after the 1st of January, 1801.

The Session was closed by the King on the 29th of July, and his Speech expressed his peculiar satisfaction at the passing of the Act of Union. 'This great measure,' he said, 'on which my wishes have been long earnestly bent, I shall ever consider as the happiest event of my reign, being persuaded that nothing could so effectually contribute to extend to my Irish subjects the full participation of the blessings derived from the British Constitution.'

The King's ready acquiescence in these last words when framed and recommended by his Ministers, may have led Mr. Pitt, however erroneously, to think that His Majesty's objections to the Roman Catholics were in no small measure mollified.

CHAPTER XXIX.

1800–1801.

Dissatisfaction of Lord Wellesley—Convention of El Arish—Battle of Heliopolis—Death of Kleber—Good faith of England vindicated—Bonaparte enters Milan—Battle of Marengo—Successes of Moreau in Germany—Overture of Lord Minto, and consequent negotiations—Their failure—Malta surrenders to the English—Differences in the Cabinet—Dearth of provisions—Pitt's broken health—His views and those of Grenville on Free Trade—Meeting of Parliament—Remedial measures for the scarcity—The *True Briton*—Battle of Hohenlinden—Treaty of Luneville—Confederacy of the Northern Powers—First Meeting of the Imperial Parliament—Roman Catholic Question—Political Intrigues—Pitt's plan laid before the Cabinet—His letter to the King—The King's reply—Pitt resigns—Succeeded by Addington.

In the course of this summer Mr. Pitt had the mortification to find that, in advising His Majesty to confer an Irish Marquisate on the Governor-General of India, he had by no means satisfied his friend. On the contrary, there came to him a letter from Calcutta full of—or rather overflowing with—complaints.

Marquis Wellesley to Mr. Pitt.

Fort William, April 28, 1800.

My dear Pitt,— .   .   .   .
With the warmest acknowledgment of the zealous and anxious interest which all my friends have taken in my success, I cannot describe to you the anguish of my mind in feeling myself bound by every sense of duty and honour to declare to you my bitter disappointment at the reception which the King has given to my services, and at the ostensible mark of favour which he has conferred upon me. . . . In England as in India, the disproportion between the service and the reward will be imputed to some opinion existing in the King's mind of my being disqualified by some personal incapacity to receive the reward of my conduct. I leave you to judge what the effect of such an impression is likely to be on the minds of those whom I am appointed to govern; and with what spirit or hope of success I can now

attempt to take that lead among the allies which it must now be the policy of the British Government to assume in India.   I will confess to you openly that as I was confident there had been nothing *Irish* or *Pinchbeck* in my conduct or in its result, I felt an equal confidence that I should find nothing Irish or Pinchbeck in my reward. . . . . . My health must necessarily suffer with my spirits; and the mortifying situation in which I am placed will soon become intolerable to me. You must therefore expect either to hear of some calamity happening to me here, or to see me in England; where I shall arrive (*si ita Diis visum*) in perfectly good spirits, in the most cordial good temper with all my friends, and in the most firm resolution to pass the remainder of my life in the country, endeavouring to forget what has been inflicted upon me, and praying—*Novos consules, legionesque Britannas, ita in Asiâ bellum gerere, ut, me consule, bella gesta sunt.*

Ever, dear Pitt, yours most affectionately,
MORNINGTON.

(not having yet received my *double-gilt Potatoe.*)

It should be added, however, that the anguish which Lord Wellesley here expresses did not at any time affect his feelings of personal friendship. He continued to write to Mr. Pitt, whether in or out of office, in the most cordial, nay, affectionate terms.

In Egypt, the departure of General Bonaparte had cast a gloom on General Kleber and the remaining troops. To return to France became at once their ardent aspiration and their common cry. On the other hand the Turkish army, which was now again advancing, had no other object than to effect the evacuation of Egypt. It was a matter of perfect indifference to the Grand Vizier how else after their departure the French troops might be employed, and he was well disposed to guarantee to them a free passage to France.

Off the coast at this time there was cruising a British man of war and French prize, *Le Tigre*, detached from the fleet of Lord Keith, and commanded by Sir Sidney Smith. Sir Sidney had no authority whatever to treat with the French in Egypt—no authority either from his superior officer, Lord Keith, or from the Ministry in England. Nevertheless he took a forward part in urging a negotiation between the Grand Vizier and General Kleber. He allowed the agents from each to meet and hold their first conferences on board his ship, these conferences being followed by others in the Turkish camp. Finally, on the 24th of January, was concluded the Convention of El Arish,—concluded with the full sanction, though without the signature, of Sir Sidney Smith. The stipulations were that the French should leave the country, and be conveyed to France in vessels provided by the Porte. They were to retain their arms, baggage, and effects; and there was no clause restraining them from immediate service in any other quarter of the world.

Meanwhile the chance of some such treaty on the part of the Turks had occurred to the Ministers in England. They did not think that England should consent to it; they did not think that the mistress of the Mediterranean (as the victory of Nelson had made her) should allow twenty-five thousand troops equipped on all points to be quietly brought home and left free to turn their arms at once against her or her allies. These general views of the British Cabinet were much confirmed by the desponding tone of an intercepted despatch from Kleber, written immediately after Bonaparte's return. Therefore, on the 17th of December, the Admiralty had sent instructions to Lord Keith, directing him not to consent to any treaty in which it was not stipulated that the French troops should lay down their arms and become prisoners of war. Lord Keith, who was then in Port Mahon, at once transmitted these orders to Sir Sidney Smith, but they did not arrive until after the Convention of El Arish had been signed. Lord Keith also announced the orders which he had received in a letter to the French General at Cairo. At the mere thought of a surrender, the martial spirit of Kleber was fully roused. He published Lord Keith's letter in the Orders of the Day to his troops, adding to it these laconic words: 'Soldiers! we can only answer such insolence by victories; prepare to fight.'

Nor was this a mere empty boast. The Grand Vizier had by this time advanced to the neighbourhood of Cairo with his Turkish hordes. At the ruins of Heliopolis he found himself assailed with irresistible fury by the French; and his raw levies, notwithstanding their vast superiority of numbers, were scattered far and wide. The Grand Vizier himself, with only a few hundred horsemen, fled beyond the desert and sought shelter in Syria. But only a few weeks later the victorious career of Kleber was suddenly closed. On the 14th of June he fell beneath the poniard of an assassin, a fanatic Mussulman, on the terrace of his house at Cairo.

During this time the British Government had become aware how deeply a British officer was implicated in the Convention of El Arish. On their knowledge of that fact their determination wholly changed. But perhaps their whole course of policy upon this subject will best be shown in the words of Mr. Pitt as addressed some months later to the House of Commons.

Mr. Pitt said:—

'Before the order alluded to [that of the 17th of December] went out, there was no supposition that Sir Sidney was then in Egypt, nor that he would be a party to the treaty between the Ottoman Porte and the French General. When he did take a part in that transaction, it was not a direct part. He did not exercise any direct power; if he had done so, he would have done it without authority; he had no such power from his situation, for he was not commander-in-chief. . . . . Sir Sidney was, at first, no party to this treaty. That he sincerely desired it to take place, that it was concluded on board his ship, and that he was a witness to the transaction, was very true; but he never affected

to do it on the part of this country. The order of the
17th of December was to signify to our officer that we
should not regard the treaty between the Turks and the
French wherever it tended to affect our state and condition in the Mediterranean ; and what was there in this
that could be considered as wrong? What legitimate
power had the Ottoman Porte and a French General to
dispose of our interest in the Mediterranean ?—Now,
upon the subject of the breach of faith he would say a
word. The order was, not that we should break the
treaty to which we were no party, but to give notice
that, as we were no party to it, there was no power to
dispose of our interest ; but, the moment we found that
a convention had been assented to by a British officer,
although the policy of it we disapproved, we sent directions to conform to it.'[1]

When, however, the new instructions of the English
Ministers reached their officers in the Mediterranean,
the views of the French at Cairo were no longer the
same. Menou, who as the senior General succeeded
Kleber in the chief command, had never been inclined
—and was still less so since the victory of Heliopolis—
to relinquish Egypt without a blow. He refused to
renew the Convention when its renewal was tendered
to him. Hostilities, therefore, were continued off the
coast, and an English expedition was preparing. To
the results of that expedition I shall come hereafter.
Meanwhile I venture to affirm that on a careful review
of all the circumstances, the case of the treaty of El
Arish, which has sometimes been urged as an imputation
against the good faith of England, will be found, in
truth, among the strongest proofs of it. The English
Ministers had resolved to bear as they deemed a substantial wrong sooner than even the slightest shadow
of just reproach. Sooner than disavow one of their
officers, even though acting without their authority, they
had sent orders to sanction a compact which they did
not approve.

[1] Second Speech of Mr. Pitt, November 18, 1800.

In Europe the hopes of Mr. Pitt, as founded on the prolongation of the war, were doomed to utter disappointment. No Russian army took the field in support of the Austrian. Since last year the capricious temper of the Czar had completely veered round. Far from warring against, he was rather inclined to side with France. And France under her new government seemed no longer the same nation which had sustained the manifold reverses of 1799. The First Consul, by his genius and his energy, carried all before him. Darting across the Alps when least expected, by a passage without a parallel since the days of Hannibal, he entered Milan in triumph, and then again darting into Piedmont gave battle to the Austrian army on the plains of Marengo. There, on the 14th of June, he gained a most brilliant victory. The Austrian chief, General Melas, a brave veteran, but oppressed with age and infirmities, found it requisite on the day but one after the battle to sign a convention, by the terms of which the French recovered—not only the fortress of Genoa, which, after a most obstinate defence, had been surrendered by Massena only a few days before,—not only the fortress of Alessandria, which might have stood as long a siege, but all their former conquests in Northern Italy as far as the river Oglio; and with such great results achieved General Bonaparte was again at Paris on the 3rd of July.

In Germany the French, commanded by General Moreau, had similar success. They crossed the Rhine and Danube; they overran the plains of Bavaria; they entered the gates of Munich. Then, as in Italy, a truce ensued for the summer months, and a negotiation was attempted.

Under such circumstances Lord Minto, the British Ambassador at Vienna, having received fresh instructions from home, announced on the 9th of August that His Britannic Majesty was ready to take part in any negotiation for a general peace. M. Otto, a French gentleman employed by the First Consul, was at this time residing in London, as agent for the exchange of prisoners. He was desired to request of Lord Grenville some further explanations on Lord Minto's overture, and a correspondence of six weeks' duration—afterwards laid before Parliament—ensued.

It was stated by the French negotiators that their armistice with Austria was near expiring, and that they would not consent to renew it unless there were also an armistice with England. They proposed a general truce, with full powers of communication both by sea and land, their object of course being to send succours, in spite of the English fleet, to their army in Egypt and to their garrison in Malta. But their object being manifest, their proposal was declined. Lord Grenville brought forward on this point a counter-project, as follows :—Malta and the maritime towns of Egypt shall be placed on the same footing as those places which, though comprised within the demarcation of the French army in Germany, are occupied by the Austrian troops. Consequently nothing shall be admitted by sea which can give additional means of defence ; and provisions only for fourteen days at a time, calculated according to the consumption of the place.'

We find Mr. Pitt in a private letter at this juncture argue strongly in favour of that counter-project, as compared to an absolute refusal—which the King would have preferred—of the French demands. Thus he wrote to the Chancellor at Weymouth :—

Downing Street, Sept. 5, 1800.

My dear Lord,— .　　.　　.　　.　　.　　.　　.　　. The question is certainly a delicate one, as any naval armistice is now, and the benefits, as far as they go, are all on the side of France. But the absolute refusal of such a measure would, as I conceive, clearly produce the immediate renewal of hostilities between France and Austria, and probably drive the latter, after some fresh disaster, or from the apprehension of it, to an immediate separate peace on the worst terms. We should thereby not only lose the benefit of a joint negotiation, at which we have so long been aiming, but should also give up the present opportunity of negotiating for ourselves in a manner much more creditable and satisfactory than would result from any direct and separate overture which we might make at a later period. . . . . The season of the year itself, independent of the articles of the Convention, as we propose them, and of the right of search which we retain, will render it impossible for them to procure any material supply of naval stores before the end of the year, and will therefore prevent their deriving that advantage which we should have most to apprehend. On the whole, I am persuaded that the inconvenience of the armistice, thus modified, would be much less than that of Austria being driven at the moment either to a separate peace or the renewal of hostilities; and that, if the modifications are rejected by France, we shall at least have shown that we have done all that in fairness was possible towards a general peace, shall stand completely justified to Austria, and shall carry the opinion and spirit of our own country with us in any measures which the continuance of the war on this ground (if such should be the result) may require. I wish W—— could have had time to have given notice to yourself and such of our colleagues as are at a distance; but the business has pressed so much to a day as to make it impossible.

Ever, my dear Lord, &c.,   W. Pitt.

At this period both Mr. Pitt and Lord Grenville flattered themselves with the hopes of speedily commencing a joint negotiation for a peace. They had already fixed on their negotiator at the intended Congress of Luneville. The Foreign Secretary proposed his brother, Mr. Thomas Grenville, and the Prime Minister readily acceded to the choice of so able a man. But all such hopes were dashed by the answer from Paris to the English counter-project. The French could not deny the parity of reasoning which Lord Grenville's note established between the Austrian garrisons in Germany and their own in the Mediterranean, but they insisted upon it 'that the maritime truce should offer to the French Republic advantages equal to those secured to the House of Austria by the Continental truce.' And finally, after many endeavours on both sides to effect an adjustment, the negotiation fell to the ground. Before its close, however, one at least of its objects was decided. The garrison of Malta, reduced to great extremities, surrendered to the English squadron early in September, after a blockade of two years.

It was impossible that this negotiation could proceed in London without bringing to light the tendencies of each individual Minister. And here a wide divergence came to be apparent. Mr. Dundas, with his usual practical good sense, drew up a 'Statement of Views in the Cabinet,' which he submitted to Mr. Pitt. This paper, still preserved at Melville Castle, bears the date of September 22, 1800.

'Some of us,' says Mr. Dundas, 'think that the only solid hope of peace lies in the restoration of the Bourbons.

'Some, without going so far, think that there should be no peace with a Revolutionary Government, and that the present Government of France is such.

'Some are for negotiating with the present Government of France, but only in conjunction with the Emporor of Germany.

'Some [it is clear that Mr. Dundas includes himself] are for negotiating on our own foundation singly, with a just sense of our dignity and honour, and of the conquests we have made out of Europe.'

Mr. Dundas observes that these differences are not theoretical, but practical, presenting themselves in every discussion either on the prosecution of war or the prospect of peace.

The Statement thus concludes:

' It is earnestly hoped that Mr. Pitt will take these observations into his most serious consideration before it is too late.'

From this Statement it certainly appears that Mr. Pitt might find it requisite to make some changes in the Cabinet before he could hope to renew the negotiation with effect.

Dundas had, at this time, besides the public, a personal motive for desiring the conclusion of a peace. There is among the Pitt Papers a confidential letter from him dated April 14, 1800. In this letter he relates a conversation between himself and a member of his family who had with affectionate anxiety urged upon him some proofs of his failing health, and, above all, 'that I had lost the talent of sound sleep, which was now always broken, and depending more or less on the current transactions of the day.' In conclusion Mr. Dundas makes it his earnest request, 'although I had promised, and should most certainly adhere to to it, to remain, if necessary, in the War Department while the war lasted, yet that if at any period previous to that you see any opening for my retiring from it sooner, with your own perfect approbation, you will embrace it.'

The division in the Cabinet on the question of peace or war was no doubt very painful to Mr. Pitt. Still more painful to him was the continued dearth of provisions, and the effect which it was producing. In some parts of the country there was disturbance; in all there was distress. At the commencement of the harvest, when the rain was pouring in torrents, and when it was feared that the entire crop might be spoiled, the price of wheat rose even to the famine price of 120s. a quarter. Combined with these causes of disquietude to the Prime Minister, there was his own broken health, requiring at this time the frequent attendance of his physician and friend Sir Walter Farquhar. We find him, under the pressure of all these feelings, write as follows to his friend the Speaker :—

Mr. Pitt to Mr. Addington.

Oct. 8, 1800.

After all, the question of peace or war is not in itself half so formidable as that of the scarcity with which it is necessarily combined, and for the evils and growing dangers of which I see no adequate remedy. These are uncomfort-able speculations, and I am not the better for brooding over them during the confinement and anxiety of some weeks past. Sir Walter Farquhar even begins to threaten me with the necessity of a visit to Cheltenham or Bath, in order to be at all equal to the Session. How long that can be deferred is not quite ascertained.

Ever affectionately yours,   W. P.

Next day he writes again :—

Downing Street, Oct. 9, 1800.

Since I wrote to you yesterday, I have been reflecting further on an idea which many circumstances have suggested to me within these few days, and in my opinion of the pro-priety of which I am very much confirmed. I see nothing so likely to prevent the progress of discontent and internal mischief as what we have more than once found effectual, and cannot too much accustom the public to look up to—a speedy meeting of Parliament. Even if no important legislative measure could be taken, the result of Parlia-mentary inquiry and discussion would go further than any-thing towards quieting men's minds, and checking erroneous opinions; while on the other hand if petitions for Parlia-ment were to be spread generally (as I have little doubt they will) and were to be disregarded, a ground would be given for clamour, of which the disaffected would easily avail themselves for the worst purpose.

Besides, I think in fact there are some measures which it would be of real advantage as well as useful in impression to take without delay—such as, particularly, the renewal of the measure of guaranteeing a given price to all corn and rice imported in the next twelve months, with a view par-ticularly to the importation of rice from India, for which we have already given directions, through the Company, trusting to Parliament to make good the guaranty. The renewal of the prohibition to make starch, and perhaps the stoppage of the distilleries (though measures of less importance), may also be useful. Other provisions of a slower but more per-manent operation may perhaps be devised for encouraging further the growth of corn; and I do not wholly despair that temperate discussion might gradually appease the in-discriminate clamour against some of the most necessary classes of dealers, and reconcile the public to confining the penalties of the law solely to *combinations*, which are always criminal, or at least to speculations which can be proved to be for the purpose of unduly and artificially raising the price. There seems at least matter enough for some substantial proceeding not uncreditable to Parliament.

With respect to the question of war and peace, I rather think good instead of harm would result from discussing it on the ground on which it is placed by our late correspondence. Pray let me know what you think of all these ideas. . . . . We shall probably decide this question by a Cabinet to-morrow.

Ever affectionately yours,   W. P.

These letters were quickly followed by a visit of the writer to his friend at Woodley. On the 19th of October Mr. Addington writes to his brother Hiley :—' Pitt is now here. He is certainly better, but I am still very far from being at ease about him. Sir Walter Farquhar is to be here on Tuesday, and it will then be determined whether he is to remain here or proceed to Bath or Cheltenham. . . . He wants rest and consolation, and I trust he will find both here.'

Again on the 26th to Hiley :— Pitt, thank God, is recovered beyond my expectations, and greatly beyond those of Sir Walter Farquhar, who strongly advised his continuance in his present quarters. . . . He seems perfectly happy, and I must say that Woodley has never been more pleasant to myself.'

And finally on the 5th of November :—' Pitt has just left us. He had been so long one of the family that the separation was very painful to all parties.'[1] At this very time moreover Mr. Pitt gave a practical proof of his regard for his friend at Woodley by naming his brother Mr. Hiley Addington to a Lordship of the Treasury.

All through his stay at Woodley Pitt was intently watching the price of corn. Thus he writes to Mr. Rose

[1] *Life of Lord Sidmouth*, by Dean Pellew, vol. i. p. 266.

October 25 :—'The market here at Reading has been very abundant to-day (Saturday), and fallen 7*s.* per quarter, which I hope augurs well for the London market on Monday.'

It is to be observed that on the questions relative to the price of corn, the opinions of Pitt and Grenville were by no means the same. Pitt held that on the primary article of the nation's food it might be justifiable and wise to depart in some measure from the strict principles of Adam Smith. He held that some regard should be had to the special circumstances of the country, and to the concurrent opinion at that time of all the parties concerned. He held that to encourage either the immediate importation of corn or its future growth among us for an adequate supply, some action of the Legislature might be properly required. Pitt therefore inclined to the principle of the Corn Laws as they have since been called. Grenville, on the contrary, maintained in the most absolute form and in the most peremptory language the doctrine of Free Trade. He had to yield his opinion in the Cabinet, but was only the more earnest in expressing it whenever he wrote to the Prime Minister. I subjoin his principal letter at this period :—

Lord Grenville to Mr. Pitt.

Dropmore, Oct. 24, 1800.

My dear Pitt,—Lord Buckingham's letter is nothing more than an exaggerated statement of my fixed and, I am sure, immutable opinion on the subject of all laws for lowering the price of provisions, either directly *or by contrivance*. That opinion you know so well, that it is idle for me to trouble you with long discourses or long letters of mine about it. We in truth formed our opinions on the subject together, and I was not more convinced than you were of the soundness of Adam Smith's principles of political economy till Lord Liverpool lured you from our arms into all the mazes of the old system.

I am confident that provisions, like every other article of commerce, if left to themselves, will and must find their level; and that every attempt to disturb that level by artificial contrivances has a necessary tendency to increase the evil it seeks to remedy.

In all the discussions with which we are overwhelmed on this subject, one view of it is wholly overlooked. Every one takes it for granted that the present price of corn is in itself undue, and such as ought not to exist; and then they dispute whether it is to be ascribed to combinations, which they wish to remedy by such means as will destroy all commerce, or to an unusual scarcity which they propose to supply by obliging the grower to contend in the home market, not with the natural rivalship of such importation as the demand might and would produce of itself, but with an artificial supply poured in at the expense of I know not how many millions to the State.

Both these parties assume that the price is undue—that is, I presume, that it is more than would be produced by the natural operation of demand and supply counteracting each other. Now I know no other standard of price than this. But if the price be really so much higher, as is supposed, what prevents the increase of the supply at home? Or what bounty could operate so effectually to increase the quantity of wheat produced in the country, as the experience of the farmer teaching him that by the increased growth of that article he can make two or three times as great a profit as he can by any other?

No man, with the least knowledge of the subject, will say that the country now produces all the wheat it could, if it answered to apply more capital to the produce. Give me my own price for it, and I will engage to produce more wheat in my kitchen garden than any farmer in this neighbourhood now does in his whole farm. But the wheat so produced will have cost so much in labour and manure, that unless it were sold at two or three times more than even the present price, I should receive no return for my capital— perhaps not even recover the capital itself.

It never has been proved to me that the price of wheat in these last two years has been more than sufficient to afford a reasonable profit on the capital of the farmer who has produced it, considering the increased expense of every article which he must consume in producing it, and the very scanty crop of last year, which gave so much smaller a quantity, while it left the expense the same as before, or rather, indeed, much increased by some of the unfavourable circumstances of the season.

It is for this reason that I detest and abhor as impious and heretical the whole system on which we are now acting on the subject.

.   .   .   .

As to tithes—when we begin to rob and confiscate, I imagine we shall not stop at corn-rents, nor will the *tithes* of the parish of Stowe be all that will fall a prey to that system.

How can any man of sense who looks at this country, and sees what has been done in it the last hundred years, pretend, or believe, that there exists in it an obstacle which will let no man employ capital in the improvement of land? Has no land been improved in that period? or how has it been improved but by the application of capital to it? The Chancellor's plan on that subject I look at with great satisfaction, because it increases instead of diminishing the power of the life-tenant over his own property; and though by this individuals sometimes lose, the public I am confident always gains by it.

Considering that I began by saying that it was useless to trouble you with a long letter, I have not been very forbearing; but my mind is full of the subject, and I cannot restrain myself till the moment comes when I may vent myself upon it, and by endeavouring to convince all the world of their ignorance, satisfy them of my folly.

Ever most affectionately yours,   G.

The Cabinet meeting which Pitt in one of his letters mentions as close at hand, had decided that Parliament should be convened on the 11th of November. It met accordingly, the House of Commons in the Painted Chamber, whilst St. Stephen's was preparing for the reception of a hundred additional members under the Act of Union. The King, in his opening speech, alleged the high price of provisions and the severe pressure upon the poorer classes as the motive why he had called Parliament together at an earlier period than was at first designed.

The question of remedial measures was at once

referred to Select Committees of both Houses. The Commons' Committee, which chose Mr. Ryder for Chairman, presented in succession no less than six Reports. They recommended that the King should be empowered to prohibit, by Orders in Council, the export of provisions. They recommended a bounty on certain articles of import. They recommended the prohibition for a limited time of corn in distilling of spirits, or in making of starch. They recommended the prohibition of any bread made solely from the fine flour of wheat. All these proposals, and some others, were passed into law with very slight discussion. Yet some might, perhaps, have been debated with advantage, and one especially (the Brown Bread Bill, as commonly called) was found so oppressive in practice as to be repealed almost at the very outset of the ensuing Session. 'For my part,' said Mr. Pitt, 'I recognize the freedom of trade in its full extent; but I do not mean to deny that some regulation may be necessary in the present situation of the country.'[1]

In the same discussion Mr. Pitt rebuked some popular prejudices of the time. There had been a loud cry against 'forestallers and regraters.' There had been in the month of July preceding a trial upon this subject in the Court of King's Bench. Mr. Rusby, an eminent cornfactor, was indicted for having purchased in Mark Lane ninety quarters of oats at 41s. per quarter, and sold thirty of them again on the same day and in the same market at 44s. The 'heinous charge' being fully proved, the Jury brought in a verdict of Guilty: upon which the Chief Justice, Lord Kenyon, thus addressed them : 'You have conferred by your verdict almost the greatest benefit that ever was conferred by any Jury!'[2]

The law laid down on this occasion did not altogether pass current. It was afterwards discussed in full Court, and the Judges being equally divided in opinion, the

---

[1] *Parl. Hist.*, vol. xxxv. p. 793.
[2] *Ann. Register*, 1800, part ii. p. 23.

benefit of their doubts was allowed to Mr. Rusby.   But
when errors like these prevailed in high places, how
could any half-educated multitude be free from them?
At Coventry, for example, the same prejudice was entertained.   Mr. Wilberforce Bird, who was one of the
Members for that city, expressed the views of his constituents in the debate upon the First Report of the
Select Committee.   He said that they would desire far
more effectual measures of relief.   He said that being
as they were under the grievous pressure of an artificial
dearth, they would bitterly feel that the great evils to
which alone it could be attributed, monopoly and ex-
tortion, were still to proceed without any check at all
from Parliament.

Pitt rose at once to answer this gentleman.   He
complained that Mr. Bird had spoken rather in the
spirit of a delegate obeying his orders than of a representative exerting his free judgment.

'There are, undoubtedly, occasions,' he said, ' on
which gentlemen who represent large and populous
places, instead of receiving instruction from their constituents, will find themselves enabled to convey to them
much useful information, and to correct their errors.
I know, Sir, that in many populous places the spirit of
Jacobinism, taking advantage of the pressure of hunger,
as it does of everything, has, with unwearied activity,
endeavoured to increase the mischief.   I know, too, that
there has been a disposition to inculcate the mischievous
idea that it was in the power of Parliament to make
every deficiency disappear—a deficiency arising principally from a succession of unfavourable seasons, whatever
other causes may have contributed to it—and at once
to produce abundance and cheapness.   I know that many
people, in suggesting remedies for the evil, have talked
about a limitation of price, and have hinted at the propriety of establishing *a maximum price of corn.* Now,
it is evident that populous places would be the first to
feel the mischief arising from the adoption of so per-

nicious a doctrine. It is well known that large manufacturing districts do not grow a quantity of corn sufficient for the consumption of their numerous population; and it is equally clear that the adoption of such a measure would necessarily put an end to transportation of grain from places where the quantity grown is greater, and where the consumption is less.'

In this Session, which was protracted till the last day of the year, the questions of the Scarcity, though the most important, were not the only ones discussed. There was a Bill carried through continuing the suspension of the Habeas Corpus. There was a motion by Mr. Sheridan relative to the late negotiation for a peace with France: it was defeated by 156 to 35. There was a motion by Mr. Tyrrwhitt Jones, which reflected on the conduct of the English Government in the Convention of El Arish; it was defeated by 80 to 12. The same persevering gentleman also brought forward an Address for the dismissal of His Majesty's Ministers. Neither Pitt himself nor any of his colleagues deemed it necessary to say a word in reply; they maintained a disdainful silence, and left the motion to be disposed of in a thin House by 66 to 13.

In the months of November and December many titles were conferred. There was a batch of English Baronetcies, one of which, ' Robert Peel, of Drayton Manor, in the county of Stafford,' is memorable when viewed in the light of subsequent events. Sylvester Douglas, who had yielded his seat at the Treasury in favour of Hiley Addington, was raised to the Peerage as Lord Glenbervie, and also appointed Governor of the Cape of Good Hope. Lord Malmesbury, in just requital of his high diplomatic services, was made an Earl.

But it was in the sister country that such favours were cast about with a truly lavish hand. Already had the Dublin Gazette of July 30, 1800, announced sixteen creations or promotions in the Irish peerage. To these the Gazettes of December 27 and 30 added, surprising as it may appear, no less than twenty-six. Great efforts had been made to reduce these lists, and no small anxiety upon this point had been manifested by the King.[1] But it was necessary to fulfil with honour the engagements which, to carry through the Union, Lord Cornwallis had thought himself obliged to make.

At the close of this year Lord Chatham appears to have called the attention of Mr. Pitt to a special attack in the *True Briton*. What that attack may have been I cannot say. I applied at the British Museum to see the *True Briton* of the date in question, but I found that by some accident there is a blank in the series for that year. Here, at all events, is Mr. Pitt's reply:—

Downing (Street), Tuesday,
Dec. 30 (1800), ½ past 2.

My dear Brother,—I had not seen the *True Briton* till after I got your note. The only paragraph I have yet found does not seem one that can have much effect; but such as it is, it is impossible for it not to be very offensive to me. I shall certainly take the most effectual measures I can to check such a conduct, but you really do not know how little means there are to keep printers in order.

Ever affectionately yours,   W. Pitt.

To this last remark of Mr. Pitt I am tempted to add another, though of different date, of Lord Grenville. He writes to his brother, Lord Buckingham, as follows, December 27, 1809: 'It has been my fate all through life to be more injured by the press in my favour than by that which has been pretty unsparingly employed against me.'

Several Ministers besides Lord Grenville might have made the same observation.

During this early Session the news from the Continent was very far from auspicious. The French at the conclusion of the armistice had resumed hostilities with vigour and success; and, although the First Consul remained at Paris for the conduct of the government,

---

[1] See the *Cornwallis Correspondence*, vol. iii. p. 257, &c.

he could still, in some degree, direct the movement of the armies. In Italy the Neapolitans were defeated along the Tiber, and the Austrians compelled to fall back behind the Mincio. In Bavaria General Moreau, who was opposed to the Archduke John, gained over him, on the 3rd of December, the brilliant victory of Hohenlinden. That battle, fought in the midst of snow, though won by French valour, is renowned in British verse :—

> Wave, Munich, all thy banners wave,
> And charge with all thy chivalry !

The Austrians had no alternative but to solicit another armistice and allow the principle of a separate negotiation. Conferences had already been opened in the town of Luneville. There Austria was represented by Count Cobentzel, and France by Joseph Bonaparte. The First Consul laid down as conditions from which he would not depart, the Rhine as the boundary of the French and the Adige as the boundary of the Cisalpine Republic.

From Petersburg also the tidings were not favourable to the cause of England. The Emperor Paul, among other fantastic notions, had conceived an idea that he was the rightful heir or head of the Knights of Malta. He had greatly resented the surrender of that island to the English. He had in a formal note made a demand for its transfer to himself, a demand which we as formally refused. Under these circumstances Paul, in a transport of anger, laid an embargo on all British ships in the ports of Russia, and actually seized above three hundred. But further still he undertook to urge against us once again the claims of Neutral Nations. In these he felt himself fortified by some recent cases at sea—the case of the Danish frigate the Freya, in July, and the case of the Swedish ketch the Hoffnung, in September. Paul accordingly determined to renew the confederacy against England which had been formed by the Empress Catherine, in

1780, on the plea of Maritime Rights and under the name of an Armed Neutrality. With this view he invited a visit from the King of Sweden, and entered into negotiation with the Courts of Berlin and Copenhagen. The result was speedily apparent. On the 16th of December there was signed at Petersburg a Convention between Russia and Sweden, to which, in a few days, Denmark adhered. It reasserted in still stronger terms the principles of the Armed Neutrality, and expressed a readiness to maintain them, if necessary, by an appeal to arms.

This new confederacy was encountered by England with the same high spirit which she had shown in 1780 under still greater difficulties and still greater dangers. On the 14th of January, 1801, there was issued an Order in Council for an Embargo on all Russian, Swedish, or Danish vessels in the ports of the United Kingdom. At the same time Lord Grenville expressed his concern and his displeasure in a joint Note to the Danish and Swedish Envoys. 'At the beginning,' he said, 'of the present war the Court of Petersburg, which had taken a most active part in the establishment of the former alliance, entered into articles with His Majesty which are not merely incompatible with the Convention of 1780, but which are directly in the face of it; engagements which are still in force, and the reciprocal execution of which His Majesty is entitled to demand upon every principle of good faith during the continuance of the war.'

In January, 1801, our navy was perhaps not unequal to that of all the other European states. By sea we might probably against all gainsayers hold our own; but by land the prospect was certainly not encouraging. The sanguine hopes in the January preceding of a successful campaign against France had melted away into air. Austria had already succumbed to superior power, and Naples was prepared to follow in her train.

Within a very few days the conclusion of a Peace at Luneville on the terms which the First Consul had dictated, and from which we were shut out, would leave us without a single ally of any value upon the Continent of Europe.

In the course of such unfavourable tidings, and amidst such lowering prospects came on the first Meeting of the Imperial Parliament. On the 22nd of January, the first day of that Meeting, Mr. Addington was unanimously elected to the Chair, and several of the following days were employed in swearing in the Members. It was not till the 2nd of February that the King opened the Session in a speech from the Throne. 'The unfortunate course of events,' in the war with France, and 'the acts of injustice and violence' of the Court of Petersburg, together with the new attempt of that Court in conjunction with those of Copenhagen and Stockholm 'for establishing by force a new code of maritime law,' were dwelt on by His Majesty. But thus continued the King: 'You may rely on my availing myself of the earliest opportunity which shall afford a prospect of terminating the present contest on grounds consistent with our security and honour. . . . . It will afford me the truest and most heartfelt satisfaction whenever the disposition of our enemies shall enable me thus to restore to the subjects of my United Kingdom the blessings of Peace.'

The terms of the Royal Speech, as framed by Mr. Pitt, were, as usual, embodied in a counter-Address from both Houses. In the Lords the Address was moved by the Duke of Montrose. Earl Fitzwilliam proposed an Amendment of a party character, alleging the waste of the public resources 'either by improvident and ineffectual projects or by general negligence and profusion.' But this Amendment was rejected by 73 votes against 17.

In the Commons the same Amendment was moved. Mr. Grey, in Fox's absence, brought it forward in a long

and eloquent speech. On the Northern Confederacy
he descanted in some detail. He was not clear that we
were really entitled to the Maritime Rights which we
claimed, and he was convinced that even the loss of
them would not produce such very serious results. Mr.
Pitt rose at once to reply: ' In following, Sir,' he said,
' the order which the Hon. gentleman has taken, I must
begin with his doubts and end with his certainties;
and I cannot avoid observing that he was singularly
unfortunate upon this subject, for he entertained doubts
where there was not the slightest ground for hesitation,
and he makes up his mind with absolute certainty upon
points in which both arguments and facts are decidedly
against him. That part of the subject upon which the
Hon. gentleman appears to be involved in doubt is with
respect to the justice of our claim in regard to neutral
vessels. . . . . . Sir, the Hon. gentleman doubts that
which has been the acknowledged principle of law in
all the tribunals of the kingdom, which are alone competent to decide upon the subject, and which principle
Parliament has constantly known them to act upon. I
ask whether that principle has not been maintained in
every war? Let me also ask whether, in the course of
the speeches of the gentlemen on the other side of the
House, ever since the present war began, any one topic
of alarm has been omitted which either fact could furnish or ingenuity supply? I believe I shall not be
answered in the negative; and yet I believe I may
safely assert that it never occurred to any one Member
to increase the difficulties of the country by stating a
doubt upon the question of Right: and it will be a
most singular circumstance that the Hon. gentleman
and his friends should only have begun to doubt when
our enemies are ready to begin to combat. . . . . . But
the case does not stop here. What will the Hon. gentleman say if I show him that in the course of the
present war both Denmark and Sweden have distinctly
expressed their readiness to agree in that very prin-

ciple against which they are disposed to contend, and that they made acknowledgments to us for not carrying the claim so far as Russia was disposed to carry it? What will the Hon. gentleman say if I show him that Sweden, who in 1780 agreed to the armed neutrality, has since then been at war herself, and then acted upon a principle directly contrary to that which she agreed to in 1780, and to that upon which she is now disposed to act? In the war between Sweden and Russia, the former distinctly acted upon that very principle for which we are now contending. What will the Hon. gentleman say if I show him that in the last autumn Denmark, with her fleets and arsenals at our mercy, entered into a solemn pledge not again to send vessels with convoy until the principle was settled; and that, notwithstanding this solemn pledge, this state has entered into a new convention, similar to that which was agreed to in 1780?

'Sir, I come now to the question of expediency, and upon this part of the subject the Hon. gentleman is not so much in doubt. The question is, whether we are to permit the navy of our enemy to be supplied and recruited—whether we are to suffer blockaded forts to be furnished with warlike stores and provisions—whether we are to suffer neutral nations, by hoisting a flag upon a sloop or a fishing-boat, to convey the treasures of South America to the harbours of Spain, or the naval stores of the Baltic to Brest or Toulon? Are these the propositions which gentlemen mean to contend for?

'The Hon. gentleman talks of the destruction of the naval power of France, but does he really believe that her marine would have been decreased to the degree that it now is if during the whole of the war this very principle had not been acted upon? And if the commerce of France had not been destroyed, does he believe that, if the fraudulent system of neutrals had not been prevented, her navy would not have been in a very

different situation from that in which it now is?   Does
he not know that the naval preponderance which we
have by these means acquired has given security to
this country, and has more than once afforded chances
for the salvation of Europe?   In the wreck of the Continent, and the disappointment of our hopes there, what
has been the security of this country but its naval preponderance?—and if that were once gone, the spirit of
the country would go with it.'

The speech of Mr. Pitt that night seems to have
displayed in full perfection what Coleridge, in describing his style, once called 'the proud architectural pile
of his sentences.' Delivered with his usual force and
fire, it produced a strong impression on the House.
With all the efforts of Grey, Tierney, and Sheridan,
the Amendment was rejected by 245 votes against
63.   Never had the Ministerial phalanx appeared more
numerous or compact.   Never did the Minister, in spite
of all foreign dangers or alarms, seem to stand more
firmly fixed at home.   Yet even then there were public
rumours of a change.   Yet on that very night Mr. Pitt
was virtually, and by his own act, out of office, and
his powerful administration of seventeen years was in
fact already dissolved.

The cause was the Roman Catholic question—the
question which then and for thirty years to come was
the main obstacle to lasting governments and united
parties in England.   I have already shown with how
much vehemence in February, 1795, the King had
expressed to his Ministers his determination to maintain the Test Act.   Not satisfied with the recall of Lord
Fitzwilliam, and apprehending a renewal of the question
at some future time, His Majesty, about a month later,
wrote to consult Lord Kenyon.   The King had doubts
whether his consent to repeal the Test Act would be
consistent with the due observance of his Coronation
Oath.   On this point he desired Lord Kenyon to obtain
the opinion also of the Attorney-General.   Lord Kenyon

and Sir John Scott, like the honourable men they were, did not permit either any bias of their politics or any hopes of their promotion to distort their legal and constitutional views. On the 11th of March, 1795, they thus replied : 'Though the Test Act appears to be a very wise law, and in point of sound policy not to be departed from, yet it seems that it might be repealed or altered without any breach of the Coronation Oath or Act of Union (with Scotland).'[1]

The conclusion of Lord Kenyon and Sir John Scott, as given in this letter, appears of unanswerable force. I am far from denying, although I was not convinced by them, that there were several weighty arguments to allege against the Roman Catholic claims. But most certainly the supposed breach of the Coronation Oath is not to be numbered among these. It has been long since, and almost by common consent, abandoned as untenable.

Unhappily, however, the King at the same time, but separately from the other two, consulted the Chancellor Loughborough. Even the warm admirers (if there be any such) of his Lordship's political career will scarcely ascribe to him any very ardent zeal on the abstract merits of the question. Through his whole life his political principles hung most loosely upon him ; he had more than once changed them on a sudden, and from the lure of personal advantage. Of his first turn in 1771, one of his successors on the Woolsack writes : ' This must be confessed to be one of the most flagrant cases of *ratting* recorded in our party annals.'[2]

In 1795 Lord Loughborough was most anxious to gratify and find favour with his Royal Master. He sent the King a written opinion stating that the Royal assent to the repeal of the Test Act might be held by

[1] See p. 14 of the Correspondence published in 1827 by Dr. Philpotts, afterwards Bishop of Exeter. Exactly to the same effect in the view of the Coronation Oath are the powerful remarks of Lord Macaulay (*Hist. of England*, vol. iii. p. 117).

[2] Lord Campbell's *Lives of the Chancellors*, vol. vi. p. 87.

implication to violate the Coronation Oath. But he appears to have carefully concealed the communication from his colleagues. It was only some years later, and after the fall of Mr. Pitt's Ministry, that we find him give an account of the affair in conversation with Mr. Rose. It is painful to add, that the statement of his written opinion, as Mr. Rose reports that statement in his Diary, is utterly and irreconcileably at variance with the written opinion itself which Lord Campbell has published from the original draft in Lord Loughborough's own handwriting.[1]

The further progress of this question, as it bears on the Union with Ireland, is most clearly to be traced in a remarkable letter which Lord Castlereagh addressed to Mr. Pitt, recapitulating for his final decision the steps which had recently passed. It is dated the 1st of January, 1801, and is published both in the Castlereagh and in the Cornwallis Correspondence. Lord Castlereagh states that when in England during the autumn of 1799, he was requested to attend the meetings of the Cabinet upon the Catholic question. He did attend them accordingly. He heard no difference of opinion as to the merits of the question itself. On these the Ministers seemed to him unanimous ; but he found 'that some doubts were entertained as to the possibility of admitting Catholics into some of the higher offices, and that Ministers apprehended considerable repugnance to the measure in many quarters, and particularly in *the highest*.'

On the whole Lord Castlereagh was at that time empowered to write to the Lord Lieutenant that so far as the sentiments of the Cabinet were concerned. his Excellency need not hesitate in calling forth the Catholic support to the projected Union. Upon this principle, then, did Lord Cornwallis and Lord Castlereagh act in Ireland. They refrained, as did also Mr. Pitt in Eng-

---

[1] Compare Lord Campbell's *Chancellors*, vol. vi. p. 297. with Mr. Rose's *Diaries*, vol. i. p. 300.

land, from any kind of pledge, or promise, or assurance
to the Roman Catholic leaders. But undoubtedly a
general hope was raised, and from that hope a general
co-operation was afforded. The Roman Catholics, as a
whole, either remained neutral or gave their support to
the Union. It seems to be admitted that had their
support been withheld, and their weight been thrown
into the opposite scale, the measure could not at that
time have been carried.

It will, therefore, be seen that when the measure
became law in July, 1800, there was no engagement to
redeem with the Roman Catholics in Ireland. But I
think it must be owned that they had a moral claim
upon the Government in England. So at least thought
Mr. Pitt. He decided that their state, and the change
that might be made in the laws affecting them, should
be laid before the Cabinet on its reassembling after the
summer recess; and he summoned Lord Castlereagh from
Dublin to attend the Cabinet meetings on this subject
as he had the year before.

It so chanced that in the early autumn the King had
gone to pass some weeks at Weymouth for the benefit
of his health. There he was joined by the Chancellor,
who at first had intended to remain only a few days,
but who, to ingratiate himself with his Royal Master,
prolonged his stay. Until then he may have thought,
as having heard no more of them, that the feelings of
George the Third upon the Catholic question had cooled
and subsided since 1795. But he soon discovered that
they were as warm as ever in the Royal breast. He determined to do his utmost in private to strengthen and
confirm them, and to stand forth in public as their
mouth-piece and assertor.

It may be asked what motive could sway this versa-
tile politician at that juncture. Some men may, if they
think fit, ascribe to him a devout and irrepressible zeal
for Protestant ascendency; others may believe that he
was secretly aiming at the highest object of political

ambition, and designing to make himself Prime Minister on the ruins of Mr. Pitt, and with the aid of some deputy in the House of Commons.

In his political movements at this time we may conjecture that Lord Loughborough did not stand alone. He was in the closest intimacy with his relative and friend Lord Auckland. Since 1798 Lord Auckland had held a lucrative office in the Home Government as joint Post-Master General. While filling that post he appears to have chafed at his exclusion from the Cabinet. He saw men far below him in accomplishments above him in position. I am convinced that he did not desire the actual downfall of Mr. Pitt, with whom he had lived in such familiar friendship ; but he might seek to enhance his own importance, and to gain a higher post in the same administration.

If, as Lord Malmesbury states, and as seems probable, Lord Auckland did take some part, for whatever reason, with Lord Loughborough, he may have brought him a co-operation even more important than his own. He was brother-in-law of Dr. Moore, the Archbishop of Canterbury. Certain it is that in the course of this autumn the Archbishop received from some quarter a private hint that a Roman Catholic Relief Bill was in contemplation, and addressed a letter to the King, at Weymouth, strongly deprecating any such design. It is said that, before the close of the year, there came also a similar representation to His Majesty from the Primate of Ireland : this was the Hon. Dr. William Stuart, who was appointed only in November of this year, and who was a younger son of the former favourite, the Earl of Bute.

It was at this period, and at the outset of these designs, that Mr. Pitt, writing in the honourable confidence of one colleague to another, addressed the following letter to Lord Loughborough at Weymouth :—

Sept. 25, 1800.

My dear Lord,—There are two or three very important questions relative to Ireland, on which it is very material that Lord Castlereagh should be furnished with at least the outline of the sentiments of the Cabinet. As he is desirous not to delay his return much longer, we have fixed next Tuesday for the Cabinet on this subject; and though I am very sorry to propose anything to shorten your stay at Weymouth, I cannot help being very anxious that we should have the benefit of your presence. The chief points, besides the great question on the general state of the Catholics, relate to some arrangement about tithes, and a provision for the Catholic and Dissenting Clergy. Lord Castlereagh has drawn up several papers on this subject, which are at present in Lord Grenville's possession, and which you will probably receive from him by the post.

Ever, my dear Lord, &c.,   W. Pitt.

Mr. Pitt did not intend as yet to submit his project to the King. It is, I apprehend, the usual and customary course that a measure should not be laid before the Sovereign until it has been matured and perfected in consultation between the members of the Cabinet. At all events it is quite certain that any previous communication should be made by and through the First Minister of the Crown. But the receipt of these papers from London gave Lord Loughborough a favourable opening for his own designs. How tempting to betray the Prime Minister, and in due time trip him up! How tempting to possess himself of the King's private ear, and become the regulator of his public conduct! With such views the Chancellor showed His Majesty the confidential letter from Mr. Pitt, thereby raising great anxiety and great displeasure in the Royal breast. That he did thus show the letter at Weymouth is acknowledged by himself in a long paper of explanation which in the spring of the ensuing year, when some rumours of his conduct began to be afloat, he found it requisite to draw up and to circulate among his friends. The original paper still remains among the Rosslyn manuscripts, and it has been published by Lord

Campbell. ' I abstain,' says Lord Campbell at its close, ' from the invidious task of commenting on this document.'[1] Seldom indeed has any document so discreditable proceeded from any public man.

Lord Loughborough having now, as he hoped, secured a strong position with the King, set off for London, and attended the Cabinet to which he had been summoned on the 30th of September. There Mr. Pitt unfolded the entire design which, in conjunction with Lord Grenville, he had most carefully prepared. ' We had formed a plan '—so writes Lord Grenville a few months afterwards—'of an extensive arrangement of this whole subject, in which we included the measure of substituting in lieu of the Sacramental test, now notoriously evaded and insufficient for any effectual purpose, a political test, to be imposed indiscriminately on all persons sitting in Parliament, or holding State or Corporation offices, and also on all ministers of religion, of whatever description, and all teachers of schools, &c. This test was to be directly levelled against the Jacobin principles; was to disclaim in express terms the sovereignty of the people; and was to contain an oath of allegiance and fidelity to the King's Government of the realm, and to the established constitution both in Church and State. All this was to have been accompanied with measures—the outlines of which I had before communicated to you—for strengthening the powers, and enforcing the discipline of our Church establishment over its own ministers; and for augmenting the income of those whose poverty now forms an insuperable bar to their residence. And a provision was also to be made in respect of tithes, which would, I think, materially operate in this country, and still more materially in Ireland, to remove the objections to that mode of provision for the clergy.[2]

The plan being thus explained and laid before the

---

[1] *Lives of the Chancellors*, vol. vi. p. 326.

[2] Lord Grenville to Lord Buckingham, Feb. 2, 1801 : *Courts and Cabinets of George III.*, vol. iii. p. 129.

Cabinet, Lord Loughborough at once stood forth as its opponent—perhaps a little to the surprise of his colleagues, who remembered his acquiescence in the preceding year. He was willing to commute the tithes, for which indeed, as he said, he was already preparing a measure with the assistance of one of the Judges, but he must maintain the entire exclusion of the Catholics from Parliament and office. Under these untoward circumstances the Cabinet broke up without any decisive resolution. Mr. Pitt adjourned the question for two or three months, hoping then to allay the Chancellor's objections, and meanwhile requesting him to mature his measure upon tithes. Lord Castlereagh was instructed to return to Dublin, and tell the Lord Lieutenant what had passed. ' I apprised his Excellency,' he says, ' that sentiments unfavourable to the concession had been expressed by the highest law authority, and that the Cabinet at large did not feel themselves enabled in His Majesty's absence, and without sounding opinions in other quarters, to take a final decision on so momentous a question.' [1]

During the interval which ensued the Chancellor was not inactive. He drew up and sent to the King at Windsor about the middle of December an able Essay, strongly urging the most popular objections to the Roman Catholic claims. The King subsequently gave this paper to Mr. Addington, and it has been printed by Dean Pellew.[2]

It might have been better for the great public interests involved if Mr. Pitt, in the course of this autumn, had freely opened his mind to his Royal Master. It might have been better to meet at once, rather than procrastinate, the main obstacle before him. The absence of the King from London, and his own depression of health and spirits, may have been perhaps among the causes that withheld him. But on the other hand, he had no reason to suspect the treachery of one of his

---

[1] Letter to Mr. Pitt, January 1, 1801.
[2] *Life of Lord Sidmouth*, vol. i. p. 500–512.

colleagues, and he had known many cases in which the King's aversion, however strong, and however strongly expressed, had been at the last surmounted. Of this three especial instances may be alleged from their past correspondence: first, the dismissal of Lord Thurlow from office: secondly, the recall of the Duke of York from Flanders; and thirdly, the negotiation of Lord Malmesbury for peace with France. On all three points His Majesty had shown not only aversion, but even anguish of mind; yet on all three he had yielded to the firm though respectful representations of Mr. Pitt, made in writing and supported by the other members of the Cabinet.

It is highly probable that on the Catholic claims George the Third would have yielded too, had he thought them, like the other, only a political question, and had not the dread of violating his Coronation Oath been recently instilled into his mind. With that conviction, chimæra though it was, implanted, we can scarcely blame him for resistance at all risks. We can scarcely blame any man for desiring to confront any danger rather than incur the guilt of perjury.

Such then was the state of the question in January, 1801, when the Cabinet resumed its sittings, and when Lord Castlereagh came back from Ireland. He addressed to Mr. Pitt, as I have already stated, an important letter recapitulating all the previous steps that had been taken. In reply he must have been authorized to assure the Lord Lieutenant that Mr. Pitt would abide by his own opinion; for a few days afterwards we find Lord Cornwallis write to Lord Castlereagh in the following terms:—'Your letter, dated the 7th, afforded me very sincere satisfaction. If Mr. Pitt is firm, he will meet with no difficulty.'[1] So ill had Lord Cornwallis, a man of but moderate abilities, informed himself! For it is certain that even if the Cabinet had been unanimous, and even if the King had yielded,

____
[1] *Cornwallis Correspondence*, vol. iii. p. 331.

there would still have been many and not slight difficulties to surmount, from the warm opposition of the two Primates and of their brother Bishops, and from the repugnance, even though as yet inactive, of a large portion of the British people.

Meanwhile the Cabinet was pursuing its deliberations. The Chancellor maintained his ground with more zeal than ever. Lord Westmorland, who had never been friendly to the Roman Catholics, but who had acquiesced in 1799, now stood forth at the Chancellor's side. The Duke of Portland had changed his opinion, and was inclining, though gently, against the Catholic cause. Lord Liverpool was absent, but declared his opposition by letter. Lord Chatham was also absent, but was understood to be also adverse. The other members of the Cabinet concurred with Mr. Pitt.

The discussions still at intervals continued, though with less and less prospect of agreement, when the anxiety of the King brought the matter to an issue. At his Levee on Wednesday, the 28th of January, the King walked up to Mr Dundas, and eagerly asked him, as referring to Lord Castlereagh, ' What is it that this young Lord has brought over which they are going to throw at my head? . . . . . . The most Jacobinical thing I ever heard of! I shall reckon any man my personal enemy who proposes any such measure.' ' Your Majesty will find,' answered Mr. Dundas, ' among those who are friendly to that measure some whom you never supposed to be your enemies.' [1]

During this conversation at the Levee several other persons stood partly within hearing, and some public rumours of course ensued.

Next day the King, in great distress of mind, wrote to the Speaker. ' I know,' he said, ' we think alike on this great subject. I wish Mr. Addington would from himself open Mr. Pitt's eyes to the danger . . . . . which may prevent his ever speaking to me on a subject upon

---

[1] *Life of Wilberforce*, by his Sons, vol. iii. p. 7.

which I can scarcely keep my temper.'[1] Mr. Addington therefore did call upon Pitt, and was not without some hopes of having produced an impression on his friend. He wrote accordingly in answer to the Royal letter, and he had afterwards an interview with the King at Buckingham House. The part of the Prime Minister was, however, already taken. After the public and vehement language which the King had so recently used, Pitt had little or no hope of prevailing with His Majesty.[2] But he thought his own course of duty clear before him. On the evening of Saturday, the 31st of January, Mr. Pitt addressed a letter to the King, containing a masterly argument on the question at issue, and asking leave to resign if he were not allowed to bring it forward with the whole weight of Government. The King received this letter on the morning of Sunday, the 1st of February, and after consulting with the Speaker, wrote his reply before the close of the same day. 'I shall hope,' so says the King, 'Mr. Pitt's sense of duty will prevent his retiring from his present situation to the end of my life;' and he proposed as a compromise that he, the King, should maintain henceforth utter silence on the question, and that Mr. Pitt on his part should forbear to bring it forward. 'But,' adds the letter, 'further I cannot go.'

In his rejoinder, dated the 3rd of the same month, Mr. Pitt declared himself unable to continue Minister upon these terms; and the King then wrote again on the 5th, accepting with grief, but from a sense of duty, the proffered resignation. These four letters were shortly afterwards shown by George the Third to Lord Kenyon, and his Lordship was at the same time permitted to transcribe them. From that copy the letters were first published in 1827 by Dr. Henry Philpotts, subsequently

---

[1] *Life of Lord Sidmouth*, by Dean Pellew, vol. i. p. 286.

[2] See on this point the letter of Lord Grenville to his brother, dated Feb. 2, 1801, when, as he mentions, the King's answer was not yet received.

Bishop of Exeter. They will be found reprinted at the close of my present volume.

Thus abruptly ended Pitt's renowned administration of more than seventeen years. It ended, as will be noticed, without a single conference between the Monarch and the Minister. None, indeed, was requisite, since opinions were well understood to be fixed on either side.

The King at once summoned the Speaker and desired him to form a new administration. Mr. Addington wavered, and went to consult Mr. Pitt. Pitt had been no party to the King's proposal; but when consulted by his friend, he warmly counselled his acceptance. He assured him of his own cordial and decided support, and as Lord Sidmouth at a later time was wont to relate, he used these very words: 'I see nothing but ruin, Addington, if you hesitate.'[1] Thus encouraged, the Speaker undertook the arduous task.

It was well understood that the members of the Cabinet who had agreed with Mr. Pitt would retire with him. So would also Lord Cornwallis and Lord Castlereagh. 'But'—so writes Wilberforce at this time—'of the younger or inferior in office as many continue as Mr. Pitt can prevail to stay in. He has acted most magnanimously and patriotically.'[2]

In the same spirit Mr. Pitt was anxious that the ties of kindred and affection might not weigh with his brother to resign. On the 5th he wrote at length to Lord Chatham, who was still absent from town; explained to him fully all the circumstances of the case, and entreated him to continue in office. He showed this letter to Mr. Rose, and it must have been of considerable interest; but it is no longer to be found among his papers.

Here is the letter which Mr. Pitt wrote to Rose on this occasion :—

[1] From 'Family Recollections' in the *Life of Lord Sidmouth*, by Dean Pellew, vol. i. p. 288.
[2] Letter to Lord Muncaster, Feb. 7, 1801.

Downing Street, Thursday,
Feb. 5, 1801, ½ past 1.

Dear Rose,—I have been occupied till this moment, and on sending found you were gone to the House. I should be very glad to see you any time in the evening; but as what I wish is to communicate to you some papers which I also want to send to my brother by a messenger to-day, I think the shortest way is to enclose them to you in the mean time, and beg you to return them as soon as you have read them. You will recollect what I said to you some days since on the Catholic question, though you will hardly have expected so rapid a result. As I wish you to know at once the whole of my real sentiments, I have thought it best to enclose with the other papers the letter which I have but just had time to finish, and am going to send with them to my brother.

Ever sincerely yours,   W. PITT.

Take care not to read these papers where anybody can overlook you. Dundas dines with me, but I shall be at leisure any time in the evening.

Mr. Pitt, it appears, had not consulted the Bishop of Lincoln on this weighty matter; and notwithstanding their ties of close friendship, they did not concur upon it. I subjoin the letter which the Bishop at this time addressed to Mr. Rose :—

Buckden Palace, Feb. 6, 1801.

My dear Sir,—I hear, and I think from good authority, that something very unpleasant is passing relative to a Roman Catholic Bill, which Government stands pledged to Ireland to introduce into the Imperial Parliament, and which is said to be disapproved by a Great Personage to such a degree that very unpleasant consequences indeed may follow. If what I hear concerning the intended measure be correct, I cannot but most earnestly deprecate it, and I am satisfied that it never can be carried through the House of Lords. I think that every Bishop would be against it : it has already excited no small alarm amongst some of our bench. I am unwilling to write to Mr. Pitt about it, and you will judge whether it be expedient for you to mention to him what I have said.

Yours ever most truly,   G. LINCOLN.

Rumours of the change had been floating for some days. On the 7th of February they were fully confirmed and acknowledged. In the City the first feeling was that of great alarm. Mr. Rose states in his Diary of that date: 'Late at night (half-past eleven) Mr. Goldsmid came to tell me that on the account of Mr. Pitt's resignation being heard in the City, great confusion followed—a fall of five per cent. in the funds, and no market for Exchequer Bills. As this appeared, in the course of the conversation with Mr. Goldsmid, to have arisen in a great degree from an apprehension that Mr. Pitt was going out of office instantly, I thought it expedient to say to him that there was no intention of that sort, and that Mr. Pitt would certainly open the Budget, and provide completely for the ways and means of the year, before he quitted his situation, which Mr. Goldsmid seemed to think would quiet people's minds sufficiently for the purpose in view.'

Next morning, however, it occurred to Mr. Rose that his last communication to Mr. Goldsmid ought to be conveyed in a more authentic form. With Mr. Pitt's approval it was announced at the Stock Exchange, through Mr. Thornton, Governor of the Bank of England; and on this assurance, adds Mr. Rose, 'Stocks fell one quarter per cent. only.' Indeed, it seems probable that in the first alarm Mr. Goldsmid may have expressed himself with much exaggeration. I do not believe that, unless in some private transactions, the Stocks had fallen five per cent. on the preceding day. The list of prices of Stock for 1801, as printed in the 'Annual Register,' shows that the fluctuation in the Three per Cent. Consols during the entire month of February was but from 57 to 55¼.

Among statesmen the opinions were of course very much divided. 'If the Speaker is employed, as is said, to make a new arrangement, it must be indeed a notorious juggle.' So, from St. Anne's Hill, wrote Fox on the 8th; for Fox, though most kind and generous to his

political or private friends, seldom in his correspondence
shows any candour to his adversaries.   Other statesmen
thought the new arrangement very frail and unpromising.   That such was the opinion of Mr. Dundas appears
from a letter which at this time he addressed to Mr.
Pitt.   It bears date 'Wimbledon, Feb. 7, 1801,' and
begins, ' I know not to what stage the Speaker's endeavours to form an arrangement have proceeded, but it is
impossible for me not to whisper into your ear my conviction that no arrangement can be formed under him
as its head that will not crumble to pieces almost as
soon as formed.   Our friends who, as an act of friendship
and attachment to you, agree to remain in office, do it
with the utmost chagrin and unwillingness ; and, among
the other considerations which operate upon them, is the
feeling that they are embarking in an administration
under a head totally incapable to carry it on.'

CHAPTER XXX.

1801.

Lord Grenville announces the resignation of Ministers—Sir John
Mitford chosen Speaker—Speech of Sheridan, and Pitt's reply—
Pitt's Budget—Pitt endeavours to allay the disappointment of
the Catholics—The new Cabinet—His Majesty's illness—The
Doctors Willis consulted—Stir among politicians—Discussion in
the House of Commons—Crisis in the King's disorder—Fox's
concert of measures with his friends—The King's convalescence
—Pitt's determination never again to moot the Catholic Question
during the King's reign—Pitt has an interview with the King,
and gives up the Exchequer Seal—He leaves Downing Street—
His friends in retirement : Mr. Rose—Mr. Canning—Lord Eldon
—Lord Mulgrave—Lord Wellesley.

Few things in our history are perhaps more to be
lamented than the inflexible determination of the King
in February, 1801, against the Roman Catholic claims.

Even the adversaries on principle of those claims would probably in the present day partake in that regret. They would argue that the concession should not have been made at all, but they would allow that, if made, it would have been attended with much greater benefit, or with many fewer evils, in 1801 than it was in 1829. How fierce and long was the intervening conflict! How much of rancour and ill-will—and not on one side only, but on both—did that conflict leave behind!

It is true, indeed, that even in 1801 there would have been a resolute resistance to the measure—a resistance headed by the Primate in England and by the Primate in Ireland. But I think it certain that, had the King been favourable, or even remained neutral, the measure would have passed, not easily indeed, but still by a large majority. The feelings of the English people had not then been stirred to any considerable extent against it. There had been none of that violent conduct and violent language on the part of Roman Catholics which at a later period provoked so much resentment upon the other side. In 1801 it would have been a compromise between parties; in 1829 it was a struggle and a victory of one party above the other. And, further still, the measure that was carried by the Duke of Wellington was far less comprehensive than the one proposed by Mr. Pitt. It did not comprise any settlement of the Roman Catholic clergy, a settlement which in 1801 might have been most advantageous, and which thirty years later became not only disadvantageous, but impossible.

But let me now revert to the events which immediately followed the resignation of Pitt. In Parliament the great change impending was at first understood and implied, rather than expressed. Pitt and Dundas had ceased to attend the House of Commons, and on the 8th Lord Hawkesbury requested Mr. Sturt, on account of their absence, to postpone a motion on the expedition to Ferrol. Mr. Sturt at first demurred. 'I

hope he will consent,' said Mr. Ryder. ' My Right Hon.
friends have no desire to avoid the subject. Their absence proceeds from circumstances which it is impossible
for me now to state, though those circumstances are
almost notorious.'

It is not very easy to discern the advantage of this
formal reserve; and next day, the 9th, Lord Grenville
announced the resignation in due form to the House
of Lords. ' May we hope,' he said, ' that our services
have contributed to the escape which this country has
made from the evils that threatened it? It is our
consolation to reflect that the same vigorous line of
conduct will be pursued by our successors. Though
we may differ from them in some points, in most there
is no difference between us; and while they continue
to act in a firm, resolute, and manly manner, they shall
have our steady support.'

The most pressing question for Mr. Addington was
to find a successor to himself as Speaker, so as to
enable the business of the Commons to proceed. He
tendered the post to the Attorney-General, Sir John
Mitford, by whom it was accepted. On the 11th, therefore, Sir John was proposed; with very little opposition
chosen; and, after the usual coy demur, conducted to
the Chair.

On the 16th, when Mr. Pitt was present, a Vote
of Thanks to the late Speaker was moved; and there
followed a discussion on the impending Ministerial
changes. Pitt spoke four times that day. To Addington
he referred in the kindest terms: ' The Right Hon.
gentleman,' he said, ' has already filled one situation of
great importance with the most distinguished ability,
and this is the surest augur of his services in another
exalted situation.'

The principal adversary on this occasion of the Ministers—both the old and the new—was Mr. Sheridan.
He referred to Mr. Pitt as follows:

' The Right Hon. gentleman took great pride to

himself for the assistance which he was about to lend to his successors in office. It was triumphantly asked, whether our allies and the people would not look for the same degree of vigour and ability from the new administration, standing on the same ground and fighting the same battle? He must certainly repy in the negative. When the two Right Hon. gentlemen (Pitt and Dundas) and a noble Earl (Spencer) should be removed, there would certainly be a great defalcation from the vigour and abilities of the Cabinet. The reasoning on this occasion was of a singular description. When the crew of a vessel was preparing for action, it was usual to clear the decks by throwing overboard the lumber, but he never heard of such a manœuvre as that of throwing their great guns overboard. When an Election Committee was formed, the watchword was to shorten the business by knocking out the brains of the Committee. This was done by striking from the list the names of the lawyers and other gentlemen who might happen to know a little too much of the subject. In this sense the Right Hon. gentlemen had literally knocked out the brains of the administration, and then, clapping a mask on the skeleton, cried, " Here is as fine vigour and talent for you as anybody may wish to see." This empty skull, this skeleton administration, was the phantom that was to overawe our enemies and to command the confidence of the House and the people.'

Here is Mr. Pitt's reply:

' I have been accused of having refused to give the House any explanation upon the subject of my resignation. Sir, I did not decline giving the House an explanation upon that subject; but I must be permitted to observe that it appears to me to be a new and not a very constitutional doctrine that a man must not follow his sense of duty—that a man must not, in compliance with the dictates of his conscience, retire from office without being bound to give to this

House and to the public an account of all the circumstances that weigh in his mind and influence his conduct. Where this system of duty is established I
know not. I have never heard that it was a public
crime to retire from office without explaining the
reason; I, therefore, am not aware how it can be a
public crime in me to relinquish, without assigning
the cause, a station which it would be the ambition of
my life and the passion of my heart to continue to fill
if I could do so with advantage to the country and
consistently with what I conceive to be my duty. As
to the merits of the question which led to my resignation, though I do not feel myself bound, I am willing
to submit them to the House. I should rather leave
it to posterity to judge of my conduct—still, I have
no objection to state the fact. With respect to the
resignation of myself and of some of my friends, I
have no wish to disguise from the House that we did
feel it an incumbent duty upon us to propose a measure on the part of Government which, under the circumstances of the union so happily effected between
the two countries, we thought of great public importance and necessary to complete the benefits likely to
result from that measure: we felt this opinion so
strongly that, when we met with circumstances which
rendered it impossible for us to propose it as a measure
of Government, we equally felt it inconsistent with our
duty and our honour any longer to remain a part of
that Government. What may be the opinion of others
I know not, but I beg to have it understood to be a
measure which, if I had remained in Government, I
must have proposed. What my conduct will be in a
different situation must be regulated by a mature and
impartial review of all the circumstances of the case.
I shall be governed (as it has always been the wish of
my life to be) only by such considerations as I think
best tend to ensure the tranquillity, the strength, and
the happiness of the empire.'

Two days later—that is, on the 18th of February—Pitt, according to his promise, brought forward his Budget and the new taxes for the year. The demands which he had to make were large indeed—a loan of twenty-five millions and a half for England, and another million and a half for Ireland. To meet the charge thus accruing, he proposed new taxes upon a great variety of objects, as tea, timber, paper, and horses of every description, not even excepting those employed in agriculture, although upon a lesser scale. On the whole these new taxes were calculated at no less a yearly sum than 1,794,000*l.*; but so clear was the necessity which Pitt established, and so authoritative and convincing was his statement, that it did not encounter even the semblance of an opposition. 'The whole,' says Mr. Rose, 'passed off with unanimity, which never happened before in the seventeen years of his administration.' 'In the evening,' so continues Mr. Rose in his journal of that day, 'I went to him at his desire, and we were alone more than three hours in an extremely interesting conversation, in the course of which he was, beyond all comparison, more affected than I had seen him since the change first burst upon me, but nothing particularly leading to any new disclosure occurred. The most remarkable thing that fell from him was a suggestion that, on revolving in his mind all that had passed, it did not occur to him that he could have acted in any respect otherwise than he had done, or that he had anything to blame himself for except not having earlier endeavoured to reconcile the King to the measure about the Catholics, or to prevail with His Majesty not to take an active part on the subject . . . . There were painful workings in his mind plainly discernible; most of the time tears in his eyes, and much agitated.'

The same evening the King wrote to Mr. Pitt an affectionate letter expressing his joy at the triumphant success of his Budget that afternoon. It is a letter of the greatest kindness from its unusual form—the only letter in the whole series which commences ' My dear Pitt.' Mr. Pitt, in answer, expressed his warm sense of the Royal condescension, and the King's rejoinder of the 20th was the close of the correspondence between them for a period of more than three years.

One of the first cares of Mr. Pitt, as soon as his resignation became known, was to allay the disappointment of the Roman Catholics in Ireland. Lord Castlereagh wrote accordingly, under Pitt's own eye, to Lord Cornwallis; and Lord Cornwallis drew up to circulate among the Catholic chiefs a paper, which, though headed only as the ' Sentiments of a sincere friend,' was perfectly well understood to proceed from the Lord Lieutenant. It was very short; indeed, in only two sentences. In the first, the Roman Catholics were warned against ' convulsive measures,' or ' associations with men of Jacobinical principles.' In the second, they were told to ' be sensible of the benefit they possess by having so many characters of eminence pledged not to embark in the service of Government except on the terms of the Catholic privileges being obtained.'

In this last clause the Noble Marquis certainly evinced very little discretion or sound judgment. Some time afterwards he had not the least scruple in departing from it, so far as his own conduct was concerned; and when, in 1805, Mr. Plowden, the author of the ' History of Ireland,' addressed to him a question on the subject, it must be owned that his explanation was of the lamest kind. ' I have not by me,' he wrote, ' a copy of that paper. If I did make use of the word *pledged,* I could only mean that in my own opinion the Ministers, by resigning their offices, gave a pledge of their being friends to the measure of Catholic emancipation; for I never received authority, directly or indirectly, from any member of administration who resigned his office, to give a pledge that he would not embark again in the service of Government except on the terms of the Catholic privileges being obtained.'[1]

The object in view, namely, the tranquillity of the Roman Catholics, was however for the present secured. They saw the exertions and the sacrifices which had been made in their cause. They forbore in general all violent proceedings, and all resentful language. They were as yet for the most part disposed to bide their time, and to rely upon their friends.

Meanwhile Mr. Addington was busy in filling up the vacant offices. Besides the members of the Cabinet who had agreed with Mr. Pitt, and besides the two Irish chiefs, there were several men in lesser office, who, notwithstanding the urgent request of the late Prime Minister, insisted on resigning with them. The principal of these were Mr. Rose and Mr. Long, the joint Secretaries of the Treasury; Lord Granville Leveson Gower, one of the Lords of the Treasury; and Mr. Canning, joint Paymaster of the Forces.

It is related in Lord Malmesbury's journal that when the new Prime Minister saw Lord Granville Leveson on this occasion, he spoke of himself as ' only a sort of *locum tenens* for Pitt.' But I concur with Dean Pellew in rejecting this story. It seems to me wholly at variance with Addington's course and conduct only three weeks afterwards; and I think that in this instance, as in some others of the same period, Lord Malmesbury did no more than transcribe a current but much exaggerated rumour of the day.

The issue of the Writs in the House of Commons was postponed until the new arrangements should be fully matured. But, in truth, Mr. Addington had little choice. The ablest men in the Government having withdrawn, and the Opposition being irreconcileable, he could only, as Lord Macaulay says, ' call up the rear ranks of the old Ministry to form the front ranks of a new Ministry. And thus,' as the same historian adds,

<hr>

[1] *Cornwallis Correspondence*, vol. iii. p. 318.

‘in an age pre-eminently fruitful of Parliamentary
talents a Cabinet was formed containing hardly a single
man who in Parliamentary talents could be considered
as even of the second rate.’[1]

In one respect, however, these appointments seem
to me highly gratifying. The statesman who for his
selfish ends had wrought all this confusion derived no
advantage from it. On the contrary, he was signally
humbled. ‘ Never,’ as Lord Campbell says, ‘ was there
such a striking instance of an engineer “ hoist by his
own petard.” ’ The King had lately seen a great deal
of Lord Loughborough. He had been glad to lean on
his Lordship’s legal knowledge and skill. But at the
same time he had become well acquainted with his
Lordship’s character, and I need not add to what
opinion a thorough knowledge of that character would
inevitably lead. So far from naming Lord Loughborough Prime Minister, as Lord Loughborough himself
appears to have hoped, the King was fully determined
that he should not even continue Chancellor. His
Majesty designed that high office for Lord Eldon, whose
perfect integrity and firmness of principle he justly
esteemed; and on this point, as on most others, Addington was compliant to the Royal will.

This appointment of Lord Eldon was settled on the
very first day between the Monarch and the Minister.
On that day, the 5th of February, Mr. Addington could
announce it to his friend Mr. Abbot, as we learn from
the latter’s Diary, and Addington added that he should
endeavour to persuade Lord Loughborough to accept
the Presidency of the Council. No wonder, if, in the
diary of the same date, Lord Loughborough is described
as ‘ all consternation !’ No wonder if, suddenly inverting
his political course, he wrote to the King earnestly
pressing His Majesty still to continue Mr. Pitt in office,
and to rely upon ‘ the generosity of Mr. Pitt’s mind !’[2]

[1] *Biographies*, p. 212, ed. 1860.
[2] This letter is not dated, but was, I think, beyond all doubt

Nearly similar was the case of Lord Auckland. Though he had sided with the King, he had not gained the King's good opinion. In a conversation some weeks afterwards, he was described by His Majesty to Mr. Rose as 'an eternal intriguer.'[1] Though permitted in the new administration to retain his office as joint Postmaster-General, he was not called to any special confidence, nor admitted to a seat in the Cabinet.

The King's wishes as to persons had been studiously consulted. To him the progress of the new arrangements was highly gratifying. He liked and he applauded every step of Mr. Addington. But at the same time His Majesty could not divest himself of deep anxiety. He must have felt that in losing Mr. Pitt he lost a tower of strength. He must have felt that a doubtful and clouded future was in view. Under such circumstances, and as if to tranquillize his mind, he reverted again and again to the religious obligation which he conceived to bind him. One morning—so his faithful equerry General Garth many years afterwards related—he desired his Coronation Oath to be once more read out to him, and then burst forth into some passionate exclamations: 'Where is that power on earth to absolve me from the due observance of every sentence of that oath? . . . . No—I had rather beg my bread from door to door throughout Europe than consent to any such measure!'[2]

Another day at Windsor—this was on the 6th or 7th of the month—the King read his Coronation Oath to his family, asking them whether they understood it, and added: 'If I violate it, I am no longer legal

written at this period; and the papers it refers to as sent by the King for the Chancellor's perusal consisted of the correspondence between His Majesty and Mr. Pitt. Lord Campbell, who first published this letter (*Lives of the Chancellors*, vol. vi. p. 317), has erroneously placed it a month later, that is, on the King's recovery from his illness.

[1] *Diaries* of Mr. Rose, note at vol. ii. p. 158.

[2] Note to Lord Sidmouth's *Life*, by Dean Pellew, vol. i. p. 286.

Sovereign of this country, but it falls to the House of Savoy!'[1]

In the middle of February the King fell ill. His illness was at first no more than a feverish cold. On the 17th he saw Mr. Addington, and on the 18th he saw the Duke of Portland. With the latter he talked very calmly on the general aspect of state-affairs. 'For myself,' said His Majesty, 'I am an old Whig; and I consider those statesmen who made barrier-treaties and conducted the ten last years of the Succession War the ablest we ever had.' The Duke only noticed as unusual that the King spoke in a loud tone of voice.[2] But it is remarkable in this conversation that George the Third discerned, what since his time has become much more apparent, how, not by any sudden change, but by the gradual progress of events, the Whig party has drifted away from its first position in the reign of Queen Anne, and come round to occupy the original ground of its opponents.

The King's calmness in this interview did not long continue. A most grievous calamity was now impending over him from all the agitation and anxiety which he had just sustained. After an interval of twelve years his mind was once more deranged. The Duke of Portland was with him again on the 20th, and was then extremely alarmed. Next day, that is, on Saturday the 21st, the mental alienation was plainly manifested. On the Sunday Mr. Addington was for a short time admitted to his chamber, and afterwards reported to Mr. Pitt that he had found the King collected on some points, but wandering on others. Unhappily the symptoms, instead of diminishing, increased, and became at last not less acute than in 1788.

It is said that one of the earliest symptoms which the King publicly showed of his mental affliction was

---

[1] *Diaries* of Lord Malmesbury, vol. iv. p. 21.

[2] *Ibid.* vol. iv. p. 44.

in Chapel, and it may have been on this very Sunday. He repeated in a loud voice and with extraordinary emphasis, as though referring to his own accession in 1760, the well-known verse in the Morning Service : ' Forty years long was I grieved with this generation, and said : It is a people that do err in their hearts, for they have not known *My* ways.'

On the Monday the King was for many hours without speaking, and, it would seem, unconscious of what passed around him. Towards the evening he came to himself, and then said, ' I am better now, but I will remain true to the Church.' Thus at every intermission of his malady his mind at once reverted to the first cause of his distress. By an Order of the Privy Council, public prayers were offered up for His Majesty's recovery ; and the three Doctors Willis were summoned to his aid.

On Tuesday the 24th, however, Lord Loughborough, as still holding the Great Seal, thought himself justified by the public exigency in going to Buckingham Palace and obtaining the King's signature to a Commission for giving the Royal Assent to an Act of Parliament. That Act was for the repeal of the Brown Bread Bill, which, as I have elsewhere shown, was passed in haste at the close of the preceding year, and which had been found very mischievous in practice. There is no doubt that all parties now concurred in desiring its repeal, and that a delay of that repeal would have been injurious ; yet even this consideration scarcely suffices to vindicate the course which, under such circumstances, the Chancellor pursued. On returning from the Palace, his Lordship said that when he had carried the Brown Bread Act to the King, His Majesty was in the perfect possession of his understanding.[1] But this was only his Lordship's public declaration. To Mr. Rose, as to a private friend, he owned that he had not seen the King at all. He had sent in

---

[1] *Diaries* of Lord Malmesbury, vol. iv. p. 17.

the Commission to His Majesty by Dr. Willis, who brought it back signed, and told him that there would be no difficulty in obtaining the Royal Signature to a dozen papers respecting which no detailed statements were necessary.[1]

During many days the King's malady did not abate. During many days he was unable to see his Ministers, either the late or the new, or even the Queen and the Princesses. Meanwhile the Government was in a most anomalous, nay, unprecedented state. Here was one Cabinet in progress of formation, and sanctioned by the King. Here was another Cabinet which had resigned, but still holding the seals of office, and alone competent to do any official act. Here was Mr. Addington Prime Minister *de jure*. Here was Mr. Pitt Prime Minister *de facto*. It was only by the entire cordiality at this time between the two statesmen that confusion was avoided. They held several familiar conferences on the painful, but, as it seemed, unavoidable and close impending question of a Regency.

It was also on this question of Regency that the Prince of Wales, so early as Monday the 23rd, commanded Mr. Pitt to attend him. ' I have sent to consult you,' said the Prince, ' on the present distressing occasion.' ' Sir,' said Mr. Pitt, ' being *de facto* in the situation of Minister, I shall have no hesitation in giving your Royal Highness the best advice and opinions in my power. But there is one thing that I must be allowed very respectfully to state : I can do so only on the express condition that your Royal Highness will forbear to advise with those who have for a long time acted in direct opposition to His Majesty's Government.' In answer, the Prince acquiesced as to the persons immediately alluded to by Mr. Pitt, but added that he should think himself still at liberty to advise from time to

---

[1] *Diaries* of Mr. Rose, vol. i. p. 315. In 1801 and the three subsequent years this Diary and the accompanying correspondence become of the greatest value to the biography of Pitt.

time with Lord Moira, as he had long been in the habit of doing.[1]

'I am afraid, from what I hear,'—so said Mr. Thomas Pelham to Lord Malmesbury—'that Mr. Pitt, when sent for by the Prince, was more stiff and less accommodating than he should have been.' It was the opinion of Mr. Pelham and some others that the two contending parties at the last Regency should each to some extent give way. Pitt, on the contrary, was determined to maintain his own ground. He saw the Prince again on Wednesday the 25th, and frankly stated his intention to propose, and press if the necessity should arise, a measure of restricted Regency, as in 1789. In this view of his duty he was supported by the members of his Cabinet, even by those who in 1789 had opposed him, as the Duke of Portland, Lord Loughborough, and Lord Spencer. This was expressly mentioned by Mr. Pitt to the Prince. 'Every one concerned,' added Pitt, 'not even excepting your Royal Highness, cannot do better than accord with what was then most evidently the clear sense of the Legislature, expressed in a manner not to be mistaken.' The Prince muttered that some of the restrictions were likely to be found extremely inconvenient, but showed no displeasure, and observed that he must take time to consider all that Mr. Pitt had said. On the whole there seems every reason to believe that if the affair had proceeded, the Prince would have acquiesced in the Bill of 1789, and that it would have gone through both Houses with no opposition, or with next to none.

In conversation at this time with Mr. Rose, Mr. Pitt expressed a strong opinion that the Regent, if appointed, should call Mr. Addington to his councils; so that the King on his recovery might find in his service the person whom he had designed to place there. On the other hand, Rose, Canning, the Bishop of Lincoln, and others, earnestly endeavoured to dissuade Pitt from giving that advice. 'It is my firm belief,' said Rose,

[1] *Diaries* of Mr. Rose, vol. i. p. 311.

' that neither your friends nor yet the public would bear such an arrangement.' It was the wish and the hope of all these gentlemen to see Pitt himself restored to power.

Great was the stir among all classes of politicians. Hopes and fears, rumours and surmises, flew from side to side.   Public discussion was, however, as by common consent, avoided.   One very foolish Member, Mr. Nicholls, did, indeed, give notice of a motion for the 27th in the House of Commons; but even his own friends did not scruple to inveigh against him.   Mr. Fox, who had emerged from his retirement at St. Ann's, and intended to take his seat on that very day, postponed it, lest he should be thought to give any countenance to that mischievous course. ' When,' says Mr. Rose, ' I went into the House of Commons [that afternoon] with Mr. Pitt, we found Mr. Sheridan on his legs, moving the adjournment of the House to Monday, to get rid of Mr. Nicholls's motion, and stating the utter impropriety of any discussion of public matters in the present uncertain state of the King's health.' Mr. Pitt, who rose next, said that he gave Mr. Sheridan great credit for his conduct.   He urged very strongly that no man with a heart, or who had the slightest feelings of humanity, or of gratitude, duty, and affection for a beloved Sovereign, would even allude to his situation at present.   At the same time he assured the House that before it became necessary to take any steps of importance in public business, the state of His Majesty's health should be investigated, if, unhappily, His Majesty should not be able to give the proper directions.   Addington was in the House, but did not speak, and the House readily agreed to the adjournment which Pitt advised. This short discussion is not even mentioned in the ' Parliamentary History,' but an authentic account of it may be derived from the valuable Diary of Mr. Rose.

To this discussion also Mr. Wilberforce in his journal briefly refers. ' House suddenly up from Nicholls's absurdity and Pitt's extreme eloquence—too much partaking of stage effect, but Pitt sincerely affected.'

On the same day, as Mr. Rose further says, ' Sir Robert Peel told me he had been urged by many independent men to state in the House of Commons the necessity of Mr. Pitt remaining in a responsible situation, and not abandoning the country. He referred plainly to the total want of confidence in Mr. Addington, and stated that to be general in and out of Parliament.'

On the 2nd of March there was a crisis in the King's disorder. His Majesty was so ill that his life was almost despaired of; but having sunk into sleep, which continued for some hours, he awoke much refreshed, and from that time steadily mended. ' On the whole,' says Mr. Rose, in his journal of the 3rd, ' the alteration for the better appeared to be most extraordinary. The King was thought so well, that the Queen and the Princesses took an airing in their carriages. This account was brought to Mr. Pitt, while in bed, before eight o'clock, by Mr. Addington. . . . . . . Mr. Addington came again to Mr. Pitt late in the day, when I was with him, and said the accounts from the Queen's House continued as favourable as possible.'

During the next two days the King's health continued, though slowly, to improve. Nevertheless, on the 5th Pitt felt it necessary to consider seriously with his Treasury intimates how far it would be possible to prolong the *Interregnum*. It was absolutely requisite to obtain, without much further delay, the Royal sanction to the foreign despatches, and the Royal assent to the Parliamentary Bills. Pitt came to the conclusion that unless His Majesty should be quite well before the 12th, that was the latest day to which he could defer an examination of the physicians either before the Privy Council or the House of Commons. In that case a Regency Bill might be brought in on the 14th, and might pass by the 23rd. This was on the supposition that it would be unopposed. And Mr. Pitt thought that it would not be safe to defer the inquiry of the physicians even till the 12th, unless it could be ascertained that no delay would be created. ' In order to which,' adds Mr. Rose, ' Mr. Pitt agreed the best mode would be to have an intercourse with Mr. Fox, either by letter or through some person who can communicate directly with him; first waiting upon the Prince of Wales again to know whether His Royal Highness will acquiesce in the provisions of the last Regency Bill, with perhaps some modifications as to Peerages, confining that to one year, or till a certain period after the commencement of the next Session of Parliament.'

Fox, like the Prince, appeared at this juncture well inclined to acquiesce without demur in the proposed restrictions. He had ended his secession, and returned to his post with great reluctance. He was most unfeignedly attached to the ease and leisure of his country life. Only a few weeks later, when summoned by his nephew, Lord Holland, to come up again from St. Ann's, we find him answer in his ever genial style: ' Never did a letter arrive in a worse time, my dear young one, than yours this morning. A sweet westerly wind, a beautiful sun, all the thorns and elms just budding, and the nightingales just beginning to sing, though the blackbirds and thrushes would have been quite sufficient, without the return of *those seceders*, to have refuted any arguments in your letter.' [1]

At the beginning of March, however, Mr. Fox having taken his seat in the House of Commons, felt it his duty to enter into some concert of measures with his remaining friends on the possibility of his being called on by the Regent to form or to take part in a new administration. Lord Loughborough appears to have done his best at this juncture to ingratiate himself with his old ally. He called upon Fox, and as a token of his confidence revealed to him the important fact that he had not seen the King when he had carried to Court the

---

[1] *Fox Memorials and Correspondence*, vol. iii. p. 189.

Commission for the Brown Bread Bill.[1] But Fox knew Lord Loughborough well. In the event of his own accession to power, he had resolved to press the Great Seal upon his old enemy Lord Thurlow, and Lord Thurlow had made up his mind to accept the offer, but without the Speakership of the House of Lords, to which he felt his health and advancing age unequal.

It must be acknowledged that at this juncture, as at some others, the character of Lord Thurlow appears to little more advantage than Lord Loughborough's. Even the melancholy condition of his Sovereign could not soften that rugged and implacable breast. Lord Kenyon told Lord Eldon at this period that Lord Thurlow had been with him, and that his conversation about the King was perfectly shocking to his ears. 'In short,' added Lord Kenyon, 'he is a beast; and the conversation ended by my saying, "I swear to God, my Lord, I believe he (the King) is more in his senses than your Lordship."'[2]

All questions of Regency, however, were set at rest by the King's convalescence. It is remarkable that the first favourable change was due to Mr. Addington, not indeed in his political, but rather in his filial capacity. He remembered to have heard from his father, the eminent physician, that a pillow filled with hops would sometimes induce sleep when all other remedies had failed; and the experiment being tried upon the King was attended with complete success.[3] Some persons have supposed that a rumour of this fortunate prescription gave rise to the nickname of 'the Doctor,' which some months later was almost universally applied to Mr. Addington; but I doubt whether the report was ever so prevalent as to produce that popular taunt, which

[1] 'This Lord Loughborough told me himself.'—*Fox Memorials*, vol. iii. p. 356.

[2] *Diaries* of Mr. Rose, vol. i. p. 311.

[3] This curious fact, first, I think, stated with authority by Mr. Adolphus (*History of England*, vol. vii. p. 457), is confirmed by Dean Pellew (*Life of Lord Sidmouth*, vol. i. p. 309).

was only, I conceive, a reminiscence of his father's profession.

On Friday, the 6th of March, the King, though much reduced in strength, was clear and calm in mind. He sat for some time with the Queen and the Princesses. He desired Dr. Thomas Willis to write an account of his convalescence to Mr. Addington, to Lord Eldon, and to Mr. Pitt. With respect to Mr. Pitt His Majesty used the following words:—'Tell him I am now quite well—quite recovered from my illness; but what has *he* not to answer for who is the cause of my having been ill at all?'

Pitt was deeply affected. It had given to him and to his colleagues, who were retiring from the Cabinet, most heartfelt pain to find that their conscientious course of duty had been the means of bringing upon their Royal Master this heavy and unforeseen affliction. Lord Malmesbury has an entry as follows in his journal under the date of the 25th of February:—'Lord Spencer very much hurt at what has passed, and feeling a great deal for the share he has had in it; and Pitt, though too haughty to confess it, feels also a great deal.'

Moved by these feelings and by the King's affectionate reproof, Mr. Pitt at once conveyed to him an assurance that he would never again during His Majesty's reign bring forward the Catholic Question. Lord Malmesbury heard that Mr. Pitt had conveyed this assurance in a letter to the King, but this appears to be an error of detail. In the first place, had Pitt written any such letter, it would certainly have called forth an answer from the King, and no trace of any such appears in the series of their manuscript correspondence. Secondly and chiefly, I think that we are enabled to trace the exact state of the case from a letter which some months afterwards Bishop Tomline addressed to Mr. Rose. At that time Mr. Rose expected to have some private talk with the King, and the Bishop wishes him to repeat to His Majesty the precise facts of the preceding spring.

Bishop of Lincoln to Mr. Rose.

Buckden Palace, Aug. 14, 1801.

My dear Sir,—I am very glad that you think of going to Weymouth, and I am impatient that you should have the conversation with the King. Recollect that when the King was recovering from his illness, Mr. Pitt saw Dr. T. Willis at Mr. Addington's; and before Mr. Addington authorised Dr. Willis to tell His Majesty that during his reign he would *never* agitate the Catholic Question; that is, whether *in* office or *out* of office. Mr. Pitt left Dr. Willis and Mr. Addington together. I saw Dr. Willis's letter to Mr. Pitt, and I suspect that the message was not properly and fully delivered. All this is of course private history, but I think it very important . . . .

Yours always most cordially,   G. LINCOLN.

But further still I am enabled to give the very letter of Dr. Willis which the Bishop mentions.

Dr. Thomas Willis to Mr. Pitt.

Queen's House, ½ past 8.

Sir,—Her Majesty, the Dukes of Kent and Cumberland, went into the King at half after five o'clock, and remained with him for two hours. They came out perfectly satisfied—in short, everything that passed has confirmed all that you heard me say to-day. He has desired to see the Duke of York to-morrow, and all the Princesses in their turn.

I stated to him what you wished, and what I had a good opportunity of doing; and, after saying the kindest things of you, he exclaimed, 'Now my mind will be at ease.' Upon the Queen's coming in, the first thing he told her was your message, and he made the same observation upon it.

I stated also the whole of what you said respecting Hanover—which he received with perfect composure.

You will not expect that I mean to show that the King is completely *well*, but we have no reason to doubt that he very soon will be so.

I have the honour to be, Sir, &c.,   THOMAS WILLIS.

Pitt made no secret to his immediate friends of the determination which he had thus expressed. But why, they asked themselves, should he then resign at all? If the Catholic Question is not to be stirred again by any Minister during the King's life, lest His Majesty's faculties should be once more subverted, where is the practical difference upon that question between Mr. Addington and Mr. Pitt? And if none upon that question, why then, when the pre-eminence of the latter is on all other points acknowledged, should the former at a period of the greatest national exigency be preferred before him?

On the grounds of public duty at a time of public danger, considerations such as these could not fail to weigh with the great Minister himself. Mr. Rose has noted in his Journal of the 6th, ' Mr. Pitt seems to admit more than he has at all heretofore done, the possibility of its being right that he should remain, or rather return to his situation; in which possible case it would become necessary to dispose honourably and advantageously of Mr. Addington.'

Mr. Pitt, however, was fully resolved to make no step of his own, no, not even the smallest, to the resumption of office. If he did resume it, that could be only at the request of others. The King must apply to him and Mr. Addington must of his own accord offer him his place. Pitt therefore remained at rest. He made no communication to his colleagues of the Cabinet, but he talked without reserve upon the subject to such intimate friends as happened to be near him. He did not mention it to Lord Grenville, who had already gone to Dropmore.[1] But he talked of it especially to Rose; to Dundas, with whom, at his country house, he passed Sunday the 8th; and to Pelham, whom he met on horseback, as on the Monday he was riding back from Wimbledon. Pelham immediately communicated to Lord Malmesbury his impression of what had passed.

<hr>

[1] See Lord Malmesbury's *Diaries*, vol. iv. p. 41.

' It was evident to me,' he said, ' that Pitt had thought the whole over and over again ; that his mind was full of it ; and that he was anxious to come in, but that his pride led him to wish that it should be by entreaty, not by any voluntary forward movement of his.'

Some friends of Pitt at this time greatly disapproved of his reserve. ' Pitt will not stir unless Addington begins,' said Canning to Lord Malmesbury, on Sunday the 8th. ' Surely,' answered the veteran diplomatist, ' this is a very erroneous idea.'—' Pitt is to blame, highly to blame, I confess,' said the young and eager politician. In the next few days, however, several common friends, though with no authority or commission from Pitt, went to call on Addington, and urged him to take measures with the King that Pitt might be invited to continue in office as Prime Minister. It can be no matter of surprise, and it should be no matter of blame, if Addington received this communication very coldly. Let his situation at the time be fairly considered. He had relinquished the post of Speaker, a post independent of all political vicissitudes, and adapted in an especial manner to his tastes and talents ; and to that post his successor was already appointed. He had relinquished that post on the understanding, and, indeed, condition, that he was to be named Prime Minister ; and he was now required to forego that prospect without being able to resume his former functions, and only left free to accept the office, if any, which it might be the pleasure of Pitt to bestow upon him. Of scarce any man could it be expected that he should entirely overlook personal considerations such as these ; above all, since the main public advantage on the other side was one which Addington of all men might be excused if he did not unreservedly admit—I mean the great superiority of genius on the part of Pitt.

With these very natural feelings, Addington replied to the gentlemen who urged him to give way, that they might open the matter to the King if they pleased, but

that he would not propose it, and he trusted they would
think fit previously to consult the King's physicians as
to the effect such a proposal might have upon His
Majesty in his present state of health.[1]

This answer was, of course, quite decisive so far as
the expectant Prime Minister was himself concerned.
Finally, Mr. Pitt put an end to the entire project,
saying that he thought any application on his behalf
utterly improper, that he was determined to give his
strenuous support to the new administration, and that
he expected his friends to do the same.

Under these circumstances, and the Ministerial
arrangements of Addington being meanwhile in great
measure matured, Saturday, the 14th of March, was the
last day of Pitt's long administration. 'On that day,'
as Mr. Rose details it, 'Mr. Pitt went to the King at
three o'clock, and returned about half-past four, and I
saw him at five for a few minutes before he went to
Mr. Addington. He had resigned the Exchequer Seal
to His Majesty. He said His Majesty possessed himself
most perfectly, though naturally somewhat agitated on
such an occasion; that his kindness was unbounded.
Mr. Pitt said he was sure the King would be greatly
relieved by the interview being over, and his resignation being accepted; adding, what I am sure was true,
that his own mind was greatly relieved.—Sunday,
March 15. Mr. Pitt explained to me much more at
large what passed when he was with the King yesterday; repeated that His Majesty showed the utmost
possible kindness to him, both in words and manner;
that His Majesty began the conversation by saying,
that although from this time Mr. Pitt ceased to be his
Minister, he hoped he would allow him to consider
him as his friend, and that he would not hesitate to
come to him whenever he might wish it, or when he

<hr>

[1] *Diary* of Mr. Abbot (Lord Colchester), vol. i. p. 258. It is
plain that Abbot's information was derived from Addington himself.

should think he could do so with propriety; adding that in any event he relied on his making him a visit at Weymouth, as he knew Mr. Pitt would go to his mother, in Somersetshire, in the summer.'

Even at a previous interview, the last before His Majesty's illness, the King had in like manner expressed an earnest wish to see Mr. Pitt frequently as a friend. 'I am sure, Sir,' answered Pitt, 'that your Majesty on a little reflection will be aware that such visits might give rise to much remark, and would be attended with inconvenience.'

I have found scarce any letters of Mr. Pitt at this period. There is mention of one to his mother, but it has not been preserved.[1] Nearly all the other persons with whom he might desire to communicate were then in town.

I have now related in full detail, and brought to a final conclusion, the story of Mr. Pitt's retirement from office in 1801. It has often been said, both in England and abroad, and even now perhaps the rumour has not wholly died away, that the cause assigned by Mr. Pitt was only his ostensible and not his real motive. It has been asserted that he withdrew from office on account of the difficulties which he experienced or expected in the way of making peace. Lord John Russell and another eminent critic have some years since sufficiently disposed of this hostile allegation.[2] The original documents bearing on the question, some of which have but lately come to light, must, I am sure, convince every careful and dispassionate reader that any such idea is entirely unfounded.

It is clear that Mr. Pitt felt himself bound, both by his past conduct and by his present opinions, to press forward the Catholic Question; that he would gladly, if

---

[1] It is mentioned by Mrs. Stapleton, writing to Mr. Rose, Feb. 11, 1801.

[2] *Memorials of Fox*, vol. iii. p. 252; *Edinburgh Review*, No. ccx. p. 354.

he could, have overcome the Royal scruples ; and that, far from seeking to escape from office, he resigned it with regret.

It is allowed on all hands that Mr. Pitt, in proposing to the King a measure which he deemed of high national importance, and in resigning when he could not obtain the King's assent to it, fulfilled the duty incumbent on a patriotic Minister. But there is by no means the same unanimity as to his subsequent course, when he promised to refrain from stirring the Catholic claims during the King's life, and was willing if solicited to remain in office. Believing as I do that his conduct at the latter period, as at the former, was not merely free from blame, but entitled to praise, I grieve to find myself at issue on this question with the eminent critic whom I just now cited. I allude to the author of two articles which appeared in the 'Edinburgh Review' of April, 1856, and of January, 1858, and which treat of the period now before us. Many persons have thought that they here discerned the hand of Sir George Cornewall Lewis; and certainly both these essays, in their discriminating powers of inquiry, their large stores of information, and their calm and sustained judicial temper, appear well worthy that distinguished man.

In the former of the articles which may thus in general with no undue praise be described, I find an allusion to the unsuccessful attempt made by some friends of Mr. Pitt to restore him to office in March, 1801 ; an attempt ' in which,' it is added, ' the conduct of this statesman does not appear to advantage.' And the second article carries the criticism further. ' We confess ourselves at a loss to justify, and scarcely even to explain, the course which Mr. Pitt pursued. Why, if he was so willing to remain in March, he was so resolved on resigning in February ; or why, if he was so resolved upon resigning in February, he was so willing to remain in March ; we are equally unable to determine.'

On the other part, I would venture, in the first place, to ask how the critic can feel the smallest difficulty in explaining at least, if not in justifying, the change which he here describes. As reasonably might he state his surprise that the Emperor of Austria was not willing to treat on the 1st of December, 1805, and was willing on the 3rd of the same month; the fact being that the battle of Austerlitz was fought on the intervening day. The intervening illness of George the Third affords, as I conceive, a no less clear, a no less sufficient explanation. When it became manifest that the proposal of the Roman Catholic claims had not only wrung the mind of the aged King with anguish, but altogether obscured and overthrown it, the duty of a statesman, even if untouched by personal considerations, and acting solely on public grounds, was then to refrain from any such proposal during the remainder of His Majesty's reign. Loyal Roman Catholics themselves could not expect, could not even desire, their claims to be under such circumstances urged. Let me moreover observe that the restraint which Mr. Pitt laid upon himself in consequence was one that came to be adopted by all other leading politicians of that age. It was on the same understanding that Lord Castlereagh took office in 1803; Mr. Tierney also in the same year; Mr. Canning in 1804; Lord Grenville and Mr. Fox in 1806. All these, with whatever reluctance, agreed that on this most tender point the conscience of George the Third should be no further pressed. And surely if the ground here stated was sufficient, as I deem it, to justify Mr. Tierney, who had never before held office, and who owed no special attachment to the King, the ground was far stronger in the case of Mr. Pitt, who had served his Majesty as Prime Minister through most trying difficulties and for more than seventeen years.

It may be said, however, that although Mr. Pitt was right to relinquish the Catholic Question in March, 1801, he should not have been willing to resume office at once upon such terms. If, however, the Catholic Question were honourably and for good reason laid aside, the special, and indeed the only, reason for calling in 'the Doctor' was gone. Under him there was every prospect that the new Government would be a weak one—even far weaker than from various causes which I shall hereafter explain it really proved. I have already shown what were the anticipations upon this point of so experienced and so far-sighted a politician as Dundas. A weak Government was then in prospect; and that at a period when the national interests called most loudly for a strong one. It was the duty of a patriot Minister to avert, if he honourably could, that evil from his country. It was his duty not to shrink from the service of his Sovereign, if that Sovereign thought fit to ask his aid, and if the question which had so recently severed them was from other and inevitable causes to sever them no more.

For these reasons I believe, and must be permitted to maintain, that the conduct of Mr. Pitt in March, 1801, is free from all ambiguity and open to no just imputation, but guided from first to last by the same high sense of duty as distinguished his whole career.

On giving up his official residence in Downing Street Mr. Pitt retired to a small furnished house in Park Place. It had lately been occupied by one of the Under Secretaries of State, and Mr. Pitt had purchased the remainder of the lease, extending to the period of one year. 'A set of dinners for Pitt : he declined them all'—so writes Wilberforce at this time. In the House of Commons, whenever Pitt attended, he took his seat—as Mr. Abbot at the time describes it —'on the right hand of the Chair, in the third row from the floor, and in the angle next one of the iron pillars.' Many years afterwards, in the former House of Commons, I have seen old Members point out the very place with something of a reverent feeling.

In the Ministerial changes of March and April, 1801, Lord Cornwallis and Lord Castlereagh had quitted their posts rather on account of their connexion with Ireland and of their engagements with the Catholics than from any especial tie at that time to Mr. Pitt. But in his retirement the late Prime Minister was followed by a small band of trusty friends who, in spite of his entreaties, would not remain in office without him. Chief among these were Long and Rose, and, above all, Canning. Of Mr. Long I have spoken elsewhere.[1] Mr. Rose had no gifts of genius nor powers of eloquence : on the other hand he was an eminently practical and most useful man of business. We find in the course of his long career persons under almost every form of difficulty apply for counsel, and seldom without effect, to his tried sagacity and shrewdness. These qualities were in him combined with a kind and generous heart. To Pitt so long as he lived, and to the memory of Pitt after he was gone, Mr. Rose evinced a devoted and constant attachment ; and to act in conformity to the views of that great Minister was, throughout, the aim and the pride of his public life.

Mr. Canning, as he was in 1801, has been well portrayed by Lord Macaulay in a single sentence, as 'young, ardent, and ambitious, with great powers and great virtues, but with a temper too restless and a wit too satirical for his own happiness.'[2] It may be added that these faults during a long period of succeeding years tended to dim the lustre of his genius, and to delay the ascendency which that genius deserved ; but in spite of them he was perhaps the favourite disciple of Mr. Pitt, and certainly the most renowned.

The following letter from that period will in some degree illustrate the restless temper which Lord Macaulay mentions :—

[1] See vol. i. p. 416.
[2] *Biographies*, p. 216, ed. 1860.

Mr. Pitt to Mr. Canning.

Park Place, April 26, 1801.

My dear Canning,—I return you your letter to Frere, and heartily wish I could do so without saying a single word on the subject to which it relates. I do not now mean to enter into any particulars on which it would be useless to dwell, but I should be guilty of great insincerity if I did not own to you that I do not acquiesce in the idea that there has been anything unkind, much less unfair, in any part of my conduct, or anything either for me to excuse or for you to complain of or to forgive. You certainly were the very first person acquainted with the determination I was likely to form; and I am much mistaken if even in our first conversation I did not express the intention—in which I have never varied—of giving the fullest support to the formation and to the measures of any administration composed of persons acting on the same general principles as I had done. In the incessant and anxious occupations of the succeeding days, it is not surprising that I did not seek a further communication with you till the business was brought more to a point; and after it was so I certainly considered myself as stating to you explicitly and earnestly both my wishes and opinions before you could have been called upon to commit yourself as to your own line of conduct. In addition to this you heard both from myself and, I believe, from others, what the line was which I had persuaded all those to adopt with whom my wishes and opinions were most likely to have weight. Under the circumstances I most deeply lament your having misunderstood me as you now appear to have done, and still more the effect which that misunderstanding has produced; but I really cannot ascribe this to any fault of mine. Having said this, I have no other wish but to dismiss this subject from my mind; and though I am aware that at present there may be some political subjects on which we cannot converse with the freedom with which we have done till lately, I trust that circumstance will not make any change in our intercourse on all other points. I am sure it has made none in my feelings of friendship and attachment to you, or in my earnest wishes for the happiness of your future life, whatever may be its course.

With these sentiments, which I state without disguise,

I remain sincerely and affectionately yours,

W. Pitt.

Many persons who had consented to remain in their old offices did not scruple to avow their strong feelings of attachment to Mr. Pitt. Such an attachment was avowed even by some of those who then accepted new office. Thus Lord Eldon, when he agreed to take the Great Seal, said in express words to Mr. Addington that 'he accepted it only in obedience to the King's command, and at the advice and earnest recommendation of Mr. Pitt; and that he would hold it no longer than he could continue to do so in perfect friendship with the latter.'[1]

Another person who at this time attached himself with great zeal to Mr. Pitt was Henry Lord Mulgrave. In 1792 he had succeeded his brother in that — an Irish—peerage; and, in 1794, was himself created an English Baron. Since that time, though filling no office, he had taken part, and with success, in the debates of the House of Lords.

But of all the personal adhesions which Pitt in his retirement received, there was none certainly of which he had greater reason to be proud than that expressed in the following letter from the Governor General of India.

Marquis Wellesley to Mr. Pitt.

Patna, Oct. 6, 1801.

My dear Pitt,—Although you have been so cruelly lazy as not to send me one line on the subject of the late unparalleled changes in the administration, I cannot allow this packet to depart without renewing to you the sincere assurance of my unalterable attachment and of the truly affectionate interest which I must ever take in any event likely to affect your welfare, with which are involved all our national greatness and honour. I trusted that you would have explained to me the causes and prepared me for the probable consequences of the new arrangements, and that you would have distinctly stated to me the part which you wished me to take in such a crisis. I rely on the testimony of my own

[1] As repeated by Lord Eldon himself to Mr. Rose, February 24, 1801.

heart that you must have felt an implicit confidence in my firm adherence to your cause under any exigency which might arise. When that cause shall cease to be the master-spring of our councils, I shall wish to retreat from the disgrace of office to whatever *fortress* you may choose to defend. My political connexion with you, confirmed by every tie of friendship and intimate intercourse of private regard and affection, is become not only the pride but the comfort of my life ; and I never can support the idea of considering you in any other light than as the guide of my public conduct, the guardian of all that I hold dear and valuable in our constitution and country, and the primary object of my private esteem, respect, and attachment. To these sentiments I would in an instant sacrifice—not only without regret, but with the greatest pleasure—the most lucrative, honourable, and powerful station which any British subject can hold. If, therefore, I had imagined, from the apparent aspect of affairs in England and from the tenor of your conduct, that the crisis had appeared to you to menace either the cause which you have so long maintained, or your own public or private honour, I should have resigned my present office without waiting for any advices from you ; leaving, however, to the Court of Directors and to the new Ministers a sufficient time for the choice of my successor in England and for his arrival in India. This degree of delay I conceive to be an indispensable duty in any person holding my present charge. The consequences of an abrupt dissolution of any existing government in India might be fatal to the power of Great Britain in this quarter. I therefore should not quit this government, even if Charles Fox were to become Minister or Horne Tooke First Consul, until I had allowed a reasonable time for my regular relief. . . . .

Ever yours most sincerely and affectionately,

WELLESLEY.

APPENDIX.

LETTERS AND EXTRACTS OF LETTERS FROM KING GEORGE THE THIRD TO MR. PITT.

Windsor, Jan. 26, 1793.

In consequence of Mr. Pitt's note, I authorize him to direct Sir George Yonge to postpone sending the letters of service to the General Officers for a few days. I shall certainly be ready to hear what Mr. Pitt may have to state against calling forward Lord Townshend; but I think it right to apprise [him] of the reasons that made me think it a desirable measure, his being the original father of the Militia, and as such a most popular character with that corps, and that his rank a little drew off the attention of the army from seeing another General Officer called forth (whom I think it best on paper not to name, though Mr. Pitt's penetration must understand), which appointment certainly is not popular with the army.   G. R.

Windsor, Feb. 2, 1793.

On returning from hunting I have found Mr. Pitt's note, by which I learn that Lord Beauchamp seconded the motion for an Address, which was only opposed by Lord Wycombe, Mr. Whitbread, Mr. Fox, and Lord William Russell. The impression of the House seems just what could have been expected; for if the occasion ever could occur that every power for the preservation of society must stand forth in opposition to France, the necessity seems to be at the present hour. Indeed my natural sentiments are so strong for peace, that no event of less moment than the present could have made me decidedly of opinion that duty as well as interest calls on us to join against that most savage as well as unprincipled nation.   G. R.

Feb. 13, 1793.

I am rather surprised that Mr. Percy Wyndham should have supported the amendment of Mr. Fox to the Address moved by Mr. Pitt, as it had been thought that Lord Egremont's sentiments were very decided in favour of the line of conduct which has been pursued. I am glad to find Mr. Thomas Grenville has taken a line so becoming of him.

G. R.

Feb. 19, 1793.

Mr. Pitt's account of Mr. Fox's five Resolutions having fallen by the previous Question attended by a division, has given me infinite pleasure ; and I doubt the Forty-Four that voted in the minority are the whole number Mr. Fox can at the present hour muster. I am glad the friends of the Duke of Portland in general joined the majority. G. R.

May 8, 1793.

It is with infinite satisfaction I have received Mr. Pitt's note communicating the sense of the House of Commons on the renewed debate on the motion of Mr. Grey, which was so clearly shown by the division of 282 against 41 ; and I most devoutly pray to Heaven that this Constitution may remain unimpaired to the latest posterity, as a proof of the wisdom of the nation, and its knowledge of the superior blessings it enjoys. G. R.

June 18, 1793.

This instant I have received Mr. Pitt's note communicating that Mr. Fox's Motion for a negotiation of peace with France on the terms of her evacuating the places she has conquered had been last night negatived by a division of 187 to 47. I cannot help observing that it seems very extraordinary that any one could advance so strange a proposition, and I trust one so contrary to the good sense of the majority of the whole nation, and such as no one but an advocate for the wicked conduct of the leaders in that unhappy country can subscribe to. G. R.

Windsor, July 13, 1793.

I return to Mr. Pitt the warrants, having signed them. By my orders Lord Amherst has directed the ditch at Walmer Castle to be stockaded, and a picket of twenty-five men to be posted there to prevent any surprise, which will enable Mr. Pitt to go safely there whenever the public business will permit. I did not choose to mention it till I had given the necessary orders. G. R.

Windsor, Sept. 14, 1793.

The misfortune of our situation is that we have too many objects to attend to, and our force consequently must be too small at each place. Yet it seems to me that the Hessian infantry are the only corps we can soon get at to send to Toulon.

Windsor, Nov. 17, 1793.

On the whole, as to active service, I incline much more to Flanders, as being more easily supplied from hence, and also, if enabled to move forward, being more able to advance to Paris.

May 17, 1794.

The conduct of Opposition on the present occasion seems most unwise. The attention of the public at large is awakened at the present crisis, and certainly must see with horror and disdain any set of men trying by mere chicane to clog the measures of Government. After what has passed in the House of Commons, I have not the smallest doubt but that Lords Lansdowne, Lauderdale, Stanhope, and Derby will hold a similar conduct this day in the House of Lords.

I believe there cannot be an impartial man who, when the papers are brought to light, will not see that if Government has erred, it has been in not stepping forth earlier. And yet perhaps the time that has been given was necessary to push on the faction to such overt acts that authorise the measures now pursuing. G. R.

Windsor, July 13, 1794.

If Mr. Pitt can find that a Marquisate would be as agreeable to Lord Howe as a Garter, I will consent to it; but having with Mr. Pitt's knowledge acquainted Lord Howe with my intention of conferring the Order on him, it is impossible, unless Lord Howe chooses the former mark of favour in preference to the latter, that I can propose it. Besides, I cannot see why on the Duke of Portland's head favours are to be heaped without measure. G. R.

Weymouth, Aug. 24, 1794.

Agreeable to what I mentioned to Mr. Pitt before I came here, I have this morning seen the Prince of Wales, who has acquainted me with his having broken off all connection with Mrs. Fitzherbert, and his desire of entering into a more creditable line of life by marrying, expressing at the same time that his wish is that my niece, the Princess of Brunswick, may be the person. Undoubtedly she is the person who naturally must be most agreeable to me. I expressed my approbation of the idea, provided his plan was to lead a life that would make him appear respectable, and consequently render the Princess happy. He assured me that he perfectly coincided with me in opinion. I then said that till Parliament assembled no arrangement could be taken except my sounding my sister, that no idea of any other marriage may be encouraged.
G. R.

Weymouth, Sept. 9, 1794.

I enclose to Mr. Pitt a copy of the letter I received yesterday from the Duke of York in consequence of the overture made to him by Mr. Windham, and am happy he sees the appointment in the same light I do of the Marquis Cornwallis, namely, of necessity obliging him to retire. I have wrote him an answer approving of his determination, as it so perfectly concurs with what I expressed in my letter to Mr. Pitt; and adding that I had not written, that he might have full liberty, should the event happen, to take the line he thought best; that I trust he will during the suspense act with the same zeal as if his command was permanent; but that in my opinion the Emperor will never agree to so novel a measure as [that] the Imperial troops should be commanded by a foreigner : that therefore I look on his remaining at the head of the troops in British pay as most probable.
G. R.

Windsor, Nov. 24, 1794.

Mr. Pitt cannot be surprised at my being very much hurt at the contents of his letter.[1] Indeed he seems to expect it, but I am certain that nothing but the thinking it his duty could have instigated him to give me so severe a blow. I am neither in a situation of mind nor from inclination

---

[1] There is no draft of that letter preserved.

inclined to enter more minutely into every part of his letter ;
but I am fully ready to answer the material part, namely,
that though loving very much my son, and not forgetting
how he saved the Republic of Holland in 1793, and that his
endeavours to be of service have never abated, and that to
the conduct of Austria, the faithlessness of Prussia, and the
cowardice of the Dutch, every failure is easily to be accounted
for without laying blame on him who deserved a better fate,
I shall certainly now not think it safe for him to continue in
the command on the Continent, when every one seems to
conspire to render his situation hazardous by either propa-
gating unfounded complaints against him or giving credit to
them.

No one will believe that I take this step but reluctantly,
and the more so since no successor of note is proposed to take
the command. Truly I do not see where any one is to be
found that can deserve that name now the Duke of Brunswick has declined ; and I am certain he will fully feel the
propriety of the resolution he has taken when he finds that
even a son of mine cannot withstand the torrent of abuse.

Jan. 29, 1795.

Mr. Pitt may be desirous of knowing whether anything
remarkable passed with the Duke of Richmond yesterday.
He certainly seemed much hurt at his intended removal, but
I thought it but justice to say that Mr. Pitt had yielded to
the arrangement to prevent any want of concert in the
Cabinet, which the Duke himself must allow would be
highly detrimental to the conduct of affairs at so critical a
time as the present. His remaining on the Staff seems to
give him much pleasure, and I hope will secure his support.

Feb. 6, 1795.

I received this morning Mr. Pitt's note on the success of
the Austrian Loan, and am glad the business ended in the
House of Commons with so little trouble.

I enclose a rough paper I have drawn up on the extraordinary but serious proposal the Duke of Portland is to-morrow to lay before the Cabinet, which I mean merely for Mr.
Pitt's own information.   G. R.

Feb. 6, 1795.

Having yesterday, after the Drawing Room, seen the
Duke of Portland, who mentioned the receipt of letters from

the Lord Lieutenant of Ireland, which, to my greatest astonishment, propose the total change of the principles of government which have been followed by every administration in that kingdom since the abdication of King James the Second, and consequently overturning the fabric that the wisdom of our forefathers esteemed necessary, and which the laws of this country have directed; and thus, after no longer stay than three weeks in Ireland, venturing to condemn the labours of ages, and wanting an immediate adoption of ideas which every man of property in Ireland and every friend to the Protestant Religion must feel diametrically contrary to those he has imbibed from his earliest youth.

Undoubtedly the Duke of Portland made this communication to sound my sentiments previous to the Cabinet Meeting to be held to-morrow on this weighty subject. I expressed my surprise at the idea of admitting the Roman Catholics to vote in Parliament, but chose to avoid entering further into the subject, and only heard the substance of the propositions without giving my sentiments. But the more I reflect on the subject, the more I feel the danger of the proposal, and therefore should not think myself free from blame if I did not put my thoughts on paper even in the present coarse shape, the moment being so pressing, and not sufficient time to arrange them in a more digested shape previous to the Duke of Portland's laying the subject before the Cabinet.

The above proposal is contrary to the conduct of every European Government, and I believe to that of every State on the globe. In the States of Germany, the Lutheran, Calvinist, and Roman Catholic religions are universally permitted, yet each respective State has but one Church establishment, to which the States of the country and those holding any civil employment must be conformists; Court offices and military commissions may be held also by persons of either of the other persuasions, but the number of such is very small. The Dutch provinces admit Lutherans and Roman Catholics in some subsidised regiments, but in civil employments the Calvinists are alone capable of holding them.

Ireland varies from most other countries by property residing almost entirely in the hands of the Protestants, whilst the lower classes of the people are chiefly Roman Catholics. The change proposed, therefore, must disoblige the greater number to benefit a few, the inferior orders not being of rank to gain favourably by the change. That they may also be gainers, it is proposed that an army be kept constantly in Ireland, and a kind of yeomanry, which in reality would be Roman Catholic police corps, established, which would keep the Protestant interest under awe.

It is but fair to confess that the whole of this plan is the strongest justification of the old Servants of the Crown in Ireland, for having objected to the former indulgences that have been granted, as it is now pretended these have availed nothing, unless this total change of political principle be admitted.

English Government ought well to consider before it gives any encouragement to a proposition which cannot fail sooner or later to separate the two kingdoms, or by way of establishing a similar line of conduct in this kingdom adopt measures to prevent which my family was invited to mount the throne of this kingdom in preference to the House of Savoy.

One might suppose the authors of this scheme had not viewed the tendency or extent of the question, but were actuated alone by the peevish inclination of humiliating the old friends of English Government in Ireland, or from the desire of paying implicit obedience to the heated imagination of Mr. Burke.

Besides the discontent and changes which must be occasioned by the dereliction of all the principles that have been held as wise by our ancestors, it is impossible to foresee how far it may alienate the minds of this kingdom; for though I fear religion is but little attended to by persons of rank, and that the word *toleration*, or rather *indifference* to that sacred subject, has been too much admitted by them, yet the bulk of the nation has not been spoiled by foreign travels and manners, and still feels the blessing of having a fixed principle from whence the source of every tie to society and government must trace its origin.

I cannot conclude without expressing that the subject is beyond the decision of any Cabinet of Ministers — that, could they form an opinion in favour of such a measure, it would be highly dangerous, without previous concert with the leading men of every order in the State, to send any encouragement to the Lord Lieutenant on this subject; and if received with the same suspicion I do, I am certain it would be safer even to change the new administration in Ireland, if its continuance depends on the success of this proposal, than to prolong its existence on grounds that must sooner or later ruin one if not both kingdoms.　　　　　　G. R.

Feb. 10, 1795.

I received yesterday Mr. Pitt's note of that day, but did not choose to answer it till I had written to Lord Amherst and received his answer.　Nothing can be more honourable than his conduct.　He has again declined the rank of Field-Marshal as well as that of an Earl.　I have in consequence directed Mr. Windham to notify the Duke of York as Field-Marshal, and place him at the head of the British Staff, and acquainted him that my son is to stand exactly in the situation till now held by Lord Amherst.　I approve of the Marquis of Cornwallis being presented to-morrow.

I do not say anything of the temporising directions to the Lord-Lieutenant of Ireland.　　　　　　G. R.

Feb. 22, 1795.

I cannot lose an instant in answering the note I have just received from Mr. Pitt, expressing what he has collected from Earl Spencer and Lord Grenville of the Duke of Portland's wish in writing to Earl Fitzwilliam to offer him in my name to continue to attend Cabinet meetings on his return from Ireland.　The whole conduct of the Duke of Portland in this unpleasant business is so handsome, that it is impossible not with satisfaction to gratify his feelings on this occasion.　I therefore authorise Mr. Pitt to acquaint him with the suggestion having been laid before me and with my cordial consent, though I doubt much whether Earl Fitzwilliam is in a state of mind to accept it.　　　　　　G. R.

Windsor, March 10, 1795.

I am much pleased with Mr. Pitt's account that both the Earl Camden and Mr. Pelham are willing to accept the offices of Lord-Lieutenant of Ireland and Secretary for that kingdom, which have been rendered more difficult by the strange conduct of Earl Fitzwilliam.　I approve of Earl Camden being nominated in the Great Council Room to-

morrow, and I trust he will understand that he is to reinstate all those who have been removed by his predecessor,
and to support the old English interest as well as the Protestant Religion. G. R.

May 28, 1795.

Mr. Pitt's account that the motion of Mr. Wilberforce
expressing an inclination for a general pacification was got
rid of by the moving the Order of the Day, which was carried by 201 to 86, is highly agreeable, particularly as the
temper of the majority appeared to be strongly in favour of
perseverance in the war. The recent accounts from France
certainly show the propriety of the opinion ; but above all,
till the bad principles propagated by that unfortunate nation
are given up, it cannot be safe for any civilised part of the
globe to treat or trust that people. G. R.

Kew, July 17, 1795.

By some mistake of the messenger in going to Windsor
instead of bringing Mr. Pitt's letter and the instructions for
the Earl of Moira here, his return is so much retarded.
I think the instructions are very proper, but doubt whether
the promise of cavalry in the letter that is to accompany
them does not go further than perhaps can be effected.

I approve much of the resolutions printed in the papers.
to which I have the pleasure of seeing my Ministers have all
subscribed ; but wish Mr. Pitt would propose to them on
account of the present dearness of provisions adding a resolution of having no *entremets* nor second course during the
present pressure. This I am certain would meet with universal applause, and everything necessary might as well be
served at one course, and without the smallest inconvenience
to anyone much unnecessary waste prevented. G. R.

Windsor, Nov. 13, 1795.

I shall now, as briefly as I can, state the substance of
the information I have received.

General Walmoden reports to me of the 4th inst. from
Nienburg that having sent Captain Berger to Brunswick to
acquaint the Duke that his troops were to return home, the
Duke upon this opened his ideas fully to this officer, and
wrote the General a letter, of which the annexed is a copy,
as a credential of the matter Berger had to communicate.

The last declarations of M. Barthélemy that France will no longer regard any lines of demarcation she had agreed to nor any neutrality, and that under pretence of marching through the various countries she will lay all under contributions, the Prussian and Hesse Cassel dominions not excepted, but that the other Princes shall repay Prussia and Hesse Cassel, the only two with whom she has concluded peace, the quota laid on their dominions : this shows how impossible it is for any country to treat with that unprincipled nation.

The Duke's ideas tend to his being authorised by England to go to Berlin, and try to bring back the King of Prussia on this strange declaration and the change of appearance by the Austrian successes (which he is aware will raise the jealousy of Prussia), and thus attempt to get an army formed to secure the flank of the Austrians, which he is willing to command, with a view of preventing the French from overrunning Germany, not on any plan of offensive but defensive operations.

Mr. Pitt to the King.

Downing Street, Nov. 14, 1795.

Mr. Pitt was honoured yesterday with your Majesty's commands, accompanying the copy of the letter from the Duke of Brunswick, and took the first opportunity of mentioning the interesting subject to which it relates to your Majesty's confidential servants at their meeting this morning.

Mr. Dundas not having then received the letter to H.R.H. the Duke of York, which has since come to his hands, your Majesty's servants did not feel themselves enabled fully to discuss so important a subject, and the consideration of it will be resumed with as little delay as possible. In the mean time Mr. Pitt cannot help submitting to your Majesty the strong apprehension which he entertains that the immense additional expense which would probably be incurred by again collecting and maintaining an army to defend the line of demarcation, added to the impossibility of depending on any concert in which Prussia is to bear a material part, will hardly admit of any encouragement being given to the Duke of Brunswick's proposal.

Dec. 4, 1795.

It is with much satisfaction I have learnt from Mr. Pitt's note that the Bill for preventing seditious assemblies has

been passed this morning on a division of 266 to 51, and
that Mr. Abbot, who spoke for the first time, delivered his
sentiments with great ability and effect. G. R.

Jan. 27, 1796.

It is but natural that I must feel much interested that
every measure of magnitude should be well weighed previous
to any decision being adopted. I have therefore put on paper
the objections that seem to me most conclusive against any
step being taken to open a negotiation of peace with France,
of which I have taken a copy, which I desire to deposit in
the hands of Mr. Pitt. G. R.

Mr. Pitt to the King.

Downing Street, Jan. 30, 1796.

Mr. Pitt was honoured with the commands which your
Majesty had the condescension and goodness to send him on
Wednesday last. The present circumstances had necessarily
led to repeated consideration among your Majesty's servants
on the line proper to be pursued with respect to negotiation.
The result of the best opinion they can form on the subject
is so fully stated in the draft of a despatch to Sir Morton
Eden, which will be submitted to your Majesty by Lord
Grenville, that Mr. Pitt does not feel himself obliged to
trouble your Majesty with much additional observation.

The return of Admiral Christian with a large part of the
convoy to Spithead (of which accounts were received this
morning), and the advanced season, make it now impossible
that operations on a large scale can be prosecuted with full
effect (though they may still be successfully begun) till the
close of the year; and it cannot be expected that Parliament
or the country will wait to so distant a period for *some*
pacific explanation. It seems equally clear that if Government takes in time steps to remove the possibility of cavil
on its real desire to make peace in conjunction with your
Majesty's Allies, on suitable terms whenever they can be
obtained, that this will ensure the continuance of a zealous
support in and out of Parliament.

On the other hand if Government delay taking steps
themselves so late as to be obliged at last to take them in
consequence of any declaration of the sense of Parliament,
all hope of good terms would be at an end. In the first case,

the issue of the war (though far from equal to all that might at some periods have been hoped) would still be honourable and probably advantageous; in the other case, it can hardly be expected to be otherwise than the reverse.

Besides this, it is to be considered that if on explanation France should avow the inadmissible and extravagant pretensions contained in the papers lately circulated by the French Agents, nothing would contribute more to a cheerful and vigorous support of the war; and in the interval any Parliamentary difficulties will be avoided, and the undisturbed management of the negotiation in its future progress be secured to Government, by their being enabled to hold a language which must silence all opposition.

Jan. 31, 1796.

I should not have felt easy had I not fully stated my sentiments against any step from hence being taken for applying to France for peace; and it is not the return of the force sent to the West Indies that can in the least alter my opinions as to the propriety of holding out till France takes some avowed step for attempting to treat; but I do not in the least mean by this to make any obstinate resistance to the measure proposed, though I own I cannot feel the utility of it. My mind is not of a nature to be guided by the obtaining a little applause or staving off some abuse; rectitude of conduct is my sole aim. I trust the rulers in France will reject any proposition from hence short of a total giving up any advantage we may have gained, and therefore that the measure proposed will meet with a refusal.

G. R.

Kew, Oct. 5, 1796.

Mr. Pitt's account of the manner with which Lord Morpeth and Sir William Lowther conducted themselves in moving the Address this day, and the general impression of the House, is as could be wished. I cannot help expressing that I was better pleased with the opinion held yesterday by Lord Grenville that no man of note ought to be sent to France, but some mere official agent, than with his thought this day of offering the commission to Lord Malmesbury, who having been advanced to a seat in the House of Peers, will probably not feel flattered with the proposal.

G. R.

Windsor, Dec. 8, 1796.

I feel much pleasure at Mr. Pitt's note, as it contains the agreeable information that the proposal for the Loan and the Taxes for the annual interest met with unanimous approbation. I own I would have wished, considering the desire for subscribing, that the Loan had been for 2,000,000*l*., as that would probably have covered all the expenses of the year. I hope Mr. Pitt will no longer let the Extraordinaries due to my Electoral troops remain unpaid. It is dreadful, the cries of poor officers and widows who are really almost starving for want of their dues ; and it is impossible to talk of the credit of the country, while, on the contrary, many individuals are exclaiming at these losses. I have this week signed Warrants for the Hessians and Brunswickers, and think my Electoral subjects have an equal claim to justice.

G. R.

Windsor, Feb. 26, 1797.

I suppose the predatory attack and landing in Pembrokeshire will rather add to the dismay of the timid. But I trust that cool firmness which used to be the natural attendant of Englishmen will again appear.

February 28, 1797.

If we are true to ourselves, and will act with vigour, and not be drawn into perplexities by the insidious advances of Prussia, which I have just read, I still hope we may bring matters to an honourable conclusion. But any negotiation for peace at this period would be destruction, for it would be entailing every evil we have been avoiding for a momentary ease.

March 4, 1797.

I believe the good news of yesterday will a little rouse the pusillanimous, and that we shall, as previous to the fatal 22nd of June, place some confidence in naval skill and British valour to supply want of numbers. I own I am too true an Englishman to have ever adopted the more modern and ignoble mode of expecting equal numbers on all occasions. When Mr. Pitt reads the instructions given by Hoche, he will, I am persuaded, feel as I do the wanton cruelty of the enemy, and equally rejoice that Lord Malmesbury's negotiation failed.

April 9, 1797.

The paper received this morning from Mr. Pitt would require much more time for meditation before any opinion was given on its purport than the press of the moment will admit, as it seems to allude to a decision of Cabinet being made on the measure in the course of this day, and I am desirous Mr. Pitt should communicate to them my view of the subject previous to their forming any final opinion : I therefore desire my sentiments may be canvassed without attending to the irregular mode in which they are stated, as it was impossible to arrange them properly when placed so rapidly on paper.

Before I enter upon the serious subject that has been this morning brought before me, one natural reflection occurs—the lamenting the mode, but too often adopted of late years, of acting immediately on the impulse of the minute, consequently not giving that cool examination which, perhaps, in more instances than one, might have been beneficial to the service.

I think this country has taken every humiliating step for seeking peace the warmest advocates for that object could suggest, and they have met with a conduct from the enemy, bordering on contempt, that I hoped would have prevented any further attempt of the same nature; from my fear of destroying every remaining spark of vigour in this once firm nation.

The news from Italy is certainly unfavourable, but too recent for us to build any sound opinion upon till further information arrives from Vienna; and certainly the language Sir Morton Eden holds looks as if the Emperor still inclines to continue the conflict, without which he must make excessive sacrifices. Would it not, therefore, be wise to wait for further accounts before we cast a die that, I fear, must for ever close the glory of this country, and reduce Austria to a small state in comparison of her situation before this conflict; besides fixing the present wicked constitution of France on a solid ground of more extent and preponderancy in the scale of Europe than the most exaggerated ideas of Lewis XIV. ever presumed to form?

If the Low Countries remain in the possession of France, and the former United Provinces continue a dependent state on the former, one may talk of balances of power, but they cannot exist; and the same claim of reasoning that will admit the above measures will, I fear, not prevent France from adding all the territory between her and the banks of the Rhine to her possessions.

As to the state of our finances, it is impossible for me to decide how far they will enable us to assist Austria. I flattered myself, after the debate on Tuesday, Mr. Pitt had viewed that measure as not difficult; but should that prove otherwise, and reduce Austria to sue for peace, I own I should rather see her make a separate peace, as that would leave us at liberty to make one with less sacrifices than if we are to make a joint negotiation, where our acquisitions must be employed to regain the territories of Austria.

I find my thoughts run on so much that I shall in the evening send some further reflections to Mr. Pitt.   G. R.

Mr. Pitt to the King.

Downing Street, April 9, 1797.

Mr. Pitt did not to fail to obey your Majesty's commands in laying this day before the Cabinet the paper which your Majesty had the goodness to communicate to him. It was impossible that they should not be strongly impressed with the weight and importance of the considerations it suggests, and deeply sensible of the dignified feelings and gracious condescension which dictated it; but a sense of the over-ruling necessity arising out of the present circumstances at home and abroad has made them feel it an indispensable though painful duty to submit to your Majesty the opinions expressed in the Minute which your Majesty will receive from Lord Grenville.

Mr. Pitt can with truth assure your Majesty that his present opinion, as far as it depends upon recent events, is nevertheless not formed without cool and repeated deliberations. It rests, however, much more on what has been long the object of his anxious attention, the gradual and increasing difficulties of finance, the real and serious hazard which may arise from their being further augmented, as well as the effect of the impressions which they may be too likely to produce in Parliament and with the public. The obstructions which these difficulties have already occasioned to pecuniary succours to Austria, the precarious footing on which they must place the continuance of these succours, added to the apparent embarrassment and extreme military risk to which that Power is exposed, though they may not render the chance of its co-operation desperate, seem to make it impossible to place any reliance on it. In this situation Mr. Pitt also feels that a separate peace concluded by Austria, instead of diminishing would increase the expenses of this country, while it would at the same time tend still more to alarm and dispirit the country, and probably leave it no adequate resources for the struggle, without having recourse to means which are to be looked to only in the last extremity, and which are likely to be supported only in proportion as all prudent steps have been used to avoid the necessity.

Mr. Pitt cannot, therefore, disguise his sincere conviction that the means now suggested are absolutely indispensable to avoid risking too nearly the ultimate and permanent safety and peace of this country itself. In this opinion he knows that none concur more decidedly than those of your Majesty's servants who have been most anxious to resist while they thought it possible the sacrifices now proposed; they can now reconcile these sacrifices to their minds on no other ground than the public necessity on which it seems to them to rest; nor could they at any rate bring themselves to be the advisers and instruments of such measures if they did not feel themselves bound, both from public duty and from gratitude and devotion to your Majesty, to submit to any personal difficulty or mortification rather than risk the existence of the present system of administration, as long as your Majesty deigns to consider its continuance as important to your personal ease and satisfaction, or to the general interests of your kingdom.

April 10, 1797.

On receiving Mr. Pitt's note yesterday evening, with the account that, though reluctantly, the Cabinet had unanimously agreed to a Minute conformable to the paper he had sent me in the morning, I thought it right not to continue the second paper I was preparing. I shall certainly not with less sorrow acquiesce in the measure, as one thought by the Ministers of necessity, not choice; and Mr. Pitt will, I am certain, not be surprised that the opinion which encouraged me to withstand the difficulties of the war is personally not changed; but I am conscious that if that remains a single one, I cannot but acquiesce in a measure that from the bottom of my heart I deplore ; and should the evils I foresee not attend the measure, I shall be most happy to avow that I have seen things in a blacker light than the event has proved.

I am certain Mr. Pitt's mind is not less hurt than mine on the occasion, and that he has had many unhappy minutes previous to forming his present opinion. The die being now cast, we must look forward, and both must do their best to put this country in as good a state by attention, and not by trying new schemes which mislead, and thus preserve a Constitution which has been the admiration of ages.

G. R.

May 9, 1797, 7.50 A.M.

When I returned from the play the last night, I found Mr. Pitt's note on my table ; but not having read the papers from the Admiralty, I was entirely ignorant of the very outrageous mutiny that has a second time broke out in the Channel fleet. I have since read the papers, and cannot in the least form an opinion as to what measures may be necessary for restoring discipline, or what more can with propriety be done than the increase of pay and provisions that has been now fully granted : I shall, therefore, very willingly concur in such opinion as may be suggested by the Cabinet on the present very distressing occasion.

G. R.

May 11, 1797.

Mr. Pitt's note of the last evening is a fresh proof of the unwarrantable conduct of the leaders of Opposition ; the smallest degree of public spirit ought to have prevented the bringing forward any censure at this hour, when silence was the only line proper. The accounts from Portsmouth, though highly unpleasant, yet certainly bear a better aspect than two days ago was expected. I hope, therefore, that the arrival of Earl Howe this day will prove very conducive to restore some degree of order.   G. R.

Mr. Pitt to the King.

Downing Street, Sept. 22, 1797.

Mr. Pitt thinks it his duty humbly to acquaint your Majesty that he has received communications from a person

(who produces as strong proofs as can in the nature of the
case be given of the authenticity of his mission) stating
that notwithstanding what has passed at Lisle, the Directory
will still agree to an immediate peace, giving to this country
both the Cape and Ceylon, on condition of their receiving a
large sum of money for their own use. The sum named is
1,200,000*l.* for Ceylon, and *two millions* for both. He under-
takes that as a further proof of the authenticity of his
mission, a conciliatory answer shall be returned to the note
now sent from hence to Lisle, and that he will bring or
send a copy of it from Paris hither before it comes from
Lisle. And he desires no payment of any sort till after the
signature of the treaty.

Mr. Pitt has mentioned the outline and substance of the
proposal to all your Majesty's servants who are in town.
The particulars, excepting names, are known to the Secretaries of State and to Lord Chatham. The names are
known only to Mr. Pitt and Mr. Dundas. It is impossible
not to consider any transaction of this sort as liable to great
uncertainty; but in such a state of things as that now prevailing in France, Mr. Pitt and all those whom he has consulted think the overture not destitute of probability, and
the experiment worth trying, as such a sum would be well
employed indeed to procure peace on our own terms without
the risk and expense of another campaign. It seems, however, essential that such a business should be conducted
with the utmost secrecy at present; and that if it succeeds,
every possible precaution should, in point of honour, be employed to prevent as far as possible the circumstance being
fixed on the French Government. Suspicion cannot be
avoided, and (as might be expected from the present state of
that country) seems to be little feared. And it has been
distinctly explained to the person through whom the proposal comes, that enough must be stated to Parliament, in
order to procure the grant of the money, to satisfy them that
it was really employed for secret service on the Continent,
with a view to the settlement of peace. Mr. Pitt is aware
that the measure is quite singular in its extent, and of doubtful success; but it seems attended with little risk of mischief,
and worth trying in these extraordinary times. He hopes,
therefore, your Majesty will not disapprove of its having been
thought right, as time pressed, to encourage the proposal.

Windsor, Sept. 23, 1797.

The demand of money is enormous, and must require so explicit a declaration to Parliament to exculpate Ministers that [it] cannot fail, and I trust will, leave on men's minds a due suspicion of the use that has been made, though it is absolutely necessary to say as little as the novelty of the occasion will permit. I certainly do not mean to prevent Mr. Pitt from encouraging the informer by assurances of the reward if the business is fully done, and no demand of restoring ships, or any alterations in our naval or commercial laws.

Windsor, Nov. 11, 1797.

It is impossible to receive more satisfaction than I have experienced at the receipt of Mr. Pitt's note, as it contains an assurance of the spirit expressed by the whole House of Commons on the subject of the Address, which undoubtedly promises the most active exertion in every measure that may be required for the public safety. I hope these will be cautiously considered before they are brought forward, for to some of those of the last year I fear may be in great measure attributed the mutiny of the navy, and the total failure of recruiting the army. I own I am still sanguine, if we will profit by the experience we have had, and act firmly, that the resources of the enemy are so totally exhausted, and the enmity now arising between Bonaparte and the Directory of France so likely to occasion incalculable events, that with the attempt now making towards Russia and Prussia, there is a foundation to expect a more honourable conclusion of the war and the prospect at a proper time of a more lasting peace than the last year had promised. G. R.

Windsor, Dec. 15, 1797.

Considering the kind of clamour Opposition is attempting to make against the Bill respecting the Assessed Taxes, I think the division of last night of 175 to 50 very favourable. I hope Mr. Pitt will be cautious not to admit any modifications in the Committee on Monday that can possibly lessen the value of the measure; for experience has fully taught me that when Government have from too much candour greatly weakened the effect of any proposition, it never renders it more palatable, and constantly destroys the value of it.

No one can dissemble that the occasion requires heavy contributions, but the cause is so great; it is to save every thing that is dear to men, and therefore must be met with firmness, for I believe the mode adopted is the most equal that could have been devised. G. R.

Windsor, Jan. 5, 1798.

I have this instant received Mr. Pitt's account of the principle of the Bill for the Assessed Taxes having been carried by a division of 204 to 75, and the Third Reading by 198 to 71, and that no further opposition will be made to this measure in the House of Commons, but that a few trifling amendments must be made this day. By this the great point is carried of introducing a new mode of taxation that may be of great utility to the finances of the country, though I doubt whether the actual Bill has been improved by the alterations that have taken place in the progress of it, for I believe Mr. Pitt brought it forward on solid ground, and that the changes must have rendered the Bill less agreeable to it; but sometimes, unfortunately, right gives way to expedience: when it does, I am ever hurt; for, as a plain man, I think right and wrong ought never to be blended for any momentary purpose, and try to inculcate that principle as much as possible. G. R.

January 23, 1798.

I am ever sorry when any proposition is made to me on which I cannot give a decided answer: the one now brought to me by Mr. Pitt is certainly of that nature; but, as I have no secret on the occasion, I shall certainly state the matter so fully to him that he can as easily as me point out what *ought* to be done; for if there is no means of effecting what is suggested, the *appearance* would certainly [be] ridiculous, when attended with an application to Parliament for the means.

My income is certainly, in proportion to the greatness of the country, inadequate to my station, for my Privy Purse at 60,000*l.* and the expense of my Household is the only real income I possess. As to the former, I have some debts, of which the sum borrowed for the late elections makes the most considerable part, which I am by instalments paying off. As to the Household, Mr. Pitt knows how much that is in debt. I have no other fund in the world. I never drew a shilling from my Electorate when in its greatest prosperity, but regularly paid off the debts that were incurred in the Seven Years' War by the very unjust manner in which the just demands on this country were withheld. I thought it prudent to call in a large mortgage, the interest of which was affixed on the keeping part of my Electoral troops : this I placed in trustees, the German Regency, to be placed in the Funds here, the interest of which goes regularly to Hanover, and I have never touched one sixpence of it, but let it answer its disposition, the payment of those regiments. Now I have been forced to borrow above two millions in Germany for my part of the army that forms the Cordon, and Mr. Pitt knows I have a large sum owing to me for the German troops whilst in English pay, that is as yet kept back here : with this he must see that whatever I could nominally subscribe can be but little, and must be again repaid me. I state this truly, and therefore leave him to judge what can be done. So far I can say, it must be out of my Civil List, to which my Privy Purse can give a small proportion. I am sorry to say the King of England is not so rich a man, and that every shilling taken from his Privy Purse must fall on the indigent; for if he has not the means, his workmen and the poor cannot but feel it to their sorrow. G. R.

January 25, 1798.

I have had a satisfactory answer from Messrs. Drummond : I therefore lose no time in permitting Mr. Pitt to subscribe in my name 20,000l. in the Voluntary Loan, to be deducted in the following manner from my Privy Purse : the 5000l. usually paid on the 1st of April to be kept for the Loan, as also that of the 1st of July, the 1st of October, and 1st of January, 1799. G. R.

February 1, 1798, 8.40 A.M.

I am sorry to find by Mr. Pitt's note that he is confined by indisposition. The Earl of Chatham yesterday mentioned Mr. Pitt's idea of the propriety of removing the Duke of Norfolk from the Lieutenancy of the West Riding of Yorkshire, and had my permission, as he intimated Mr. Pitt's not being able to come out, to express my thorough concurrence in the proposed removal. The Chancellor, whom I had previously seen, was strong of the same opinion :

I therefore authorized Lord Grenville to desire the Duke of Portland at the Earl of Chatham's dinner to send the usual letter for that purpose to the Duke of Norfolk. I entirely agree with Mr. Pitt that the Earl Fitzwilliam is the most proper person for the Lieutenancy, but that whoever is appointed must previously know that he must remove the Duke of Norfolk by my command from Colonel of the 1st Regiment of West York Militia. Should Earl Fitzwilliam decline, which I do not expect, perhaps the Duke of Leeds might be the most proper person, as he would be glad of commanding the regiment, which would vacate the East York Lieutenancy, formerly held by the Earl of Carlisle, who naturally would again be appointed. G. R.

February 1, 1798, 5 m. past midnight.

On coming to my room I have found Mr. Pitt's note. I am clear that the Earl of Westmoreland's conduct in Ireland gives him the best claim to the office of Privy Seal, and that the Earl of Chesterfield cannot but feel gratified at being Master of the Horse, and that Lord Auckland will fill the vacancy in the Post Office very properly : I therefore authorise Mr. Pitt to take the necessary steps for effecting this arrangement. G. R.

Windsor, May 13, 1798.

It gives me infinite satisfaction to find Mr. Pitt can recommend, on the vacancy of Master of Trinity College, a person, according to the character he gives me of Dr. Mansel, so exactly qualified to fill that arduous though honourable station. I flatter myself this appointment will restore discipline in that great seminary, and a more correct attachment to the Church of England and the British Constitution than the young men educated there for some time have been supposed to profess. G. R.

May 30 (1798),[1] 7.43 P.M.

By the note I have just received from Mr. Pitt, I am sorry to find his not appearing to-day at St. James's was

[1] The original MS. of this letter bears the date of year 1797, in a perfectly clear hand. But this must have been a slip of the King's pen. It is evident that the first paragraph has in view the same illness of Mr. Pitt as the succeeding letter of June 4, 1798; and it is no less evident that the second paragraph must refer to the duel with Mr. Tierney.

occasioned by the continuance of the complaint in the stomach. I fear it is some inclination to gout, and will probably not be entirely removed till a regular fit takes place.

I certainly said nothing to Lord Chatham but what my mind dictated, and I trust what has happened will never be repeated. Perhaps it could not have been avoided, but it is a sufficient reason to prevent its ever being again necessary. Public characters have no right to weigh alone what they owe to themselves; they must consider also what is due to their country. G. R.

June 4, 1798.

I return the Warrants which I have signed. I am sorry to find Mr. Pitt's complaint still continues; indeed I fear, without he will take the decision of going for a couple of weeks to Bath, that it will not be removed; that what he now takes can alone be termed palliatives, whilst those efficacious waters taken with caution would strike at the root of the disorder. I had desired both the Earl of Chatham and Lord Grenville to mention this to Mr. Pitt, but I would not omit so good an opportunity of doing it myself. G. R.

Windsor, June 10, 1798.

I have signed the messages to Parliament for a Vote of Credit, which must at this time be a very necessary precaution.

By Mr. Pitt's not mentioning his health, I trust there is some amendment.

This country remains in a very naked state by the large detachment sent to Ireland, which nothing but the greatest necessity can justify; but I cannot think any forces sent there can be of real avail unless a military Lord Lieutenant, and that the Marquis of Cornwallis, with Mr. Pelham as his Secretary, be instantly sent there. The present Lord Lieutenant is too much agitated at the present hour, and totally under the control of the Irish Privy Councillors, whose hurry has been the real cause of the two failures, which, if repeated, will by degrees teach the Irish rebels to fight. G. R.

G G 2

Windsor, June 11, 1798.

Since the first breaking out of disturbances in Ireland I have not received so pleasant a moment as the receipt of Mr. Pitt's letter, as it contains the Marquis Cornwallis's consent to accept the Lord Lieutenancy of Ireland. I trust Mr. Pitt will do his utmost to persuade Mr. Pelham to return as Secretary; no one could fill the office so well: but Lord Cornwallis must clearly understand that no indulgence can be granted to the Catholics farther than has been, I am afraid unadvisedly, done, in former Sessions, and that he must by a steady conduct effect in future the Union of that Kingdom with this. I trust that Lord Cornwallis will consent to be nominated in Council on Wednesday. I cannot help again urging that he as Lord Lieutenant, and Mr. Pelham as Secretary, is certainly the best arrangement.

G. R.

Windsor, June 26, 1798.

The draft of the intended Speech at the close of the Session seems very proper. I certainly shall be willing to attend the first day that the Parliament can be prorogued: if that is Friday, it will be as agreeable to me as any other.

I am sorry Mr. Pitt makes no mention of his health; but I must insist on his now not longer deferring taking such remedies as his physician may think most likely to reinstate it. I understand Cheltenham first, succeeded by Bath, is what he means to propose. If my information is just, I desire this may without delay be submitted to, for the allowing bile or unformed gout to undermine a constitution may lead to the most fatal consequences.

I write thus openly from the very great consequence of the subject, and that real affection I bear Mr. Pitt.　　G. R.

Windsor, Nov. 17, 1798.

The draft of the intended Speech on opening the Session of Parliament on Tuesday fully answers my warmest expectations. I can assure Mr. Pitt if it equally calls forth the ardour of those to whom it is addressed as it has mine on perusing it, I am certain it will have the most salutary effect. I entirely coincide in opinion as to the propriety of not as yet alluding to a proposed union with Ireland. That the measure will, when it can be effected, prove salutary to both countries, cannot bear a doubt; but that it will not be obtained on either side of [the] water with the case Mr. Pitt expects, I should fear will prove but too true.   G. R.

Windsor, Dec. 12, 1798.

Nothing can be more advantageous than that, by a motion of Mr. Tierney calculated to discountenance the making any fresh engagement on the Continent, the sense of the House of Commons should have been felt on this subject, and that Mr. Canning should have had so fair an opportunity of exerting his powers of oratory, and the motion have been negatived without a division; but I cannot conclude without highly approving that Mr. Pitt did not speak : it certainly was by no means necessary; it might have lessened the merit of Mr. Canning's performance ; and the speech last week on the finances of the country was too excellent to require Mr. Pitt's holding forth till a more formidable opposition is made to the measures he must propose. I expect that on Friday more of them will attend, when he probably will find it necessary to exert himself, but with the heartfelt satisfaction that his endeavours are for the good of the public—theirs for the destruction of all that is valuable.

G. R.

January 24, 1799.

It is impossible to calculate the improprieties of Mr. Sheridan ; or his having taken up the last evening the time of the House of Commons in objecting to an Address that merely expresses that attention which every Message observes, and which binds the House of Commons to no specific measure, would seem extraordinary.

Mr. Tyrrwhitt Jones seems to have got that habit of holding forth on every occasion that I suppose he could not withstand the pleasure of hearing himself, whilst the Opposition in the House of Commons is not more formidable. I think the great measure now coming forward rather gains respect by the transactions of yesterday.

I cannot help at the same time expressing to Mr. Pitt some surprise at having seen in a letter from Lord Castlereagh to the Duke of Portland on Monday an idea of an established stipend by the authority of Government for the Catholic Clergy of Ireland. I am certain any encouragement to such an idea must give real offence to the Established Church in Ireland, as well as to the true friends of our Constitution; for it is certainly creating a second Church Establishment, which could not but be highly injurious. The tolerating Dissenters is fair ; but the trying to perpetuate a separation in religious opinions by providing for the support of their clergy as an establishment is certainly going far beyond the bounds of justice or policy.

G. R.

Weymouth, Sept. 23, 1799.

This morning I have received the draft of the Speech to be delivered to-morrow. It seems very proper for the occasion. As to any great event arising in Holland previous to my delivering it to-morrow, I cannot say I think there is much reason to expect it. The country the troops have to pass through is much intersected, and if the enemy avails himself of these natural difficulties, our advance must be slow. I believe the passing the duties substituted for the Land Tax and the Malt Tax will prove a salutary measure; and if all the despatch that can be used is exerted, that it will not long delay the Session, which is certainly very desirable.

G. R.

Windsor, Feb. 10, 1800.

Having signed the accompanying warrant, I forward it to Mr. Pitt. I have looked with interest at the new publication of Mr. Marsh, and have inquired of Dr. Fisher, who was of St. John's College, concerning him, who assures me he is a man of considerable learning and talents ; that he is the particular friend of Dr. Cookson : therefore any further inquiry Mr. Pitt may wish to make can be easily obtained through the channel of Mr. Wilberforce.   G. R.

Windsor, April 26, 1800.

Mr. Pitt's account of the fate of Mr. Grey's motion for an instruction to the Committee on the Irish Articles of Union to provide for the independence of Parliament, meaning a Parliamentary Reform, is most satisfactory, as it shows the wisdom of the House of Commons on that fallacious subject.

The fourth Article of Union having passed without division, after a short discussion, I should hope, indicates that with diligence this business may be speedily concluded and returned to Ireland.   G. R.

May 6, 1800.

The information of the last night from Mr. Pitt that all the resolutions on the Articles of Union with Ireland had been agreed to by the House of Commons, and ordered to be communicated to the House of Lords with an Address, laying them before me, gives me sincere satisfaction : I therefore trust there can now be no doubt that either on Thursday, or at latest on Friday, I shall receive the joint Address of the two Houses, which will, I trust, effect one of the most useful measures that has been effected during my reign, one that will give stability to the whole empire, and from the want of industry and capital in Ireland be but little felt by this country as diminishing its trade and manufactures. For the advantages to Ireland can only arise by slow degrees, and the wealth of Great Britain will undoubtedly, by furnishing the rest of the globe with its articles of commerce, not feel any material disadvantage in that particular from the future prosperity of Ireland. G. R.

Windsor, June 18, 1800.

As to the regulations proposed in the office of Clerks of the House of Commons, I fully authorise Mr. Pitt to give my consent to the Bill proposed, as it has the approbation of the worthy and excellent Speaker of the House, who would not countenance the measure if not advantageous to the public.

Windsor, June 28, 1800.

Nothing can be more true or just than the ground on which Mr. Pitt objected to Mr. Sheridan's motion, and the House of Commons showed their concurrence in that opinion by the great majority for rejecting the Call. For the same reason I own not approving of the Minute of Cabinet of Thursday, as it will encourage Austria in treating with the enemy instead of in making exertions to recover the mischief that may have arisen, but of which we do not at present know the true extent. No disaster can make me think the treating for peace either wise or safe whilst the French principles subsist. An armed neutrality is the only thing that can be obtained, and that I look upon as most fatal, for no confidence can be placed in the present French Government. My opinion is formed on principle, not on events, and therefore is not open to change. G. R.

Windsor, July 19, 1800.

Since my note to Mr. Pitt from the Great Lodge, I have received from the Bishop of St. David's an explicit acceptance of the Primacy of Ireland, which I look upon as essential to the quiet of the Irish Established Church, and to the promotion of religion and virtue in that island. I believe nothing but my own exertion on this occasion could have effected this right measure.

Windsor, Oct. 11, 1800.

My opinion fully coincides with Mr. Pitt's on the propriety of meeting the Parliament on the 11th of November, for the sake of examining what may be necessary to be done with regard to the high prices of corn and provisions. I hope on canvassing the question fully, that no strong measures will be attempted, for I hear what was done the last Session rather increased the evil.   G. R.

November 28, 1800.

It gives me infinite pleasure to find by Mr. Pitt's account that Mr Tierney's motion for a Committee on the State of the Nation was rejected by 154 to 37, which cannot but be of use both at home and abroad : indeed, I have not the smallest doubt of the good sense of the country at large, and that however the weight of taxes may be felt, that every one judges that in the present state of France no secure peace can be made, and that consequently the continuance of the war is highly necessary.

The strange conduct of the Emperor of Russia in a second time laying an embargo on the British trade from his dominions loudly calls for the measure of a prohibition from the Privy Council to the merchants trading [with] Russia from answering any bills of exchange from that empire, which Lord Grenville proposed the last night to me, in consequence of which I have desired him to give notice that I will hold a Privy Council here at as early an hour as may be convenient, that the merchants may acquaint their correspondents by this night's post of the injunction under which they are placed.   G. R.

Windsor, Dec. 18, 1800.

The application forwarded to me by Mr. Pitt's note of the Marquis of Buckingham's request that I would grant an Irish Barony of Nugent to the Marchioness of Buckingham,

with a remainder to her second son, on whom the Marquis
will settle his Irish estate, meets with my approbation ; but I
trust the Irish estate will at the same time be settled on
Lord George Grenville, not left to future disposition.

G. R.

Jan. 23, 1801.

The general tone as well as matter of my proposed
Speech for Tuesday meets with my fullest approbation, and
no amount of exertion shall be wanting in me to deliver it
with the force it deserves. I trust, therefore, that Mr. Pitt
will not make any material alteration in it, and that I shall
find it as perfect when, on Monday, it will be communicated
here to the Cabinet as it has come this morning from him.

G. R.

A.[1]

Mr. Pitt to the King.

Downing Street, Saturday, Jan. 31, 1801.

Mr. Pitt would have felt it, at all events, his duty, previous to the meeting of Parliament, to submit to your
Majesty the result of the best consideration which your
confidential servants could give to the important questions
respecting the Catholics and Dissenters, which must naturally be agitated in consequence of the Union. The knowledge of your Majesty's general indisposition to any change
of the laws on this subject would have made this a painful
task to him ; and it is become much more so by learning
from some of his colleagues, and from other quarters, within
these few days, the extent to which your Majesty entertains,
and has declared, that sentiment.

He trusts your Majesty will believe that every principle
of duty, gratitude, and attachment must make him look to

[1] The following letters, marked A, B, C, and D, are those which
were transcribed by Lord Kenyon in 1801, and published by Dr.
Philpotts in 1827. The three subsequent ones, not hitherto
printed, of Feb. 16, 18, and 20, concluded the correspondence for
upwards of three years ; the King's next letter in the series bearing
date May 5, 1804.

The note of Feb. 18, 1801, beginning ' My dear Pitt,' is the only
one of the whole series which thus commences, and seems to have
been both intended and accepted as a token of especial regard.

your Majesty's ease and satisfaction, in preference to all considerations but those arising from a sense of what in his honest opinion is due to the real interest of your Majesty and your dominions. Under the impression of that opinion, he has concurred in what appeared to be the prevailing sentiments of the majority of the Cabinet,—that the admission of the Catholics and Dissenters to offices, and of the Catholics to Parliament (from which latter the Dissenters are not now excluded), would, under certain conditions to be specified, be highly advisable, with a view to the tranquillity and improvement of Ireland, and to the general interest of the United Kingdom.

For himself, he is on full consideration convinced that the measure would be attended with no danger to the Established Church, or to the Protestant interest in Great Britain or Ireland :—That now the Union has taken place, and with the new provisions which would make part of the plan, it could never give any such weight in office, or in Parliament, either to Catholics or Dissenters, as could give them any new means (if they were so disposed) of attacking the Establishment :—That the grounds on which the laws of exclusion now remaining were founded, have long been narrowed, and are since the Union removed :—That those principles, formerly held by the Catholics, which made them considered as politically dangerous, have been for a course of time gradually declining, and, among the higher orders particularly, have ceased to prevail :—That the obnoxious tenets are disclaimed in the most positive manner by the oaths which have been required in Great Britain, and still more by one of those required in Ireland, as the condition of the indulgences already granted, and which might equally be made the condition of any new ones :—That if such an oath, containing (among other provisions) a denial of the power of absolution from its obligations, is not a security from Catholics, the Sacramental test is not more so :—That the political circumstances under which the exclusive laws originated, arising either from the conflicting power of hostile and nearly balanced sects, from the apprehension of a Popish Queen or Successor, a disputed succession and a foreign Pretender, and a division in Europe between Catholic and Protestant Powers, are no longer applicable to the present state of things :—That with respect to those of the Dissenters who it is feared entertain principles dangerous to the Constitution, a distinct political test, pointed against the doctrine of modern Jacobinism, would be a much more just and more effectual security than that which now exists, which may operate to the exclusion of conscientious persons well affected to the State, and is no guard against those of an opposite description :—

That with respect to the Catholics of Ireland, another most important additional security, and one of which the effect would continually increase, might be provided by gradually attaching the Popish clergy to the Government, and, for this purpose, making them dependent for a part of their provision (under proper regulations) on the State, and by also subjecting them to superintendence and control :—

That, besides these provisions, the general interests of the Established Church, and the security of the Constitution and Government, might be effectually strengthened by requiring the Political Test, before referred to, from the preachers of all Catholic or Dissenting congregations, and from the teachers of schools of every denomination.

It is on these principles Mr. Pitt humbly conceives a new security might be obtained for the Civil and Ecclesiastical Constitution of this country, more applicable to the present circumstances, more free from objection, and more effectual in itself, than any which now exists ; and which would at the same time admit of extending such indulgences as must conciliate the higher orders of the Catholics, and by furnishing to a large class of your Majesty's Irish subjects a proof of the good will of the United Parliament, afford the best chance of giving full effect to the great object of the Union, —that of tranquillizing Ireland, and attaching it to this country.

It is with inexpressible regret, after all he now knows of your Majesty's sentiments, that Mr. Pitt troubles your Majesty thus at large with the general grounds of his opinion, and finds himself obliged to add that this opinion is unalterably fixed in his mind. It must, therefore, ultimately guide his political conduct, if it should be your Majesty's pleasure that, after thus presuming to open himself fully to your Majesty, he should remain in that responsible situation in which your Majesty has so long condescended graciously and favourably to accept his services. It will afford him, indeed,

a great relief and satisfaction if he may be allowed to hope
that your Majesty will deign maturely to weigh what he has
now humbly submitted, and to call for any explanation which
any parts of it may appear to require.

In the interval which your Majesty may wish for consideration, he will not, on his part, importune your Majesty
with any unnecessary reference to the subject ; and will feel
it his duty to abstain himself from all agitation of this subject in Parliament, and to prevent it, as far as depends on
him, on the part of others. If, on the result of such consideration, your Majesty's objections to the measure proposed
should not be removed, or sufficiently diminished to admit of
its being brought forward with your Majesty's full concurrence, and with the whole weight of Government, it must be
personally Mr. Pitt's first wish to be released from a situation
which he is conscious that, under such circumstances, he
could not continue to fill but with the greatest disadvantage.

At the same time, after the gracious intimation which
has been recently conveyed to him of your Majesty's sentiments on this point, he will be acquitted of presumption in
adding, that if the chief difficulties of the present crisis should
not then be surmounted, or very materially diminished, and
if your Majesty should continue to think that his humble
exertions could in any degree contribute to conducting them
to a favourable issue, there is no personal difficulty to which
he will not rather submit than withdraw himself at such a
moment from your Majesty's service. He would even, in
such case, continue for such a short further interval as might
be necessary to oppose the agitation or discussion of the
question, as far as he can consistently with the line, to which
he feels bound uniformly to adhere, of reserving to himself a
full latitude on the principle itself, and objecting only to the
time, and to the temper and circumstances of the moment.
But he must entreat that, on this supposition, it may be
distinctly understood that he can remain in office no longer
than till the issue (which he trusts on every account will be
a speedy one) of the crisis now depending shall admit of your
Majesty's more easily forming a new arrangement, and that
he will then receive your Majesty's permission to carry with
him into a private situation that affectionate and grateful
attachment which your Majesty's goodness for a long course
of years has impressed on his mind,—and that unabated zeal

for the ease and honour of your Majesty's Government and for the public service which he trusts will always govern his conduct.

He has only to entreat your Majesty's pardon for troubling you on one other point, and taking the liberty of most respectfully, but explicitly, submitting to your Majesty the indispensable necessity of effectually discountenancing, in the whole of the interval, all attempts to make use of your Majesty's name, or to influence the opinion of any individual, or descriptions of men, on any part of this subject.

B.

Queen's House, Feb. 1, 1801.

I should not do justice to the warm impulse of my heart if I entered on the subject most unpleasant to my mind without first expressing that the cordial affection I have for Mr. Pitt, as well as high opinion of his talents and integrity, greatly add to my uneasiness on this occasion; but a sense of religious as well as political duty has made me, from the moment I mounted the throne, consider the Oath that the wisdom of our forefathers has enjoined the Kings of this realm to take at their Coronation, and enforced by the obligation of instantly following it in the course of the ceremony with taking the Sacrament, as so binding a religious obligation on me to maintain the fundamental maxims on which our Constitution is placed, namely, the Church of England being the established one, and that those who hold employments in the State must be members of it, and consequently obliged not only to take Oaths against Popery, but to receive the Holy Communion agreeably to the rites of the Church of England.

This principle of duty must therefore prevent me from discussing any proposition tending to destroy this groundwork of our happy Constitution, and much more so that now mentioned by Mr. Pitt, which is no less than the complete overthrow of the whole fabric.

When the Irish Propositions were transmitted to me by a joint message from both Houses of the British Parliament, I told the Lords and Gentlemen sent on that occasion, that I would with pleasure and without delay forward them to Ireland; but that, as individuals, I could not help acquainting them that my inclination to an Union with Ireland was principally founded on a trust that the uniting the Established Churches of the two kingdoms would for ever shut the door to any further measures with respect to the Roman Catholics.

These two instances must show Mr. Pitt that my opinions are not those formed on the moment, but such as I have imbibed for forty years, and from which I never can depart; but, Mr. Pitt once acquainted with my sentiments, his assuring me that he will stave off the only question whereon I fear from his letter we can never agree—for the advantage and comfort of continuing to have his advice and exertions in public affairs I will certainly abstain from talking on this subject, which is the one nearest my heart. I cannot help if others pretend to guess at my opinions, which I have never disguised: but if those who unfortunately differ with me will keep this subject at rest, I will on my part, most correctly on my part, be silent also; but this restraint I shall put on myself from affection for Mr. Pitt, but further I cannot go, for I cannot sacrifice my duty to any consideration.

Though I do not pretend to have the power of changing Mr. Pitt's opinion, when thus unfortunately fixed, yet I shall hope his sense of duty will prevent his retiring from his present situation to the end of my life; for I can with great truth assert that I shall, from public and private considerations, feel great regret if I shall ever find myself obliged at any time, from a sense of religious and political duty, to yield to his entreaties of retiring from his seat at the Board of Treasury.   G. R.

C.

Mr. Pitt to the King.

Downing Street, Tuesday, Feb. 3, 1801.

Mr. Pitt cannot help entreating your Majesty's permission to express how very sincerely he is penetrated with the affecting expressions of your Majesty's kindness and goodness to himself on the occasion of the communication with which he has been under the necessity of troubling your Majesty. It is therefore with additional pain he feels himself bound to state that the final decision which your Majesty has formed on the great subject in question (the motives to which he respects and honours), and his own unalterable sense of the line which public duty requires from him, must make him consider the moment as now arrived when, on the principles which he has already explained, it must be his first wish to be released as soon as possible from his present situation. He certainly retains the same anxious desire, in the time and mode of quitting it, to consult as much as possible your Majesty's ease and convenience, and to avoid embarrassment. But he must frankly confess to your Majesty that the difficulty even of his temporary continuance must necessarily be increased, and may very shortly become insuperable, from what he conceives to be the import of one passage in your Majesty's note, which hardly leaves him room to hope that your Majesty thinks those steps can be taken for effectually discountenancing all attempts to make use of your Majesty's name, or to influence opinions on this subject, which he has ventured to represent as indispensably necessary during any interval in which he might remain in office. He has, however, the less anxiety in laying this sentiment before your Majesty because, independent of it, he is more and more convinced that, your Majesty's final decision being once taken, the sooner he is allowed to act upon it the better it will be for your Majesty's service. He trusts, and sincerely believes, that your Majesty cannot find any long delay necessary for forming an arrangement for conducting your service with credit and advantage, and that, on the other hand, the feebleness and uncertainty which is almost inseparable from a temporary Government must soon produce an effect both at home and abroad which might lead to serious inconvenience. Mr. Pitt trusts your Majesty will believe that a sincere anxiety for the future ease and strength of your Government is one strong motive for his presuming thus to press this consideration.

D.

Queen's House, Feb. 5, 1801.

The box from Mr. Pitt contained two letters, and a warrant in favour of Mr. Long. I cannot have the smallest difficulty in signing the proposed warrant, as I think him a very valuable man, and know how much Mr. Pitt esteems him.

I had flattered myself that, on the strong assurance I gave Mr. Pitt of keeping perfectly silent on the subject whereon we entirely differ, provided on his part he kept off from any disquisition on it for the present, which was the main object of the letter I wrote to him on Sunday, we both understood our present line of conduct; but as I unfortunately find Mr. Pitt does not draw the same conclusion, I must come to the unpleasant decision, as it will deprive me of his political service, of acquainting him that, rather than forego what I look on as my duty, I will without unnecessary delay attempt to make the most creditable arrangement, and such as Mr. Pitt will think most to the advantage of my service, as well as to the security of the public; but he must not be surprised if I cannot fix how soon that can possibly be done, though he may rest assured that it shall be done with as much expedition as so difficult a subject will admit.

G. R.

Feb. 16, 1801.

The services of Sir Sidney Smith certainly deserve the public notice Mr. Pitt so properly proposes. I therefore return the Message, which I have signed. G. R.

Feb. 18, 1801, 8 P.M.

My dear Pitt,—As you are closing, much to my sorrow, your political career, I cannot help expressing the joy I feel that the Ways and Means for the present year have been this day agreed to in the Committee without any debate, and apparently to the satisfaction of the House.

G. R.

February 20, 1801.

The King is much pleased at hearing from Mr. Pitt that on Mr. Sturt's Motion for a Committee to inquire into the failure of the expedition against Ferrol, Sir James Pulteney made a very able and satisfactory explanation of his conduct.

His Majesty cannot help expressing infinite satisfaction at Mr. Pitt's feeling the expressions of the note the King wrote to him on Wednesday evening. They were only the effusions of the real affection His Majesty will ever have for Mr. Pitt. G. R.

END OF THE SECOND VOLUME.

Spottiswoode & Co., Printers, New-street Square, London.

www.ingramcontent.com/pod-product-compliance
Lightning Source LLC
Chambersburg PA
CBHW052347110726
47901CB00005B/1397